THE BRIDESMAID'S BROTHER

OLIVIA LOCKHART

For the invisible women...

I see you

And you are amazing

ONE

*W*eddings. Often the culmination of the romance novels I'd lose myself in, and accordingly, I adored them. The decor, the stories of how the couple met, the reflections of them in the venue and food choices. Even so, I'd agonised over whether I should skip this one.

It wasn't an ex or an unrequited love, and I wasn't the black sheep at a family do, nothing like that. I just wasn't exactly a beacon for true love at the moment, having discovered precisely how deceitful a boyfriend could be. 'Boyfriend', the word made me scoff, I was too old for boyfriends at forty-four, but equally 'partner' sounded stuffy and regimented.

Not that it mattered anymore, I was done. My heart had enough scars and stitches, I was over men, forever. But I didn't want my own failures to be a dampener to someone else's joyous day. I wasn't willing to bring a fake date like some ridiculous book character, nor did it seem necessary to drag a random male friend along for safety in numbers.

So, I shrugged off the fact that I didn't have a plus one for today's nuptials, it didn't matter. I was here with my book club, and how lucky I was to have been welcomed into their ranks almost three years ago. The eight of us had bonded over fiction, consoled each other through life's ups and downs, and become firm friends in the process. Our differing ages, incomes, and backgrounds faded away when compared to our mutual obsession with reading as much as possible. My own 'to be read' pile threatened to engulf my bedroom; it was a good job I was single, there'd be no space for a boyfriend.

And today, one of our own would be walking down the aisle. No matter my personal relationship predicaments, I knew true love when I saw it, and Zoe and Emma were absolute soul mates. Then again, I'd always been a fanciful daydreamer; my school report had admonished it every single year.

Zoe was the one who'd invited me to book club, we'd gotten to know each other at the local library as I borrowed book after book, and attended rhyme time with my little girl, Lucy. Zoe wore glasses, but apart from that she was no stereotypical librarian. The glasses were Dolce and Gabbana, framed to perfection by her black bob with its electric blue streaks which matched her unique eyes, and I'd never once heard her tell someone to shush!

The wedding was taking place in an exclusive country hotel, and my drive up to the Lake District had been peaceful. With the air-con on full, my favourite playlist on shuffle, and nobody to interrupt any of it. It wasn't that I'd purposefully avoided any of the car sharing but I'd stayed pretty quiet while those conversations were going on. Time alone was a blessing at the moment for my muddled mind, at least as long as I could keep it on the right subjects.

And so that hot, summers day, I was wedged into a pew alongside my book club friends, wiping a happy tear aside as Zoe and Emma exchanged their vows. Zoe projected her words with confidence, as if the whole world needed to hear of her love. In return, Emma murmured in her quiet, Irish lilt, gazing up at Zoe with utter adoration through her long, dark lashes.

The vows were emotive and intimate. For a moment, I imagined writing something similar for *him*, if only he'd been as invested in our happy ever after as I had. It had been four months since we broke up and I despised the fact that he continued to wander around in my thoughts with his lazy arrogance. He routinely interrupted my day with memories, plans that now wouldn't happen, thanks to his ultimate lie, and the rippling effects it continued to have on my life. There was one consequence I was glad of, however; my vow to make *that* my last break up. My final heartache. I was adamant, I would never put myself in that position again. Ever.

He'd done quite a job on my self-esteem, I mean really, who gets their heart broken by a dentist? A wanker of a dentist at that. I was forced to remind myself that I wasn't a failure. I had a good job, a beautiful child, a loving family. The only new man in my life was the puppy I'd brought home a couple of weeks back. Lucy, my six-year-old daughter, had been asking for a dog for years, and this was the perfect time to make *her* wish come true and give *me* a walking buddy, night-time snuggler-upper, and general life companion while Lucy was at school or with her dad on alternate weekends. Her dad and I had separated when she was just a baby, I thought *that* would have been my worst breakup, in my naivety I hadn't realised there was more to come. The dating pool in my neck of the woods had not been kind.

"Earth to Penny?"

"Hmm?" I asked, confused as I looked up and snapped out of my depressing thoughts.

"Wakey-wakey," teased Bea. "Come on, file out after the happy brides. We're not far off Champagne time now." Bea always made me smile with her zen-like calmness and thoughtful nature, always looking out for people. She was the one who'd founded our book club, trekking up and down the streets of our corner of the town with her flyers, until she'd found like-minded bookworms who also loved a gin.

I joined the procession of up-dos and fascinators as the guests flowed out of the cool church into the hazy summer heat. And as we posed for photographs, threw confetti, and bestowed congratulations in the beautiful August sunshine, that wanker-dentist sauntered away from my thoughts, without so much as a backwards glance to see the middle finger I metaphorically held aloft to him and his screwed-up morals.

The beauty of the function room drew a gasp from the gaggle of guests as they entered. This was a million miles away from our regular book club meetups which took place in the local pub, tucked away at the back, far from the screens showing dreary football matches, but close enough to the bar that we could top up on gin at regular intervals.

A stunning, semi-circular room encapsulated by floor-to-ceiling panoramic windows which looked out over the lake. It shimmered, azure as it sparkled in the sweltering heatwave, as though glitter had been sprinkled all over it in celebration of the day. The top table stood in front of a giant 'Mrs and Mrs' sign; it was bedecked with tropical flowers – hibiscus, orchids, star flowers, and so many more in all the colours imaginable. The scents drifted to me, as if on a balmy ocean breeze, and for once even *he* couldn't intrude on my thoughts; he'd backed away into the box labelled 'lying little shits' that I desperately wished he'd remain in.

The seating plan was attracting all the attention. I knew the old problem of who to seat where had played havoc with Zoe and Emma in the last couple of months. Which auntie shouldn't be near which cousin? Who was liable to drink too much and grope a bridesmaid? Who would heckle during the speeches? I felt it best to let everyone else sort their places out, then I could hotfoot it to my seat unnoticed in time for the drinks to be served.

I ducked down the short corridor which led to the ladies' room, a little niggle of guilt surfacing before relief washed over me as my friends' chatter faded into the distance. I was hot and, in all honesty, more than a little emotional. I needed a minute. Simply for me, not for *him*. For me.

August was always going to be humid, of course it was, but the temperature today was fierce. I was relieved I'd opted for cotton when choosing my outfit. The navy-blue halter-neck dress was as cool as I could hope to achieve. I would've been a sweaty mess in silk or anything too dressy and didn't envy the bridal party in their get-ups, beautiful as they were. My skirt was full and long and I couldn't wait to dance in it. The only complication had been the bow fastener at the back of my neck, not easy to get a nice symmetrical loop when fastening it up alone, but I'd managed.

The hubbub outside quietened down as I touched up my lipstick, pressing my lips back and forth against each other as I appraised my reflection. It wasn't bad per se, I'd just lost faith in myself somewhere along the way, over the years. Eyes of the darkest brown, deep plum hair that I'd curled this morning so it bounced past my shoulders, freckles that I secretly loved even if they weren't seen as desirable by Instagram standards. I'd inherited good bone structure, if I smiled at myself right now I'd see enviable cheekbones, I knew this, but... smiles weren't always forthcoming.

He'd been obsessed with how I looked, and it had bestowed me with new-found confidence, for a time at least before it all crashed down. I'd never been called gorgeous, beautiful, or stunning in such quantities as I had while we were together, and he'd sucked me in with every word. He'd loved my eyes, worshipped my figure, and sang hallelujah over my scent. As we'd lain in bed, he'd press his face to my neck and breathe me in as he fell asleep. He bought me lingerie, drooled over every curve, longing to trail his mouth over each inch of my skin. I'd been so sure that he was 'the one.' Sometimes when my eyes opened in the morning, still in the remains of a dream, I'd feel the ghost of his fingers in the lengths of my hair.

And *that* was precisely why I was booked into the salon next week to get it chopped and changed. I'd never be 'his' again.

His loss - that's what I told myself. He'd screwed it up, not me. With a decisive nod, I fastened my delicate clutch and headed out in search of my assigned seat. Two ladies clustered around the sink I'd vacated, whispering about some guy that had been sat near them in the church. My ears picked up on 'gorgeous' and 'he's the bridesmaid's brother', but I was both ravenous and in dire need of a large, chilled pinot grigio, those things trumped any gossip about gorgeous men.

"There you are," chided Bea as she pushed a wine glass towards me. I was sipping at it before my bum had even touched base on the ivory chair cover, this was precisely what I needed to help stitch my poor, broken heart together and remind me how to smile again. "I thought you'd got lost. Let me introduce you to everyone."

I giggled, relaxing in the familiarity; this was typical Bea. Of course she knew everyone at this table already, she'd be in their family WhatsApp groups by the end of the night, with a heart of gold and not a shred of wariness about her. I checked out the room; the book club ladies had been split between tables, we'd have been too raucous on our own, or started reading some new release and obsessing.

"Everyone, this is the lovely Penelope." She gestured theatrically around my aura, which was the type of thing she liked to keep an eye on. "Penny – meet Margot, Geoff, Sally, Noah, Jessica, and Ryan."

"Hi everyone," I replied, inhibited and awkward. This was akin to an icebreaker at some corporate training event, where I'd be put on the spot and asked to describe myself as my favourite food, or something equally ridiculous. "Nice to see you again, Jess."

She raised a hand in greeting before plonking her empty glass down and whispering to the man next to her whilst gesturing towards the bar. This didn't surprise me; I'd met Jess on the hen do, and at odd parties with Zoe, and she had made me look like a drinking amateur. I'd never known someone to do shots *that* early in the morning and still function by mid-afternoon. She and Zoe had become best friends at high school, which had earned her a brides-maid role today. My eyes tracked across to her husband as he listened to her; she'd told us all about him on the hen do, they were newlyweds themselves. He was very good-looking, as was she. One of those power couple types with their tall, dark, handsome/beautiful thing going on. He looked older than her, but in that sickening way that so many men did, whereby they only get better with age. I, on the other hand, seemed to sag and wrinkle more by the day ever since I'd turned forty. His wedding ring glinted under the mirror ball above us, set up for the evening reception no doubt, as he stood and asked if anyone wanted anything from the bar. We all refused, still on our first drinks, with a flurry of shaken heads and a polite 'thank you anyway.'

A fierce growl erupted from my stomach as plates of hot salmon starters were delivered to our table. Bea pinched my knee under the table. "You ok, sweetheart?"

I nodded, and for once meant it as I replied. "Absolutely perfect, thank you."

"You never know, the man of your dreams might be here. Lots of people meet at weddings."

"Book boyfriends all the way for me, Bea..." I announced as I tucked in. "All the way..."

TWO

The sharp clink of a knife tapping against a glass interrupted my conversation with Aunt Margot, as she insisted I call her. She'd been telling me all about her life in Scotland. The family, all seated with us, had a small-holding near Perth and it sounded equal parts blissful, yet terrifying. I'd even managed to secure myself an invitation for a trip up there next summer. Aunt Margot was a sweet-heart, but boy, could she talk. I'd barely said a word to anyone else at our table between her chatter and the sump-tuous feast that began with the salmon, moved on to crispy pork belly, and ended with a chocolate and caramel cheesecake that I gladly would have thrown my current paperback out of the window for a chance to eat second helpings of. I would dream about that dessert. Again, who needed men in a world when dessert like that existed?

As my eyes flitted around the table, they met with Ryan's. He smiled, and I wondered if Jess had told him about me; was it a pity smile? Glasses of Champagne were filled by dutiful waiters, the fizz of them audible as a second of anticipatory silence transitioned into the beginning of the speeches. Freshly poured bubbly had to be one of the best sounds in my world. That insistent whispering as the throng of bubbles crashed around, reckless, and giddy as they attempted to swim to the top of their crystal flutes, one of which would be making its way toward my mouth as soon as we toasted the happy couple.

Emma's father rose to his feet. I'd fully expected emotion but this wonderful, genuine man from Cork had the gift of the gab and one hundred per cent brought the craic. Everywhere I looked, tears streamed from guests' eyes as they roared with mirth at his tales and jokes. Emma and Zoe practically had to drag him back to his seat to end the speech before time ran over or the Champagne ran out.

Their own speeches were next; they repeated their vows with a back story on how and why they'd written them. Utterly beautiful and the moment threatened to crack my heart open again, so I resorted to my usual trick of letting my mind meander away as if it were in a book. I pondered the paperback I'd left on my bedside table and what would happen next in the twisting, turning plot, my gaze settling across the table as I did so. Jess and Ryan were locked in a tight embrace. I looked away, not wanting to disrupt their moment as they perhaps recalled the emotion of their own recent wedding.

"To Zoe and Emma!"

I flinched back to reality, full of guilt that I'd zoned out and missed the ending. We were almost ready for the final speech. I hurriedly raised my glass before taking a deep gulp, feeling like an utter idiot. Ryan sighed as he placed his now empty glass down on the table. Jess strode towards the top table alongside her fellow bridesmaids, Roisin and Rebecca.

"We know it's not traditional for the bridesmaids to make a speech, but... with no best man and three best ladies, there are a few things we wanted to say." Jess's voice wavered as the bridesmaids lined up and began. Well-rehearsed and bursting with nostalgia, they brought affection and friendship into the heart of the moment. It left me thinking of the friends I didn't see enough of nowadays, how busy lives meant plans got postponed and cancelled – that needed to change.

"One last thing. Our darling brides here chose artificial blooms today for their own wedding bouquets. They want to keep them as a memento, not watch them waste away, which I think is genius." Jess winked towards the brides. "But that means we can't throw them in that traditional way we all love. I caught a bouquet one month before my husband proposed and I want to give someone else that chance. So, I volunteer mine." She brandished her spray of tropical flowers in the air. "All the single ladies to the dancefloor please!"

A DJ had appeared from out of nowhere as the afternoon reception seemed to morph into a practice run for the frivolity of the evening do. Beyonce's tones blasted out of the speakers and my heart sank. The bouquet toss, how had I forgotten there would be a bloody bouquet toss?

"Off you go!" Bea pushed me out of my seat and ushered me towards the cleared space in front of the top table. I dragged my feet, muttering under my breath.

"Single by choice, remember?" I grumbled. "I don't want to catch the sodding bouquet!"

"I can't hear you, Penny. The music's too loud." She giggled, as she deposited me on the spot and scurried back to our table with a spring in her step.

I was mortified as I glanced across at the tables to my left to see who else was getting up. Nobody. A quick look to the right, avoiding my own table and smug Bea. Still nobody. An awful sense of dread crept up my body, and I could feel the burn of a blush on my face. As I looked up at the bridesmaids, I could see the confusion in their eyes as they weren't sure what to do. This was so much worse than any anxiety dream.

I twisted around to see which 'single ladies' I was in competition with. All I saw were the friends and family seated at their tables, some looking on in abject horror, some with laughter, as it became abundantly clear that I was the only sad singleton in the room. Alone, on the dance floor, in honour of a bouquet I didn't even want. Fantastic. Truly.

"Erm..." I mumbled, my eyes racing between Jess, Roisin, and Rebecca. "There's no need, honestly, I'll sit back down." My voice quivered and it hit me how close to tears I was. Maybe I wasn't the 'proud to be single' version of me, not quite yet.

Zoe stood, mouthing something that looked like, "I'm so sorry." Then I felt movement at my side, cool cotton brushing my arm as a deep voice spoke.

"I thought we did equal opportunities, Jessica? Why is it only single *ladies*? What about single men? I demand to join in."

"Let's get this over with," sighed Jess as she turned her back to us. "Three, two, one... Catch!"

I half-heartedly raised my arm in a vague attempt to catch but, in reality, wanted the ground to swallow me up. As it was, the bouquet sailed by, way too high, and I watched it zoom right out of the tall, open windows and towards the lake beyond. Half the guests dashed out to see where it went, the awkwardness of me being alone forgotten as the next spot of drama began.

I gulped back the tears that still threatened, as I took in the dark suit in front of me. With a crinkled, confused forehead, bitten lip, and teary eyes, I raised my head to see who the other singleton was.

"Ryan?" I asked, bemused.

"Penny, right?"

I nodded. "Thank you for saving me from standing here on my own like a massive idiot, it's hugely appreciated. But surely catching your own wife's bouquet wouldn't count?"

His face paled and I saw the flash of a deep gulp in his throat. "My wife?" he asked, his voice timid for some unfathomable reason.

"Yeah, Jess. You two got married a few months back, right? She told me on the hen do the other week."

"Oh…" He blew out a deep breath, relief flashing over his face. "No, no. Jess is my sister. Her husband, Matt, came down with food poisoning yesterday. She was going mad, some dodgy kebab after football. She asked me to come in his place. She's my sister. She needed a plus one."

"You're the bridesmaid's brother?" Another hot flush ran up my chest. "Well, that's a faux pas and a half. Apologies for implying anything incestuous," I garbled with a forced laugh, wishing I could shut myself up but knowing, with this level of mortification, that anything was liable to pass my lips. "Still, you're not single though, are you?" I pointed at his wedding band, wondering if he took it off to chat other girls up like my wanker dentist ex. "Either way, the gesture is very, very much appreciated." I went to curtsy, before stopping mid-knee bend as his words hit me, like tiny bullets burrowing deep under my skin.

"My wife died. So… yeah… I wear a wedding band, but if you wanted to argue it in a court of law, I'm single for the purposes of the bouquet toss."

I think I stopped breathing, from incest to mentioning his dead wife in under a minute. Was there still a chance that the ground would open up and take me away from this?

THREE

*R*yan coughed and I realised I'd remained crouched, as if about to propose or do something equally ridiculous. Given the things I'd said in the last two minutes, it probably wouldn't be as offensive.

I smiled, it was more of a rictus gurn, as I straightened up and met his gaze, unable to read the emotions on his face as his grey eyes focused in on me.

"I really didn't mean to offend you. What an awful thing for me to have said."

"Not at all. You couldn't have known. To be honest, I'm relieved you didn't say you were sorry. Nine times out of ten, that's the first thing people say. 'I'm sorry'. What are they sorry for? It wasn't their fault."

A loud cheer erupted outside, followed by a splash, and I guessed someone was wading into the lake to retrieve the cursed bloody bouquet that had started this.

"Well, I think your sister's inhumanly strong throw has distracted the crowd from my pathetic single lady moment. And I am truly, truly grateful you stepped in there. Can I buy you a drink to say thank you?"

He exhaled, long and slow, intent for a moment on the kerfuffle outside. Beyonce's dulcet tones had wrapped up, and the DJ was playing some mellow jazz selection as background noise.

"To be honest, I'm a bit weddinged out right now. It's not the easiest," he admitted. My mind flashed back to the embrace with Jess - she'd been comforting him, of course, it all made sense now.

"That's OK," I began, not wanting to make this more awkward or weird than it already was, if that was even possible.

Ryan shook his head. "No, I need a drink, a drink would be great, just not here. There's a resident's bar on the floor below this one, want to escape there?"

"Definitely, I'm weddinged out too. That's a great phrase."

We headed down an elegant staircase together, then along a plush corridor to the opposite end of the building, whereupon Ryan held a large, wooden door open for me. The bar beyond it was a world away from the function room, the stellar opposite. As light and bright as that area was, this one was dark and warm, with a mishmash of comfortable-looking upholstered chairs and dark cushions and throws. It felt like some upper-class country establishment, where hunters and their hounds (not that I approved of them) would barrel in at any point.

"Thank god for that air conditioning," he murmured, closing his eyes, and raising his face to the vent above us.

Its blissful ultra-chilled air was winning the battle against the oppressive summer heat.

"What can I get you?" I asked. "To drink?"

"Spiced rum, straight, with ice, please."

"Coming right up. You grab a seat."

I fumbled around in my delicate clutch bag and grabbed my debit card as I approached the bar.

"Hey, Penny?"

I pivoted around, secretly impressed with the swish of my dress, to see Ryan smiling at me. "Yep?"

"Thanks. For the drink. And for coming here, I appreciate it."

"Least I can do after you saved me from Beyonce and your sister. That bouquet could have hit me right in the face." I smiled, as I ordered two spiced rums and anticipated sinking back into one of the chairs to savour mine, hiding here from the wedding party for the foreseeable. Maybe this day wasn't so bad after all.

But as I sat back down, I found myself at a loss for words. My mind was blank of any kind of 'safe' conversation. So, we smiled politely and sipped at the drinks – delicious by the way, but how do you follow up a conversation that involved Beyonce, incest, and death?

"You can ask, you know? It's fine." He blurted out, without warning after a pause in our chat.

"Ask what?"

"How long has it been? Was it cancer? All the normal stuff people ask as soon as they know. I swear the whole world thinks nobody under forty dies of anything but cancer."

"I'm not very normal." I clinked the ice around in my glass, trying to keep my eyes off his; I felt too intrusive. "I didn't mean to bring up bad memories with my stupid comment. Especially when you were trying to do a nice thing for me."

"You didn't bring the memories up. They're always there, sometimes I quieten them, but not for long. Jess always nags me to get out more, and I think she thought this would be good for me. It should be, but it's a bit much." He downed his drink and placed the heavy tumbler down onto a pristine beer mat. "The only way I can face going back up there for the evening do is if I've sampled *many* more of those. Care to join me?"

He smiled, still tense around his eyes but the action was infectious, and I hoped I could make amends because, no matter what he said, I felt like I'd ruined his day. I could still picture the colour draining from his cheeks as I mentioned his wife's bouquet.

"You know, I think that's the only way I'm going back in there too. But when I do, I'm asking that DJ to play Beyonce again and I am gonna dance the *crap* out of it."

"Are you a good dancer?" he asked.

"Completely awful until the second bottle of wine, then I'm a goddess. Imagine a badly co-ordinated five-year-old on a sugar rush."

"This I need to see. Stay there, I'll be two minutes."

My smile persisted as he walked away. This was refreshing; physically he was exactly my type. Tall, dark hair (even the grey bits suited him), mysterious eyes (crinkly from smiling, he obviously hadn't always been sad), expensive, well-fitted suit. My vow of celibacy was firm, and it was obvious he wouldn't be looking to catch anyone's eye, but it was freeing to be able to spend time with a guy and have a laugh, knowing there'd be no weirdness or expectation. How often did the opportunity to wear a pretty dress and get tipsy with a hot man come up? I planned to make the most of this.

I had no idea of the time because I now measured it in trips to the bar. I'd bought two rounds, as had Ryan, and my sides ached from laughter as he finished up more tales of his childhood and how he and Jess had tortured each other, to the point that he had ended up stuck on the roof one night as a teenager. I glanced at my phone and saw multiple messages and calls from the book club ladies, in a panic that I was upset and had run off home. With a quick reply, that I'd see them in a few minutes and reassurance that I was OK, I turned my attention back to Ryan, now a little dishevelled, but infinitely more relaxed and, dare I say, attractive. Being sworn off men didn't mean I couldn't appreciate the good-looking ones.

"Makes me glad I was an only child," I said, still chuckling at the image of them and their childhood warfare.

"Yeah, we never grew out of it. One more? Shall we?" he asked, holding his empty glass aloft.

"My friends were worried." I motioned towards my phone as it beeped with another message. "I'd better go and let them know I'm OK. I think I'm almost ready for dancing anyway. You going to come up?" I let it sound casual, but I hoped he would return. We were having such a lovely time and it felt good to laugh like this, with no pressure.

"Of course, I am. Need to see this dancing, Penelope." He exaggerated the pronunciation of my name, his tongue rolling across every syllable in such a way that I had to force the flutter in my stomach away.

I huffed, enjoying the tease. "I told you; Penelope is my Sunday name." I wobbled as I stood from the chair, the warm, tipsy effect of the rum shooting straight to my legs.

Ryan's arm shot out as he steadied me, a look of concern on his face. He gripped my waist as he spoke. "Careful. You ok?"

Damn, now he was this close I couldn't help but notice how incredible he smelled, almost like cherries and chocolate but sharp and arousing, not sweet and sickly as it sounded. Had that tiny hint of dark, five-clock shadow been there before? Ugh, I had to stop these thoughts, they wouldn't lead me down a good path.

Ryan coughed; I think I had beaten my own record for making a man feel awkward so many times in one afternoon. Now stable on my feet I faced him, only to see his eyes fly up to my face from my cleavage, which to be fair had been pressed against him as I wobbled.

"Thanks, getting to be a habit, you saving me," I murmured.

"Anytime." His eyes stayed intent on my own, but his brow twitched, creating a little furrow along the bridge of his nose. "Who knows... maybe one day I'll see you on a

Sunday and can use the name without getting told off." His hand was still on my waist, his words almost like an invitation.

I laughed it off, tipping my head back as we stumbled towards the function room. I needed to find my friends and stop getting the horn about this guy. I was off men. Forever. Absolutely forever.

The reception room had been transformed, partially by the hard-working team of hotel staff but more so by the sun itself. Hovering over the surface of the lake, it painted the sky with pinks and oranges. The large balcony was like a fairytale, illuminated by strings upon strings of large glass bulbs, each one stuffed full of tiny, sparkling lights in warm white. With such amazing views outside it was almost possible to skip your eyes over the interior, although that was captivating in itself. The dance floor was illuminated, with all the tables from the wedding breakfast pushed to the sides, allowing more room for dancing. Tall, elegant displays of flowers, also entwined with fairy lights, led the way along a short path to a photo booth and the beautiful wedding cake, which I could see had been ceremonially cut during our absence.

The bar bustled, as a barrage of extra evening guests attempted to catch up on the drinks. In the background, I spied a long table laden with stacks of plates and pots of cutlery. I licked my lips as, despite the lavish feast of the afternoon, those many rums had left me ravenous.

My book club friends bopped away to some random

eighties track, absolutely loving life. I waved and was beckoned over but mouthed, "five minutes," hoping it would buy me time to figure out what to do. Because I should have been dancing around my bag, drinking too much wine, and crying in the lady's loo later about *him*. But what I actually wanted to do was continue talking to Ryan. It unsettled me, wanting that, but I couldn't deny it.

From the corner of my eye, I glimpsed Jess beckoning him over. He raised his hand before turning to look at me. It sounds ridiculous, but he was the perfect height to look at me. I didn't get a sore neck, nor did I feel we were similar sized. He was in that goldilocks zone for sure. Perfect man height for my distinctly average 5' 5".

"Hopefully, nothing else embarrassing will happen," he said with an air of reluctance. "But shout if it does and I'll step in."

I grinned, like a total idiot, but the unexpected afternoon had made me gleeful. "I'm expecting a dance later, you better be ready."

His eyes darted to the dance floor and back to me. "Erm... yeah... I have an urgent call so..."

I tapped him on the arm playfully before he backed away, laughing, his eyes still on mine for another moment before he turned and headed to Jess and the other bridesmaids.

"Hey, gorgeous," shrieked Zoe, as bridal and tipsy as they come. She careered into me and enveloped me in a warm hug.

"Congratulations Mrs." I kissed her cheek. "Hope you're having the best day?"

"Loving every minute. Fully utilising my bridal privileges and being the centre of attention, it's marvellous." She fluttered her eyelashes before moving closer, her voice lowered a notch. "I'm so sorry about before. Jess, the bouquet, I had no idea."

"Don't worry, I'm OK. Got my big girl pants on. Did they get the bouquet out of the lake in the end?"

"Nah, bollocks to it, there are two more. But we won't repeat the game, don't worry." she slurred as she motioned at the barman for a glass of Veuve Cliquot from the bridal stash behind him. "Bride privileges, I get served first. Now you, lady, drink this and I want to see nothing but smiles, OK?"

"Deal." I nodded and raised the glass to my lips.

"Where were you before by the way?" she asked as she backed away, looking towards a new group of guests entering the room. "You were gone ages."

"Oh, I was about. Just needed some space." She threw me an understanding nod before she was engulfed in hugs and congratulations. She was in her element. I smiled as I leaned on the bar, enjoying the fizz of cold bubbles in my mouth. "How's your evening going?" enquired the barman as he moved towards me. It's not nice to judge people, I know, but the first thoughts that crossed my mind were - too young, too smarmy, bet he tries to pull a guest at every wedding. So that definitely made it time for dancing.

My friends grabbed me within a second of my big toe crossing onto the sparkling dancefloor. Arms flailed, hips swung, and every lyric of each song was shouted out as we held hands, jumped up and down, and generally acted like utter fools. Shoes were discarded, more drinks were ordered, and surely every calorie of that cheesecake must have been burned off in the process.

The balls of my feet burned, and no air conditioning in the world could fight the sheer quantity of bodies and the hot, evening air which flowed in from the open doors. I motioned that I needed a break, grabbed my bag, and headed onto the balcony, knowing it was about time to Facetime my little girl who would be heading to bed at her dad's house about now.

"Hey, sweetheart!" I beamed into the phone as her face came into view. She was tucked up in her bed and I could just see her dad's arm behind her as she cuddled into him.

"Mummy, you look so pretty!"

"Thank you. I can't wait to show you all the photographs of the wedding. Have you been having a lovely time with Daddy?"

"Yes, we've been to the cinema and then we got chicken nuggets."

"Mmm, nutritious," I joked, sticking my tongue out at her.

"And what are you reading for bedtime story?"

"*Ten Minutes To Bed, Little Unicorn*," she replied, holding it up to show me, as if I hadn't read it a hundred times myself.

"I love that story."

"I know, you can read it again when I'm home."

"I'd better let you get to sleep, it's late. I was dancing with Bea and got carried away."

"I'll call you tomorrow," she grinned and blew kisses into the phone. "Love you!"

"I love you more, always will."

"Never will," she giggled before ending the call.

I slid my phone into my bag and looked out across the lake. The sun was now out of sight, ready to illuminate the opposite half of the world. In its place hung the stunning moon, illuminating the clear and beautiful night sky. A breeze blew over me and I smiled, inhaling as it rushed over my hot skin.

"Is it waning or waxing, I never did figure out the difference?" I jumped at the voice, twisting around to see where it had come from, only to spot Ryan tucked away in the corner of the balcony, the one unlit section, gazing at the moon as I had.

"It's waning gibbous, to be precise," I replied with a warm smile, as I stepped towards him. "You hiding out?"

"Yeah, only so much polite chit-chat I can take." He shrugged in resignation.

"Sorry, I'll leave you in peace. Was about to melt with heat exhaustion inside."

"You were throwing some moves," he laughed, his fingers running over his stubble as he shuffled around on the bench. "I didn't mean *you*, by the way. About the chit-chat."

"Ladies and gentlemen!" The DJ's voice boomed from inside, and the scratching whine of feedback made me wince. "The pizza buffet is served. Go, go, go!"

Glancing at the table in front of Ryan, I noticed a bottle of Veuve that looked as though it had been liberated from the special stash behind the bar. "Stay there," I said. "I'll be back in five minutes, maybe ten. Just stay."

"Are you always this bossy?" he asked, leaning back with a raised eyebrow.

I glanced over my shoulder, my smile enlivened as I headed away, maybe with a tad more of a hip swish than was strictly necessary. I couldn't help the spirited giggle that escaped me, and I was gratified to see the smile that infiltrated Ryan's lips as he returned to his moon-gazing.

This wedding grew more interesting by the minute.

FOUR

I scooted around the edge of the room and managed to wriggle in near the front of the queue. The pizza smelled divine, this place was renowned for its stone-bake ovens and homemade dough. I'd been thrilled when Zoe had said they were forsaking the usual buffet fare for Italian perfection. The staff were re-filling the burning hot ovens within seconds of pulling out fresh baked pizza that oozed with cheese, herbs, and every combination of topping imaginable. They were boxed up, as if from a takeaway, but the boxes had the names of the brides and the wedding date in beautiful calligraphy across the top. I grabbed one labelled 'pepperoni and spicy honey,' before retracing my steps back out to the balcony, hoping not to be intercepted.

As I approached, Ryan looked up from his phone, sliding it onto the table as his eyes roamed to the pizza box. His jacket had been discarded and his sleeves were now rolled up to the elbow, the golden cufflinks that had held them in place discarded next to a beermat and ashtray that wouldn't be needed.

"You're not vegetarian, are you?" I asked, plonking myself down next to him and placing the box in front of us.

"Even if I was, I think I'd give it up for whatever is in there. It smells amazing."

"So, you'd like me to share my pizza, is that what you're saying?"

"Penny…" He leaned in close to me, a lazy, tipsy smile on his lips. "It would be my honour to share your pizza."

His breath brushed over my cheek, why did it feel so nice on me? I could sense my cheeks warming up and hoped the expensive foundation I was wearing would disguise the blush, as I busied myself opening up the fancy pizza box.

"You can share my Champagne, but alas, I only have one glass…" His eyes didn't leave mine as he spoke, but I glanced at the table, confirming there was indeed one solitary glass. "Do you think I'm the kind of girl who shares a glass with a man she just met?" I asked, aware I was borderline flirting but seemingly unable to stop. I was flirty by nature anyway but, after a few hours of drinking, I had no hope.

"We bonded over Beyonce, we're fine." He nudged me with his elbow, before he filled the glass and offered it to me.

"Is this stolen Champagne?" I teased.

"Yep, from my sister. Is that a problem for you?" He made it sound like a challenge, and I wanted to play. Oh, how I wanted to play, vows of celibacy were all well and good until you found yourself looking at the moon with a handsome man who made you laugh.

"No problem here." I wriggled my nose at him, hoping it looked sexy bewitched rather than a weird itch, before I grabbed the glass, drained it, and licked my lips. "I love to share."

"Oh my god..." I moaned, utterly satiated. My taste buds had barely recovered from the orgasmic qualities of the pizza sauce as I licked my fingers clean. "That was better than sex. Spicy honey on pizza, where the hell has that been all my life?"

"Was it?" he asked.

"Was it what?"

"Better than sex?"

"Right now, yes. Is it me or are the stars spinning?" I leaned my head against the cushioned back of the bench, but the sky only seemed to sway more.

"I'm not entirely sure I remember sex accurately. So, pizza is good for now."

"I remember March 21st." I murmured into the glass.

"What happened on March 21st?" he asked, as he held his hand out for our shared drink.

"I spent the afternoon in bed with my boyfriend, thinking we were completely in love. He left around teatime because Lucy, my little girl, was due home and I wasn't ready for them to meet. I had no idea what was coming."

"What went wrong? If it's not too personal a question?"

"A few hours later his wife turned up at my house, screaming and shouting, threatening me. Lucy was petrified, I can still picture her face." I sighed, weary from the memory. "I wasn't expecting a wife, or some sort of double life."

"What the… what a shit." He shook his head as he topped up our shared glass.

"Well, I knew he was married. When we met, he told me they'd been separated for two years and were waiting for their youngest to finish high school before they divorced. Turns out that he hadn't thought to mention this little nugget of information to his wife."

"Well, no wonder you're off men. But we're not all bastards, you know?"

"The boyfriend before that left me for another woman, a woman he'd sworn was nothing more than a colleague for six months. The boyfriend before him was a compulsive liar. And before that was my husband who slept with my friend. Don't know if I was more pissed at him or her." I shrugged and grabbed the glass from him with a smile. "But sod them all. I don't need a man. I have a great job, a lovely family, wonderful friends, and a bottom drawer sponsored by Lovehoney. Penelope Archer does not need a man."

I stabbed my finger into the table to make sure the point was properly made; it hurt.

"You sound proud to be single now we're many, many units of alcohol in. But," he added gently, "You weren't happy on the dancefloor earlier, thanks to my little sis."

I sighed, watching the stars as they sparkled. "I'm still adjusting to it. Bad days and good days. It's like my heart has been stitched up after what he did, but it doesn't take much for the stitches to loosen, or tear."

"I get that," he said as he slouched down in the seat, the side of his head rested against mine.

"I hate that he made me the 'other woman.' I'd never knowingly interfere in a marriage. It's the worst bit sometimes. That her and her friends, and their family, their kids, will always think it was my fault, that slutty other woman. That's who I am to them."

"He can only make you that if you let him. I don't think you're that at all."

"What am I, then?" My voice quivered, and I knew this conversation was turning my mind to places I didn't want it to go.

"You're Penny, my new friend." He said it so simply, as he took hold of my hand, that all those stitches on my broken heart tightened up a notch.

"That's one of the loveliest things I've ever heard. But how about you?" I asked, trying to lighten the mood and stave away the tears that had pricked the edges of my eyes. "Do you remember the dates you had sex?"

He laughed, one little burst. "I don't, but I know it hasn't been since…" His sigh was full of defeat. "It doesn't feel right. Not yet. I don't know if it ever will."

"What happened to her?" I put my hand on top of his, trying to bring some comfort as we shared this moment.

"It was a car crash. A normal, mundane workday, except she never came home. Nobody was to blame, just an accident that left me with a million what-ifs. What if I'd driven her? What if it hadn't rained that morning? What if she'd decided not to wear her new shoes and had run back into the house to change? It's enough to drive a person insane."

"I almost said it then…" I whispered, and he turned to me with a sad smile.

"Everyone does, but what else is there to say?" He closed his eyes, leaning his head back and my heartache faded into nothing in comparison to his.

"How long ago was it?"

"A little over two years."

I tried to think what to say, what to do, but my mind was blank. Grief wasn't something I'd been through, not really, I counted myself lucky, blessed even. So, I did the only thing I thought could provide any comfort at that moment, for the brief second of time that was all I could affect.

I tucked my knees up under me on the seat, raising myself as I turned to face him before pulling him into a hug. I tried to channel my most nurturing thoughts, to give him any kind of respite from his pain.

He turned his face into my neck as he hugged me back, a shudder running down his spine as he let out a long breath. I wanted to soothe him, even if only for a moment. Time passed and I remembered an article I'd read about not being the one to end a hug, as you didn't know what the other person needed. After two or three silent minutes, Ryan pulled back and resumed his position gazing up at the stars. I mirrored him, smiling as he linked his fingers through mine once more.

"Nobody hugs me anymore. When it first happened they did, but I didn't want it then. Losing affection is another loss, I guess. The hugs turned into pats on the back, or a sympathetic touch on my arm. Then even that stopped. Everyone else's lives carried on but mine didn't, not in the same way, not the way it was meant to." His fingers squeezed mine tight. "After a while, never being touched, it becomes an issue. I don't mean in a sexual way, but the simple things people take for granted, like a hand to hold, hair to ruffle, the warmth of a body next to yours. Hugging someone who isn't your mum or your sister, that's kind of unexpected."

"Everyone needs affection. For what it's worth, I'm available for hugs at short notice due to my non-existent life. Just not on book club nights please."

"Be careful, I might take you up on that. Not sure how today would have been without you here. Jess is on a mission to get me out more, but she doesn't get how hard it is sometimes."

"Well, I like talking to you. And just so you know..." I grabbed his arm and pulled him up. "It's time to dance some of this booze off."

It transpired that Ryan's footwork was as bad as mine, hence much hilarity ensued between us as we budged onto the packed dance floor and claimed a corner. There were some whispers as people watched us together, a few raised eyebrows, but I didn't care. Drunk or not, two people were allowed to become friends and dance, and that's all this was. No men for me. Too soon for him. It made no difference that he looked absolutely adorable and was so bloody sweet that I wanted to squeeze him.

The fast beat of retro, familiar tunes faded out as the last orders at the bar were announced and everything slowed down, the very air seeming to still as a different vibe came over the room. The first notes of the next song played, and we found ourselves surrounded by couples. I realised this was one of the bride's end of the night dances, 'Come Away With Me,' by Norah Jones. The two lovebirds swayed together at the opposite end of the dancefloor, lost in each other, as it should be.

I blew a stray hair from my face and took half a step backwards, feeling exposed and also aware I was desperate for a glass of water. It's never good when you're still awake as your hangover starts to creep in.

"A dance is a little like a hug, isn't it?" Ryan asked, as he stepped forward into the space I'd created, his arm outstretched.

I stepped towards him with a wide smile. This evening had felt like all my troubles had lifted. I leaned closer to reply, my lips close to his ear as my arm wrapped around his waist. "It is indeed. It's a moving hug I believe. They take a lot of skill, but I'll give it my best go."

I tried to stop it, I really did, but each heartbeat of the dance set another butterfly off in my stomach. It felt like a constant fizz within my fingers where they touched his and, as we turned, his stubble brushed against my face. Plus, that scent… he smelled incredible, it set sensations off in me.

Except it couldn't, I couldn't let it.

"Penny?" he whispered, bringing me back from my muddled mind.

"Yes?" I replied, the word barely more than a breath

passed through the miniscule space between my mouth and his ear.

"Would you… I wondered…" He sighed and pressed his face into my neck. It was difficult to disguise the goosebumps that the intimacy of the action had brought out of me.

"What's wrong?"

His words barrelled out with such speed that it took me a moment to digest them. "I don't know what for, or why, or if it's a good or bad idea but I wondered. Would you come and stay with me tonight? I know you've got your own room and everything, but I don't want to be on my own. It's a stupid thing to ask and… forget it, please, just forget I said anything."

"Ryan," I replied as I twisted my head around to look at him. His eyes were sleepy and rum-soaked, but they tore at my heart so that it wasn't really a decision. "Of course I will."

FIVE

"This way, I think..." Ryan's forehead wrinkled on one side, as he tried to recall which end of the corridor his room was situated on. I'd nipped into my own room to grab my overnight bag but, as Ryan had one of the bridal party suites on the executive floor, that's where we headed.

I had no idea what I was doing, only that my gut told me this was right and that I was safe. My mind whirred into a familiar cycle of overthinking as I followed him, closing my eyes momentarily only for Ryan to stop, as I crashed into him like a bumbling idiot.

"Sorry!" I gasped, eyes springing open to see him fumble with a room card and the door sensor.

"Hmm?" He seemed oblivious as he almost tripped into the room, missing the slot for the key card which activated the lights. I grabbed it from him and slid it into place.

"Wow," I mumbled as the room came into view, lamps and spotlights bursting with a warm, bright glow. "This is so much nicer than mine."

"The bridesmaids all had these suites booked. I told Jess I was only coming if I got the big room. She's sharing with Roisin; said it'd be more fun anyway. I fully expect they'll crash some other party soon regardless. You know what they're like."

I nodded, but I didn't really. I also wasn't sure what to do now I was here.

"Drink?" called Ryan, his voice muffled as he peered into the minibar.

"Can I have two?"

"You didn't say you were that high maintenance!" His head popped out from the minibar with a drunken smile.

"I just meant, can I have water to try and stave off my hangover? But one more proper drink would be lovely, a nightcap? I'll have whatever you're having." His head returned to the cold fridge. "You ok if I get changed in the bathroom?"

"Mmhm." His hand waved around in the air for a moment, and I took that as a yes.

My shoes were off in seconds, for which my feet thanked me, and in the spirit of not overthinking, I decided to make this quick. Lock the door, dress off, freshen up, perfume reapplication, brush teeth, fix hair, rub mascara smudges from under eyes, pyjamas on, job done. This wasn't sex prep or anything, I didn't need to stress, I was simply spending time with a friend, in his hotel room. That was all. I was glad I'd treated myself to the expensive pyjamas though and hadn't packed some old, tatty Winnie the Pooh set from a Christmas long ago. Organic cotton, cream with a pink stripe, a button-up shirt, and bottoms that scraped the tops of my feet. Cute, cool for summer, and also perfectly respectable for a friend.

The bedroom was lit more sedately as I exited the bathroom, about half of the many, many lamps having been turned off making it warm and tranquil. The curtains were drawn, and Ryan sat with his back to me on the cosy, squashy-looking sofa which lay opposite the bed. The tv was on, set to a random music station which played at a quiet volume and, on the coffee table in front of Ryan sat two heavy tumblers.

"Is it ok if I charge my phone?" I asked, as I padded barefoot across the room.

"Of course, go for it." He turned and smiled; he was still in his shirt, but the tie was gone, and the top button was undone, his sleeves still rolled up from earlier in the evening, showing off those very masculine arms.

I plugged the phone in near to the door, thinking next to the bed might look presumptuous, and then took a seat next to him. I twisted on the sofa, which was indeed as squashy as it looked, and turned to face him as I grabbed my drink.

"What have we got?" I asked, raising the glass to eye level as I checked out the colour.

"Rum again. Figured it was a good way to end the night. Shit... I haven't put anything in it, you can swap them if you prefer. I wouldn't do that, I promise."

He sounded so flustered, that I tried to reassure him as I reached out and touched his arm. "I never thought you would! Think I would have come here if I didn't trust you?"

"No, I think you're much cleverer than that. And also,

39

you have great taste in pyjamas. I could do with a matching pair, they're nice."

"Thanks," I beamed. "I love pyjamas, I tend to put them on straight after work, much to my shame."

"What do you do?" he asked as he sipped at his drink, taking it much slower than we had earlier.

"I work at the planning office at the town hall, I'm one of the managers."

"No way, I'm always submitting plans to that place. I'm an architect."

Our grins matched, as we took in the coincidence. "That's so crazy. I don't see the applications anymore, it's all more strategic and to do with council planning, but when I first started, I used to speak to the architects all the time. It's an electronic process now. I guess there isn't as much talking?"

"Not unless there's a problem. Have you heard of Grayson & Williams?"

"I have."

"I'm the Grayson."

"Small world." I clinked my glass against his. "Sorry, I assumed you were a Baxter because that's how I know Jess, Jess Baxter. But of course, we already established you didn't marry your sister."

"Yet you keep going there." He rolled his head from side to side with a tease of a smile.

"I'm surprised we haven't met through Jess," I pondered. "Her and Zoe have been friends forever and, with it being a small town, it's strange we haven't crossed paths."

"Did you go to Zoe's thirtieth?" he asked.

"No, I met her after that when our book club formed about five years ago. I've seen the photos of the stripper though."

"*Everyone* has seen those photos. I was there, it was horrendous. Tara loved that night." He looked down into his drink as he smiled.

"Your wife?" I asked.

"Yep, don't worry, it's nice to remember happy times like that out of the blue. That party was feral, she threw up non-stop the day after." He chuckled.

"Have you got children?"

"No, we hadn't got round to it. Stupidly assumed we had forever. To be honest, I think that's a blessing. No little kid should go through losing a parent. You mentioned a daughter earlier, didn't you?"

"Lucy, she's six. She's with her dad this weekend. Me and him get on pretty well now, and we agreed when we split that we'd never make her suffer for it. Can't abide those parents who bad mouth the other one to the child, it isn't fair."

"Agreed." He raised his glass to mine with another clink. I liked all these little toasts; they made me feel like we had a secret club.

"I should tell you about the man in my life though. It's pretty serious, to be honest."

"What?" His forehead did that adorable crinkle up once again. "Not the married one?!"

"Let me get my phone and you'll see. I attempted to jump up, but this sofa was too squashy, and it took a push from Ryan to get my tipsy butt out of it. I jogged over to the door, retrieved the phone, and flopped back down onto the seat, grinning as Ryan's drink sloshed about, the ice cubes clinking in his glass.

"He moved in with me this summer, and I promised I'd love him forever."

I turned the screen around on a recent photo and Ryan's face went from furrowed concern to absolute delight. "What breed is he? I think I just fell in love."

"A barbet. I'd never heard of them but a friend of my parents down in Cornwall had a litter, so I went and picked him up, took Lucy for a trip while she was on school holidays."

"You must get stopped every five minutes when you walk him. He's the cutest puppy I've ever seen. Between him and you..." His words petered out, as he swiped through photos of my adorable little guy.

"What do you mean? Between him and me?" I was puzzled, as I pulled the phone away in case he swiped onto anything dubious.

"Well, he's adorable and unusual, and you're... well..." His hand waved up and down in front of me and I was bemused.

"What?" I laughed as I scooted forward towards him. "What am I?"

"You're one of the most beautiful women I've ever met. Anyone seeing you, out with a puppy like that, wouldn't be able to stay away."

"Seriously?" I scoffed. "Your beer goggles are well and truly on, Mr! You're not noticing the pudgy tum or the dark circles under my eyes."

He leant towards me, the aroma of rum from his breath

breezing over my mouth as he spoke, his pupils dilated in the dim light of the room, as a familiar throb began in my pyjamas that I knew I had to chase away. "Don't focus on negatives. As someone who only met you a few hours ago, this is what I see. The biggest chocolate brown eyes. The exact right amount of freckles scattered over beautiful cheekbones. You say pudgy tum but trust me, every single person who eyed you up today, and there were plenty, saw all the right curves. And as for those lips..." He ran his thumb across my bottom lip, and I had to stop myself from jumping into his lap.

Then, just as fast as that surreal, hot-as-hell moment had begun, he pulled back, the blush on his face visible even in the dim light.

"Sorry, that was wildly inappropriate. I meant, don't put yourself down. You're stunning, truly. Plus, lovely, that's a rare combination and anyone who cheated on you or lied to you is a complete dick."

I sank back against the sofa, downing the rest of my rum with an audible gulp. I'd wanted him to kiss me so bad, which was utterly foolish and also in direct violation of my no-men rule. But really... the way he'd described me, the hot air between our mouths. That was going into the memory bank for future use.

"I've made things weird, haven't I? I didn't mean to," he said.

"No, don't worry. We're good. Friends can say stuff like that to each other. Absolutely." I stood up, not at all graceful, but at least I didn't need a push this time. "Is there more in the mini bar? Last drink before bed?"

The room seemed cosy as we savoured our final drink.

There'd been too many that day, but it was one of those weird occasions where the prolonged consumption seemed to mean you weren't rolling around like you might have otherwise. How did it feel so natural to touch him as we leaned into each other, yet also innocent? Even though that little devil part of me wanted very much to err away from innocence.

Ryan's arm was wrapped around me as I finished my drink. I turned away as a long yawn overtook me. "I'm wiped out, long day. Shall I sleep here? Do you still want me to stay?"

"If you want to go, I completely understand. But if you stay, come sleep in the bed. It'd be nice to have someone next to me for once. A friend."

"Size of that bed you could get about four friends in it," I joked.

"Ha, maybe one day, hey?" He winked, but I saw no humour in his eyes at the throwaway comment.

I gulped from my bottle of water as I threw cushions to the floor and pulled back the sheets that were tucked in so tight I almost broke a nail.

With the covers pulled up around me, I couldn't decide which way to face. This was the weirdest situation I'd gotten myself into for a long time yet, somehow, I wanted to play along, to see where it would go. My silly, whimsical mind always liked to tell me that fate often intervened, and some things were meant to be, all that crazy foolish stuff that got my heart hurt so often.

The final lamp went out and I felt the mattress dip as Ryan climbed in. The bed was huge, so space wasn't an issue. In all honesty, I was glad for the darkness and the quiet. My head still echoed with the beat of loud music, and the rum/Champagne mixture had made everything a little hazy. Ryan turned. I could barely make out the shadow of him as he faced me.

"How old are you?" he asked in a whisper, as though we were kids on a sleepover trying not to wake the adults.

"Forty-four. I hate it."

He laughed. "Don't stress it. I see things different now, don't dread your birthdays, celebrate you made another one. None of us knows what our last number will be."

"That's true." I mirrored his position. "You're very wise."

"That's because I'm so young, you'll be jealous."

"You gonna make me guess?" I enquired, attempting a flirty eyebrow raise, before realising he wouldn't see it in the dark anyway.

"I'm Forty-two. Friends can be any age, doesn't matter, does it?"

I shook my head, the pillowcase crinkled beneath it. "Not at all, I think age matters less and less the older you get."

"Night, Penny." He wrapped an arm around me and squeezed me into a tight hug, before rolling away. "I liked making friends with you today."

"Me too," I smiled to myself as I turned over, my eyes already heavy and drowsy. "Night, Ryan."

I sat bolt upright as a loud bang echoed around the room, followed by raucous female laughter.

"What was that?" I gasped, confused and sleep riddled

as Ryan sat up beside me. He switched on the torch from his phone and moved it around the room. The door was shut, all was peaceful. For a moment at least. Then the loud laughter burst out again and I realised it was from the neighbouring room.

"For fuck's sake, it's like living at home again. That's my sister, she must be next door to us. Ignore her."

His phone went dark as he placed it on the bedside table, before wriggling back under the covers and turning to face me. I snuggled back down, so warm and sleepy, I yearned to find that cosy spot I'd been inhabiting. "How long have we been asleep?" I yawned each word.

"It's gone three. You want me to find some earplugs?" he whispered as the hilarity next door continued.

"I'm good, thanks, at least we know they're not going to have noisy sex. Be worse if her husband was in there."

"That's true, I'd have to retreat back to the bar." He shivered and I laughed, edging closer as I hoped for another sneaky hug to send me back to sleep.

"That felt way too good, by the way," he murmured.

"What did?"

"Not being alone when I woke up."

I was at a loss as to how to reply because yes, it had felt good, and my mind wasn't awake enough to think through the consequences of that. So instead, I squeezed him tight, his words from earlier about how much he missed affection still floating in my mind.

His skin was hot, as he wrapped his arms around me in return. I wanted to hook my leg around his but stopped myself. This wasn't *that* type of hug, and I couldn't cross lines. For my sake and for his.

Except then, his fingers brushed the side of my face. I looked up, aware of the pressure of his eyes upon mine as we watched each other. Even in the dim light I was aware of his gaze dropping to my mouth and, despite every insistence that I was done with men, I pressed myself forward until my lips met his.

It was one single kiss, lips to lips, slow, clinging, warm... As he pulled back, it was as though my mouth tried to grasp onto his. I licked my lips, testing if this were real, and his eyes focused in once more. Quick as a flash, he covered the breath he'd left between us and pressed a second kiss to my lips, causing my body to push against him in a response I had no control over.

Neither of us moved for what felt like the longest time but was in reality mere seconds. Eyes locked, mouths connected by the barest breath, oblivious now to any noise, light, or interruption.

It wasn't kissing as I'd imagine it, the plural, the lips moving against each other in some kind of rhythm. Instead, soft, individual kisses were drawn out, and prolonged. My mind was flooded with him, awash with thoughts of Ryan that I couldn't stop.

My fingers stroked at his neck, and I felt the deep swallow that accompanied a long breath out, before he seemed to make a decision and shift closer to me. His hand landed, gentle on my hip, light as a feather, as he stroked and those tiny, solitary, sweet kisses continued.

Three...

I didn't know why I counted them, but it seemed to make sense in that moment. As if I wanted to remember the kisses, cherish them. Number four, and his warm hand rubbed my side, tickling the skin between my hip and my ribs, as my pyjama top rode up; but I didn't laugh, I didn't squirm, I sank into him.

The previous kiss had scarcely finished before he pressed his lips to mine for the fifth time and, as our mouths connected, his hand brushed across my chest. With a torturous slow touch, he traced one finger around my exposed nipple, springing it to attention and drawing a long sigh of pleasure from me. My leg took this as a sign that it no longer needed to behave, as I slid it up and over his hip, creating more connection between our bodies.

Just as I was ready to beg for kiss number six, Ryan pulled away from me and sat up in the bed, his hands raking through his hair.

"Shit. Sorry, I'm sorry." He threw his head back, facing the dark ceiling above us. "I didn't mean to do that. I don't know what's wrong with me tonight, this isn't like me."

My head whirled with a disorientating combination of lust and confusion. My body was desperate to carry on, but I could sense that wasn't going to happen. I couldn't push this, he'd made it clear he wasn't ready and, besides, at least this way my vow of celibacy remained intact.

"There's no need to apologise. I think that was my fault. I'm sorry too." I smiled and rubbed my hand over his shoulder. "Don't worry about it, any of it. Get some sleep before I start snoring," I joked, trying to lighten the mood, even as my lips tingled for more kisses I couldn't have.

"Yeah, sleep. Good idea. Goodnight... again."

"Night, Ryan," I whispered as I turned away from him, my legs squeezed tight together, willing my hormones to calm down. That wasn't even proper kissing, not in the grand scheme of things. That's what I tried to convince myself of as I drifted to sleep, unable to think about anything but numbers one to five.

SIX

"Hello? Earth to Penny." I shook myself out of a trance to find Bea waving her hand in front of my face. "You with us? Kate asked what we all thought of the final chapter. Did it leave unanswered questions for you?"

I looked down at the pristine paperback on the pub table, placed at right angles in front of me alongside my now empty gin and tonic. Everyone else had well-thumbed pages and sticky notes. I was loathe to admit I'd struggled with this one. "I didn't make it to the end, I'm sorry. I found it quite dreary, it brought me down."

"Oh, that's not like you." Bea's eyes whizzed around my face, as if looking for some physical sign of discomfort.

"It's a funny time of year, back to school madness, end of summer, all that stuff. I'm sure I'll love the next book." I plastered my best smile onto my face. "Shall I go and get a round in while you all discuss the ending?"

There was much enthusiasm at that suggestion, and I wandered to the bar. There was football on, again, so the pub was packed. I was happy to wait though, to have a few minutes where I didn't have to respond to questions or think too much. My head felt so full lately, I couldn't keep track of everything.

I couldn't care less how the book had ended in all honesty; all I could think about was how *that* night had ended. It was all I had thought about, despite two weeks having passed. In so many ways the wedding had been amazing, and meeting Ryan had knocked the other idiot from the forefront of my mind, but now I was pining. Pathetic for a middle-aged woman, but I missed him. Part of me regretted that we hadn't had time to swap numbers or discuss what had happened in the chaos that had ensued the next morning, but it was probably for the best. I'd only complicate his life and he was already going through enough.

"Four gin and tonics, a lemonade, and a large merlot please," I said to the young woman behind the bar. She seemed to have singled me out over the football crowd and their many, many pints. I guessed it was refreshing to serve someone a little less leery.

The morning after... It had been weird after the loveliness of the three a.m. kisses – all five of them. I awoke with the all too familiar post-alcohol thud in my brain and a mouth so dry I'd drink bathwater. The thudding hadn't been my headache however, it was a persistent banging on the hotel room door.

I had an awful, nauseous moment of imagining it was *his* wife again, until I remembered where I was, and who I was with. Ryan and I both sat up, how the hell does someone look that cute when they've just woken up, hungover as hell? He was all creased face, ruffled hair, and sleepy eyes, I longed to pull him back under the covers.

"Ryan Grayson!" A shrill voice boomed out. "Are you in there? You've missed breakfast. I need to get home, you're driving us. Remember? You'd better be in there."

"Shit." He rubbed his hands through his hair. "We must have overslept. Sorry. Wait there, I'll be five minutes." He jumped up from the bed and I averted my eyes from my first daylight view of his naked chest above his pyjama bottoms. He grabbed a robe and jogged to the door, wrapping it around himself as he turned and called back to me with the brightest smile. "Don't move!"

He opened the door a mere inch, apologising to Jess for oversleeping as he did so, but patience was obviously not his sister's strong point. The door burst wide open as she ploughed into the room wearing torn jeans and a green hoody, her hair still bundled up in her bridesmaid do, albeit messy and tufty in places. "What happened to not being able to sleep past five a.m.? I'm glad you slept, god knows you needed it, but we have to get going. Checkout is in fifteen minutes." The speed of her words was too much for my semi-awake brain to contend with. "Also, you missed the most amazing breakfast, they had a pancake station..." Her words faded out as she spotted me in her peripheral vision.

She turned to Ryan, mouth agape, but all words stopping in their tracks. Slowly, her head twisted around to me, in her brother's bed, the duvet askew and trailed onto the floor, which at least proved I was covered up by pyjamas before, quick as a flash, her attention snapped back to him.

"What the fuck, Ryan? What happened to not being

ready? When I tried to set you up with Ivy you were adamant it was too soon." She barked, the tell-tale wear and tear of last night's singing and screeching blatant in her voice.

"Not that it's any of your business, but nothing happened. Let me get dressed, I'll be down in ten minutes."

"You know she was sleeping with a married man not long ago?"

I gasped, what had happened to the girl code? I'd told Jess all about it on the hen do and she'd been sympathetic, taken my side. I sprang up out of bed, ready to blaze across and give her a piece of mind, as Ryan ushered her outside into the corridor and closed the door, throwing an apologetic glance my way.

I stormed into the bathroom instead, slamming the door as I tore my pyjamas off. One of the beautiful pearl buttons flew into the sink, but I didn't care as I pulled my jeans and t-shirt from my overnight bag and threw them on, biting my lip to stop the threat of tears.

As I washed my face and brushed my teeth, I could hear them bickering through the thin walls. "She didn't know he was married; she did nothing wrong and that's got sod all to do with you anyway. Neither does who I do or don't sleep with by the way, Jessica." Her name was bitter on his lips. I didn't hear her reply, as I flushed the toilet and bundled all my belongings into my bag, without care for creases or dirty high heels.

I shoved my feet into my tatty, familiar Converse as I held onto the hotel room door, ready to walk out and determined not to give Jess the satisfaction of a reaction.

"It's been two years!" I heard her squeal as I opened the door.

"It's been two years, seven months, and fourteen days. I got the phone call at about midday, so I can work it out to the minute if that makes you happy. For fuck's sake..." He sank to the floor, leaning his head back against the cool wall, his eyes closed.

I glared at Jess and dropped down next to him, abandoning my bag next to her feet, one of which tapped on the carpeted floor at high speed.

"Do you want me to stay?" I asked, as I took hold of his hand.

Ryan opened his eyes to look at me, and the sadness in them almost broke my heart. "I don't want to drag you into this shit show." He attempted to squeeze my hand, but it was as though the strength had been sapped out of him.

I heard Jess tut, but I didn't care as I pressed a warm kiss to his cheek. I didn't want to say goodbye, but once again I was left without an idea of a response, so that solitary press of lips against his stubbly skin seemed all I could do. Jess, however, got an absolute death glare as I strode away; there were so many things I wanted to say to her, but I would never wish to make the situation worse for Ryan.

I'd never scurried out of a hotel so fast; with a toss of my key card into the express checkout box, I was gone. Somehow, I didn't let one tear fall until I got home, and then, boy, did they fall.

"I said, that'll be £26.75." The barmaid glared at me. I must have ignored the first time she had asked for payment. I dangled my card against the contactless point and waited for the far too perky beep that indicated a successful transaction.

"Want me to help with that?" asked one of the football crowd with what he must have thought was a winning smile, as he motioned at the drink-laden tray. I shook my head and made my way back to the book club corner, trying to spill as little as possible.

All the book chatter had concluded and, as always, the last section of the evening was a melting pot of gossip and news. Things were quieter without Zoe, who was still away on her honeymoon cruise around the Greek islands. There was lots of talk about the wedding, of course. I joined in and smiled and laughed at the appropriate intersections, but I had this weird feeling in my stomach that I couldn't quite displace.

This was precisely why I'd sworn off men, too bloody complicated. To make it worse, I'd gone and made Ryan's life more difficult when that had been the last thing I had intended. Although the way Jess had reacted was downright weird, and a complete overreaction.

Bea walked home with me, her place only two streets over on our small and cosy estate. "You sure you're ok, sweetheart?" she asked, as she gave me a hug at my front door.

"All good, promise."

"Is Lucy at her dad's all week?"

I nodded in response. I'd been all too aware, as we had wandered home, that I had an empty house waiting for me, well apart from Rocket of course. I only left him alone in short bursts and I prayed he hadn't chewed the kitchen door again. My mum had watched him while I was away for the night at the wedding, and I think she'd let him get away with murder, those puppy dog eyes were too irresistible.

"If you want to go out for tea one night, or, watch that new movie we talked about, just let me know."

"I will," I replied with a smile, always happy on the outside at least. I also had no idea what movie she was going on about. I must have missed that bit of the chat. "Night, Bea."

"Night, Penny." She gave me a wave as she wandered off towards her place, the first nips of autumn making themselves known in the late evening air.

Working from home had multiple advantages. My favourites were not dealing with rush hour traffic or the foulness that was a communal office fridge. However, when you were also living alone for half of every week, it could get lonely.

This was the secret reason I'd acquiesced to Lucy's wishes and gotten a puppy; he was the best company. Always up for a cuddle, playful, gorgeous, and he loved me unconditionally without complication, whether I shaved my legs or not. Plus, definitely not married.

"Rocket," I called as my meeting ended. He bounded over from his bed, all legs and fluff, his tongue stuck out comically. He was the most ridiculously cute puppy I could have imagined. Every time I walked him now, and anyone stopped to talk, I couldn't help but hear Ryan's words in my mind. Maybe they were the events I needed to keep hold of from that wedding, not the myriad of things that *could* have happened, but the good things that *did* happen. Ryan truly did make me feel beautiful. Not in the overly sexualised way that Mr 'oops I forgot I was married' had, but in a way that felt like he saw the real me.

It had taken an age to instil into my friends and family that they couldn't pop around for coffee whenever they were at a loose end, because I had actual work to do. My mum had been a nightmare for popping around or inviting me out for a slice of cake when I had back-to-back meetings over Zoom. I therefore jumped out of my skin when the doorbell rang and tore my mind away from the spreadsheet I'd been working on for far too long.

I glanced at my make-up-free face and messy bun, as I passed the hallway mirror and sighed, sure that the postman had seen worse. Checking that Rocket wasn't able to escape, I reached for the lock. As I opened the door, my smile dropped and a heavy weight settled in my stomach, all too familiar to that dreadful day I had opened the door to a seething woman earlier in the year. For on my doorstep today, stood Jess.

SEVEN

"*P*enny," she began with a tense smile, her lips pinched at the edges just as I'd seen with Ryan, the familial resemblance very apparent. "Can we talk?"

"How do you know where I live?" I asked, my stomach tight with suspicion.

"Zoe. I hope you don't mind. Please? Can I come in?"

I blew out a long breath, buying myself some time. "That depends on what you want to talk about. If you're here to warn me off your brother or accuse me of any untoward behaviour, don't bother."

"I'm here to apologise. I want to explain why I acted that way. I was out of order." She at least had the good grace to look ashamed.

"It took you two weeks to realise that?"

"Please hear me out, it's important."

I glanced at my watch, just gone eleven thirty. "OK, I can have an early lunch break, but I won't have long."

She followed me into the hallway and pulled the front

door closed behind her. Rocket was in the living room where I'd set up my office that morning, and I decided to leave him there and take her through to the dining room instead. It may have been petty, but I didn't feel that she deserved to meet a cute puppy, not with the way she'd spoken to both me and Ryan.

"Tea?" I asked as I flicked the kettle on. I always left it filled and ready. She nodded, and I opened the cupboard above, which housed all the mugs and hot drinks. As I turned my back to her, I smirked at my special mug. Zoe had bought it for me, it looked pretty and respectable until you raised it up and the person opposite saw the message on the bottom – 'Leave me the fuck alone!' Zoe had given it to me because I had said I never got any peace while I read, but it was perfect for situations like this too. I'd be a grown up though, try and make peace, so instead I pulled out two matching navy and silver mugs, which I'd treated myself to in the sales.

An awkward silence ensued as I made the drinks, broken only by the normal questions of "Milk?" followed by "Sugar" – it was a yes, followed by a no, the same as me. She wrapped her hands around the hot mug as soon as I placed it in front of her, her eyes darting around my kitchen.

"Your house is beautiful," she said.

It was, I knew it was, because I had worked day in and day out to make it so for Lucy and me. But that wasn't what she'd come round for, and I wasn't going to bend over to flattery and make this easy.

"That morning," she continued. "I was still drunk, Roisin and I, we didn't go to bed until five, I shouldn't even have been up and about, but I'd promised Zoe I'd be at breakfast. I never would have spoken that way otherwise."

"To me, or to Ryan?" I asked.

"To either of you. When he didn't come down for breakfast, I was worried he'd left in the middle of the night. He doesn't sleep, he hasn't since Tara died, not properly. He's always awake at four, five in the morning, and he struggles with his thoughts during those times."

I rested my chin on my hands, my elbows on the table as I listened, and worried.

"When Ryan said he'd slept in I was made up, I knew the wedding would be tough for him and I thought maybe that meant it had helped, that I'd finally done something useful. You don't know what it's like to have been so useless through all of this. To see your brother in excruciating pain and not be able to help. And of course, I miss Tara like mad too, but I don't even feel like I can say that, because it's nothing compared to what he goes through every day. My grief is negligible compared to his."

At this point she burst into tears, her face hidden behind her hands as she sobbed, still apologising. I pulled a pack of panda tissues from a kitchen drawer and passed them over to her before I sat back down and sipped my tea, remembering the pleading Lucy had subjected me to in the supermarket because she wanted the panda pack and not the plain tissues.

"Thank you," she said with a teary smile and, as much as I wanted to remain distant, I couldn't. I reached my hand across and squeezed hers tight inside mine.

"Carry on, I'm listening."

"I've not been able to do anything to help him, and then

I saw you in his bed and he'd actually got some sleep, he looked so happy and perky. I got jealous, which sounds stupid and wrong, I know. All I could remember was you telling me about that guy with the wife, and I thought there's no smoke without fire, you know? That you must have known, and the thought of anyone hurting him after what he's been through, it made me so mad. I shouldn't have judged you."

"The only person who hurt him that morning was you, Jess."

"I know, and it's taken me this long to get him really talking to me again. He said you deserved an apology as much as he did." She blew her nose on a panda wearing a bow tie and it seemed too surreal.

"So, you're only saying sorry because he told you to?" I queried.

"No! No, that came out wrong. I'm apologising because I was a bitch and there was no need. I wanted to explain what was running through my idiotic head. Basically, I wanted to protect him."

"There's nothing going on between me and your brother. But one day he *will* meet someone, and you can't expect them to be perfect. You can't be sure they'll never hurt him. It isn't that simple. And what if he did meet the perfect woman, and you pulled some stunt like that and scared them off?"

"I know, I know." Her head sank into her arms on the table, and I pulled my hand away. "I truly am sorry, and I wouldn't do something like that again. He told me you didn't sleep together; I shouldn't have jumped to conclusions."

"You shouldn't, but even if we'd been in there having sex all night, it wouldn't be your place to comment." I was ten years older than her, but I felt like we were worlds apart, her reaction had seemed pretty immature. Did she want her big brother to herself? I couldn't tell.

She looked up at me, her eyes grey and so similar to his, although now pink from the sobbing. "I've not seen him as relaxed with anyone as he was with you, I kept spotting you talking. Did he open up to you?"

"He did, but it was private. I'm not going to share the things he told me."

"I don't expect you to." She shook her head and wrapped her hands back around her mug of half-finished tea. "I'm glad, he doesn't talk to me or my mum about it anymore. I know he still sees the counsellor, but he always looks so defeated. He was different at the wedding, and I don't want to be the one who stops you two from being friends or whatever."

"Jess, I appreciate you coming to apologise and explain but, for the record, we didn't swap numbers. I don't think he wanted to stay in touch."

"I think he does, but won't admit it to himself, not yet. I wondered, can I give you his number?"

I drained my tea as I contemplated, glancing at the kitchen clock, knowing I had to be back at work soon; plus, Rocket could be chewing the sideboard right now or, even worse, my laptop. I wanted to see Ryan again, I really did, but I'd promised I wouldn't open myself to heartache again. And surely, if he wanted to see me, he could have found me? After all, Jess did.

"No." I said bluntly.

"No?" She recoiled a little as she stood. "Do you not like him?"

"That's not the point, you can't go around interfering in his life and giving out his number once you decide people are up to standard. That's not right, Jess."

"I guess…" She stood, wiping another tear from her cheek and I did feel for her, but her interest in this situation didn't seem healthy. "What shall I say to him then?"

"Personally, I think you should tell him you apologised, as he asked, and leave it there. It's up to him if he wants to find a way to contact me. For all I know, he's mortified by the things we said or the stupid dancing and is relieved I'm out of the picture. I don't know, but that's up to him."

She nodded and I led her back out to the front door, aware of the yipping of Rocket as he threw himself at the living room door, desperate to greet a new visitor.

"Take care, Penny," she said as she turned to walk up the path, away from my house. "I do want him to be happy and meet someone, but I'm scared for him."

"I can tell how much you care about him. You have to trust him to find his own path through this. Just be there when he needs you."

She nodded, as she tucked her hands into the pockets of her jacket and walked swiftly up the road. After closing the front door, I leaned back against the wall, unsure if I'd done the right thing. Jess wasn't a person I particularly wanted to be involved with. Zoe loved her, but I knew she was a temperamental character, and seeing her at the odd party and special event was more than enough for me.

And as for Ryan. My heart said yes. My head said no. And let's not even involve my body or raging hormones.

For once, I had to listen to my brain, listen to reason. Future me who was crying on the sofa with ice cream, wine, and baggy jogging bottoms would be grateful for this sensible decision.

It was good Jess had made up with Ryan though, he needed her. He needed someone. Just as I let my eyes close and my mind meander to memories of those kisses, I heard the shrill ring of a Zoom call on my laptop. Maybe it was a sign, maybe it was for the best, that those beautiful memories remained in the past.

EIGHT

"*I*t looks incredible, I'm mad with jealousy," I confessed, curled up on Zoe's suede corner sofa as she air-played her honeymoon photos, the family-friendly version, onto the huge screen she'd had mounted on the living room wall. For a book-obsessed librarian, she also loved her movies and box sets. Another week had passed, and I was glad to have my friend back home.

"I can't believe I have to go back to work tomorrow," she groaned. "It sounds stupid, I know, but it's been like a fairy tale. The wedding itself, the amazing trip, even all the lead up to the big day." She threw herself back on the sofa like an absolute drama queen. "I mean, I've got used to a certain amount of Champagne every week, I don't want to wait until Christmas for more."

"We can drink Champagne anytime you like, don't worry about it. How's Emma?" I inquired as I sipped at my latte.

"A bit more pragmatic than me," she replied, a definite glint in her eye as she spoke about her new wife. "She was fine going to work this morning, it's me that's dreading tomorrow. Speaking of jealousy, I'm in love with your hair, when did that happen?"

I ran my fingers through my newly styled hair, flustered at the compliment. I never quite knew what to say in response to admiration. "Last week, I'm still not used to it. Feels short."

"It's still plenty long, and the colour is pretty, like caramel and chocolate brown. It's weird seeing you without the plum, but I love it."

"Thank you, I didn't want it to be the same as when I was with *him,* does that sound daft?"

"Nope, makes perfect sense. Hope the sneaky fucker is still leaving you in peace?"

"He is," I said. "Don't worry."

"Have you got time to help me put the last of the wedding stuff away in the spare room?"

"For you, always. Lucy's not due back for a couple of hours yet."

"Shall we drink Champagne while we tidy up then? After all, you did say anytime...?" Zoe sang the last few words as a mischievous smile appeared on her lips.

"Have you got some?" I asked, my interest piqued.

"Yeah, there was *loads* left after the wedding, we were too busy to drink as much as we thought we would. Got a few bottles as gifts too, but I'd better save those, or Emma will kill me."

Zoe was one of those people who made every task feel like the most fun thing you could have chosen. When she did rhyme time at the library the kids sat entranced, as she brought the books to life for them. Even when it was tidy-up time, they skipped around as though it was happy hour in a soft play centre.

Emma, always organised, had boxed everything up in clear tubs to protect them; the wedding cards, the seating plan, her precious folder which contained every booking, receipt, and plan you could imagine from the day they'd got engaged. After a short amount of work, it was now all stashed at the back of the built-in wardrobe in the spare room. Zoe and I slumped down on the double bed, Champagne in hand.

"I can't wait for the proper photos; we need a book club night around here, once I've got them. Bore you all senseless again. That photographer took hundreds."

"It'd never bore me." I smiled and drained my glass, which she promptly refilled along with her own.

"You had fun then? I was worried." Her head tilted to one side, and I spotted the tell-tale sign of pity. I'd seen it a lot since my grave error in judgement.

"I had an amazing time, barely thought of that wanker-dentist at all."

A raucous guffaw escaped her as she clinked her glass against mine.

"What's that box behind you?" she asked, peering around my side.

"Didn't spot that one sorry," I replied, grabbing it, and putting it between us on the bed. "It's got the hotel logo on it, is it a gift from them?"

"Oh, I remember now. They sent it over while we were away. Lost property." She giggled. "How funny is that, like we're at school losing our jumpers."

"People were pretty pissed, I wouldn't be surprised if they left all sorts behind."

"Right, let's see what we have." She tipped it out onto the crisp, white bed covers. Such a stylish spare room, unlike mine which was crammed full of books, photo albums, and boxes of Lucy's baby clothes that I couldn't stand to let go.

We began picking up random items, attempting to guess whom they might belong to. Some were simple, the fluffy toy kitten that a little girl had been carrying on the dance floor. A pair of long, turquoise feathered earrings that Emma's boss had turned up in, complete with matching shawl – it had certainly been eye-catching. Some could be binned, a random pack of dental floss, a stack of cards for free spins at the casino in a nearby town; but others looked sentimental, such as the delicate silver bracelet with an angel wing charm. I continued to root through the diverse collection, when my hand brushed against a cold and heavy item, a golden cufflink. I picked it up and turned it around in my fingers, noticing the tiny R.G. monogram. As much as it shouldn't, it made my heart thud. The identical one was over by Zoe and, with what should have been an audible 'ping,' an idea shot into my mind.

I gathered everything up and dropped it back into the box, Zoe frowned in confusion. "I know what'll be easiest, save you worrying about this stuff," I began, placing the lid on the box with a decisive tap. "You had a WhatsApp group for all the wedding guests, didn't you?" She nodded, still bemused. I hadn't joined the group, because I was in a complete grump at the time, but now would be perfect.

"Add me into it, and I'll post pictures of this stuff, get it reunited with the owners for you. How does that sound?" I plastered a winning smile on my face.

"That'd be lovely, thank you. Aww, I missed you!" She wrapped her arms around me in a squishy hug.

"Not a problem. Add me in and I'll sort it tonight, once Lucy's in bed. Need to start the new book club read tomorrow. Georgie's choice, you know what that means?"

"Saucy as hell? Perfect." She grabbed our empty glasses with one of her trademark winks and I followed her downstairs, clutching the lost property box.

"No need to see me out, Zo. Good luck with work tomorrow, I'll message you."

I'd stayed at Zoe's longer than planned; fortunately, it was less than a ten-minute walk back to mine, so no worries about being late for Lucy, who would be dropped home by her dad. She'd been tiny when me and him had split up, she didn't even remember us being together as a couple. She was completely comfortable with the fifty-fifty custody situation, so didn't bat an eyelid about swap overs. We both adored her, she had two gorgeous bedrooms, two sets of pocket money, double the holidays, and double the presents. For a six-year-old, that girl was definitely living her best life.

My split from her dad, my ex-husband had been horrible, but she'd been oblivious, and we'd always made sure that even when we despised each other, we never showed it in front of her.

Nowadays we got on pretty well, in passing at least, although I'm not saying I'd like a week in Wales with the guy. Simon, the ex, now lived with his fiancée, Jane. She was kind-hearted, so I had no worries about Lucy being with them, and I knew she was well looked after, as she was with me. I guess it just smarted that, even though he'd been the cheater who had ended our marriage (that wasn't Jane!), he was also the one who'd ended up happy and settled, while I stumbled through phases of disastrous dating and wanker, married dentists.

Still, I wouldn't swap it for the world, my little girl was my absolute sunshine, the light of my life. I drew in a deep breath, as her head nuzzled against my chest upon returning home.

"Missed you, baby," I whispered, kissing her soft, dark hair.

"I missed Rocket. But we went to Nando's!" And then she was off, taking me on a whirlwind tale of every single thing that had happened the past few days, with barely a breath and far more detail than was necessary, but I loved it. Her enthusiasm and excitement were contagious. The world would be a better place if more people could channel their inner six-year-olds, long forgotten in the cynicism and fog of adulting.

Tummy full of chicken wraps, she was fast asleep in record time after a hot bubble bath and clean pyjamas. Leaving her door ajar, and with the landing light on, I crept downstairs, careful to avoid the squeaky floorboards in case they woke her, or worse, Rocket. He'd perfected the knack of nudging the door open to get upstairs this week, and the last thing I needed was him running in and jumping on Lucy. I'd never get her back to sleep, she was besotted with that pup. In fact, they were the only tears she'd had about going to her dad's, not wanting to leave Rocket behind. But no way was I sharing joint custody of *that* little guy. Simon could buy his own puppy if he wanted one.

With little point cooking for one, I grabbed a large glass of Sauvignon Blanc, accompanied by a huge bowl of sweet chilli Kettle Chips, and plonked myself down on the sofa. Rocket was curled up fast asleep in his new bed - the first one had been chewed and destroyed within forty-eight hours of bringing him home. With the tv on for background noise, I retrieved my phone from the coffee table and began to take photos of all the lost property.

I knew full well what I was doing – concocting an excuse to talk to Ryan. I also knew it was a stupid idea, but I wanted to give it a go. To make sure he was OK, if nothing else.

Zoe had, as promised, added me to the group, and, by nine-ish all the photos were uploaded with a cheery message to get in touch if they belonged to you and you wanted to be reunited. I sat, poised, waiting for replies but none came through. I guess the wedding WhatsApp group wasn't so popular now, or maybe it was a little late for a Sunday evening?

With a weary sigh, I checked all the doors and windows were locked, turned everything off and headed to bed, grabbing a top-up of wine on the way. If I was going to make a start on the dirty book, I wanted a drink to go with it. My pyjamas had been donned at the same time as Lucy's, so I settled straight in under the covers, wine in one hand, e-reader in the other – I was trying to save space by reading e-books before my house sank with the weight of my paperbacks.

One paragraph in, and my phone pinged. I cursed myself for not silencing it as I usually would when in bed. A quick glance told me it wasn't the wedding group, but an unknown number, so down the e-reader went and up raised my eyebrows.

UNKNOWN NUMBER

> I hope you don't mind, I saved your number from the wedding group. I didn't want to own up to what was mine in such a public forum.

The message was very formal, but I could sense a playfulness behind it, and I thought I might know who the unknown number was.

PENNY

> I don't mind at all. What precious item can I reconnect you with? Is it the fluffy bunny?

UNKNOWN NUMBER:

> If it had been the fluffy bunny in my bed that night, it might have been easier to forget.

Cue heart flipping over, stomach tying itself in knots, and legs pressing together tight. Before I could reply, a further message came through.

UNKNOWN NUMBER

I also have something I wanted to reunite you with, Penelope. (I can call you that, can't I? It is Sunday after all)

I saved his contact, now absolutely sure that this was Ryan.

PENNY

I will let you off, purely because it's Sunday but don't push your luck. What could you possibly have that's mine? I didn't forget anything?

It was true, I hadn't forgotten a single moment about being with him. Especially those kisses, certainly not his hand as it leisurely wandered inside my pyjama top. I had a lot of time to recall this, as the three little dots to show he was typing started and stopped multiple times, making me wonder if he was actually going to send another message or not.

PENNY

Do you keep typing and deleting?

RYAN

Caught me! I thought this sounded cute but now I realise it sounds ridiculous.

PENNY

Aww, I bet it doesn't, tell me the cute thing!

I grinned like a crush-riddled teenage girl. Even my wine had been abandoned as I lay on my belly, focused entirely on my phone.

RYAN

Ok... so I was going to say that we had a Cinderella moment.

A photo appeared under his message, of a single pearl button held between his thumb and forefinger.

RYAN

I met a lovely, amazing girl. But she had to run away from the ball after my ugly sister (Don't ever tell her I said that!) behaved more like a wicked stepmother. All I had left of her was this pearl button, from her gorgeous pyjamas. I found it in the bathroom sink before I left. Almost missed it.

That was the singularly most amazing message I'd ever received, from anyone, in my entire life, and it set bits of me on fire that really shouldn't be.

PENNY

Best. Message. Ever.

I sent that with a grinning emoji, although it struck me that he wouldn't be an emoji man himself.

RYAN

Phew. That could have gone the other way. So...

My anxiety peaked as I waited for the next message, those little dots teasing me with a million possibilities. God, it felt good to be talking to him again, even if only through WhatsApp, too good.

RYAN

I could visit all the ladies in the town and see if this button belongs to their pyjamas, but it would take a long time - and my car isn't nearly as fanfare-worthy as pulling up in a carriage - and frankly, I don't think my reputation would survive it. So, Penelope, you would be doing me a huge favour if you let me visit you first, to confirm I have the right button, the right pyjamas, and the right girl x

That message had a kiss.

A kiss – I tried not to read too much into it, after all my boss had once sent me a kiss by mistake and had been mortified. People put kisses on everything nowadays, it didn't mean a thing. How to play this though... I wanted to send my address and get him here right now, but I'd look eager and pathetic, plus Lucy was here and I never had men in the house (not like that!) when she was home. Also, what if I was reading in a flirty tone, and he wasn't actually flirting at all? Maybe he simply did think it was amusingly like Cinderella.

RYAN

Penny, you there? Did I creep you out and bollocks that up?

I giggled, full-on schoolgirl again as I replied.

PENNY

Nope, sorry, was desperately trying to think of a good response and I failed. You win at WhatsApp, you are a message connoisseur x

RYAN

You have no idea how wrong you are. I considered putting – My fingers, your pyjamas? And realised that would be fast track to a restraining order x

PENNY

Maybe I'd like your fingers in my pyjamas? x

He wasn't the only one who could send kisses... although I couldn't believe I'd said *that*. How to sound slutty, what an idiot, and it was too late to delete it, two blue ticks were next to it.

PENNY

Sorry! That sounded so forward and awful. Forget I said anything x

RYAN

It sounded adorable, and I won't be forgetting it, far from it. In all seriousness, could we meet up and swap? Cufflinks for a button? You pick when and where x

My mind whirred through options and how to play this. A bar? A restaurant? Invite him round maybe? It all seemed a bit datey, or presumptuous, and his flirtiness on WhatsApp tonight contradicted what he'd said about not being ready to date. Or was I just looking for more than there was in his words? Fortunately, I had someone who would be a great distraction should we meet, and he have no interest in me. Someone furry and adorable.

PENNY

Are you free Saturday? Fancy meeting me AND the gorgeous pup? I normally take him to the country park on a Saturday, are you up for a walk and a coffee? x

RYAN

Sounds perfect, but I can't promise I won't try to leave with the puppy x

I was betraying myself and my vow of celibacy, but I hoped he'd want to leave with me.

PENNY

He has bad taste in pyjamas. I don't think you'd like him. Also, hairy legs x

RYAN

It's so good to talk to you again xx

Two kisses! I was winning.

PENNY

And you xx

RYAN

I better let you get some sleep, school night and all that! Looking forward to Saturday xx

PENNY

Me too. Sweet dreams, thanks for messaging me xx

RYAN

xx

I was swooning over WhatsApp, what the hell was wrong with me? I could see other replies had come through on the wedding chat, but I didn't care to look. I downed the last dregs of wine and got ready for bed. It was only after I finished brushing my teeth that it occurred to me, wanker-dentist hadn't even crossed my mind. This was progress.

I wished I could control my dreams, and they would one hundred per cent involve Ryan and my pyjamas, except with more buttons coming off than going on. With a smug, satisfied smile, I switched off the lamp and disappeared under the covers with only one thing on my mind.

NINE

*H*ad a walk in the countryside ever been agonised over to this extent? So many pairs of jeans and jeggings tried on with every pair of boots I owned – too many – to try and get the perfect autumnal combination that made my bum look good *and* suited the black cashmere jumper I'd already decided to wear. It was snuggly soft, and somehow very flattering in the boob area.

Not that it should matter what he thought of my bum or boobs, but I was overthinking everything to the extreme. It would have helped to talk it through with a friend, but I didn't want to 'fess up, not after the fuss I'd made about 'no men' and how I was staying single for good. Maybe there wasn't even anything to confess to anyway. It wasn't even a date, just friends meeting to swap cufflinks for a button, completely normal.

Overthinking was my unofficial Olympic sport, and I took gold every time.

Four weeks had passed since the wedding, yet it felt like so much had changed. That hazy heat wave was over, and the leaves had begun to plummet at a pace, leaving a glorious amber-brown crunching pathway on the ground. The sun was bright today, but cooler, so much fresher, and that crisp feeling only found at this time of year invigorated me as I took deep breaths.

I'd arrived ten minutes ahead of time, partially because I was early for everything. I'd been that way my whole life, the thought of being late stressed me to hell, but also because I wanted to give Rocket a chance to settle down. He was still a baby, extremely bouncy and excitable, and the smells of leaves, squirrels, and other dogs were just enough to tip him from playful to downright naughty.

As predicted, he'd bounced around so much that his lead was now in a tangle between his little legs. I couldn't help but laugh as he looked up at me with those huge, brown eyes, all helpless and confused. I knelt down amongst the leaves, trying to figure out what he'd managed to do.

"Rocket!" I play-scolded. "Keep still." Obedient as ever, he jumped up and licked my face before spotting what must have been an irresistible twig nearby and lunging for it. Thankfully, I had his lead in my other hand which stopped him from escaping. Instead, he lay on the ground, guarding his special twig as a tall shadow loomed over him.

"Morning."

I looked up, my stomach fluttering as my eyes dusted over Ryan. He was far more casual than I'd seen him before, yet still altogether gorgeous in dark jeans and a forest green jumper. His hair wasn't styled, as it had been at the wedding, and so flopped over his forehead. It should have looked scruffy, but it was endearing; boyish. I wanted to tuck it back.

Before I could reply, he knelt down next to Rocket who began to back away, his tail between his legs and the twig forgotten as he focused on the tall stranger in front of him. My pup wasn't the bravest with new people.

"Hey, Rocket," he purred, holding his fisted hand out slow and steady. "Your mum didn't tell me your name, but I think I heard it right." Rocket sniffed him tentatively as his retreat to me ceased. "I think she did that on purpose, worried I'd remember your name and not hers. As if I could. What do you think?" Rocket moved up to sniff him closer, happy as Ryan began to stroke his back with his free hand.

The lead tugged in my fist as Rocket reached up to lick Ryan's face, his tail wagging so hard the entire back half of his little body wobbled. It was adorable, very Hallmark, cute guy and puppy melting hearts all over the place, if there had been anyone else here to watch the scene.

I rose slowly, trying to make it look deliberate when, in fact, I was hoping to stop my knees from cracking like an old lady. Ryan was in front of me in two strides, Rocket following at his heels and sitting between us, panting happily as I dropped a couple of training treats from my pocket for him.

"Hi," Ryan smiled. I'd forgotten how the expression warmed his entire face, one of those smiles that drew you in, made you feel part of a special club.

"Hi, it's good to see you," I said casually, feeling anything but. "I was thinking that if we follow the blue path, it leads to the café - a twenty minute walk. Rocket will be tired by then, so we could grab a coffee, chat, do the swap?"

"Sounds like a plan." He glanced towards the wooden posts which marked the blue path before turning back to me, his grey eyes taking on a hint of green in mimicry of the jumper he was wearing. "You changed your hair." His fingers curled inwards, as though he stopped himself from reaching out to touch it.

"Yeah, I'm still getting used to it." I combed my fingers through the length. I'd had a fair bit cut off and hoped he wouldn't say he preferred it the other way.

"It's beautiful. As chocolatey as your eyes, now, I'm blaming you when I put weight on."

"So, I *shouldn't* offer to buy you hot chocolate at the café then…?" I asked, my heart still racing, no matter how much I told it to calm down.

"Hot chocolate is absolutely what I want. Offer away." I couldn't tell if he was flirting or not, and when he got me like that, I found it hard to focus. I blew out a short breath, my lips forming a tiny 'o' which his eyes dropped to in an instant. Did he want to kiss me again? I wanted him to, even though I shouldn't, I couldn't help it.

He coughed as if about to speak, but the moment was broken by Rocket barking with delight as a tiny sausage dog trotted across the leaves towards him. They sniffed noses and bottoms, living their best lives, before it meandered back to its owner, with the twig that Rocket had been so proud of.

"This way," I said with a smile, as we followed the trail. It ended up taking nearer thirty minutes after a few leg tangles (Rocket), one boot stuck in the mud (me), and coming to the aid of a little girl with a frisbee stuck in a tree (Ryan). But as we pottered along, it didn't feel as if time mattered.

I guess we both avoided talk of *that* morning, but he told me how his week at work had been, and I filled him in on the holiday plans I was narrowing down, torn between what Lucy would like best.

Rocket had slowed down a little as we neared the café and, as we rounded a corner, my hand brushed against Ryan's. I closed my eyes for a split second as a tingle shot up my arm, and then a warmness spread as Ryan took hold of it, wrapping his fingers around mine.

"Is this ok?" he asked, looking down at me with an arched eyebrow.

I nodded, happy, and moved closer to him as we continued to walk, quieter now, as we held hands like shy schoolchildren.

The café looked almost empty as we approached but it was still early and, by late morning, the place would be packed. I preferred to get here when it was quiet, especially while Rocket was still training. Usually, I'd bring a book and get a quick chapter in with a coffee while he rested before the walk back, but no book today, just Ryan.

"You don't mind sitting outside, do you? He gets a bit giddy if he can smell the sausages cooking in there," I said, motioning towards Rocket.

"I know how he feels, to be fair. I don't mind at all. What can I get you?"

"No," I said, holding out Rocket's lead. "I'm buying. You sit with Rocket, I'll go in. Hot Chocolate? Or was that all talk?"

"Bring it on. I can handle it." He smirked, as he sat down at one of the benched tables and looped Rocket's lead onto the stake underneath. This place was all geared up for dog walkers.

Five minutes later, I slid onto the bench beside him and placed two mugs of hot chocolate down, complete with creamy tops, plus a dog treat for Rocket.

"If you give him that, he'll love you forever." I said. "He's obsessed with them."

"If only people were that straightforward," he replied with a smile, as he passed the treat down to Rocket, who promptly lay down with it between his front paws and began to chomp away. "So…" he reached into his jeans pocket. "I believe this is yours?"

He placed the button on the table between us and I laughed as I picked it up. "I can't believe you kept that."

"Well, it all felt a bit surreal. This was tangible evidence."

"Is surreal bad?"

He shook his head. "No, not bad… hard to explain. I'm not usually like that, it was spontaneous and fun and sexy if I dare say it. And then it got ridiculous when Jess turned up. I didn't know if I'd see you again. The button was something to hold on to, I guess it reminded me that good things could still happen to me."

"They can, and they will. You're a great person, you deserve good things." I reached into my own pocket and placed the two golden cufflinks between our mugs. "I believe these are yours."

"Thank you," He sipped at the hot chocolate, his hands wrapped around the warm mug.

"It's getting chilly, isn't it?" I said with a glance at his hands. "Summer seemed to bugger off without warning. How were we boiling in a heatwave only four weeks back?"

"I'd say autumn has chased it away." He reached down to the floor, then brandished a conker in the air with a flourish. "I used to collect these when I was a kid."

"Sort of looks like you still do," I teased, grabbing it from him. "I love the colours of a conker, and they're always so shiny."

He grabbed it back with a grin, my reflexes too slow to stop him. "Gorgeous, glossy brown like your hair?"

"Shush," I felt my cheeks heat up. "My hair is nothing like that. Plus, the conkers don't need *their* roots doing every six weeks."

"If we find another one, we can play conkers next time we meet," he said, looking around earnestly as if he were a schoolboy.

"Next time?" I asked.

"I hope there'll be a next time. Or are you done with me, now you've got your button back?"

I avoided answering that and instead moved to the subject that I couldn't help but wonder about. "Are you and Jess ok? Did she tell you she came to see me?"

"She did. She's an absolute arse when she's drunk, I don't know why she reacted like that."

"I guess I can't blame her, Jess wanted to protect you from the dodgy woman she met on the hen do. Nobody really believes that I didn't know about his wife, I see it in their eyes."

"I don't care what other people think or say. I believe

86

you, hand on heart, never doubted it. And Jess won't behave that way again."

I drained my hot chocolate, watching him over the rim of my mug, I couldn't spot any hidden agenda or sign of deceit. Why did I have to meet someone so lovely, just at the point I'd sworn not to? Couldn't he have come before all the other idiots?

"That sky looks awful," I said, as a cold breeze blew and set goosebumps aflame up my arms. "We're only five minutes away from the car if we pick up a pace, shall we head off?"

Ryan agreed, and we strolled away as the first, freezing drops landed on the café tables. Then, as if on cue, the heavens burst open, spilling a deluge of rain upon us. We were soaked within seconds. I screeched, as an ice-cold drip ran down my back. Quick as a flash Ryan scooped up Rocket, sheltering him under his jumper as we ran towards the car park.

I ran for the car, never so happy to hear the 'beep' as the doors unlocked. Ryan wrenched the back door open and deposited Rocket onto the waiting towel on the seat.

"Jump in!" I shouted, battling to be heard against the relentless drum of torrential rain on the car roof.

I slammed the door closed as soon as I was in the driver's seat, Ryan followed and took up the passenger seat. We both burst out laughing as we looked back to see Rocket already asleep on his towel, a dampened face the only sign that he'd been caught in it. Meanwhile, Ryan and I were dripping and had no towel between us.

"Where's your car?" I asked, as I reached back and clipped the doggy seat belt on Rocket's harness.

"I walked, regretting that now." His hair dripped as he spoke.

"That's OK, I can take you home. Where do you live?" I asked as I turned the heaters to full, pointing the vents at us rather than the windows.

"Yewtree Avenue, you know it?"

"Yep, off we go." Did I know it? I knew of it, but I'd never stepped foot in a house around there. Those roads, Yewtree, Silver Birch, Aspen Way, Willow Brook, all bordered the country park and were way out of my price range, one of the very poshest parts of town.

"We bought it a few years back, it was a bit of a wreck, it's been a hell of a project to get it up to standard." He said, as if reading my thoughts.

"What number?" I asked, as we turned onto the road.

"Seven," he replied. "The one with the black car in the drive." The 'black car' was a very sleek Lexus. "Pull right up by the front door. Come in and get dry, I can't let you drive off when you're soaked through."

"You sure?" I asked, worrying about my poor cashmere sweater. "I'd have to bring Rocket in too, I can't leave him."

"Of course, Rocket too. The rain was all part of my evil plan to get the puppy in my house." He grinned, before sprinting out and unlocking his front door.

I picked Rocket up in his towel, trying not to focus on the beautiful Victorian house I was about to enter. Nice guy, really cute, amazing house... my vow of celibacy was a loose vow, wasn't it?

TEN

$\mathcal{I}$ crouched down on the wooden hallway floor to towel-dry Rocket, keen to prevent him from shaking mud all over what I assumed to be an expensively painted hallway. But in reality, all I did was make him wetter as my hair dripped with sploshes, whilst I kicked my drenched boots off.

"Where's best to put Rocket? I don't want him to wreck your house." I stood, barefoot and soggy, facing Ryan. My mouth slid into a smile as his dripping wet face came into view; I forgot that mine looked as daft.

"Come through to the kitchen," he said. "He'll be fine, he won't destroy anything, I'm sure." Ryan swiped a raindrop from the end of my nose with a smile and headed down the hallway, past a staircase and an archway, then through a heavy, oak door which he closed behind us, after ushering me politely in.

Rocket scampered off to sniff every square inch of the floor, leaving me to glance around whilst trying to not be obvious that I was checking the place out. It was huge.

Obviously an extension on the back of the house with a sloping, glass roof, ultra-modern kitchen and one of those islands I longed for but couldn't fit into my place. The other half of the room was like a cosy den, with a fireplace, shaggy rugs, and a large, grey corner sofa which pointed towards a wall-mounted television.

"I'm so sorry about the mess, I wasn't expecting company. Please don't think I'm an absolute slob." He gathered a pile of clothes that were crumpled at the side of the sofa and threw them through a doorway, dropping a sock on the way which he grabbed and tossed out of sight.

He rubbed my arms, his hands coming away damp from the cashmere that hung heavy on me now, drenched through as it was. "You're going to freeze, you're soaked."

"So are you," I pointed out, a shiver running down my spine.

"Yeah, but I'm more worried about you. I'll keep an eye on Rocket, you go have a hot shower. I'll find you some clothes to wear while your things dry. You'll get ill otherwise."

I wanted to say no, because I felt awkward and like an inconvenience. But I truly was glacial, and a shower sounded amazing. I nodded in agreement, more drips falling onto the floor.

"Upstairs, second door on the left. Help yourself to everything, no rush, get warm, OK? And I'll tidy this mess up, so sorry!"

I smiled gratefully, heading out of the kitchen as I heard Ryan chattering to Rocket, something about lighting the fire. In all honesty 'the mess' was fairly standard, dirty plates and mugs, some takeaway packets – exactly what I'd expect from a guy who lived alone. My kitchen was similar at times when work was taking up all my hours.

The stairs didn't even creak, unlike mine, as I tiptoed up, admiring the dark blue and grey striped carpet. Beautiful black and white photographs, set in slate grey frames, lined the walls of the staircase. Ryan and, I guessed, Tara, looking content and loved-up in various settings, weddings, holidays, and Christmases. I gulped down the wave of nausea that the sheer thought of his loss brought to me and hurried to the bathroom, not wanting to be nosing at things I shouldn't be.

The bathroom... Oh, this was the bathroom of my dreams. A freestanding, clawfoot bathtub, so deep I'd get through at least two chapters of a book while I filled it, sat on top of a shiny black and white tiled floor. A tall frosted-glass window stood next to the sink, with the toilet tucked away behind an outcropping of tiles. Twisting to my side, I spotted the huge, walk-in shower, easy big enough for two with its floor to ceiling glass and sleek shelves discreetly displaying expensive shower gel and shampoo. This room was spotless, too spotless, no toothpaste smears around the sink or water marks on the shower screen. I briefly pondered why, but the desire to get warm was more important.

I undressed, draping my jumper over the heated towel rail, before turning the dials to full power and high heat. My upper arms and thighs were coated with goosebumps, and it took a good few minutes of the hot water pummelling me before my skin warmed up.

I washed with one of the large luxury bottles of shower gel, the smell growing more and more familiar, as I recognised the undertones of it from the few hugs I'd shared with Ryan; peppery and spicy. I was going to need to buy some of this. His shampoo was the same brand so, after a quick hair wash, I combed the knots as best I could with my fingers and reluctantly turned the blissfully hot shower off.

Towels were stacked on a high shelf next to it, and I wrapped a large, fluffy black bath sheet around my body after rubbing myself dry, tucking it in under my arm as I patted my hair with a hand towel. After checking my reflection in the mirror and thanking my lucky stars for waterproof mascara, I unlocked the door and peeked outside. All clear, no sign of Ryan, but a little bundle of clothes had been left outside the door for me as promised.

I had an awful moment of panic that they might be Tara's, as that would have been very weird; also, judging by how petite she was in the photos, they'd never fit me, but these appeared to be Ryan's. Soft flannel pyjama bottoms and a cosy white t-shirt, which was fine except my knickers and bra were soaked and there was no way Ryan would have spare of those.

I pulled the pyjama bottoms up; if I held onto them at my hip they wouldn't fall down, and at least the t-shirt wasn't tight, so unless I pushed my chest out for any random reason, I wasn't displaying huge amounts of nipple or anything untoward. It would have to do. I wrapped my wet clothes in another dry towel, making a mental note to offer to take the dirty laundry home, then wandered downstairs, slower this time, smiling as I heard Ryan playing with Rocket.

My eyes lingered on a wedding photograph, Ryan and

Tara looked absolutely enthralled in each other. They were at the top table, her in a stunning, slinky dress and him in black tie; someone stood behind them with a microphone, mid-speech, and the two of them were laughing, pure joyous laughter with wide smiles, but their eyes were locked on each other, completely in love, anyone could have seen it from a mile away. I couldn't help but compare myself to Tara, and I couldn't see how I'd be Ryan's type. She was tiny, both in height and figure, like a little doll with her blonde pixie cut and a smile so wide it filled her face. It was impossible to know her eye colour from a black and white print, but they were bright and sparkling. Loads of guys loved tiny women like that, a far cry from my big-boobed, wide-hipped figure and, for a split second, I could imagine him throwing her around the bedroom in ways he never could me.

I shook the thought away, it was both inappropriate and unnecessary, plus I *had* to stop thinking about him in a sexual way, it was getting weird.

I wandered back into the kitchen, wondering if I could leap over to the sofa and hide under a cushion, but then if I leapt, the pyjama bottoms would no doubt fall down, and I'd be left with my bottom on show in his kitchen. *Classy.* Not.

"Hey." Ryan looked up from Rocket with a handsome smile. "You find everything OK? Sorry I didn't really have much that I thought would fit you, those OK while we get your clothes dry?"

"They're great, thank you. You got showered too?" I asked, noticing his dry clothes and slicked-back hair. The dirty dishes had also disappeared, and the sofa cushions were arranged in place, far from their haphazard positions earlier.

"Yeah, there's a wet room down here, I never use the main bathroom." Of course there is, I thought, falling more victim to house envy. "Pass me your clothes, and I'll put them in the dryer." I passed him the towel with everything parcelled inside. My knickers were tucked inside my jeans so he wouldn't see them.

"This can't go in the dryer," I said holding onto my jumper, which had my bra hidden inside. "Is there somewhere I can hang it to dry?"

"I'll hang it in the utility room, gets very warm in there when the dryer's on." He reached out for the soggy jumper.

"I'll do it," I squealed, mortified at the thought of him hanging my bra up.

"It's fine, honestly," he insisted; he took the jumper as my face burned hot. "What's wrong?" he cocked his head as he looked at me.

"There's a bra too," I mumbled.

His mouth morphed into a lopsided grin, as he backed away with the soggy parcel of damp clothes. "Penny. I'm a middle-aged man. I've seen bras before, I'll be fine." He smirked. "No bra in the dryer then?"

"Jeans and kickers are good in the dryer, socks too. Bra and jumper no. And don't look." I'd never been so grateful for a matching underwear set. I'd felt foolish wearing such an expensive set for a dog walk, but it was always better to be prepared, and it had paid off today. If they'd been some old, greying set, I'd have hurled them out the window before I let him touch them.

His face was so comical as he laughed good-naturedly.

"No looking at Penny's knickers... noted. Go pour some coffee, I'll be two minutes."

I placed my phone and keys down on the kitchen counter after grabbing them from the pocket of my jeans, then headed to the sofa. Rocket trotted along behind Ryan as if they were best pals, leaving me two minutes to arrange myself on the sofa so that I looked decent. Ryan had placed a large tray on the corner section with a cafetière, mugs, and milk; it smelled divine, rich, strong, and heavy on caffeine.

I filled both mugs and tucked my legs up under me, appreciative of the fire that was now lit and blasting warmth towards me. Sinking back, I looked up to the glass roof, where rain still poured and pounded against the glass. It was a sound I'd always found comfort in.

"You'll be glad to know the bra didn't get me," teased Ryan as he sat down and reached for a mug from the tray. As his body stretched in front of me, I could smell the same shower gel I'd washed in. "But the dog now belongs to me."

I smiled as I looked over at Rocket, who had curled up in front of the fire and fallen asleep. I was in that weird state of being lost for words again, shy and wanting to sound interesting and grown up, but knowing I'd probably say something stupid about incest or knickers again.

"Why don't you get a dog? We could walk them together."

"Worried about getting too attached, I guess." He shrugged, his eyebrows pulled together as he disguised a frown.

"To me, or the dog?" I wrinkled my nose up in an attempt to lighten the mood, but his gaze felt very intense as he watched me over the rim of his mug. "I saw your wedding photo on the stairs, it's beautiful."

"Some days, I try not to look at it when I pass by, is that bad?" he asked.

"No, I don't think so. I know it's different but, after my divorce, I never wanted to see mine again. Now though, I can look at them and remember it was a happy day. Whatever happened afterwards doesn't change the fact that we were in love on that day."

"I like that I can talk about it with you. People assume that, after a certain amount of time, it's business as usual, and that I'm OK. Or that Tara can't ever be mentioned again." He sighed. "Would you ever get married again?"

"Swore I wasn't even going to date again, never mind get married, but I don't know, you never know what's around the corner I guess."

"You might get swept off your feet yet," he said with a sad smile.

"What about you? Would you marry again?"

He rubbed his forehead, his thumbs tracing circles around his temples. "Tara and me, we had chats about the future. We made wills and got life insurance and all that stuff. We never knew death was around the corner, we assumed it was fifty years away. We both always agreed we'd want the other one to move on and be happy, to find love again, but that's easy to say when none of it is real. How can you expect someone to accept how much grief stays with you? And then there's the guilt..."

"I can't speak for Tara or anyone else but, if it were me, I'd want my partner to find happiness. Of course, you'll always still love her, nobody should ever expect anything else, nor should they expect you to forget her, she'll always be a part of you. That doesn't mean it's the end of your story though."

"What if that ended the same way? I couldn't go through it again." He sighed and leaned his head against my shoulder. I began to stroke his almost-dry hair, baby soft and fluffy; as I sat up straighter, his head fell against my chest. I'd never sensed a person need solace like this, the way he did, comfort and affection.

"What do you think matters more?" I asked. "How something starts or how it finishes? I think they both pale in comparison to what happens in between, those millions of moments that form the maze of a relationship between two people. The memories, the touches, the smiles, the love. That matters so much more, and that can't be taken away, even by death. Love and memories stay."

"I'm scared to start again." He said it so quietly, as if it were the first time he'd voiced the words.

"I know, me too," I whispered, as we both remained silent, the only sound in the room the crackle of the fire, the drumming of the rain, and the tiny, occasional baby snore from Rocket.

Ryan wrapped his arms around me and squeezed tight, before sitting up and smiling. "Want to stay and watch a movie? I don't think that rain's stopping any time soon. Or do you need to be home for Lucy?"

"She's with her dad. I'm starving, though. Have you got movie snacks?"

"I still want sausages after you teased me with the prospect of them at the café. You in?"

"Definitely." He pressed his hand onto my thigh as he

pushed himself up and off the sofa. My head was jumbled with what to do, he was so vulnerable, but I got the impression more and more that he liked me, and I really liked him, there was no point trying to deny it anymore. It wasn't worth it, in the same way that I couldn't deny the chemistry between us, every time he looked at me. I wanted to kiss him, and as much as I tried to push the feeling away, it grew with every moment that I was in his presence.

ELEVEN

*G*od, this was comfortable. And warm. *So* warm. I must have been having the most amazing dream of my life as I woke from it fully content and beaming, cosy and snug.

My eyes flicked open a fraction to the dark room, dimly lit by the remnants of the fire. I blearily made out the hazy shape of Rocket, still curled up happy with his own puppy dreams. I didn't want to wake up and go out into the rain, which still pitter-pattered down onto the roof. Just five more minutes, I was sure Ryan wouldn't mind. It was very sweet of him to leave me here resting; falling asleep during movies was an awful habit of mine, I should've warned him.

With a long, languid stretch I rolled over onto my right side, my back to the fire now as I curled up. Yet, instead of finding myself against the back of the sofa, I found myself face to face with a very sleepy, toasty warm Ryan.

How on earth was I waking up next to him again? Did

twice mean we were forming a habit? I didn't even care at that point, it felt so good that I decided to go with the flow.

I wriggled a smidge closer, smiling as Ryan's arm, which had been under me, wrapped around my middle, his fingers rubbing softly at my waist. My own arms were tucked in front of me a little awkwardly, but I didn't want to drop them down in case I brushed against anything I shouldn't; but mirroring Ryan seemed like it would be acceptable. I raised my left arm and placed it on his hip, hoping this wasn't too much.

One stormy, grey eye peeped open and a drowsy smile appeared on his lips. "Hey, sleepy," he mumbled. "What happened at the end of the movie?"

"I have no idea," I whispered as our breath mingled together. "I always fall asleep, I'm sorry."

"Don't say sorry," he pulled me close, and it sucked the air right out of my lungs. "Apparently I only sleep when I'm with you, this is good."

My face was now nestled against his neck, I had such a weakness for necks, all soft skin, and pheromones with that masculine Adam's apple full of promise. This wasn't a safe place for me to be, my hormones were all thrummed up into a cyclone in the pit of my belly. I was glad I hadn't had wine, there'd be no going back.

Ryan shifted his body and, as he did so, my lips brushed against his neck. I didn't kiss or move, I simply left them there against his warm skin, his scent swarming into my nose and leaving me giddy.

He sighed, not an impatient sigh, more of a relaxed, unrushed exhale. I waited, pulling back a breath so my lips closed, their contact with his skin broken. For someone who was allegedly off men, I sure was panicky about rejection right now.

His hand lifted from my waist, and I was certain he was about to stand up, that the moment was over but, instead, he trailed his fingers down the sides of my face before they teased their way into my hair. Then, he kissed me.

Kiss number six. Would I count them forever? I hoped there'd be so many they were impossible to tally up because *this* was luscious. His lips pressed against mine, applying just the right amount of pressure so that if I'd wanted to stop, I could have. But I did *not* want this to stop, far from it.

I kissed back, my lips rhythmic against his as my hand stroked over his hip. I flicked my tongue into his mouth, tentative, testing; was I going too far? In response, his hand slid further down my body and slipped inside the baggy pyjama bottoms, whether on purpose or by accident I'd never know, they certainly gaped around my hips. He gripped my lower back with both hands, pulling me tight against him as his mouth crushed mine and our kiss became heated and tangled. The tiniest gasp escaped his mouth, mingling directly into me. It spiralled me into pure lust as I wrapped my leg around his hip, my hand sliding up as I ran my nails down his side, wanting to touch him, feel him, know him.

The kisses on the wedding night had been delectable, but this felt like a whole new phase between us. He held a string, unknowingly, that connected him to my very centre, and he could pluck at it as he desired and reduce me to a quivering wreck who would beg for more. These thoughts reeled through my mind, drowning out the scared whimpering of the girl who'd given up on men and heartbreak.

He turned me onto my back, stopping our kiss momentarily as he moved above me. Our eyes met for a fleeting moment and then his lips were upon me again, my vision blurred with darkness, all the sensations overtaking me.

"Did I tell you how beautiful you are?" he mumbled as his mouth slipped to my neck, pressing kiss after kiss to my skin.

"I'm not sure, maybe you'd better start again, just in case?" I teased, as his hand tickled my waist, drawing delighted giggles from me.

"Is this OK?" he asked as his hands grabbed at the white t-shirt I wore, *his* t-shirt. He lifted it an inch, looking at me for consent which I was only too happy to give.

"Yes," I confirmed. "As long as we even it up." I gripped at the hem of his top and he pulled it off, throwing it to the side before he focused his attention back on mine.

"And to think you didn't want me to see your bra…" He bent down and kissed my stomach as his hands slowly, torturously pushed the t-shirt up. I smirked with anticipatory pleasure and pushed myself up, lifting my arms above my head for him. Ryan didn't waste a second, whipping the t-shirt off and discarding it with his own. To his credit, his eyes remained trained on mine, and not the bare chest he'd uncovered, but his forefinger traced around my nipple, as it had that night in the hotel room bed.

I threw myself at him, a wanton woman by this point as I pressed him against the cushion-back of the sofa and straddled his thighs. With the t-shirt gone and the too-large pyjama pants slipped down around my upper thighs, it would have been easy to feel exposed, but I felt safe with Ryan and, at that moment, cared about nothing but getting as much of him as I could.

Our tongues tangled, as damp lips crushed against each other. Then I was momentarily disoriented as Ryan's mouth left mine. He slid down the sofa, moving below me as his tongue licked along my collarbone. His hands gripped my hips tight, holding me in place; it began to pinch but the very sensation of it dizzied me in all the best ways. And regardless, any discomfort was forgotten as his tongue followed the same pattern his finger had earlier.

He pulled me down to him, his mouth centred on mine as I shuddered, wanting more.

"Penny..." He whispered my name into my ear, nibbling at my ear lobe. I sensed a change in the speed, a slowdown. "I've barely stopped thinking about you. This..." He blew out a breath, his lips grazing my neck in a slow, deliberate kiss. "This feels so good. I want this, but not just this, I want more and I just..."

His words ran out and I pulled his mouth to mine and kissed soft and slow, more like we had at the hotel. Trying desperately to control myself when in actuality I longed to hump his brains out.

"I understand," I said, in between the delicate kisses, which he returned to me over and over.

"I don't want to 'get the first time over with,' or 'jump back on the horse,' or any of that stupid advice people feel the need to plague me with," he gulped. "If we do this. *When* we do this..." He pulled back and tapped the end of my nose in a playful fashion. "I want us both to be sure. I don't want to disappoint you, do you understand what I mean?"

"That was an incredible way to wake-up. I'll never be disappointed by waking up like that."

"It was the nicest," he replied. "Don't move, one sec." He reached behind the sofa and pulled a soft blanket out. He wrapped it around us both and tugged me back to my original position, so my head rested in the crook of his shoulder, my legs still around him.

My heart hammered ten to the dozen, mirroring his as his pulse beat against my cheek. He swiped my hair from my face, pressing a soft kiss to my forehead. Everything was still but for our heartbeats and the rain, with the occasional crackle of a log.

"Penny—" he began, as my phone burst into a noisy tune, the tune I allocated to Lucy's dad, Simon. He'd never ring for a chat; he must need me.

"Sorry!" I gasped as I jumped back from his knee and darted over to the kitchen to grab my phone from the worktop where I'd abandoned it earlier. I almost face planted as the baggy bottoms began to fall to the floor, I grabbed them with a nervous shriek and tugged them up just in time. It must have looked the exact opposite of sexy.

"Simon, is everything ok?" I asked, as I answered moments before the voicemail could kick in, my fist still clutching at my waistband.

"Yeah, didn't want to worry you. Listen, Lucy seems to have come down with a bug. She's alternating throwing up and running to the toilet, she can't go fifteen minutes without one or the other."

My heart sank, my poor baby. She'd been fine when I

dropped her off this morning. "We're looking after her, but she keeps crying and asking for you. She wants to go back to yours, is that OK?"

"Of course. No problem at all." Ryan walked up behind me and wrapped the blanket around my shoulders, before heading out of the door that I presumed led to the utility room. Only then did I realise I'd been in the middle of his kitchen topless; thank goodness his house wasn't overlooked by neighbours.

"Can you get her ready, maybe send some towels for the car in case she doesn't make it back in time? I'll be there within half an hour, I'm at a friend's place."

"Yep. Sorry to ruin your weekend, I'd keep her here, but she wants her mum."

"It's never a problem. I'll be there as quick as I can. Let her know."

I ended the call as Ryan headed out of the utility room with my clothes; a quick glance at the time on my phone and I realised I'd been here for hours with him.

"Ryan, I—"

He shushed me. "Don't worry, I heard. Go get dressed, sounds like your daughter needs you."

"Thank you," I mouthed as I ran back up to the bathroom and dressed, leaving the blanket and pyjama bottoms stacked by the door, god knows where the t-shirt had ended up.

I hurried downstairs to find Ryan had Rocket all harnessed up and ready for me, waiting with a smile at the front door.

"You're amazing," I said as I tugged my boots on, which

the absolute sweetheart had left on a radiator, so they were dry and warm. "Tha—"

Before I could thank him again, he kissed me, so soft and sensual that it sent my stomach into somersaults once more.

"Mmmm," was all I could manage, sucking on my bottom lip as he pulled away.

"Let me know when you're back home and she's OK?"

I nodded in agreement as I hurried outside with Rocket, the rain thankfully more of a drizzle than a flood now. Ryan stayed at the doorway as he waved me off, all barefoot and hot looking in jeans and a t-shirt; he must have retrieved our discarded tops. It was only then I remembered that he was going to say something before my phone rang. Would I ever find out what it was, or had the moment passed?

TWELVE

*W*itnessing my poorly little girl in such a bad way, hour after hour for a day and a half was torturous. I felt helpless that all I could do was mop her brow and tell her I loved her in between putting the washing machine on over and over again, as we got through every sheet and towel in the house. Jess's words came back to me, how she'd felt helpless to comfort Ryan and it resonated. But Lucy would be better very soon, Ryan was suffering from something that had no real cure. How many times had I read that you never get over a death, you simply learn to live with it?

Ryan had messaged a couple of times over the weekend, but I'd had no chance for anything other than scant replies. I hadn't even been able to walk Rocket, who was having to make do with the back garden, as Lucy wasn't well enough to leave the house and walk, nor was she old enough to be left for even five minutes, especially whilst poorly.

By the time Monday morning rolled around, I was akin to a zombie, and not even a freshly minted one. At least a six-month-old walker, all dried up and husk-like. Lucy had stopped vomiting at about one in the morning and had slept through since, but as my alarm went off at seven-fifteen, I knew there was no way I could manage work today.

I called the council absence line, certain there'd be no one there at that time and I could leave an answerphone message; they'd call back if any problems, but I was hardly ever off sick, and I was sure it would be fine. As I ended the call, a message popped up, bringing a smile to my face.

RYAN

Morning, how's she doing? x

PENNY

Seems to be on the mend, she crashed out at about 1am, so I'm letting her sleep all day if she needs to x

RYAN

And you? x

PENNY

I'm OK, just tired. Not working today x

RYAN

You need looking after too, can I come round and help with that? x

I sat back against the headboard; he'd caught me unawares. I hadn't thought about him coming here at all, which was weird considering how much time I'd devoted to thinking of nothing *but* him.

I'd never before let Lucy meet any of the men I'd dated, not that Ryan and I were dating. I'd never wanted to be one of those women who introduced her child to a new guy every couple of months. Simon felt the same, and Lucy had only been introduced to Jane when she and him were a good few months into their relationship.

But Ryan was a friend first and foremost and, as much as he made my knees weak, I had no idea if things would go further, so was there any harm? Plus, the idea of being looked after sounded perfect. I desperately needed a shower and some food. The coffee had run out and this was disastrous to me, plus poor Rocket did need a good walk or a run in the park.

PENNY

Don't you have work? x

RYAN

It's one of the joys of being co-owner of the company. Is that a yes? x

PENNY

I want to say yes but the house stinks - and Lucy isn't at her best x

RYAN

Open some windows, leave her to rest in bed, send me a shopping list and I'll be there for about 9.30 x

PENNY

You're the best, thank you x

I smiled, as I heaved myself groggily out of the bed, knowing Rocket would be desperate to get into the garden and pee against every tree. The phone beeped once more, and I peeped at Lucy who'd been asleep next to me. She was still out like a light, her beautiful, pale face calmer now, not all bundled in reaction to the painful stomach cramps.

RYAN

Just realised I don't know your address x

I sent it to him with a short shopping list as I was desperate for coffee and milk. I suspected, based on previous bouts of illness, that Lucy's appetite would come back with a vengeance, so added her favourite cereal, some fresh bread, and chocolate digestives, although they were secretly for me.

As soon as Rocket had completed his tree pees and wolfed down his breakfast, I opened all the windows and then jumped into the shower. I mean, it would have been rude to have a friend - because that's all I told myself Ryan could be, for now anyway - turn up and find me looking like a slobby hermit.

Once the shower had worked its magic, I threw on a casual black t-shirt and some grey jeans. As I was making my eyes look more awake with some mascara, Lucy stirred, sitting up and stretching, with a confused look in her eyes.

"Hey, beautiful girl," I said as I rushed over and hugged her. "You had a big sleep."

"Did I sleep in your bed, Mummy?" she asked, her big, chocolate button eyes focusing in on the room.

"You did, you feel better, baby?"

She nodded and snuggled back down with her teddy.

"I'm going to dry my hair, is that OK?" I asked, not wanting to disturb her if she needed more sleep.

"Yes, Mummy," she murmured. "Then can we have breakfast before school?"

"You're not going to school today, sweetheart, and I'm not going to work. Duvet day, how does that sound?"

"Duvet day!" she exclaimed happily as she grabbed my phone, navigating straight to her favourite colouring game, which I was happy to let her play while I dealt with taming my wet, tangled mane.

By nine, we were both downstairs on the couch, teeth clean, hair brushed, me dressed and her in llama pyjamas. The room smelt so much better, but I'd only let her have sips of very weak juice for now, just to make sure the vomiting didn't start again.

She curled up against me, still clutching her teddy as we re-watched one of her favourite movies, but my eyes flicked to the window every time I heard a car engine in case it was Ryan's. It was exciting to see an adult after a weekend with a sick child, that was my only reason for the eagerness, at least that's what I told myself.

"What are you looking for, Mummy?" Lucy asked, turning to me, her forehead furrowed up as she questioned me.

"One of my friends is coming over, he heard you were poorly, and he's bringing some things to make you breakfast."

"That's very kind of him, you have nice friends." She went back to watching the movie, her beautiful, trusting mind not looking for any ulterior motive as an adult might.

As it was, I didn't hear his car approach until it pulled up behind mine on the driveway. It was either very quiet or electric. It was only as he came into view, heading towards my front door that I realised the last time I'd seen him I had no top on; my cheeks burned hot, and I tried to think of something else, as I dashed through to the hallway. Rocket bounded after me excitedly, probably expecting the postman (whom he loved) or the Amazon delivery guy (whom he mistrusted and growled at with each delivery).

I was at the door, which thankfully contained no glass for him to spot me through, before Ryan even knocked. Rocket yipped and jumped up exuberantly and I cringed at his claw marks on the varnished wood.

With a deep breath and a tuck of my hair behind my ear, I tried to portray a casual smile as I pulled the door open, Rocket tucked behind my legs. Fortunately, he was still enough of a puppy to be scared to let me out of his sight, so I was confident he wouldn't run off into the quiet street.

"Hi," I said, like an idiot as I gawped at him.

"Hi," he replied, smiling as he held up an M&S food bag. "Grocery delivery."

I grinned, joyful at seeing him again. Rocket's tail battered my ankles as he wriggled; I think his crush was as big as mine.

"They were giving these away free at the till, only for beautiful ladies who've had a tough weekend," he said as he pulled a bright and colourful bouquet of Gerberas from behind his back.

I was taken aback and thrilled as I accepted them, as pleased as a giddy schoolgirl who'd been passed a note in maths saying, 'my friend fancies you.' He leaned forwards and kissed me on the cheek.

"Am I allowed in? Or is this like a Deliveroo?"

I laughed, stepping aside so he could come into the hall-way, at which point Rocket jumped up at his legs, thrilled to see him again, instantly forgetting everything we'd learned at puppy class about good behaviour.

"Hey, buddy!" Ryan knelt down and made a fuss of him, completing the obligatory belly rub as I closed the front door. As he stood up and looked at me, I had to remind myself that my daughter was on the sofa, and I couldn't pin him against the wall and snog the brains out of him.

"Wanna come meet Lucy, then we'll make coffee? You don't want to know the things I'd do for coffee right now." I cringed as I said it, noting the innuendo, but he simply smiled, that twinkle back in his eye, as he replied.

"Lead the way."

"Hey, gorgeous," I said as I sat next to Lucy and took hold of her hand. "This is Ryan."

"Hi Lucy. It's lovely to meet you."

"Hello," she glanced at him as she spoke, still pale.

"Ryan brought some food. You feel up to eating?"

"Can I have toast, please? And cereal?"

"Let's try toast to begin with. I'll be back in five minutes, darling. Just this once you can eat it on the sofa."

I waited for a reaction, but she mumbled along with the words to the same movie she watched every week; her own little rendition that was nonsensical but made her very happy.

Ryan followed me into the kitchen where I flicked the kettle on and leaned back against the cupboards.

"It's so kind of you to come over. I hope I haven't interrupted your day?"

"It's fine, didn't have much on. I was more bothered about making sure you were alright?"

"I'm good, just tired. So relieved she seems better." I motioned towards the living room where the sounds of Lucy's movie played on. "She was so upset, poor baby."

"Want me to make the toast?" he asked, opening the thick sliced loaf as I pulled mugs from the cupboard.

"Yes please." I slid the butter dish towards him. "Coffee?"

"Definitely."

We moved around each other in companionable synchronicity, me reaching for the milk, him grabbing a knife, both of us smiling, his eyebrows arching up in the most delicious manner every time we passed too close. It was almost like a dance, a flirtatious dance based around coffee and toast in this case.

"Sorry, there's not much space in here, a bit cosy compared to your place."

"I like it. Mine is… aesthetically pleasing but troubling."

"Well, that's a statement and a half. Your house is beautiful, stunning. You don't like it?"

"It's too bittersweet, I think. We got this huge mortgage for the place, and it was a real labour of love getting all the work done. Neither of us earned so much then, we scrimped and saved and did so many jobs ourselves over a few years. As our careers picked up. and we could afford it, the renovations sped up, but the bills were still huge."

I nodded. "Yep, they never stop, do they?"

"Some do. Tara's life insurance paid out with no issues, we'd taken out good policies, to pay off the entire mortgage should anything happen to either of us. Of course, I never expected it would."

My heart sank, how did I always seem to make a stupid comment?

Ryan continued. "It's a wonderful house, and I have no financial worries at all. But I also feel… bound to it, and not in a good way. How could I ever walk out on all those memories? But at the same time, living under the weight of them each day is difficult."

The toast popped up and I jumped like a nervous wreck. I wanted to say sorry but knew it didn't fit. "I'd never thought of it like that. I guess you have to give it time, you'll know when it feels right to decide either way."

Before he could reply, Lucy padded into the kitchen, barefoot as she clambered onto one of the barstools, pulling the plate of toast to herself the instant Ryan finished buttering it, before tucking in as if she'd never been fed.

"I like your pyjamas," Ryan said, as he sipped at his coffee. "My friend owns a llama farm."

She dropped the toast on the plate in full-on six-year-old dramatic style. "Llamas are my favourite thing *ever*!"

"Maybe if I tell your mummy where it is, she could take you to meet them. There'll be babies in springtime."

"Can we, can we, can we, can we?" she sang at me, and I had to steady her on the stool for fear she'd slip in her excitement.

"I'm sure we can. Once you've eaten that though you need a bath, smelly girl."

She stuck her tongue out at me and continued to plough into the pile of hot, buttery carbs.

"Were these for you too?" Ryan asked her, holding up the chocolate digestives.

"No, I'm not allowed them. But my mummy eats loads," she volunteered as she downed a glass of juice, her stomach cramps obviously dispersed.

"Thanks Lucy," I whispered, blushing again as Ryan grinned at me. "Ryan, I'm sorry, you've already helped so much, but could I ask a favour?"

Lucy, plate empty and glass drained grew, bored of our company and meandered back into the living room, Rocket following her, looking for crumbs.

"Of course you can," he said, his eyes seeming to drink me in as he realised we were alone again.

"Would you mind walking Rocket for me? While I get Lucy in the bath? He's not had a proper walk since we took him on Saturday." It felt like an age since we'd wandered around the country park together, hard to imagine it had only been this weekend.

"What if I don't bring him back?" he asked, taking a step towards me. "He's pretty adorable."

"He is, but…" I took a step forward in response, my eyes drawn to his. "I think you'll want to come back for the thank you."

"How are you going to thank me?" he asked, his head cocked to one side.

I bit my lip, concentrating. I wasn't good at this, and I had to stop thinking about kissing him and being topless on his knee, plus all that other amazing stuff that made my stomach flip. His eyes were now trained on my lips, and I released the bite with a deep breath.

"Let me buy you dinner? That new French place?"

"I was going to settle for a chocolate digestive, maybe two, but who am I to turn down dinner?" He leaned closer to me, and I felt like we were about to kiss when Lucy burst into laughter at her movie, breaking me from the trance he'd caught me up in.

With a cough, I passed him Rocket's lead and busied myself with the gorgeous flowers and my best vase, as he headed out with my spare keys, the treat pouch, and a roll of little plastic bags – the ultimate romantic accessory.

The flowers took centre stage on my dining table. I pulled Lucy away from the movie and into a bubble bath, as I tried to make some sort of sense of what was going on with me and these thoughts about Ryan.

First, I wasn't his type, I was sure of that; he was probably just remembering how to flirt or something, because sometimes he was the most flirtatious guy I'd ever met, other times very serious and brooding. The way he confided in me about his wife and his grief was how you'd confide in a friend, not someone you were interested in. Plus, there was the fact that he'd said he wasn't ready at the wedding.

Then there was me and all my complications. I barely had time to maintain a social life as it was between work and Lucy, looking after Rocket, and doing the shopping for my parents who hadn't been very well lately, plus driving them to appointments and so on. It didn't sound like he'd ever dated anyone with kids, that was a whole world of custody agreements, dance classes, and school trips he'd be blissfully unaware of, and I was certain he wouldn't need these intruding on his life. He was used to doing whatever he wanted, when he wanted, and he needed a girlfriend in the same situation, not someone with my baggage; and that was before we even got to the heartbreak and trust issues that I'd acquired.

I ducked a handful of bubbles that were hurled my way with a giggle from Lucy. I was relieved to see her smile again, as my phone beeped in my back pocket. It was a photo message from Ryan, Rocket jumping excitedly at a tall tree in the park.

RYAN

He met a squirrel x

PENNY

I reckon the squirrel would win in a fight x

RYAN

Me too, but don't tell Rocket. Heading back soon x

. . .

I returned the phone back to my pocket with a sigh, he was such a nice guy. Why couldn't I have met him earlier, before all the knobs I'd come to know? But that wouldn't have worked, would it? If I'd met him earlier, he'd have been happily married, we couldn't have got together anyway, and he wouldn't have even looked at me. There were so many parties, events, and occasions where we might have met, but never did; was the universe holding us back so we could meet now?

I needed to get a grip, this wasn't a swoony book on my bedside table, it was real life, and it never went how I expected it to. We'd probably remain friends and, in a years' time, he'd fall in love with some gorgeous blond with legs for days and a wit to match, and I'd still be here.

But I'd have my baby girl, my books, and Rocket, so life wasn't all bad, that's what I needed to remember.

But... sometimes in life, you just had to take a chance.

With Lucy dried off and in a clean set of llama pyjamas – she'd insisted they had to be more llamas as Ryan had commented on the other pair – we returned to the living room where the movie marathon continued, Lucy wolfing down a huge bowl of cereal before she fell asleep, her little body still recovering from the exhaustion.

I covered her in a soft blanket and closed the door to prevent a Rocket licking attack upon his return, which I suspected would only be five minutes away. Just enough time to make more coffee and open the digestives. Absolutely not time to admire Ryan in any way, shape, or form.

It was impossible not to chuckle though as I heard him

chatter away to Rocket as he wiped his muddy paws on the doggy towel that now lived next to the front door.

Ryan smelled of the crisp autumn air as he took a seat at the dining table, his cheeks reddened and smile wide. "He's such a good dog," he enthused as he took the coffee I slid in his direction.

"Most of the time," I agreed. "Thanks so much for that, I appreciate it."

"Is Lucy OK?" he asked kindly.

"Yep, she fell back asleep. Think she might need another day off tomorrow to recover, she can sit with me while I work."

"Was she watching a movie when she fell asleep?" he teased, and I'm pretty sure I blushed again.

"It's obviously genetic, what can I say?"

"You could tell me more about dinner." He patted the seat next to him and I scooted around to face him as I placed my coffee down on the table, near to the newly arranged flowers.

"Erm... There'll be garlic bread... and wine?"

"So, garlic bread and wine, plus me and you?"

"Well, it's a thank you. I could send you a voucher if you prefer?"

"Is it just a thank you?" he asked, taking my hand in his and rubbing it.

I contemplated him, his body language, the way we always seemed to end up touching. "I..." I paused, not knowing how to finish the sentence. What I really wanted to do was blurt out how much I fancied him, that I wanted it to be a date that ended with me in his bed, but I didn't want to overstep.

He sighed subtly, raising his eyes from our linked hands as he met my gaze. "I was thinking that I'd like to ask you out, that's all. But you're off men, sooooo…"

He drew the word out so that his lips formed a perfect little 'o,' and I couldn't help but place a delicate kiss on them, smiling bashfully as I pulled back.

"How about the starter is a thank you and the main course is a date?" I said, our heads were still so close together in the quiet kitchen that there was no need for volume.

"What's dessert?" he asked, as he copied my soft kiss. There were no words I could reply with that would answer better than the deepening of the kiss as he pulled me to him, and I once again felt my resolution crumble at his touch.

THIRTEEN

*B*ea flipped her notebook shut with a nod of her head; the 'business' end of book club was done, and she'd be at the bar ordering a large gin within ninety seconds.

"Best score we've had in ages, that," said Zoe, nodding towards the stacked-up copies of this month's read, which would be distributed to little free libraries around the town.

"It was the sex scene in the pool, we all know it." I grinned and topped our wine glasses up. The bottles were on offer at the moment, so we'd ordered two, as it saved walking back and forth to the bar.

"Next month's will be different, a murder mystery, doubt there'll be much action."

"You're a newlywed," I nudged her with my elbow. "You don't need books for action."

"And what about you, Miss? You've been a mysterious one lately, don't think I didn't see you grinning inanely at your phone earlier. Please tell me it's not wanker dentist."

"God, no! Don't even say that."

"So... spill. Who's making you smile?" She leant forwards, her chin rested on her hands, glasses tipped down her nose as she caught me in her glare and demanded an answer.

"It's nothing, really. We've been spending a little time together, that's all."

"You and who?" she narrowed her eyes.

"Ryan," I mumbled, not because I felt any shame, it simply didn't feel real enough to mention to anyone, even to think out loud.

"Ryan Grayson?" she exclaimed, causing me to shush her. "Jess's brother?"

"Try that again? Not sure the entire pub caught it," I snarked.

"But... but..." It took a lot to suck words away from Zoe, I was secretly impressed. "I mean, I know you were dancing at the wedding, but whenever Jess mentions him, it sounds like he's still struggling with what happened to Tara."

"Jess doesn't give him enough credit." I shrugged and sipped my wine; that woman hadn't quite been removed fully from my shit list, although I did understand her reasons.

"What's going on between you two then? What happened to no more men? Off relationships for life?"

"I know what I said, and I meant it but there's something there, it's hard to explain. He helped me out when Lucy had that stomach bug, I said I'd take him out for dinner on Saturday night to say thank you."

"Have you slept with him?" she whispered, not quietly enough as I saw Harriet's ears twitch towards us.

"No, I have not! Zoe!" I expected nothing less from her, but these questions made me feel protective of him, of us, of whatever this was. It felt private and personal, I didn't want it to be the talk of the pub like so many other things had been, including wanker dentist. Normally I'd sit and discuss the literal ins and outs, but it didn't feel right now.

"Don't you worry it will be a bit impossible?"

"How do you mean?"

"Well, might you always be second best to Tara? I mean, wanker dentist at least couldn't stand his wife, Ryan adored Tara, and with her dying so young…" She paused, a deep dent appearing between her eyebrows. "She'll always be perfect in his head; how can anyone live up to that?"

I drained my glass and glared at her. "Zoe, you can't make assumptions like that, it's complicated. How can you be so judgemental?"

"I don't want you to get a broken heart. Again." She rolled her eyes and, whilst it normally wouldn't bother me, today it absolutely pissed me off. Maybe we shouldn't have bought two bottles of wine after all.

"Apologies if I annoy you with my failed love life!" I snapped, my voice harsh as I stood up and gathered my jacket, the rest of the table watching us open-mouthed. "How rude of me to bore you with my cheating ex and that lying shitbag of a dentist. If this all goes wrong, I'll spare you the details. But…" I pointed a finger, my hand shaking with indignation. "For your information, he doesn't compare me, I don't feel second best and actually, it's nobody's business but ours."

I stormed out, Zoe calling my name and the clatter of chair legs scraping on the floor, but I chose to ignore it, all of it. That entire exchange had me fuming. I strode towards home, stopping halfway to catch my breath from the power walk. I had two missed calls, one from Zoe and one from Bea, but I didn't want to talk about it, not right now.

I slowed my pace, my initial fury lessening as her words swirled around and around. I guessed her comments had hit a nerve because I'd worried about those precise things myself. What if I would be a consolation prize? Or worse, if I was a practice run before he started dating properly. The whole reason I'd sworn off men was that I couldn't face another heartache, but was I setting myself up for one with Ryan?

My mum had watched Lucy for me and was surprised to see me home so early. I feigned tiredness, hugging her and saying thank you before I clambered into bed, cosy in the pyjamas I'd worn on the wedding night, still with the missing button. I had a lot of skills, but sewing was not one of them.

I stroked the little tuft of cotton that remained, without its button. I hated how these doubts crowded my mind. It was basic fear though, and I couldn't bear to let it control my life, not when this attraction to Ryan was so strong. I glanced at the clock, not too late to message.

PENNY

Hey, still OK for Saturday night? x

RYAN

Of course, are you? I hope so. Isn't it book
club tonight? x

PENNY

Yeah, we finished early. And yes, I'm
looking forward to Saturday, just wanted to
check x

RYAN

Are you sure you don't want me to pick
you up? I'll be getting a taxi, can swing by
your place x

PENNY

I'll meet you there, I get to be mysterious.
See if you can spot me holding a white
carnation or something random x

RYAN

I'd spot you anywhere, Penny Archer x

And there went another explosion of butterflies.

RYAN

How's Lucy? x

PENNY

She's all good now, thank you. I better get
some beauty sleep. See you Saturday
night x

RYAN

Sweet dreams x

Simon hadn't picked Lucy up until gone five and, as I was meeting Ryan at seven-thirty, that didn't leave much time for getting my glam on. I'd had my hair in curlers since lunch and the all-important dress and shoes were picked out, so I needed to shower, do my make up, and finish my hair. I'd even splashed out on waxing yesterday, not that I wanted to assume anything, but it had boosted my confidence. Rocket was already ensconced at my parents; they weren't supposed to have pets in their retirement flat, but one night wouldn't matter.

I'd gone for the little black dress look, it was classic for a reason. The wrap dress left just enough cleavage on show, whilst cinching in my waist and, as the skirt sat on my knee, showing enough leg to be promising without wanton. Alongside my favourite black heels, it was the perfect mix of sexy but sweet, in case dessert did get heated.

My only quandary was my underwear. I stood in front of the full-length mirror in my bedroom, the curtains drawn and the lights off. I didn't want to see myself semi-naked really, some things were better off not known. I'd put on a very seductive, jade green lingerie set that I'd bought last year, all skimpy thong and lace-covered nipples. It was sensual, there was no denying that, but it didn't feel right for tonight somehow.

I pulled every bra out of my drawer, flinging them onto the bed and scouring through them for items that sat between everyday underwear and a cougar who wanted some action. As I threw them behind me, forming a reject pile, I spotted a very pretty, pale pink bra I'd bought in a sale and had never worn before.

It had full coverage, was very demure, but was also edged by intricate lace and spaghetti straps. I recalled the other half of the set were classical bikini style bottoms, delicate and beautiful. Unthreatening, unassuming, subtle, understated, and feminine. I swapped into them, happy they were the correct choice as I slipped the dress on over the top, ensuring no visible seams or lines. Perfect.

My phone beeped as I pulled the curlers from my hair. I read the message as I fingered the tight spirals into loose coppery, chocolate waves that fell around my shoulders.

ZOE

Have a great night. You deserve to be his queen, don't forget it x

I sent back a sad face. The two of us hadn't fallen out before, so I was glad she'd reached out, but her words had hurt me. Just as I was about to throw the phone into my bag, it rang and Zoe's cheesy grin appeared on my lock screen, a contact photo I'd saved on a picnic last summer.

"Hi," I answered. "I'm heading out soon, can't really talk."

"Give me five minutes, I don't want you going and thinking bad of me. I handled it all wrong, I'm sorry."

I sighed, spotting my sad reflection in the mirror,

knowing it was best to sort this now, as I didn't want any of that sadness to be in place when I saw Ryan.

"It was me too, I got all defensive. Normally we laugh about stuff like that, I know, but it felt wrong somehow."

"I do have concerns but, I'll be honest, I'd have concerns about you meeting anyone after the crap you've dealt with."

"I know, but I can't tar everyone with the same brush, they're not all wanker dentists."

"I've known Ryan a long time, me and Jess used to wind him up something chronic when we were little, then as we got older, we were constantly trying to get info on his cute mates in sixth form."

"That sounds like you," I grinned, imagining her forcing out names and numbers.

"I was at their wedding, you know? Him and Tara, if you ever had questions or anything."

"We've talked about her a lot, I'm not going into this with my eyes closed. I don't even know if anything will happen between us but, if it does, I'm fully prepared for the fact it won't be straightforward, as much because of me as him."

"He's a good guy, that much I know. And I'd accept nothing less for you, Pen."

"Thanks Zoe. Listen, I have to go, or I'll be late. Do you and Emma want to come round Monday night? I'll cook Mexican and we can talk more?"

"Definitely. Enjoy yourself, OK? Relax and enjoy. Oh, and Penny…"

"Yes?"

"Stop overthinking it all, I know you."

I laughed as we said our goodbyes, relieved that we

were OK. She only had my best interests at heart, it had just all come out wrong at book club, from both of us. And her call meant I could forget about it for tonight, and concentrate on what was happening between me and Ryan.

With my finest smokey eye makeup and burgundy red lips, set on skin that appeared flawless thanks to the wonders of luxury foundation, I was ready. The table was booked, and the taxi app showed my car was two minutes away. All I had to do was turn up and see where this merry little dance Ryan and I were involved in would lead us.

FOURTEEN

*E*xhaling slowly in an attempt to calm my nerves, I followed the waiter through the beautiful restaurant as he led me towards a row of tables set for two, over in the vicinity of the bar.

This was a stunning building, an old bank, as were half the cafes and restaurants in the town. With its high, vaulted ceilings and large chandeliers, it almost seemed too grand to cater to middle class diners. Floor to ceiling windows let in light from the street outside, but in my mind also left the guests over there on display. Plenty would love that, but I was glad to be ensconced away on the other side. I wasn't the type to want my life to be a show, I mean, I loved a bit of Instagram as much as anyone else, but tonight was about us, just us. Figuring all of this out.

My heart skipped as I glanced over and saw that Ryan was already seated, rubbing absentmindedly at his stubble as he looked at a menu. I got the impression he wasn't taking it in. I tried to hold my back straight whilst still walking normally and maintaining a façade of relaxed, happy, and pretty. It was too complicated and, instead, I broke into a wide smile as he stood up, looking perfect to me.

He wore midnight blue jeans with a caramel-coloured shirt, buttoned up but open at the neck with no tie. A suit jacket in the same shade of blue covered the shirt and took the outfit to a new level. His hair was styled as it had been at the wedding, with the slight patches of grey at the temples giving him a distinguished look; the man had no signs of thinning hair at all. His eyes crinkled up at the corners as he looked at me, and it only made me beam even more, his happiness was contagious.

He kissed me on the lips, once, before I sat down in the chair the waiter had pulled back for me. Ryan took his jacket off and hung it on the back of his own seat, drumming his fingers as the waiter poured wine from the bottle already present on the table, before backing away.

"You don't mind that I ordered the wine, do you? I didn't want to be presumptuous, but I know you like this one and I was desperate for a drink and, *holy fuck*, Penny, you look amazing." He garbled the words out in one long string, not pausing for a breath and it absolutely melted my heart. I wanted to get up and hug him, thank him for being so lovely, but how weird would that be?

"The wine is perfect," I said as I sipped, as desperate for a drink as he was but not about to admit that. "And thank you, you look pretty good yourself."

"I've not seen you in lipstick like that before, its... erm... captivating?" He laughed self-depreciatingly and rubbed at his hairline. "Can you ignore me? I'm nervous and talking utter rubbish because you look like that." He gestured his hand up and down, as he had in the hotel room that night, and my stomach swam with warm emotion.

I reached across and took his hand in mine, squeezing lightly. "Then pretend we're on a dog walk, you and me and Rocket in the woods, no pressure, no expectation, with only some overpriced, watery hot chocolate to look forward to."

He smiled, his eyes roamed over me again, filling me with delight that he liked what he saw, that I didn't have to be a mirror image of what he'd lost to be attractive, to be desired. "OK, but can I just say holy fuck one more time?"

I grinned and clinked my glass against his. "You may. So, have you already Googled the menu and chosen? I have."

That first glass of wine relaxed us both as our starters arrived. Lindisfarne Oysters for him, honey-glazed goats' cheese for me.

"You want to try?" he asked, proffering his dish towards me.

"I don't do seafood," I declined.

"You're not allergic, are you?" He looked aghast.

"No, no, it just weirds me out a little."

"I could have ordered something else, you should have said."

"Don't be silly, the starter is my thank you, remember." I smiled as I spoke. "You enjoy. I'm sure your wonderful toast skills helped Lucy recover."

"Where is she tonight? With her dad?"

"Yes, she comes back to me Monday after school. I'm home alone until then." For fucks sake, why had I said that? Made it obvious I was after an invitation back to his place. Ryan didn't seem to notice, but I needed to compose myself.

"I'll be back in a minute," I said as I stood, wiping my lips on the heavy, cloth napkin as my eyes sought out the sign for the ladies.

"Shall I order more wine?" Ryan asked, as he split the dregs of the bottle between our glasses, before upending it in the copper ice bucket.

"Definitely."

I surveyed myself in an intricate, antique-style mirror as I washed my hands. No mascara smudges, all was good. After drying my hands, I reapplied the lipstick Ryan had admired and fluffed my hair up a little. I was having such a good time, a ridiculously good time. He was kind and sweet and attentive, vulnerable, shy at times, yet fiery and flirty at others. He oozed sex appeal, but not in a nauseating way that got everyone's attention, it's like it was reserved for me. Was this too good to be true? I didn't know but, for tonight, I was going to dive in.

I smoothed my dress down as I took my seat, noticing how his eyes watched my hands as they ran over the black material. The wine bucket had been replaced and our glasses were full.

"So, how's your week been?" I asked, giving him my devoted attention.

"Good, finished those plans for the office building I told you about. Then it was my week with Caroline, the counsellor, so I saw her yesterday."

"How did it go?" I asked.

"Different, I guess," he replied, and we were both quiet as our main courses arrived – fillet steak for him with Café de Paris sauce, and coq au vin casserole for me. I didn't touch it though, not at first, as I wanted to hear what was different.

"You want to talk about it, or not?"

"I do..." He hadn't touched his steak either. "We've passed the thank you starter now so... is this the date part?"

I nodded. "I think so. I hope so."

"I hope so too, and that's what we talked about, you."

"Should my ears have been burning?" I smiled, pushing a chantenay carrot around my plate.

"Only in a good way. We talked about recovery guilt, it's been on my mind."

"Do you feel guilty when you're with me?"

Ryan placed his cutlery down. "When I met Tara, it felt different. I'd had a couple of relationships, done the usual chasing girls at uni, but when I met her..." He drew in a deep breath. "There was this feeling I couldn't pin down, a sensation, that she was special, and this was different from everything that had come before. Some people never find that, I know I was lucky to, even if she was taken away too soon."

I sensed he needed to talk, not listen to my awkward responses whilst I tried to avoid saying I was sorry, so I continued to slide the carrot around my plate.

"I've been living half a life since then, going through the motions," he continued. "And I assumed I'd carry on that way for the rest of my life because people don't get that lucky twice. They don't meet a second person who makes them feel that way, that's what I'd resigned myself to. I never even planned to look, why would you look for something that can't exist? But then *you* appeared, out of nowhere, and I feel it again, I truly do."

I tried to stop the emotions that welled up inside me and bubbled out in the form of a tear that slipped down my cheek. This wasn't my sadness, I had no right to his grief, but it spilled into me somehow. I didn't want him to think I was trying to take any of it from him with my tears, or make this about me, when nothing could be further from the truth.

"What do I do with that? That's what Caroline and I discussed in our session. Part of me feels that it's wrong, like I'm betraying Tara. But the other part of me is screaming out because I'm so drawn to you, I've barely stopped thinking about you. I worry I'm not strong enough to do it all again, and I know I couldn't handle the pain of loss again. It's petrifying."

He took a focused drink of wine before he continued.

"When you lose someone, like I did, you lose more than the person. Your memories of the past feel clouded, your plans for the future are ripped apart, and the present feels unbearable. It's like there isn't a direction you can go in, so you move through each day, aimless, ticking them off with no goal in sight, going through the motions. Until this beautiful, kind, sweet woman shows up and the monochrome of that monotony bursts into colour, into life, and you can see a future and love and happiness again, but you're too scared to grab it."

"What conclusion did Caroline help you come to?" I asked as my stomach fluttered. "Is this a first date or a last date?"

"You're my future, Penelope Archer."

At this point I wanted to say something clever and witty, but I was grinning so inanely that I don't think my lips could have formed the words even if my brain had been able to provide them.

"It's not Sunday," I said as I took his hand, rubbing my thumb over his fingers. "But I think I'd be happy to be your Penelope seven days a week anyway. It isn't just me though, you understand that?"

"I do. Lucy's amazing, she's so like you, I want to get to know her better. Build something together. There's only one thing I'll say no to – I'm not joining book club."

I raised my glass to Ryan's. "You wouldn't meet the criteria anyway, and maybe I shouldn't mix bookish romance with real life romance. So…here's to many more dates…" He clinked his glass against mine and I took a long glug of wine, my eyes rooted on his, and our smiles said it all. We picked at our main course for a few more minutes, far more interested in each other than the food. When the waiter came to take the half-nibbled meals away, Ryan asked for the bill before any questions about dessert or coffee could even begin.

He paid, I didn't even think to argue the point as I usually would have, my mind whirling with his words. *I was his future.* The taxi rank was a five-minute stroll from the restaurant, and we headed there hand in hand. His jacket was hung over his arm, neither of us seeming to note the cool, autumn air as we entered into this new phase. Officially.

A lone, dark taxi sat at the rank. It was barely gone ten, the youth of today wouldn't even go out this early, and not many were heading home yet, just us. We slid into the back, Ryan holding the door open for me; he turned to me as it closed, locking us into the warm interior.

"Where are we going?" he asked, his mouth hovering close to mine.

"My place?" I said, my heart palpitating, scared of rejection, despite all we'd discussed tonight.

He rattled my address off to the driver, before turning to me and placing one long, loving kiss onto my lips. He tasted of wine and every possibility under the sun.

I knew if I kissed him again I wouldn't be able to stop, so I sat politely in the back of the cab as it made its way through the pretty estate towards my house. I got my bank card out, determined I'd pay for this as he'd paid for dinner and, as my phone came into view, I shut it off, knowing I didn't want a single interruption. Just for this one night, I needed to be me, not on call for daughters or puppies or parents.

The taxi sped off, eager for another Saturday night fare. Ryan turned to me as we stood on my garden path, our feet surrounded by fallen leaves, as he swept my hair behind my ear. "That lipstick, seriously, it's driving me to distraction."

"Do you want to come in?" I asked, although I felt the answer was certain.

"I do, I absolutely do." He replied before kissing me, his

tongue crashing into mine in an act of pure lust without ceremony or manners as we careered towards my front door. I smirked as we passed my video doorbell, then I let my mind clear of everything but him.

FIFTEEN

*T*he front door slammed closed in our wake, and, for the briefest second, I was thankful that my house was detached, but then Ryan's lips were on mine and every single other thought in the world merged away into nothingness.

He pressed me against the wall, his fingers tangled in my hair as his breath caught up inside my mouth, his body pressed against me. I was as desperate for this as he was, but we needed some semblance of control.

"Come with me," I whispered, stroking his hair before taking hold of his hand.

I led him upstairs, our fingers intertwined as we entered my bedroom. Thankfully, I'd had the sense to shove all the discarded bras back into the drawer; my bed sheets weren't ironed but I didn't think he'd care.

The room was dark, so dark. I'd always preferred that, wanting to keep fleshier bits and bumps hidden but now, it didn't seem to matter, I wanted us to see each other, everything about each other.

I flicked my bedside lamp on, smiling as his grey eyes focused on me. He was a little tipsy, we both were, but just enough to instil confidence, nothing more. We'd remember this, every second of it, of that, I was sure.

Ryan stepped towards me, taking my hands in his as he kissed my ear, tugging gently on the lobe with his teeth. "I'm so out of my depth," he chuckled, the high pitch betraying his nerves. "I don't want to confess how long it's been since my first time with someone. Do we need to worry about using anything?"

God, he was so cute and nervous that I wanted to scoop him up and hug him, reassure him and then, of course, ravage him. Instead, I wrapped my arms around him, bringing my mouth close to his ear as I replied. "I have an IUD, so no worries there. We're both grown-ups, so I'm happy as we are, if you agree?"

He swallowed, his head nodding. I didn't even need to ask about his past, there'd been nobody but Tara for years and years and I had no concerns about him.

I began to unfasten his shirt buttons, spreading soft kisses around his mouth and neck, checking back on his eyes in between to ensure I could see no signs of reluctance; as it was, he appeared as enthralled as me.

His fingers danced their way up my back, stroking at the nape of my neck before he took hold of the zip at the rear of my dress and pulled it all the way down. From there, he ran his warm hands up and across my shoulders, pushing the dress off them so it pooled on the floor around my ankles. I knew then that the underwear had been the correct choice because I felt feminine and confident, not ashamed, or overly sexualised. I was still adjusting to being away from the toxicity of that in my last relationship.

Ryan's hands ran down my sides. Up and down, tracing over the shape of me and running around the lace barrier he found. His last button was now undone, and he shrugged his shirt off, letting it fall to the ground.

I stepped out of my shoes, instantly three inches shorter as he reached down to kiss me once more, his hands cupping the back of my head and holding me to him as I reached for his belt, pulling it tight to unbuckle before it loosened and fell open.

His hands ran over my back, and I reached behind and unfastened the hooks of my bra. His mouth lowered to my collarbone, kissing along the hard ridge as he'd done at his place, then he pulled the bra straps down my arms, allowing the soft silk to peel away from my body as it dropped onto the carpet.

This felt so intense that my stomach butterflied I tried to kiss him again, but he held a finger to my mouth with another nervy sound, as he bent down and pulled his socks off.

"Sorry," he whispered. "I thought you taking them off might ruin the moment. Nobody needs to touch my socks. Is this all OK?"

"So good," I sighed as I took a step towards the bed, followed by Ryan. I faced him, the mattress against the backs of my knees as I undid the buttons of his jeans, tugging them down and ensuring I grabbed his boxers at the same time. With a delicate touch, he pressed me down onto the bed. I watched as he kicked the jeans and pants off, leaving them atop the pile of discarded clothing.

Then his fingers hooked inside the waistband of my delicate underwear as he dropped to his knees, his mouth pressing hot kisses all over my stomach as he took that final item of clothing from me. His fingers skimmed my ankle as he pulled down and it sent a delicious shiver all the way up my body, reminding me of a Victorian lady receiving her first, illicit touch as she bared her elegant lower leg.

"Wriggle up," he whispered as he motioned towards the stack of pillows further up the bed, and I did so as he clambered above me, chasing me with kisses and smiles. We stayed on top of the duvet, not feeling the cold, not aware of anything but each other.

I'd never made it a secret that I loved sex. I'd had a lot of good sex, but I did find it hard to switch off, as many women do - *Does my stomach look awful? Is he enjoying it? Was that a weird noise I made? Does he want me to go faster or slower?* Historically I'd questioned everything with every partner. Yet, with Ryan, that didn't happen. It was as though I sank entirely into him, into us. I managed to empty my mind and be purely and wholly in the moment, that instant of sheer perfection as we crossed a point from which I knew we couldn't ever come back.

The soft jersey sheets rubbed against my skin, I ran my hands down his arms, memorising the outline of his muscles as he held himself there, his weight over me, his intent clear as he looked at me and I mouthed, "yes," barely there but giving him all the approval to continue.

My eyes closed as he pushed inside of me, I was consumed by his scent in my nose, the sound of his breath, his taste bursting in my mouth, and the quiet gasps of pleasure from us both that mingled and danced in the hot air trapped between our bodies.

His fingers tangled into mine on either side of my head as he lay upon me, his mouth placing soft kiss after soft kiss along my neck and collarbone, flipping to my mouth and back. Each kiss left a spark on my skin and, for the first time in my life, I didn't overthink or worry, I simply let every natural sense take over.

As Ryan moved inside of me, a build-up of pleasure began, every individual spark pooled together, swirling, and coalescing within me as we created pure magic. I wrapped my arms and legs around him, silently willing him for more as my breath shifted, coming from some-where deeper inside of me; I couldn't speak, couldn't think. That swirling mass of sparks exploded inside of me, pulsating like a dying star, pulling him in and drawing those same shuddering gasps of breath to match my own. Was this why they called it the little death? My head swam, not with drink or dizziness, but a satiating pleasure that I'd never known before, not like this, never like this.

A timeless period passed, probably seconds but it could have been hours to my body. I came back into the room, aware of our clammy skin stuck together, of the wet patch on his shoulder where I'd clamped my mouth in passion, of his hair tickling my neck as he buried his face into me and attempted to catch his breath. I trembled beneath him, my breath shuddering in short gasps as if I couldn't suck enough oxygen into me. All I could feel was him – Ryan Grayson, here in bed with me.

I felt lost as he withdrew and lay on his back, and then he gathered me to him, pressing kiss after kiss to the top of my head as he held me tight. I wanted to be like that with him every day, I wanted to love him, and what scared me was how very close to that I'd already come. Neither of us spoke, there was no need for one of those chats, 'how was that for you?' I think we both knew; it was absolutely everything.

SIXTEEN

I fully expected some catastrophe to come and pop our blissful morning bubble, but it didn't. No disasters, no snotty sisters, no vomiting bugs, and no rainstorms. We woke up snuggled together, warm, and blissful. I'd never been a cuddly sleeper, but I adored the sensation of being his little spoon.

When he awoke moments after me, Ryan pulled me to him and kissed me. Yes, there was morning breath and garlic but more importantly, there was him, and I invited his tongue to play with mine. The first touch of it awakened every nerve between my legs as my body jumped to attention, eager for a repetition of last night, for more of him. I grinned like the Cheshire Cat as I caught my breath, watching the lazy Sunday morning sun seep in through the curtains and give the room, and Ryan, a mellow glow.

"Have you any plans today?" he asked as his arm wrapped around me and I huddled against his chest.

"Nope." I ran my finger up and down it.

"Did you say Lucy's with her dad again tonight?"

"Yeah, she'll be home tomorrow after school," I replied, thankful for this weekend's custody arrangement.

"I didn't mean that in a bad way, as if I didn't want her here, I just wouldn't want her walking in on this, you know?"

"I know, don't worry," I reassured him. I hadn't thought that for a moment. "I was worried, to be honest, that me being a mum would put you off."

"Not at all, I love how devoted to her you are. And I was hardly expecting you to have been sat around in a chastity belt waiting for the right guy. Being a mum is a wonderful aspect of you. If anything, it's being a widower that's the problem, I thought that would have scared you away. I guess that's why I was so blunt about it at the wedding, get it out there and watch you make excuses and head off like other people do, except you didn't."

"Do people seriously do that?"

He nodded, his chin pressing against me for a moment. "Yeah, you can see their whole demeanour change."

"To be fair, it distracted from my incest comments, so I was glad of the change in direction."

"*Does* it bother you? Truthfully?" he asked.

"Honestly, I don't think it does. I have hang ups and reservations and worries, but they stem around me mostly, not your past. Not what happened."

We were both quiet for a few moments. I had no idea of the time but could hear the occasional car door slamming outside on the street.

"What's a Penny Sunday usually like?" he asked.

"Well, normally a big walk in the countryside for Rocket, followed by a full English and some very strong coffee somewhere. Then, if Lucy's here, she often has a party to go to, or I'll be roped into Playdoh or Lego. If she's at her dads, I tend to meet Zoe in the pub for a couple, and then spend the evening in a bubble bath with a book. How about you? Tell me about Ryan Sundays."

"I work a lot. I wake up early, might have a roast dinner with Jess or my mum or whoever is feeling sorry for me that week. I guess the silver lining of me having no life the past couple of years is that the business is doing well. Plans and blueprints and projects, I can lose myself in them, forget my actual problems and think logically about the task."

"Jess said something to me about you waking up early, what's that about? I haven't seen it, we always seem to end up asleep."

"I've been determined to stay off sleeping pills, but I haven't slept properly since it happened. I reached the point where I could fall asleep at night fine, but then I'd wake up at about four and nothing would get me back to sleep. Four a.m. is pretty lonely, makes you feel like the world has forgotten you. I tried running, I tried reading, I tried long drives, it was easier to build a home office and get half my work done before anyone else even woke up."

"I'm the opposite, when I'm in a state about anything I can't work. Ended up on a warning at work earlier in the year."

"Because of wanker dentist?" he asked.

"Yep, that's his name."

"The only times I've slept properly, and all the way through, are when I've been with you. That came up in counselling too."

"Should my ears burn?" I asked.

"Should mine?" he retorted. "Dread to think what Jess was like, and Zoe saw way too much of my teenage years. Bet she's told you all sorts."

"I like how we can talk about the past. We don't have to pretend we have these perfect pasts or promises of shiny futures, we can just be us."

"Isn't that one of the joys of your forties? You stop giving a fuck?"

"True." I grinned. "If it's not presumptuous of me to assume we'll spend today together, how about I pick Rocket up and we take him to the beach for a walk? I know it's cold, but he loves the beach."

"Sounds perfect, but one issue…"

My heart sank. "What's wrong?"

"I was so nervous last night I couldn't eat, and then you've worn me out twice. I'm starved. Can we get breakfast first?"

I laughed and twisted on top of him, kissing him in between smiles and giggles. "Deliveroo?"

"I love it when you talk dirty." He stretched contentedly.

"Get used to it…." I replied, pressing against him as I straddled his knee, knowing breakfast might take a little bit longer than he'd anticipated.

Eventually, we came to the agreement that we'd go to the drive-through on the way to pick Rocket up, then head straight to the beach and let him have a good run. It felt ridiculously clichéd, huddled in my car with the heaters on, munching on hash browns and sausage muffins whilst grinning like teenagers. We didn't say much, didn't need to, it felt comforting there together, cosy.

Rocket ran wild on the beach, for every step Ryan and I took, hand in hand, he covered at least two hundred as he ran rings around us, splashing in and out of the waves as they sloshed onto the shoreline.

It felt a little like history repeating itself as Rocket settled asleep in the back of the car and I closed the door, leaned back, and looked up into Ryan's grey eyes. But everything had changed since the last time we found ourselves in this position, and today there was no rain, just a subtle wind that lifted his hair a touch as he retuned my gaze, that and half a tonne of sand deposited in the car via Rocket's fur and paws.

"I can't believe you didn't mention my panda eyes this morning," I teased. "You could've told me!" The downside of smokey eyes was the mess the next morning when you'd dragged a man to bed instead of cleansing with micellar water before sleep.

"They were too adorable, and you were too distracting. You look sleepy," he said, as he linked his hands with mine.

"I can't think why." I feigned innocence as he leant down and kissed my lips.

All too soon he pulled back, which was probably for the best before I mounted his leg like a hormonal puppy. I could give Rocket a run for his money.

"You looked amazing last night, but I think today you're even more beautiful. This light is perfect on you." I giggled like a teenage girl at his compliment, before he kissed the top of my head. The moment was then rudely interrupted by the ringing of his mobile phone. "Sorry, give me one minute."

He backed away a couple of steps to answer, and I kicked as much sand off my boots as I could before taking a seat and starting the engine, another yawn capturing me as I did so. Moments later, Ryan was in the passenger seat next to me.

"I'm so sorry, that was my mum. I think she's blown a fuse in her apartment; she's stressed as anything. I'm going to have to go help her."

"Don't worry, want me to drive you?"

"I'll end up there ages, she'll suddenly tell me about the other fifty jobs she's been meaning to ask about, happens every time. You ok to drop me home and I'll grab my car? I really am sorry."

"Of course," I replied, as he stroked the side of my face, a serene look crossing his features. "It's not a problem, surprised it wasn't my folks on the phone needing some-thing. I understand."

"I'll call you later."

"I might answer... we'll see." I stuck my tongue out and he grinned, before turning to fasten his seatbelt.

After some drawn out goodbye kisses in the front of the car, I was soon home and, with Rocket settled, I ran a deep bath, sinking gratefully into the steamy, hot water. My muscles ached, but every little twinge reminded me of the night before. How his lips had felt on my neck, the way his hands had grabbed at my waist, how good it had felt as my legs stretched around him.

Letting out a long, lustful breath, I disappeared under

the water for a moment, attempting to control the rapid fluttering in my stomach.

I hoped it hadn't happened too fast for him. I knew it had been a big step, a step he'd thought he would never take. It went against everything I'd sworn to myself too, but if there was one single person in the world worth breaking my promise for, I was utterly assured that it was Ryan Grayson.

SEVENTEEN

*B*y nine thirty that evening, I was tucked up in bed with a bottle of San Pellegrino and a new book. I was out of practice where wining, dining, and bringing the guy home were concerned, and the stamina of my youth had apparently deserted me.

I hadn't heard from Ryan, but I tried not to stress. There was a point in my life when I would've been in bits, checking my phone every thirty seconds, but something about this situation gave me assurance. I looked back at my twenties in horror sometimes, so needy and demanding as a girlfriend, all insecure and jealous. I felt like I'd mellowed into the actual version of me, the real me who didn't need to pretend to like a certain band or hang out with people I'd rather not. So, it was fine to wait after all; the best things in life were certainly worth it.

I'd re-read the same page three times before I gave up and put the book on the bedside table, yawning vociferously. I glanced at the pillow next to mine and wondered if it smelled like Ryan; it wouldn't hurt to check, surely? I lay on my side, smiling to myself as I turned over and cuddled the spare pillow that I never used, inhaling deeply. Hmm… I wasn't convinced.

Just then my phone rang, I bolted upright, smoothing down my hair and smacking my lips together, as I saw it was a facetime call from Ryan. I took a deep breath before I answered.

"Hi," I said, as the blurry image stabilised and his tired, creased, very stubbly, utterly gorgeous face filled the screen.

"Hi," he replied with a smile, as he tilted his head back onto his sofa. The room was dimly lit but I could see flashes of colour along the edges, probably from the television. "Have you got my favourite pyjamas on?"

I glanced down at myself and laughed. "I do, pure coincidence."

"Did you fix the button yet?"

"Erm… My skills lie in places other than sewing." I began to twirl my hair around my finger. "Did you replace the fuse?"

"I did indeed, and put a shelf up, nipped to the shop for tea bags, and agreed to drive her to the theatre on Thursday night."

"You're a good 'un," I teased, unable to stop smiling.

"Are you reading an interesting book tonight?" he asked with a subtle smirk, as he changed the topic of conversation.

"How did you know I'd be reading?"

"Because you're you."

"Fair point. And yes, a very good book actually."

"What's it about?"

"It's a re-telling based on the legends of King Arthur. It's a romance, about Tristan and Isolde. Have you heard of them?"

"I have, but I don't know much about them."

"It's all about forbidden love. Tristan is there to escort Isolde, or Iseult, from Ireland to Cornwall. To marry his uncle. Illicit love is one of my favourite tropes."

"Is this a book club read, or did you choose it?"

"I chose it. The staff in the bookshop in town know me better than my work colleagues do." I grinned, picturing the bulging loyalty card app on my phone. I'd been saving up for a spree for months now.

"Can we talk second dates?" he asked with a small sigh, as he sank further down into his sofa.

"Mmhmm," I replied, as I lay back down, holding the phone on the spare pillow, which I now wanted to call *his* pillow.

"Could we maybe go to the bookshop together? I think you could introduce me to some new authors. And there happen to be about fourteen coffee shops nearby, so caffeine, cake, and literature... Would that be of interest to you?"

"You missed an item from that list," I replied, somehow managing to keep my voice steady, despite wanting to jump up and down on the bed with delight.

"I did?" He looked confused, as his forehead wrinkled up. I wished I could lean forward and kiss it. As it was, I giggled and then chided myself again for sounding anything but mature.

"Caffeine, cake, literature, and you."

"Ahh, but I don't think I score as highly as those three things."

"You score exceptionally high. Even if you didn't buy me any crème brûlée." I managed to keep my poker face on, even though the tone of this conversation, as innocent as it was, had somehow turned my insides to mush.

That lazy, seductive smile appeared on one side of his mouth. "Well, now I feel very ungentlemanly. Apologies, did I misinterpret your dessert preferences?"

"You didn't misinterpret a single thing."

"If someone had asked me in August if this, if *you*, could happen to me, I'd have laughed in their face."

"Me too," I said, then felt awful for even putting my stupid breakup in the same place as what had happened to him. 'Not that it's the same, but... you know?"

"Is it wrong to say I wish I was there with you?"

"Nope. I was thinking the same thing." I nibbled on the length of my thumbnail as I observed him.

"I could be there..." he said, every syllable beating like a drum within me as I knew I wanted that, I wanted him, I didn't ever want this to end. Every ounce of tiredness I'd felt during the evening had dissipated.

I gulped, unsure how to word my response. "Would you like to come over?"

"Yes, but I don't have crème brûlée."

I grinned, thankful I'd had that long bath and pamper earlier. "Come over then, I'll read to you from my book."

"Yes, because it's your book I'm interested in." He rolled his eyes as I saw him stand. "Be there in about fifteen minutes, Penelope."

"You and that bloody Sunday name!"

He blew me a kiss, ended the call, and I sprang into action.

As I heard the subtle drone of his electric car, I hurled my hairbrush back into the drawer and slammed it shut with a wince, hoping I hadn't woken Rocket who would demand more of Ryan's attention than I was willing to share.

I glanced at my phone; sixteen minutes, it had been sixteen minutes, in which time I'd brushed my teeth again, fixed my hair, added a little mascara, run to the bathroom, and moisturised my legs.

I danced around on the staircase, as I waited for the doorbell to go, not wanting to seem as though I'd been waiting impatiently for him, even though I had been. When the familiar 'somebody is at your door' sounded out from my phone, I took a deep breath and headed downstairs, tugging my pyjama top down so that the missing button, my Cinderella button, displayed a nice amount of cleavage.

"Hi," I beamed as I opened the door, all enthusiasm and eagerness.

"Hi," he replied. I couldn't even tell you what he was wearing, I was so caught up in his gaze as I stepped back into the hallway, him following me.

"I missed you," I whispered as he wrapped his arms around me, his face nestled into my neck.

"I missed you too," he replied as his lips met mine. Every insanely sexy moment of last night flashed through my mind and I longed to recreate them all, over and over, I felt as though I could never get enough of him. "I love these pyjamas." His fingers eased the buttons through the holes, slow and teasing, as I walked backwards towards the staircase, him matching me step for step.

"Really? I could do without them." As I stood on the first step of the staircase, I tucked my thumbs into the waistband and pulled the bottoms down, delighting in the soft catch of his breath that he couldn't disguise. I wriggled my foot loose from the material as I stepped up, my eyes now level with his.

"Penny…" was all he could manage as he followed me, more of a whisper as his lips chased mine, his hands fumbling at the remaining buttons as I continued to climb, loving the game, craving him.

I felt empowered; after having had every bit of confidence knocked out of me, he'd somehow revitalised it. And it was because I felt he was my equal, where previously there'd always been someone who held the power; with him, it felt matched. We were right, we were even, we could play this either way and it was enchanting.

By the time I was two steps from the landing I had shrugged the top off, his hands aiding me as he pushed the soft material down my shoulders. I had no worries that I was naked in front of him, the moonlight shining in through the uncovered landing window; none of it mattered because I felt like he truly saw me. Not just as a friend, not simply as a sexual conquest, but as some wonderful culmination of so many things that we could be together.

He remained two steps below me as he kissed me, hard, forceful, completely deliciously. His hands were in my hair as he tugged and pulled, moving my mouth around his. I was lost in a tangle of tongues as those hands slid to my shoulders and urged me down onto the floor. I sank down, weak against his touch, his hands brushing my chest as my back rubbed against the plush carpet. My eyes were closed, and I didn't see him kneel, simply felt his tongue snaking down my belly, a place I had previously felt so paranoid about. However, with him I felt like a goddess.

His hands gripped at my hips as his lips kissed lower and lower, my legs opening as if on autopilot, as his destination and intent became clear. For the briefest moment I pondered the situation…my hair ruffled up on the carpet, in front of the radiator where I hung Lucy's socks on winter mornings to get them warm before school. This was surreal, a different way to be in my house, with someone new, and before thoughts of what was right or wrong could even penetrate my mind, he was dissolving every conscious thought I had with his mouth.

For everything we'd done last night, this hadn't been on the list and, oh my god… it should've been. The fact that the top stair was hard against my spine, that my head was millimetres from banging against the wall, none of it mattered as his mouth moved over me. He was so in sync, and not at all averse, as my fingers tangled in his hair and moved him to where I needed him the most. Over to the right… down lower… that absolute perfection as his tongue flicked inside of me and I was gone… moaning and writhing on the top of my staircase as his hands pinned my hips down and he drove me over the edge.

My whole world had spun by the time he stopped, all appreciation of time leaving me. I didn't know what was up or down, only that my thighs clamped around him felt so good I never wanted to move. He pulled himself up, grabbed my arms, and tugged me towards him, as his mouth covered mine and, between us, we dragged every item of clothing from his body.

Then I was walking backwards once more, towards my bedroom which he now knew well. I'd crumbled like a soft cake under his touch, but now I wanted some control back. I wanted to be his equal so, as we approached the bed, I twisted around, pushing him down onto the mattress.

His hands were instantly on my behind as I straddled him, his back against the headboard. "Ryan…" I whispered, even though the house was empty save for us and a sleepy puppy. I moved against him, as we became a tangle of kisses and touches, heat and urges.

I pulled my forehead back from his, our hot skin damp, clinging in places as his warm breath misted over my face. It drove me insane. I lifted myself, so that the length of him rubbed over the nerve endings that were currently buzzing like bees around nectar. I needed to get him in the exact right spot, and he was so, so close.

"Don't move," I gasped as the tip of him brushed that point that held so much promise until I was crashing over the edge again, lost in total pleasure to his body, his heat, his everything.

A million emotions raged throughout me, things that I knew I shouldn't feel at this point but was unable to deny as he grabbed hold of me, driving deeper inside as I still shuddered with pleasure. He joined me within moments, catching his breath, as he tucked my hair behind my ear with a smile and pressed a kiss to my shoulder.

"I'm a bit disappointed," I teased, chuckling as his face

shot up to meet mine, his eyebrows raised in question.

"In what way?"

"Well, I thought you were coming over to ask me to go on a bookshop date. Instead, you got all… you know…"

"I *was* going to ask you on a date but then you seduced me. Again. It's a filthy habit, Penny."

I cradled his head against my chest. My legs were still wrapped around him, his back flush against my lilac-grey headboard, we were completely covered in each other.

My heartbeat whooshed around my head, sweeping in and out as it pumped blood that was pure lust around my body. At some point it had started to rain once more, the drops pounding against the window, and I was amazed at how much I loved the sound, repeating on and on, as he raised his face and looked into my eyes.

Silent seconds stretched languidly between soft kisses with no words spoken. His fingers stroked my hip as if this was the most normal thing in the world now, so 'us.' Where had 'us' suddenly appeared from?

It scared me, but it also felt inevitable. The way we'd met, the way all of this had happened – if I stopped and focused on how lost in it all I was, it was as though my breaths couldn't fulfil me, because only he could do that. I was fixated, on a knife edge, and even my fear, my scarred heart, my ridiculous pledge to never love again – none of it could stop me as I teetered, ready to free fall completely into him.

I reached behind the stack of paperbacks on my bedside table and pulled out a bag of Minstrels – my go-to book chocolate because they'd never melt in your hand and leave chocolate on the precious pages.

"You hungry?" he asked.

"Sex *always* makes me want chocolate. As does reading, coffee, and tiredness. Basically, I always want chocolate." I popped one of the smooth, glossy discs between his lips as I shifted, our tangled limbs still sticky and warm. "That's why I'll never have a flat stomach."

He crunched on the chocolate, before reaching into the bag and pressing two into my mouth, his fingers rubbing against my lips as he slid them open. "Your stomach is sexy, everything about you is. Don't even worry about it."

Chocolate-scented kisses somehow evolved into a whole new level of intensity. My body was warm and malleable, moulded by him. I wanted to be this way forever, absorb him, learn everything about him, be completely his.

We lay cuddled up together, our breaths slowing, before he asked me what I was thinking.

"Honestly, I'm so glad you don't mind that I eat chocolate in bed. What about you, what are you thinking?"

"That you're very self-assured in bed, and I like it."

"I never used to be. I faked orgasms all the way through my twenties, always too worried to let go. People change though."

"I want to discover everything about you."

"I want to let you." I smiled and cuddled up to him once more.

He kissed the top of my head, before yawning. I had no idea what the time was, we'd been lost in the night, but I was aware we both had work tomorrow and, as uncomplicated as these times between us were, real life was waiting to edge in again as the sun rose.

EIGHTEEN

"*P*enny? Are you OK to take that action?"

My manager's voice woke me from a daydream, as I pulled the chewed pen from my mouth and focused back on the zoom call that I'd joined an hour ago. I must have coasted through it on autopilot because not a word had stuck in my sleepy, love-drugged mind.

"Of course, sorry, bit of a bad connection here," I replied, scribbling nonsense onto my notepad to make it look as though I knew what was going on.

"Great. Same time next week then everyone, thank you."

A chorus of goodbyes rang out, which always brought Rocket running to my desk as the team members logged off the call. I clicked the red button and dropped to the floor, ready for a puppy cuddle. I was so tired that, in all honesty, I'd have curled up in his bed with him for a nap.

Caffeine would have to do though. I took a large mug of coffee into the garden and sat on the bench, watching Rocket race around, in and out of bushes as he burned off his excess energy. I groaned, as I rested my head back on the wall behind me; why had I offered to cook dinner tonight? I was too exhausted for anything more than a chippy tea, except it wasn't even open on Monday, the big tease.

The morning had been a flurry of blushes, smiles, and kisses as we woke up too late and then Rocket, upon realising we had a visitor, jumped all over Ryan and then peed on the kitchen floor in excitement. All too aware I had meetings from nine, there'd been no opportunity for much conversation.

My phone pinged and I grabbed it greedily from my pocket, hopeful for a Ryan fix. Disappointment sank in as I saw Zoe's name, and I immediately felt guilty. She confirmed they'd be round by seven thirty. I replied with a predictable thumbs up emoji as I drained the last of my coffee and considered what I should eat for lunch. That made me think of my stomach, which made me recall Ryan's words last night, and then my appetite was forgotten as my stomach lurched into pleasurable sensations.

Another ping, I sighed, expecting Zoe to tell me off for having used her least favourite emoji.

RYAN

Do I still get a bookshop date, or do you remain horribly disappointed? x

My toes jiggled around in my socks, as a Cheshire Cat grin formed on my face. I would have looked deranged to any passers-by.

PENNY

I think a bookshop date is the only thing that could rid me of the disappointment, to be honest. That and crème brûlée x

RYAN

Do I need to up my game? x

PENNY

My favourite thing about this is that we're not playing games x

RYAN

Damn, I thought you'd found your favourite thing last night! x

PENNY

Funny... (but kinda true!)

RYAN

So, when? After work Thursday? They open late x

PENNY

You did your homework! They do open late, and I'd love to, but Lucy has Brownies. Plus, you said you were taking your mum to the theatre? x

RYAN

Good point, I forgot. I have nothing on this Wednesday, could you sneak away from work? x

PENNY

I've got a half day but I'm meeting my mum and dad, sorry. Sunday? x

RYAN

We're all going for dinner at Jess' new place on Sunday, big family thing, it'll be hellish I have no doubt, but I won't hear the end of it if I don't go. Saturday? x

PENNY

Lucy is with me this Saturday. Finding free time isn't the easiest, sorry. I do want to, maybe we just need to wait another week? x

RYAN

Does Lucy love books as much as you do? x

PENNY

She does! x

RYAN

So why don't we all go? Bookshop, coffee for us, milkshake for Lucy. Make an afternoon of it? x

This took me by surprise. I hadn't considered bringing Lucy into the situation. I'd never let her meet any of the men I'd dated before, and I guess, looking back, that had been because I'd known in my heart that none of them were right.

But Ryan... God... it felt so different. And they'd already met at the house, although Lucy had been blasé about it. She'd love it too, I knew she would, she'd be in her element with books and sugary dairy products.

RYAN

Sorry if that's too much I understand. We
can wait x

PENNY

It's not too much at all, it sounds perfect x

RYAN

It's a date then x

PENNY

Can't wait! Back to work now, I'll call you
later x

Zoe and Emma arrived at seven on the dot, clutching bags
of Monday margarita ingredients. I'd collected Lucy from
after-school club at five, and she'd giddily awaited their
arrival, knowing she'd get a virgin margarita for herself.

I let her have half an hour of fun with them both before
I had to be the bad guy and tell her it was bedtime; it was a
school night after all. And that's when she turned those big
puppy dog eyes on us all.

"Do you know what I'd love?" she asked, in her most
grown-up voice. I swear the girl had been on this earth
before, some of the phrases she came out with.

"Go on..." I said, bending my knees to crouch down
and talk to her.

"A story from Emma," She murmured, a shyness
coming over her.

"As long as Emma doesn't mind, that's ok," I replied,
knowing Emma would love the opportunity. "Then I can

finish cooking the food with Zoe. I'll sneak up for a kiss afterwards, that OK?"

"Yes, Mummy," she said as she wrapped her soft, warm arms around me for a tight hug, before grabbing Emma's hand and pulling her towards the staircase. Rocket toddled after them, and I didn't have the heart to stop bedtime puppy cuddles, despite the fact I'd been insistent he wouldn't be allowed upstairs.

"Honeymoon period still blissful then?" I asked Zoe, as I gathered all the food, hastily purchased from the over-priced shop around the corner on the way back from school, my plans for a big shop at the weekend having gone out of the window.

"We've lived together for five years, it's exactly the same but with rings." She fixed me with a pointed look. "Much more interested in you! How was Saturday night? You've been quiet, not so much as a hungover gif on WhatsApp. Spill."

"It was…" I sighed, as I splashed olive oil into a pan that was supposed to be for paella. "Really nice."

"Really nice. That's not a very 'Penny' description. Tell me." She sashayed around the kitchen, so she remained in my eye line as I spooned the peppers and onions into the sizzling pan. "If I went to your room right now and sniffed your pillows, would there be Eau d'Ryan?"

I gawped at her. "Zoe! You can't go sniffing peoples' pillows!"

"I notice you didn't deny it though," She wriggled her nose at me.

"He may have stayed over…" I bit my lip, as I added the fajita spices and chicken, which had been cooked earlier.

"On Saturday night?"

"And maybe Sunday too..." I mumbled, continuing to stir as if my sanity depended on it.

"Wow, not a teeny-peenie then? I know I was fishing but I wasn't expecting that."

"Zo! I'm not discussing his penis. I know you don't exactly approve but—"

Zoe cut me off. "It's not that. I don't want to see you hurt again. But he's a good guy, if this is what you want, you know I'll support you all the way."

"It's one hundred percent what I want." My mouth reverted back to its inane, happy grin.

"So where are you both? Is it just sex? Is it casual? Are you about to declare undying love?"

I pondered this, as I poured the contents of the large pan into a duck egg blue ceramic bowl. The table was already set with the guacamole, salsa, sour cream, cheese, and extra jalapenos for Emma who was definitely the spicy one. A bowl of salad was also in place alongside the second round of margaritas that Zoe had prepared. I just needed to retrieve the warm, floury tortillas from the oven.

"I don't know, he wasn't ready... I wasn't either, but we seem to be pulled together. And I can't tar every man in the world with the same brush, can I? I have to move on from what happened."

"*Is* he ready though?"

Zoe's phone rang, saving me, I didn't know *how* to answer in all honesty. She held five fingers up and headed out the back door, leaving me a few minutes to make the dining table beautiful and snap a photo. Normally it would be for Insta, but there was only one person I felt like sharing with at the moment.

PENNY

> Do you wish you were here? x

I attached the photo of the table and smiled, involuntarily, as I saw the dots appear on the screen to show that he was replying.

RYAN

Well, it does look good, but I think you'd prefer to be here x

A photograph of his living room opened up; the fire was lit and looked so warm and cosy. His legs were outstretched onto the large suede footstool and in his hand was what looked to be a spiced rum, the glass half full of large chunks of ice.

PENNY

> I think those two mixed together would be a pretty perfect evening x

RYAN

I know you have friends around; I don't want to intrude. Why don't you call me when they're gone? x

PENNY

> It might be late, don't want to disturb you x

RYAN

I'll be up, don't worry. Call me x

PENNY

> xx

I placed the phone on the kitchen countertop as Zoe returned, followed by the tell-tale creak of my stairs that indicated Emma was heading down, followed by Rocket. A goodnight kiss and a hug for Lucy, then it was time to eat, drink, and survive the Spanish inquisition. Fortunately, Ryan Grayson was my favourite topic of conversation.

———

It had been midnight by the time the newlyweds left, and I knew I'd be exhausted once again the next day but somehow, it didn't seem to matter at the moment. Ryan imbued me with some sort of adrenaline that counteracted my lack of sleep this weekend.

There'd been a fair amount of tequila consumed and, by the time I stumbled into bed, ready to call Ryan, mischievous thoughts had invaded my mind. So maybe I'd worn a very loose t-shirt that slipped to one side, exposing neck and shoulder and collarbone. And possibly I'd kept my nice eyeliner on and roughed up my hair, not for any specific reason.

I grinned madly before I even started the Facetime call. I couldn't control myself around Ryan, but I was determined he was not coming over tonight. Lucy was fast asleep, I wasn't ready to have sleepovers when she was in the house. Plus, I did need some rest, and had to focus on work tomorrow.

It seemed too late to call, but he'd told me to go ahead, that he'd still be awake, so with a final adjustment of my hair, I pressed the green button.

"Are you working?" I asked in shock, as the screen

blurred into view and I saw the background of Ryan's office.

"Yeah, been a bit side-tracked this past week, thought I'd better catch up."

"Things *are* very distracting, I have to admit." I smiled, happy to see him again even if not in the flesh. "You look sleepy though, I know I am."

"It was quite the weekend…"

"It was…" I said back, biting on my bottom lip as I recalled it in all its naked glory. "I wanted to ask you about it."

"What do you mean?" He asked, his head tilted down to the right, or was that left? I could never tell what was and wasn't reversed on these calls, especially after tequila.

"Well, us, I guess…" I stammered. "I know we said slow, and I'm not expecting anything signed and sealed in writing. I wondered where we are? Where you think we're going?"

"You know I'm terrible at all this stuff." He raked his hand through his hair which then stuck up in all kinds of directions, comedic but ultimately sweet. "I think that we've been dating longer than either of us realised. Maybe Saturday was the first official date, but since the wedding, we've grown closer and closer."

"I think so too."

"I never thought relationships would be more perplexing in my forties than in my teens. But then I found myself here, with you. I want this to be a relationship, I want us to be together, but I worry."

"That it wouldn't work out?" I asked, my heart hammering in my chest. I knew I'd been getting carried away with my thoughts of him, but I realised now as he wavered, how invested I was in the situation.

"No, not really. More that I'll end up back in a bad place and that you'll suffer because of that. I wouldn't want to do that to you. I'm OK at the moment, but I still see the counsellor, I still have the sleep issues, and I know at any point I could slip back into the darker stages of this."

I wished I could reach out and stroke his cheek. "I get that, and I know it's different but it's not exactly smooth sailing here either. I worry you'll get fed up with my childcare schedule, my job, and my lack of free time. I do also have ridiculous hang-ups thanks to previous experiences, which I try to never project onto anyone else, but sometimes they slip in."

"Penny," he began. "I love that your life is so full, how devoted you are to Lucy, how you manage to make everyone feel seen. I'd never hold that against you, and I'd never expect you to put me ahead of others, especially Lucy."

"You know that part of a relationship is taking bad times with good, right?" I smiled. "I get that there'll be bad days, bad weeks, times you need something I can't give you. But I wouldn't walk away, I want to be there for you. I…" I blew out a long breath, wishing this were in person and not over Facetime. "I want us to be together. Despite everything I swore to myself, I just want you. And that isn't the tequila talking, although I have had more than is respectable for a Monday night."

That slow, slanted smile was back upon his mouth. "I want that too, I want *you*. I knew it from the wedding, and I battled it, I tore so many thoughts apart. But then every time I saw you, it all made sense. And why is it that I sleep well when you're with me?"

His voice faltered ever so slightly and, in a vague attempt to lighten the mood, I came out with a ridiculous line. "That would be my wit and charm. I've been known to send a man to sleep in ten minutes."

"As if. You look incredibly sexy right now, by the way." He scratched at his beard.

"I mean, I tumbled into bed like this, it's how I landed," I grinned.

"I like how you landed the past two nights, personally."

"Don't," I groaned and pressed a pillow to my face. "Tequila makes me mischievous."

"We need a Mexican night. I like the sound of this."

I laughed, as I threw the pillow away. "If it's like the French place, we may as well have gone to the café up the road for all the attention we paid to the food."

"So, Penny." His voice was back to normal, as I'd hoped. "Me and you, you and me... Are we doing this?"

"Yes," I replied without hesitation. "And that's not the tequila talking."

"I know." He sighed. "I also know your days are crazy busy, but you always walk Rocket at lunchtime, don't you?"

"I do, I have a recurring appointment in my calendar, so the time is blocked out each day."

"So, I could come and join you tomorrow? I know we can't be as spontaneous as you might like, but walking with you and Rocket is one of my favourite activities."

"You could definitely join us." I beamed into the phone. "I'd love that. Meet me here at one?"

"Perfect. Now, stop distracting me with the bare shoulder, I know what you're doing."

I noticed myself in the little screen at the bottom of the phone and realised I was lip biting again. "Night, Ryan."

"Night, Penny."

With a blown kiss, we ended the call, and I sank into my pillow. I was a lost cause, and I couldn't stop smiling.

NINETEEN

Saturday finally arrived. I understood now why Lucy got so anxious and twitchy in the build-up to birthdays or Christmas, she desperately needed the day to arrive right this minute.

Ryan and I had managed two dog walks and about seventy-four phone calls. I'd also had a lovely time with my parents on Wednesday afternoon, where I'd told them I was seeing someone, but it was early days. They knew me better than to push for details as it was the one thing guaranteed to make me clam up. I'd had to work late Friday to catch up, but now it was the weekend, and I was beside myself with anticipation.

"Where are we going today, Mummy?" Lucy asked, half distracted by the 'adopt a baby' game on my iPad, as I coerced her dark hair into Dutch braids.

"You remember Ryan?" I asked, as I pulled a clip from between my teeth and smoothed down the last of her stray curls.

"Yes. Are we going to the llama farm?!" She jigged

around.

"What? No... Lucy, keep still." I chuckled with my sweet girl. "I'd forgotten you'd even talked about that. We'll visit there when the weather is better. Ryan knows I love books, and I told him that you love them too, so he's taking us to the bookshop today."

"Can I get the next one in the Rainbow Girl series?" She gasped, holding her breath.

"If they have it in stock and you're good, yes. But you do need to sort some books out to donate to the little library. Your shelves are overflowing."

"Yours are worser." She grinned at me, her tongue poking out from the gap her front teeth had left when they fell out two nights ago. Ryan had saved me, again, when I realised at gone ten that I had no coins from the tooth fairy. He'd dropped some round for me, along with some kisses of course.

"Hmm, well maybe I'll donate some too. I need your help though, sweetheart. Red top or green?"

I held up two of my favourite jumpers, both fairly well fitted and with V necks, one a beautiful cranberry red and the other a deep emerald green. Either one would look good with the long, black silky skirt I'd already picked out.

"That one." She pointed at the green and returned to her game. "The other looks like Christmas."

Ryan had offered to pick us up, but the faff of fitting Lucy's car seat into his pristine leather interior had filled me with dread, plus I'd have needed to get it professionally cleaned in case I lifted it up and eight million Wotsits fell out of the bottom. Instead, we were meeting him there. It was also less pressure in case Lucy didn't take to him, although she seemed very unphased about the situation. Divorcing while she was so young had been a blessing, even if it hadn't felt that way at the time. She didn't seem to have any memories of Simon and I being together, and she'd not been witness to any animosity or plate throwing, although there had been plenty of both for a while.

Her little hand was gloriously warm and soft, encased in mine as we wandered up the wide, pedestrianised high street. Lucy chunnered away about a boy who'd stolen the teacher's pen at school and how very cross Miss Baxter had been. The butterflies in my stomach performed a jig as I spotted Ryan outside the shop. He wasn't engrossed in his phone like all the other men who loitered, waiting for wives, girlfriends, and daughters to come out of Primark or River Island. Instead, he was looking up at the sky. I noticed how blue it was, how clear, loving the nip of cold that the cloudless sky brought to the day. Rosy cheeks all around.

"Hi," I said as we approached, seemingly unable to walk naturally or control my lips.

"Hello," he replied with a slow smile, his gaze lingering on me before he looked toward Lucy. "Morning. You look much better than the last time I saw you."

"That was *ages* ago, when I was sick." She wafted her hand in the air, drawing a chuckle from us both.

"True, silly me," he replied. "Want to show me where these rainbow books are? Your mum told me all about them."

"I know exactly where they are!" she said, letting my hand drop as she grabbed onto his sleeve and marched him inside, intent on getting to the large children's section as quickly as possible.

I followed on with a wide smile, amused by Ryan's slight panic as he looked my way. If he thought Rocket had a lot of energy, he was in for a shock with Lucy! They rushed ahead, but I meandered leisurely, drawing in a deep breath as I inhaled the scent of all these books, all those magical parcels of bound paper that held an infinite number of stories and ideas inside them, escape and knowledge for anyone who opened the pages. The store was bustling, and it warmed my bones to see people of all ages browsing, from the lady with her walking stick in the true crime section, to the teenage boys poring over graphic novels. This place excluded nobody; I'd even heard the staff recommend a library to a family recently who'd been trying to choose between books as they only had a birthday gift card with enough credit to pay for one. Books were for everyone in my opinion and deserved to be loved, read many times, and cherished. I wasn't the type to leave them on a shelf, untouched and gathering dust.

The duo eventually came crashing back over to me, as I trailed my fingers over some beautiful hardbacks with sprayed edges in the Fantasy Romance section, a favourite hangout area of mine.

"What did you choose, sweetheart?" I asked, noting the one book Lucy held, as opposed to the four or five stacked in Ryan's arms.

"Is six books too many?" she asked, sucking her lips into her mouth as she waited for the answer.

"Definitely. You know this."

"But you got that parcel last week and it had more than

six in, I saw it!" The slightest hint of sulkiness had crept into her voice, and I prayed she wasn't going to be awkward in front of Ryan. However, she did have a point; I bought more books than was entirely healthy.

"How about we all get two each?" I countered. "That's six in total."

"Okaaaaay…" She twisted her toe into the ground, before plonking herself on the floor with all her choices, beginning the harrowing task of narrowing down her selection.

With his hands now free again, Ryan brushed his fingers over mine and I longed to kiss him as I wrapped my little finger around his. "What are you choosing?" he asked.

"I was choosing one for you actually. You said you wanted to expand your reading. I think you need some epic, mythical romance in your life."

And there was that smile again, the smile that I was certain I could never tire of. I handed him a hefty hardback, its cover covered in intricate, swirling patterns.

"That's… chunky." He turned it over, looking for the blurb which was hidden inside the jacket.

"It's my favourite series. You want to get to know everything about me, you need to understand about my book boyfriends."

"I better get this read then, suss out my competition."

"As if there's any…" I said quietly, aware that Lucy was at my feet.

"What would you like me to read? Please don't say horror, I can't do horror."

"Crime? 1920's New York. That's what I was thinking."

"For you? Absolutely."

We stood there for a moment, smiling inanely at each other, likely much to the annoyance of anyone else who was looking for some steamy romance for the weekend, before Lucy jumped up, pushing two books into my hands. "These two," she confirmed with a nod.

After taking the unlucky remaining four back to the children's section, I grabbed a cosy mystery I'd seen rave reviews for, and Ryan chose a non-fiction book about the changing geography of the planet. That was our six books. Until we got to the till and Lucy convinced me she needed the activity pack that was on offer. I wouldn't normally give in, but it did increase the likelihood of her sitting in the café for longer, thereby increasing my time with Ryan.

So, after an hour and a half in my most treasured of retail establishments, we hurried into a cosy coffee shop, arms laden down with heavy bags of books. The café was tucked away down a quaint, cobbled street, away from the large shops that dominated the main road. It was quirky and individual and I much preferred that to a large chain. Despite their ease, apps and loyalty points, they couldn't compete with the pretty fairy lights that hung over the hand-painted sign, or the personal touches from the owners who seemed to work every hour to keep the place viable. It really deserved more customers than it got, but people didn't seem to leave the main high street these days, oblivious to the delights away from the big chains that dominated the best spots.

A bell jangled above the doorway as I opened it, immediately wrapped in the glorious scents of coffee and gooey chocolate brownie. Every table sported a different table-cloth in colourful prints, with mismatched plates, teapots, and cups adding to the colourful exuberance. The walls were a classic dark blue and, every now and then, in beautiful golden calligraphy, you could spot some wonderful quotes from Alice in Wonderland, which I'd learned on an earlier trip was the owner's favourite. They'd often have 'eat me' cookies, tied up with little ribbons which I'd forever be unable to resist.

Ryan had insisted on paying for all of our books but had used my loyalty card which filled me with delight as I thought of that complimentary book shopping spree I was still saving for. Therefore, I hadn't had to argue *too* much that this was on me. I was also starved, again, so along with the vanilla latte, the mocha, and the chocolate milkshake, I'd ordered panini's, brownies, and rocky road. My appetite had been ridiculous since I was tiny, this was why I'd given up on being thin - slightly rounded and full of cake was far more me – who needed a thigh gap anyway?

I could hear the two of them chattering away and, as I approached with the loaded tray, it warmed my heart. I'd never expected to be introducing my baby girl to someone like this, someone so important to me, but it all felt natural and right. I had to pinch myself at times. As Ryan spotted me, he sprang up, grabbing the heavy tray and placing it on the table between the three of us. We'd managed to bag one of the big round tables with the squashy leather seats around it, near to the window, which left us under the soft glow of the fairy lights. It was my dream to get a little window seat for reading at home, draped with lights and soft cushions, but there wasn't a good spot for it at my place.

Lucy grabbed the activity pack from the bag. Although

her reading was coming on in leaps and bounds, she wasn't yet at a stage where she could read a book to herself, but this she'd have no trouble with. She arranged it alongside her milkshake and food and then got to work, her forehead furrowed in concentration.

"That'll keep her busy for hours." I nodded towards Lucy as I focused on Ryan, crossing my legs as I twisted around to face him. "She's had a great time."

"She's so like you."

"What, is she making you sleepy?" I teased, loving the smile on his face that rewarded my efforts. "Important question – which panini do you want? Mozzarella and Pesto or Cheddar and Tomato?"

"Is this a test?" He leaned closer, making me desperate for a kiss I couldn't have here in front of Lucy; he knew that well, and I planned to pay him back for this at a later date.

"Yep. Wrong choice and you're gone."

"In that case..." Ryan grabbed the knife and cut both into two, arranging them on the plates so we had half of each one. "I'm hedging my bets."

I let my fingers graze over his, as I smiled. "Clever."

"Not just a pretty face..."

I almost lost myself in him again when the bell above the door tingled into life, followed by a deep voice calling out.

"Ryan?"

We both turned. A tall, well-built man took the few short steps towards us. He was clean-shaven, wearing glasses, and looked very respectable, clutching a paper bag from a healthcare shop nearby.

"Rob? Hey, good to see you." He stood up and they clapped each other on the shoulders in that way men so often seem to do.

"You too, you should have said you were in town today, we could have gone for a drink. It's been months."

"I know, time gets away with me. I already had plans today anyway," he said, and Rob's eyes headed in my direction. I cradled my Mocha, sipping from it as I tried to look innocent.

"Rob, this is Penny, and her daughter, Lucy. Penny, this is Rob."

"And Rob is...?" I asked, as I smiled and shook his outstretched hand.

"He's so rude, isn't he?" Rob smirked as he spoke to me. "We met at primary school, bonded over lunchtime football matches and we've been friends ever since."

"I've seen you in photos, of course. Hi!" I replied, remembering some of the pictures I'd seen at Ryan's place. Rob had featured in a few of them, definitely the wedding ones.

"You got time to join us for a drink?" Ryan interjected.

"I do, Grace is off at some spa weekend, so I've no need to rush back."

"I'll come up with you, I could do with another. Penny, you want anything?"

"No, I'm good, thanks," I replied with a brief nod, guessing he wanted some privacy for a moment as he explained to Rob who I was, as it didn't seem as if Rob had heard of me. That was OK though, I knew that any lack of explicitly telling people about us wasn't for any other reason than this was so new, and we were both coming into it from a difficult past. Plus, it felt magical, secret, and sweet as we snuck around together, lost in our own little bubble.

I made a fuss of Lucy while they queued, cutting her up a square of each piece of cake and assisting with a tricky word search. She was such a good girl, I sometimes felt bad that she'd not had the opportunity of siblings, but then neither had I and I was OK. She loved her books, her games, and some time to be quiet and enjoy them. It had been a godsend when schools were closed and she had to entertain herself, while I worked from home for the first time, before it had become the new norm.

A glance across to the counter showed me Ryan and Rob talking animatedly while the barista pulled handles and pushed buttons on a large, bronzed machine that looked as complicated as piloting a jumbo jet to me. Ryan's gaze brushed across mine as they turned, and I felt my cheeks heat up a little as I focused my attention back to Lucy, who was cramming rocky road into her mouth at an impressive speed.

"Good job I bumped into you all, or he would have kept you to himself, Penny." Rob smiled, as he lifted his latte glass to his mouth. He put me at ease, I'd seen the way he'd placed a hand on Ryan's shoulder as they had talked at the till, it was obvious he cared. "Hey, Lucy," he continued. "Have you heard of Hillview Primary?"

She nodded, her big eyes looking up as she wiped crumbs from her mouth onto her sleeve. "Ruby Farmer left our school to go there," she said.

"Hmm, I don't know Ruby, but I teach Year 5 at Hillview. And I love buying books for the class, can I see what you chose?" He pointed to the large paper bag next to her and she grinned, before pulling everything out onto the table.

We'd shuffled positions to accommodate Rob, which meant Ryan and I were now nestled together on a small sofa. It was no hardship as his fingers linked with mine, our hands squashed together between our legs. Another hour of this lovely Saturday passed by at a pleasurable place as we chatted, before Rob glanced at his watch and stood, needing to go, but not without a promise that we'd meet him and Grace, his wife, for dinner soon.

"Let me know which book is best, Lucy, don't forget!" He gave her a little salute as a parting gesture and she squealed, tipping all the books back into her bag haphazardly, which I have to confess did make me cringe.

"I'll walk you back to your car," Ryan said as we zipped up jackets and collected our belongings. I tidied all the empty mugs and plates onto the tray, smiling at the barista as we headed outside. The afternoon had darkened, and a definite had set in; it would be a perfect day to be snuggled in front of a fire with a nice glass of red, warming toes and holding hands.

Lucy held my left hand and Ryan held my right, plus the bag in his spare hand, bless him. Life felt perfect, I was waiting for something to pop the bubble, but also praying that it wouldn't.

"Mummy…" Lucy began as my car unlocked itself upon our approach.

"Yes, sweetheart?"

"Is Ryan your boyfriend now? I would only hold hands with a boy if he was my boyfriend."

Ryan squeezed my hand tight in assurance.

"I think he should be, how about you?" I knelt down, so I was at her level, and stroked an errant chocolate-brown curl from her forehead.

"I think so too, but won't Daddy mind?" Her little nose crinkled up.

"Daddy won't mind at all, he's Jane's boyfriend, after all. Daddy wants us all to be happy. Are you happy?"

"I am. I love Rocket so much." She grinned, still all gappy teeth and pink gums, before opening the car door and clambering inside a most undignified fashion.

I was used to her tangents, how one conversation would flip to another. Ryan looked a little more bemused.

"Don't worry," I said as I looped my hand back into his. "That was the seal of approval. If she wasn't happy, we'd be discussing it for hours, she doesn't hold back, my little girl."

"Well, that's a relief." He popped a delicate kiss onto my forehead. "Want to come back to mine? I can light the fire and find a movie for all of us to fall asleep to?"

"I really, really want to but..." I rested my head against his shoulder, as he wrapped his arms around me. "It's gone well today, and I don't want to push it. Lucy needs baby steps as much as we do."

"That makes sense. Call me tonight then?"

"I will. But you know, I think Rob would've liked a drink with you. Why don't you go meet him? Catch up? Make my ears burn."

"Maybe. I'll see."

"It was good to meet him, you don't talk about your friends much."

"I let a lot of them drift away, it's a small circle now." He shrugged.

"For me too, but that's nothing to be ashamed about. Quality over quantity every time. Was Rob your best man?"

"He was. I was worried about his speech for weeks." He smiled at the memory, and I felt it best to leave it there.

"Thank you for today, Ryan. It was as close to perfect as Saturdays get."

"It was. Go on, I'd better let you go or else I'll want to keep you."

He leaned down and kissed me on the lips, a sweet kiss, not a tongue-swirling public display in front of my daughter and the car park attendants, then wandered away with one of his sweet little waves.

I strapped Lucy into her car seat and stowed the bags of books safely in the boot, before driving home, my heart thumping out the rhythm of his name.

TWENTY

*W*e sank deliciously into a relationship which seemed to be equal parts lust and equal parts deep understanding. I was delirious about it, drunk on it, and I struggled to think of anything but Ryan.

Rocket walks became our fix of each other, as many days as we could manage around the multitude of our other commitments. Actual dates were more troublesome to arrange but we watched movies, visited a stately home and devoured scones with clotted cream and jam, and kissed at every single opportunity. Every day or night we *could* spend together, we did. And when our day-to-day lives didn't allow it, we worked around it.

The illicitness of it made it all the sweeter. We'd discussed the fact I wasn't happy for him to stay over when Lucy was with me, not yet. She was adapting to the relationship well and I wanted to keep that going, letting her adjust over time. Some nights though, we couldn't help ourselves. I'd message Ryan once Lucy was asleep; she'd always been a deep sleeper, very rarely would she wake overnight. I'd leave the front door on the snib and head into the living room, where the curtains would be drawn, and the lights dimmed.

Soon after, Ryan would gently tap on the front door and everything else was forgotten. How bad the day had been, how tired I was, how many jobs I still had to do, or what a mess the kitchen was. Nothing mattered from the moment his fingers tangled in my hair until the second he withdrew from me, breathless, hot and so ridiculously happy. Then I'd be ushering him out, all kisses and giggles, before I locked up with a sickeningly smug smile.

On the nights that Lucy was with her dad, I'd sometimes stay at Ryan's house. I'd been apprehensive the first time; after all, it was where he'd lived with Tara, but he made me feel so at home, so wanted, so secure, I needn't have had a doubt. Plus, he doted on Rocket, who was also always welcome.

There were days, inevitably, when Ryan was quiet, almost on edge. It seemed to build up as his counselling appointments became due, and then afterwards he'd be exhausted, drained, before the next day returning to 'my' Ryan as I thought of him.

We still talked about Tara a lot. I didn't want him to ever feel that that part of his life had to be put away or closed off, far from it. A new chapter beginning shouldn't ever stop the previous chapters from existing, the past shouldn't be overwritten.

Lucy had never been the type to divulge what happened at her dad's place, she didn't keep anything from me, but neither did she overshare. I'd always thought of it as a positive sign that she was well-adjusted to the 50/50 custody split. I should have known Ryan would be mentioned at some point to Simon, though, and that he'd have questions. It probably would have been wise to have spoken to Simon earlier, but he had been nowhere near the top of my 'to do' list for years now.

That Thursday, Simon was due to bring Lucy back to mine after she'd been to Brownies. I had expected him at just gone seven. Instead, his car pulled onto the drive a few minutes after six, and I realised my error.

"Hi," I said suspiciously as I opened the front door, my face devoid of makeup, hair shoved up in a messy ponytail. "I think you're an hour early and without a child?"

"Funny." He rolled his eyes. I didn't understand how I used to find that attractive in him, now it made me grimace. "Got time for a brew?"

I nodded and held the door open for him, smirking to myself as Rocket jumped up on his clean jeans, leaving tiny scratchy marks with his claws. He'd never been an animal person; he and Jane had no pets, good job really with their white sofas.

"How can I help you then?" I asked as the kettle boiled and I sloshed the water over teabags, still remembering now that he liked his tea weak and milky, which should have been a red flag from the start.

"Lucy mentioned you had a boyfriend, and I was a little surprised. I wanted to talk about it." He took the mug from me as he glanced around the kitchen, as if suspecting the infamous boyfriend would be hidden in a cupboard or down the side of the fridge.

"You're surprised someone would want to be my

boyfriend? Actually, can we use the word partner? I feel too old for boyfriend."

"No, I'm not surprised somebody would want that. I know you've been in relationships since us, but you've never, ever involved Lucy. Which is why I'm wondering what's different now. A warning would have been nice. I told you when I was introducing her to Jane."

"I'm sorry, you're right." I acquiesced, fully aware that if this was the other way around, I would not be impressed. "I should have spoken to you, it's been a bit manic."

"Oh... well... OK..." he stammered; perhaps he'd been expecting me to disagree. "Lucy said he's called Ryan."

"Yes, Ryan." I replied slowly.

"I did some digging—"

"For fuck's sake, Simon!" I exclaimed. "That's not your place, you're unbelievable."

"It is my place when he's around *my* daughter!"

My fists clenched at my sides, breaths bursting in my chest with fury. It had been ages since he'd got me this wound up, but I could feel all the animosity returning.

"What did you find then, Simon?" I sneered his name as I gulped at my drink, determined not to show my discomfort as it burned my tongue.

He sighed and plonked himself down onto a bar stool. "Nothing that worries me with regards to Lucy, but Pen..." I bristled as he used a too-familiar term for me. "I saw the news stories about his wife, that's... heavy going."

"You Googled it? You're unbelievable."

"Only because I worry about you both! It's not long since you had some enraged wife banging on your door and scaring my daughter witless, remember?" He slammed the mug down and tea sloshed over the top. He'd gone too far, a line had been crossed, and I didn't mean by the spilt tea. The clatter startled Rocket who ran between my legs. I reached down to rub his ears as I composed myself.

"If only you'd worried about us both as you fell into bed with my *friend*." I sneered at the word, I couldn't help it. "That would have been a better time."

"Jesus Christ, Penny. Can we not go there again?"

I raised an eyebrow and surveyed him, still so uncomfortable with his actions it made me laugh. It had been years since we'd talked about it, our steady truce held in place by focusing on Lucy and not what a cheating arse he'd been.

"Is that what she said?" I snapped, disappointed at myself for being childish but also revelling in the fact she'd left *him* within weeks of *him* leaving me.

"You weren't exactly on top form at the time!" He stood, his hands gesticulating wildly.

"Not on top form?! What the actual…. I had a six-month-old baby, Simon. *Our* baby! I apologise if I wasn't flouncing about in sexy lingerie and sucking your cock on a daily basis!"

He sank down onto the stool once more, his breaths rapid, his anger seeming to dissipate at the same speed as my own rose. "Penny, please. I didn't want the chat to go this way. I just… you've made some bad decisions, you know that. I want to make sure you're both OK."

"You know what, Simon? The worst decision I made wasn't you, it was trusting that *she* was my friend. Yes, there's been failed relationships since then, but that has nothing to do with you. You're lucky Jane is so accommodating, given your history."

"It's not that long since his wife died..."

"You need to go," I snarled. "That is so out of order I can't even..." I felt sick as I backed away, consumed by frustration and anger. "He is more than you could ever hope to be. I want to keep things civil, as they have been, for Lucy's sake. So, with that in mind, I'd suggest you leave. Immediately." He stared at me, pulling some alpha male shit as he refused to back down. "Now, Simon," I repeated before he screeched his stool across the floor and stormed towards the front door, slamming it behind him.

I sat down, Rocket nestled up on my knee. He wasn't used to shouting, other than when he'd been in the mouthing stage of puppydom and had elicited multiple shrieks from me with his nippy teeth.

I hated what had happened. I was annoyed that I had less than an hour to get myself under control before he brought Lucy back. Most of all... I hated the thought he'd been partially right, because yes, I should have spoken to him earlier. Maybe if I had, things wouldn't have escalated as they had.

"He's still an arse though," I mumbled into Rocket's fur as I soothed him with a cuddle. I never had been any good with conflict, regardless of whose fault it was.

By the time Simon returned with Lucy, who was giddy from Brownies, we had our grown-up, co-parenting champion faces on again. I pushed his comments to the back of my mind and only at odd moments would they resurface. Lucy adored Ryan and Simon couldn't take that away.

October rolled into November as Ryan and I continued in our idyllic little bubble. People close to us knew, but other than that we kept it to ourselves. Not out of guilt or shame, rather we were so engrossed in each other that the outside world seemed to fade in comparison. Of course, the problem with idyllic bubbles is that they can't last forever.

I was enjoying the cosiest spoon of my life, Ryan was of course the big spoon, when his phone rang. I sighed, as he peeled his skin off mine and grabbed the phone from the bedside table.

"Jess," he said as he answered. "Why are you calling so early?"

I hated to eavesdrop, but phones these days were so bloody loud and he was close to me, there was nothing I could do to *not* listen.

"It's not early. Are you still in bed?"

"Yeah, it's the weekend."

"As if that makes a difference to you. I can imagine why you're still in bed, but anyway, that's why I'm calling." Her voice sounded as barky down the phone as it had at the hotel that morning, to me at least.

"Jess…" His voice held a warning growl that I found insanely sexy.

"Mum noticed the change in you, and she worries about every little thing. Would you bring Penny to meet her? Put her mind at rest? Sunday lunch at The Oaks?"

"Sunday lunch, as in tomorrow?" I heard the scratch of his nails against his stubble.

"Yep," she replied.

"Let me check, I'll message you later."

"Ok. I wanted to see everyone too, so if you can be there, that'd be appreciated."

"You OK, Jess?" he asked, the concern in his voice sliding through.

"Yeah. All good. Just let me know so I can book the table." Her tone seemed soothed. Their relationship was complex, and I wasn't sure, as an only child, that I understood the love/hate aspects of it.

"Will do, bye for now."

"Smell ya later."

That mature exchange apparently ended the call, as Ryan moved away again and I heard the plink of his phone on the bedside table, before his arms wrapped back around me, full-on spoon.

"Guess I don't need to repeat that?"

I twisted around so I faced him, my leg hooked over his hip as I kissed him.

"It was kind of hard *not* to hear."

"Are you free? Is meeting my mum something you want to do? I understand if not, don't worry."

I smiled and stroked his hair from his forehead. It was overdue a trim, but then so was mine. "I'd love to. I guess if we're doing meet the families, I'd better arrange for you to meet mine?"

"Yes." His gaze dipped, before raising it back. "Everything's good between us, isn't it?"

"The best," I said, which was the understatement of the century given how I obsessed about him night and day.

"I know you wanted, and we both needed, to take it slow, so I don't want to force you into a big step."

"You're not at all. Ryan... I..." I sucked in a deep breath, quivering as he placed a soft kiss on my forehead.

"You can say anything, you know that."

"I want to say... let's fall in love, let's plan our forever." I rubbed my nose against his, hoping to hide the blush that I felt spread across my face even for mentioning the 'L' word in his vicinity.

"Penny..." he pressed his lips to mine in the sweetest, chaste kiss. "I think I already did."

Lost... did I mention lost? And now officially in love.

I'd never been to The Oaks before, a pub situated within a nearby country club. You didn't *have* to be a member to go there, but I'd never wanted to be the stranger who walked into the 'local' place, the very posh local place. It was also a bit of a trek from mine and there were multiple other lovely pubs nearby, without the social class dread and a cheaper stumble home.

It was another reminder that Ryan's social standing was a million miles from mine. I'd done well in my career, and I earned more alone than some couples did combined, but I was still firmly from a working-class background, and a little apprehensive of Ryan's middle-class family roots.

I'd finally settled on a Joules dress in a delicate sky blue with some wedge heels and silver jewellery. Nothing says middle class like Joules, right?! Ryan had booked a taxi, so we could both drink, and he held my hand in the backseat as we turned into the country lane that led towards The Oaks.

"I love you, don't worry," he said, as he lifted my hand to his mouth and kissed it softly.

"I'm OK, honest. Just hungry. They better have Yorkshire puddings." I joked, when in all honesty, I was anxious that I wouldn't fit in. Not into their lives, their expectations, or their standards. Single mum… was that what his mum would want for her widowed son? Wouldn't she prefer he met someone younger and start his own family?

The building was beautiful. Large and airy, the interior was awash with natural light which bounced off whitewashed wood and calming sea-foam walls, very Farrow and Ball.

As Ryan led me towards the table, I gulped down my nerves. But the lady before me was less Hyacinth Bucket and more smiling Judi Dench. Elegant, yet approachable, as she stood and held her hand out to me.

"You must be Penelope. So nice to finally meet you." She threw daggers at Ryan which made me chuckle, to my horror. "I'm Elsbeth."

"Call me Penny, please," I replied as I shook her hand. "I've been looking forward to meeting you."

"I've dispatched Jessica for drinks." She gestured towards the grand bar behind us. "What's a Sunday without gin?"

As I turned to take in my surroundings, I spotted Jess heading back towards us, a man at her side balancing a full tray. I guessed he was the husband; it made more sense now than when I'd assumed it was Ryan at the wedding. This guy was much younger, more her age, sort of tough looking, with close shaved hair and two full sleeves of tattoos.

"Hi, Penny," Jess said as she took a seat. "This is Matt, my husband. Matt, Penny."

He nodded towards me, as he put the tray down and Elsbeth began pushing Copa glasses full of ice, and what looked to be double measures of gin, towards each of us, swiftly followed by premium brand tonic in glass bottles.

"Nice to meet you," I replied, reaching for my gin. Matt busied himself on his phone, as Jess and Elsbeth continued what seemed to be an ongoing conversation about the new couple who'd moved in next door and their strange comings and goings.

Ryan poured tonic over the ice in my glass, as he leaned close to me and whispered. His breath tickled against my skin. "We can disappear once we've eaten, don't worry."

His sheer proximity had sprung goosebumps all over me, as I turned to reply. "It's OK, don't worry. It's fine." I laced my fingers into his atop the table, before noting Elsbeth's gaze track to the sign of affection between us.

"So," she began. "Where did you two meet?" She'd cut off the conversation with Jess, whose face resembled thunder.

"At Zoe's wedding, you know this," Ryan said patiently.

"Yes, I do, it's not wrong for a mother to want to hear it again, is it?" She smiled at him, and the playful slant on her features was good to see. I could understand her being protective, seeing your child go through trauma like that, losing your daughter-in-law, it must have been life-changing for them all.

"Your son was extremely chivalrous," I said. "Saved me

from an unfortunate moment and the more time we spent together, the closer we grew."

She glanced between us both, as if appraising how we presented as a couple. "Yes, I did hear my darling daughter caused that unfortunate moment. Well, I hope you're not vegetarian, the roast beef here is to die for!"

Her conversation with Jess resumed, although not before a fierce eye roll from the latter, and Ryan shrugged at me with a short laugh; it appeared the brief 'interview' was over, and I was accepted. It was all a mystery to me, but I would have sat through a hundred awkward dinners to be with this man. Plus, I couldn't deny that Elsbeth had been right, the roasted joint *was* insanely good. Ryan even got me an extra Yorkshire pudding, sod the podgy belly, he seemed to like it regardless.

Another round of gins had been consumed and I was a teensy bit lightheaded, so when Ryan asked who wanted coffee, I was first in line. Matt had excused himself to take a phone call outside, and Elsbeth leaned over the table to talk to me.

"Jess, Ryan, go get the coffee, look over the dessert menu. Give Penny and me a few moments together."

My stomach bubbled with nerves as they headed away, Ryan's fingers brushing over my upper arm in reassurance as he went.

"It's good to see him relaxed and smiling." She poured more tonic into her glass as she spoke. "I didn't think I'd see the day. I worry about him endlessly."

"I know, he's been very open about everything."

"I lost my husband seven years ago, to cancer. It was devastating, but he was older, we'd had our children, lived our lives, and had our dream holidays. To have lost Tara in the prime of her life…"

"It must have been hard for all of you," I said as I reached forward for her hand, her gaze jolting up at me in surprise.

"It was, it is, but we focused on getting Ryan through it, through the worst of it at least. There isn't really a resolution, more acceptance, perhaps? I'll never forget the words of our late Queen – 'grief is the price we pay for love'. It truly is."

"We've talked about Tara a lot. I know she'll always be a part of him, I'd never want to take that away."

"I understand that he's a grown man, a middle-aged man, and it isn't my place to say but…" Her breath shuddered. "Please don't hurt him; no matter how grey his hair gets or how many birthdays he celebrates, he's my little boy and he's had a lifetime of hurt on his shoulders since the day Tara was taken."

"I understand. I have a little girl, Lucy, and the first boy who breaks her heart will have me hammering on his front door." She smiled and I withdrew my fingers from her hand. "Ryan is an amazing man, I love him. Nobody can predict the future, but I'd do anything for him, I really would."

She blew out a stiff breath and finished her gin, just as the siblings returned to the table. "They'll bring the coffee over," announced Ryan before turning to me. "Everything OK?"

I nodded. "All good."

Jess flopped a couple of dessert menus onto the table. "Just going to find out where Matt's disappeared to."

"Is he always so... absent?" I asked Ryan, as Elsbeth reached gracefully for a menu.

"No, to be honest..." He lowered his voice as he leaned into me once more. "I think they're having some problems. She wouldn't admit it to me, but there's something off."

"Maybe next time I have Zoe over, I could ask Jess too? See if she opens up?" I needed to try with her, much as she wasn't my cup of tea. It was weird how Zoe was so close to both of us, when we were so very different.

"You don't have to, you're dating me, not my family. Don't feel you have to be friends."

"We got on OK at the hen do, it just all went a bit weird from then on. She probably feels as awkward as I do."

The coffee arrived, rich and deep aromas that oozed with wonderful caffeine. Jess and Matt returned; their faces gave little away but considering they hadn't been married long, I didn't see much affection between the two of them.

I showed photos of Lucy and Rocket as we drank the coffee, Jess nagging Ryan for extension ideas which only made Matt roll his eyes and exclaim that they couldn't afford it at the moment. Elsbeth took it all in, the archetypal matriarch. She wasn't the tactile type, that much was obvious, but I liked her, I felt respect for her, and she obviously adored the family and wanted to keep them safe – that I could relate to entirely.

Jess headed outside discreetly, grabbing her handbag from under the table. She'd been vaping non-stop at the hen do and the wedding, but I realised she hadn't done it at all today; maybe it was one of those little habits she didn't want her mum to know about. I gave Ryan's hand a squeeze and followed her out, thinking this might be a good time to suggest a get together.

As I opened the door that led to the beer garden a family entered, and I held back a moment, holding the door for them, not realising there were grandparents, cousins, and all sorts behind them. By the time they all got inside, I could see the tell-tale plume of steamy mist in the air floating toward me from around the corner.

"We haven't even been married a year, what the hell am I supposed to say?"

I stopped, frozen to the spot, as I heard Jess hissing the words, my stomach sinking as my mind cycled through a thousand scenarios.

"I can't carry on this charade in front of her. He says it'll all work out but I'm not seeing it. At least Ryan's little play-mate is taking her attention off me for a while..."

I stepped back quietly, not wanting her to know I'd followed her. Scurrying back indoors I headed briskly to the ladies' room, splashing some cool water onto my wrists and temples. I felt hot and guilty which was ridiculous, but really... what was Jess hiding? And what was I supposed to do now?

TWENTY-ONE

*C*hristmas soon loomed on the horizon, with all its glitter and promise. It could be the loneliest time or the most magical time, and I felt like all would be perfect, finally. My arrangements with Simon were in place. This year I'd have Lucy for both Christmas Eve and Christmas Day which was incredible, then on Boxing Day Simon would take her away for ten days to stay with his parents in Spain and top up on some vitamin D.

I wanted to take Ryan away for those days but needed to find a way to sneakily book it and ensure his work schedule was clear. The only way I could envisage doing that was with the aid of his sister and mum.

There was a beautiful garden centre about a half-hour drive from my place and it was infamous for its delectable afternoon teas, the place I loved to bring my parents as a treat. I'd messaged both Jess and Elsbeth and invited them, expecting polite refusals, but both had agreed. When I told Ryan, minus the plans to book a trip, he'd been bemused but pleased. Our relationship had grown more and more loving as autumn flowed along its gradual path into winter, sweeping us up with it as if we were errant leaves always reaching for each other.

I couldn't help the nerves that bounded through me as I pulled into the car park and spotted Jess' sports car with its private registration. I parked a little further back in case there was any awkwardness when we left. I'd tried to go for a middle-class, countryside tweak as I chose my outfit. It probably hadn't worked, but I felt nice regardless in my black jeggings, cream blazer, and knee-length boots.

I'd booked the table online and, despite being ten minutes early, Elsbeth and Jess were seated, chunnering away as I walked into the tearoom.

"Penny!" Elsbeth exclaimed, standing up to embrace me. Jess copied her action, but I didn't quite feel the same heart beneath it. "So lovely to see you, your invitation was darling, thank you."

"Well, it's nice to get together on our own sometimes, no men," I smiled as the waitress fetched over thick cloth napkins and beautiful china teapots and cups.

"It is indeed. Speaking of which, you must bring Lucy next time. Ryan was telling me about her school project, it sounds like he's having a wonderful time helping with it?" she asked as she poured.

I pulled out my phone to show her a photograph of the two of them working away. "He's an absolute treasure, in his element. Each of the pupils have to make a Tudor House. I'm sure hers will be the most detailed by miles."

"He never shows me photographs. She looks so like you." Elsbeth was smiling, as she took in all the detail of the picture.

"Why don't you come to mine and meet her one weekend? She'd love that," I offered, before being interrupted.

"Is it true he's stopped his counselling appointments?" Jess asked brusquely.

"Erm, well…" I was taken aback by her bluntness, although Elsbeth didn't seem to notice any aggression in the tone. "He told me he feels ready to stop. I said it might be better to drop to maybe once a month and take it from there. But ultimately, it's his decision."

"He's in a good place, I can tell each and every time I speak to him." Elsbeth pushed away Jess' obstructions, and I could see the scowl take root on her face. She was obviously troubled at the moment, and the overheard conversation from the country club played through my mind again. I'd not mentioned it to anyone, but maybe I should broach it with Jess.

"Jess," I beamed as she looked up at me from across the table. "How are you anyway? What's going on in your world?"

"Um… All good, I guess. We decided not to get the extension, Matt wants to build the business up some more, so we'll see in a year."

"He's a builder, right?" I asked, and she nodded.

"I bet he and Ryan could work well together."

"Yeah, but Ryan doesn't tend to do plans for houses anymore, it's all offices and city regeneration projects."

"But the other architects at his company do standard house plans, I'm sure they could point clients in Matt's direction for a quote."

"What a marvellous idea," chipped in Elsbeth.

"You two should come for dinner at mine one night,

talk about it. You know where I live, don't you?" I continued, knowing full well she did.

Before she could reply, the waitress returned with two
ornate afternoon tea stands. One was filled with sandwiches – smoked salmon with cream cheese, poached
chicken with mayonnaise, then treacled ham for the third
choice with mustard on the side and savouries such as mini
quiches and bitesize sausage rolls. The second contained
still-warm scones, jams and clotted cream, plus a selection
of teensy patisserie – mini eclairs, millefeuille, and gateaux.

After the obligatory umming and ahhing, as we
sampled bites of every item and drank our complimentary
fizz, I decided to get to the point.

"Lucy will be with her dad for ten days from Boxing
Day," I explained. "I wanted to book a surprise trip for
Ryan as a Christmas present, but I don't know how to
make sure he's free at work. I can't exactly call his boss
when he *is* the boss. I wondered if either of you could
help me?"

"They pretty much close the firm over Christmas
anyway, well, Joshua does. The last few years Ryan has
worked, but that's through choice," Jess said. "Joshua
moved to Edinburgh last year to be with his wife. He and
Ryan mostly meet over Zoom."

"I could give you his details?" offered Elsbeth. "I'm positive he could help you. Ryan needs a proper break."

"Thank you," I said as I plucked a teensy pastry from a
tray. "That would be wonderful."

An hour later, Elsbeth made her excuses and headed
away. A friend was picking her up for bridge club. I felt
accepted as she embraced me and air kissed my cheeks

with a genuine smile. Jess was gathering her things together, as I suggested we head out together.

"If you want to come round for a glass or two of wine one night, you'd be more than welcome, you know? Sometimes it's nice to talk…" I began apprehensively, as we wandered out into the car park.

"Yeah, maybe… There's a lot going on at home at the moment."

"Is everything OK?"

Her eyes flashed to mine. "Of course. Why would things not be OK? What do you mean?"

"Sometimes the expectations after you've got married are tough. I remember everyone suddenly asking about babies and I got so stressed. I just meant; if you want to talk about anything, you could talk to *me*, that's all."

Her forehead remained set in a frown, but there were distinct tears in her eyes. She fished around in her handbag for sunglasses, despite the dimness of the cloudy afternoon.

"I'll keep it in mind." She sounded frosty, but it wasn't a no. "Let me know if you don't hear back from Joshua."

And with that she headed to her car with a wave. I wasn't reassured at all, yet still didn't feel I could broach it with Ryan, maybe it was just me projecting some worries?

He was coming over later in the evening; we were seldom apart for a night now, having spoken to Lucy about him staying over. She loved the idea of sleepovers and didn't seem perturbed. So, with what was left of the afternoon, I sat and penned an email to Joshua, introducing myself and my dilemma – could he somehow make Ryan 'free' for those dates without giving it away?

I bumbled around the house tidying for a few minutes, when my mobile trilled into life with an unknown number. It had been months, and I'd changed my own number, but somehow a sickened ache still spread into my stomach, in case it was *her* spewing her hatred at me again.

"Hello?" I answered, ripe with nerves.

"Penny!" A cheerful voice boomed. "It's Joshua, I picked up your message. Hope you don't mind me calling, it's easier than all that email stuff."

"I don't mind at all, I didn't mean to bother you though, there's no rush."

"Ahh don't be silly. I've been nagging that bastard to take a holiday for ages now, your email was music to my ears. I had an idea though," he said. "If you fancy a trip up north?"

"What idea?" I asked, as I slumped onto the couch, toes wriggling in my socks.

"Me and the wife will be away for some of those dates you mentioned, the annual skiing trip. She's stressed about leaving the bloody dog, she's a cavapoochon or some such concoction. So, I was thinking, why don't you two come spend Hogmanay here? We'll piss off on our trip, and you can stay here with the dog? Edinburgh is a beautiful city."

"That sounds incredible, but I have my own puppy, I was going to book a dog-friendly cottage—"

"Bring the mutt! Show mine what a proper dog looks like. Assuming yours isn't some fancy lap dog too?"

I laughed. "No, he's a proper dog, promise."

"Have a think, then drop me a line and let me know. We could sell it to Ryan as a business meeting and then surprise him on New Year's Eve."

"It sounds like a good idea, let me look into it. I'll get back to you."

"I'll look forward to it Penny. I've heard a lot about you, be good to finally meet."

I said goodbye and chucked the phone onto the floor next to me. Rocket sniffed, then ignored it when he realised it wasn't anything edible. New Year's Eve in Edinburgh with my man and my puppy – it sounded like a perfect combination.

TWENTY-TWO

"*A*nd you *have* to go?" Ryan asked for the umpteenth time.

"I do. I know it's only a Christmas party, but Ken will be retiring next year, and I'm ready for directorship, I really am. I need to be seen, make myself known."

"You know you don't even have to work," he stated, knowing it made no difference.

"It's not about the money, it's about being a role model to Lucy, about showing *them* that you don't have to be a fifty-year-old white guy to get to that level," I said.

"Showing who, though?"

"Anyone, everyone. You don't get it Ryan because you're exactly who they'd promote to the top. You don't have the battle that I do, you don't have to fight to be listened to, to be seen as more than a pretty girl with boobs."

"Call me when you stop for a break, and then again when you get there?" he pleaded, having lost the battle to keep me at home.

"I will," I promised, sensing his pain through his words.

"I'll be safe, I'm not in a rush. I'll take my time and keep you updated. The hotel details are on the coffee table in case you need me."

He lifted my small suitcase into the car boot and pushed it closed, before wrapping me into a tight hug. "You sure you don't want me to come?"

"You'd be bored senseless. Plus, Rocket needs you and I know you have your own work." I glanced behind him. Rocket bounced around at Ryan's front room window, giddy in his second home. "I'll be back Friday afternoon, they always do these events on a Thursday so everyone can slope off for the weekend early."

"I love you," he whispered, his mouth nuzzling at my neck before he kissed me, slowly, deeply, sucking the sheer breath out of me.

"I love you too," I replied, holding his hands in mine, wishing I could stay but at the same time knowing I wouldn't be gone long.

As I drove away, I swallowed a lump of guilt. It was understandable that he'd panic about me driving long distances, but I couldn't go my whole life without such journeys. The works Christmas event was at a beautiful country hotel in the Lakes, there wasn't a train station anywhere near, so I had to drive or send apologies. I simply had to be there; I wasn't going to put my career on hold because I'd fallen in love.

Lucy was with Simon and Jane. Rocket was with Ryan. My mum and dad had all their shopping, and the housing association was holding a Christmas quiz evening, they'd be fine. All was good, the dress and shoes were packed, and there was nothing to worry about. Nothing at all.

I could never be far from a book of course so, on the journey, which I expected to take around three hours, I'd selected an audiobook to listen to. I liked to devote December entirely to Christmassy books, all miracles and romance and reunited families. I'd read one last week that took place in Lapland. I was still desperate to travel there while Lucy was young enough to be enthralled by Father Christmas and all the snow. I'd hoped to take her this year, but finances and time had gotten away with me. Maybe if we went next year, I could invite Ryan along.

For December the weather was mild, no ice, no rain, no scary storms, and so I made good progress on the motorway as I headed further north. Fully appreciative as the scenery grew greener and rugged, the air less claggy and full of the scents of nature.

With some time to spare, I stopped halfway to stretch my legs and fill up on caffeine. I also knew Ryan would appreciate the update. I grabbed my phone from the centre console as I switched off the engine, about to send him a message that I loved him and all was good, when I was greeted by an urgent text from my boss, the aforementioned Ken, about an urgent call he needed me on. There were sudden problems with a huge town centre re-assignment from a nursery to a leisure unit, some major players were involved, and they would not be happy if this venture went south.

"Shit, shit, shit…." I repeated, worried the whole project was about to fall apart, as I dropped my phone back into the console and grabbed my handbag. My laptop was in the boot and would be better for joining this call which was due in…. I glanced at my watch… fifteen minutes.

Hopping out of my car, I grabbed the laptop bag and sprinted towards the services, hearing the car auto-lock behind me. I managed to grab a venti Starbucks and situate myself near the window in time to join the call.

Thirty minutes later, we all disconnected from the meeting with many, many actions. I could see my weekend plans going out of the window, but the deal seemed salvageable, that was the main thing. I needed sugar after the stress, without a doubt.

As I stood in the queue, eyeing up an espresso and a brownie, I rummaged around in my bag for my phone, my heart plummeting when I couldn't find it, before I remembered throwing it back into the centre console in my work-induced panic. I tried to breathe, sure that Ryan, Rocket, Simon, Lucy, my parents, and everyone who counted on me would have been OK for the short time that I was out of contact. The weight of everyone overwhelmed me at times, but I understood I was blessed to have them all.

Clutching my cute little cup and paper bag, I headed back into the car park. The light had already begun to fade in the wintery afternoon and the temperature had certainly dropped as I wandered towards section E, the laptop bag heavy on my shoulder.

Hmmm, I was sure I'd parked in E... I wandered up and down but couldn't see my silver car; of course, it was a common colour which didn't make the job easy. Perhaps I'd been mistaken, and it had been section F? I continued to search, as panic bloomed and invaded my chest when I saw no sign whatsoever of my vehicle.

I plopped myself down on a bench at the grassy edges

of the car park, glancing around, trying to avoid the obvious thought but, as time went on, it was too apparent. My car was gone. I pulled the contactless car key from my jeans pocket – how could it be gone if I had the key? It made no sense, but it wasn't here. Which meant... neither was my suitcase, dress, or shoes.

I fumbled around in my bag once more, vaguely hoping to see my mobile phone but it was definitely in the car. I was alone, in a random Cumbrian service station, with no phone. It was at that point that the tears flowed.

A coach pulled up nearby, and I wiped my eyes as what appeared to be hordes of retired couples disembarked and made their way inside. My head was back in my hands as I sensed a shadow stop over me.

"Are you OK, dear?" a kind voice asked.

I glanced up to see a couple in front of me, they looked to be in their late sixties and were holding hands, which I always found adorable.

"I'm OK," I replied before bursting into spluttering sobs.

"What's happened? Are you hurt?"

"I... No... No, nothing like that." I looked up, taking the tissue she offered as I wiped my eyes. "I was inside doing some work and my car's been stolen. I don't understand how though as I have the key here." I held it out in the palm of my hand; it was useless, but I clung to it as if it would save me.

"Oh, is it one of those contactless ones? They're cloning them all over the place. Bank cards too, you need to be careful, we carry ours in special pouches." She proceeded to pull multiple items out of her large handbag to show me, but I couldn't focus on anything but her phone. She saw me looking.

"Do you need to make a call?" she asked kindly.

"I do," I sobbed. "But I don't know anyone's number. My partner is going to be so worried."

"For a start, why don't you call the police?" she said. "I'm Joan; this is Eric, my husband. He'll get us some tea. We've got half an hour before our coach leaves, so let's see what we can do for you."

"You're so kind," I said as I took her phone. "I'm Penny."

Fifteen minutes later, I'd given all my details to the police and was sipping on a strong tea, chatting away to Joan and Eric, even though my mind was in total panic.

"Is there nobody on your computer who can help you?" Joan asked. "I feel awful leaving you, but we can't miss the coach. We're on a trip to Scarborough, a little turkey and tinsel celebration."

"I can message my boss," I replied with a smile. "That's a good idea, thank you."

"You look after yourself my love." She rubbed my arm. "Merry Christmas."

"Merry Christmas," I replied as they walked away, hands interlocked again. I opened up the laptop and logged into Teams to message Ken and explain the situation, plus beg for help.

As bosses went, he wasn't the worst. He was already at the hotel, and I assumed at least two drinks in as he insisted I call a taxi and he'd approve the expenses payment in the new year.

It still took an age, as I tried to find someone at the services to give me a number and make the call – had every payphone in the country been removed already?! This wasn't exactly London with an abundance of Ubers vying for customers. This was Cumbria on a Thursday afternoon in December.

Even if I'd known Ryan's number off by heart, I don't think the staff here would have let me make another call. They seemed very untrusting of a woman with no phone and no money, I didn't know why. The police crime number seemed to do little to persuade them, but then, I guess nefarious deeds happened at service stations all the time and they had to be on their guard.

The drive to the hotel, once the cab did turn up, was another ninety minutes. I didn't know if he was taking the long route on purpose or if it was just genuinely a long trek, but I grew more and more tense as time went on. I was definitely not in the mood for a party now. I wanted to be home and cosy with Ryan, Lucy, and Rocket; it was a battle to stop myself from crying.

When I eventually sloped into the hotel lobby, down-trodden and emotional, I could hear the laughter of my colleagues from the bar, but all I wanted to do was collapse in my room. Check-in was thankfully brief; I was beyond desperate for a wee and a sob, so found myself on the loo with my head in my hands as I cursed everything and wished I'd stayed home as Ryan had suggested.

I flopped down on the bed, turning to the side and cuddling a pillow, wracking my brains as to what Ryan's phone number was and berating myself for not memorising it. There was so little need to, these days. My gaze caught the landline phone next to the bed and I shot up with a smile.

Zoe was one of the only people in the world I knew who still used her landline, she had some weird attachment to it. When I'd first found this out, she'd told me it was because she'd managed to keep the same number she had at home as a teenager, and it felt special. When read out, the number sounded like a cute little rhyme and I could remember it, miraculously!

I grinned, as I grabbed the receiver and dialled her number, not caring about the automated message informing me of the charges.

"Hello." Zoe's confident, smooth voice rang out and I pumped my fist in pleasure that I'd caught her at home.

"Zoe! It's Penny! I need your help!" The words all came out in an explicit jumble, too fast, but she knew me well, she'd know I wasn't arsing around.

"Penny, what's wrong? Why are you on the landline?"

"I'm in the lake district. My car got stolen, and my phone and I don't have Ryan's number and I don't know what to do, Zoe!" I exclaimed, before I was overtaken by sobs once again.

"What the fuck!? Are you OK? Did they hurt you?"

"I'm OK, I wasn't there when it was stolen. I was in a bloody work meeting. The twats."

"Work or the robbers?" she asked.

"Both," I sobbed. "Everyone is at the party but my dress, shoes, makeup… they were all in the car. I haven't even got clean knickers." More tears ran down my cheeks.

"Hey, shush. You're OK." She soothed. "Was it in the lakes? I can come up. Do you want me to get you?"

"I want Ryan, but I don't know his number. Will you call Jess? Get his number for me?"

"Of course. Give me ten minutes, ring me back."

"Thanks, Zo."

"Go find a mini bar, you'll be OK. Promise."

It turned out there was no minibar, much to my dismay, but after a quick call to reception and a tearful explanation, they took pity and brought a delicious double gin and tonic to my room, even though room service wasn't an actual thing here.

I counted down the minutes on the digital screen displayed on the television, alongside the "Welcome to your room Mrs Archer" message. It pissed me off that even post-divorce I was still Mrs to the world, but never mind. That wasn't my priority right now.

The second that ten minutes had passed, I dialled Zoe's number again, humming the little tune of the digits in my mind.

"Penny?" she said as she answered.

"Did you get his number?" I asked like a desperate, needy woman.

"I spoke to him. He was worried sick. He's driving up. I said I'd look after Rocket, is that OK?"

"He's driving here?" I asked, my heart hammering, I knew he'd hate the journey, but I equally felt safer in the knowledge he was on the way.

"He was kinda frantic."

"I feel horrible, this is the last thing he needs."

"This is *not* your fault, don't do that. Listen, he'll be a couple of hours, get some rest, you must be drained."

"I am." I agreed. "Is he dropping Rocket to you?"

"Yeah, he'll be here a minute, I'd better go, can't see the door from here, damn wires."

"Zoe, I've never been more grateful for your retro phone or landline. My room number is 112, can you write it down for him? He won't remember if he's all stressed. Also, tell him to drive slow and—"

"Penny!" she interrupted me. "I need to go, can hear someone. It's fine, chill, he'll be there soon."

The call ended abruptly and I placed the receiver down, rubbing my hands across my face. I hated the thought of him driving such a long way, while worried. I went to check the weather forecast and the traffic updates on my phone before realising again that I didn't have it.

I didn't want to join the party. Instead, I logged onto my laptop and began to notify my bank and mobile company, plus car insurance. I'd never had anything stolen like this before, it all felt too surreal. Once I'd got my head together a little, I realised I could access my backup on the cloud and could still see my mobile contacts, meaning I was able to call Simon and my parents to let them know. I downplayed how stressed I was, but wanted them to have the phone number for my hotel room in case of emergency.

After that, I flicked through the five predictable channels that were available on the TV; to be honest, though, the Bolshoi Ballet could have put on a private show for me and I still wouldn't have been able to focus.

I splashed water on my face and wished I could brush my hair and teeth, but I had nothing with me. No doubt reception might have had mini complimentary kits, but I didn't want to go down there and bump into colleagues. I didn't feel strong enough to explain all this right now. without dissolving into tears again and the last thing I needed was them to see me looking all weak and needy, better they not see me at all than *that*.

I rested my forehead against the mirror feeling like an out and out failure; days like these I realised how bad I was at adulting. Then a firm, insistent knock sounded out, spooking me as I jumped back, before dashing to the door. My fingers were clumsy as I fumbled to open it, then Ryan was in the room with me.

We collided, that was the only way to describe it. He stepped into the room, reaching for me at the same time as I bounded into his arms and burst into tears as my every emotion and vulnerability flowed out.

His arms squeezed me tight as he kissed the top of my head over and over, walking me backwards, kicking the door closed behind us.

"I was so worried about you." His voice broke as he spoke, his hands clutched at my cheeks as he held my face and looked into my eyes. "I didn't know what to do when I couldn't get hold of you, I..." He sighed, his eyes closed as he pressed his forehead to mine, but not before I saw them fill with tears.

"I'm so sorry, I didn't mean to worry you," I sobbed.

"It's not your fault, it's not your fault..." He pressed his mouth to mine, kissing me as I felt the wetness on our cheeks mingle together, damp skin rubbing against damp skin.

Then his hands lifted my top over my head as we tumbled into the bed, swiftly removing all clothing from each other, wanting and needing to feel every bit of each other without barrier, to know we were both still here.

Afterwards he clung to me, his arms tight around my

middle as my head cradled against his chest, listening to his heartbeat, too fast and too loud, I was all too aware that I'd filled it full of stress. I howled inside at the thought I'd unwittingly brought those awful memories back to him, caused him to feel fear, loss, and panic.

"I love you," I said as I kissed his chest. But even as I said the words I could feel the shudder from him. He untangled himself from me and moved to the edge of the bed, his head in his hands as he struggled to slow down his erratic breaths. "It's OK, Ryan. I'm safe, you're safe, we're both OK."

I pulled him to me, rubbing his back in a slow motion, trying to soothe his ragged breathing, to slow his mind down, to centre him back here with me. I felt nauseous, absolutely sick to my guts as the full reality of what he must have been reliving in his mind became apparent.

Eventually, he raised his head, his hands, still damp from tears, reaching around me and pulling me to him. "I couldn't stop thinking it was happening again. I'm sorry, Pen. I'm meant to be here for you, and I end up like this."

"You never, ever have to apologise. Never."

He pressed a kiss to the top of my head with a forlorn smile.

"Zoe sent some clothes for you, I left them in the car." He pulled on his jeans and searched for his top as he spoke. "Let me go get them…" He glanced around, hands patting his pockets until he found his keys. "Then, time for a stiff drink."

My hands shook, as I pulled my underwear on and fumbled with my bra clasp. At this point, I couldn't distinguish if it were due to shock, fear, passion, hunger... or a toxic mixture of them all.

I pulled a towelling bathrobe from the wardrobe and wrapped myself in it, before heading to the bathroom to wash my face. My eyes were pink from crying and the smudged mascara made me look as if I hadn't slept for a month. A far cry from the perfect foundation, smokey eyes, and big lashes I'd planned for tonight.

I heard the door open and popped my head out of the bathroom to see Ryan place a small holdall on the bed. "I don't know what's in there," he said. "Zoe passed it to me in exchange for Rocket, I was gone within a minute."

"Thank you,"

"I really..." He wiped his brow with a nervous laugh. "Really need a drink. I'll wait in the bar for you, is that OK?"

I nodded, all too aware of the slouch in his shoulders as he closed the door on his way out.

Zoe's wife, Emma, travelled a lot for work, so there were always mini toiletries and travel-sized goodies in their bathroom. Zoe appeared to have thrown a random selection into a bag for me. I grabbed some makeup wipes and cleaned the smudges from my cheeks and eye sockets before spraying myself with deodorant and brushing my teeth. She'd sent clean underwear; jeans and a long tunic top I recognised from her work wardrobe. I breathed in as I zipped the jeans up, jealous again of her slender figure, but at least they fit. I wished I could message her and say thank you but, once again, no phone. I was so bloody dependent it was pathetic.

There was no hairbrush, but I did have a bobble around

my wrist from earlier so pulled my hair back into a pony-tail and, with a long sigh, left the room to search for Ryan in the bar.

I kept a low profile as I made my way there, not wanting to bump into anyone and be drawn into a conversation or explanation. Fortunately, I only saw strangers; the party would be in full swing in the marquee, which had its own bar, so I could remain anonymous if luck was on my side.

As I stepped into the bar, I saw Ryan over in a dark corner, near the fireplace. He was at a small table, with a glass of amber liquid cradled between his hands. A second sat on the table, waiting for someone to claim it.

"Hey," I said. "Is this for me?"

He nodded and, as I sat down, he pushed it across the table to me. I took a long gulp of the spiced rum, revelling in the burn along my throat as it distracted me from the ruined evening.

"I'm sorry you've had to come all this way and..."

"Penny, stop, please stop." He sighed and ran his hands through his hair. "It's not your fault. One of those random coincidences that it was your car they took. It just..."

He didn't finish the sentence as he took another long drink, and I remembered the day he told me about the crash. How it hadn't been Tara's fault, how it was a random, unfortunate chain of events.

"If I'd had any way to let you know I was OK, I would have done. Please believe me."

"I do believe you, I do." He reached his hand for mine and I could feel the tremble within him. "Today was...

tough. For both of us, I'm not trying to make this all about me."

I sat back in my seat, completely out of my depth and not knowing what to say. Everything felt surreal.

"Another?" he asked.

"Can we take them up? I feel drained."

He nodded and we stood at the bar together, my head resting on his shoulder as he paid for the drinks. "Have you eaten?" he asked.

"No, it's fine, I don't feel hungry."

"You need to eat…" he urged, his eyes full of concern.

"Kitchens closed now, mate," said the barman as he placed the two glasses down. "Just got the snacks on the shelf there."

Ryan grabbed some random bags of crisps and nuts and paid with his phone. As we wearily traipsed up the stairs to bed, I couldn't help but feel that a barrier had gone up around him, and what really scared me was that I didn't know if he'd let me inside it again, now that all his pain had been brought back to reality.

TWENTY-THREE

We soon found ourselves side by side in bed, both in t-shirts due to the random state of our overnight bags, or lack of. I tried not to crunch my crisps too loudly, as Ryan flicked through the disappointing choice of channels, all of which seemed to show something cute and Christmassy.

"You OK?" I asked.

"Yeah, can't find anything to watch."

"You know I'll fall asleep anyway," I said with a smile, remembering easier times, but his frown increased as he stopped the channel surfing and settled on a comedy quiz.

"Did you put a stop on your phone?"

"I did, managed to do most things on my laptop. Replacement sim is already ordered, I just need to get a handset." I gasped, suddenly feeling dread.

"What? Penny, what's wrong?" Ryan sat up straight, knocking crisps all over the duvet.

"Those arseholes had better not spend my bookshop loyalty points!"

He looked aghast for a moment, then burst out laughing. "Sweetheart, I'll buy you all the books you want, always."

"I know, but I've been saving them." I pouted but couldn't truly look sulky when I was happy to hear him laugh for the first time tonight.

"Here." He handed me his phone. "Log in on there and change your password. Then even if they access the app on your phone, it'll need logging back into."

"Thank you." I stretched up and kissed his cheek.

It took me a good ten minutes to remember my original password and then log in and change it. Ryan was very quiet and, considering he was watching comedy, there wasn't so much as a chuckle from him.

"Are you mad at me?" I asked as I handed his phone back.

"No, god no, you've had an awful time. I'm mad at myself, I think, for letting intrusive thoughts defeat me today." He sighed and turned his lamp off. "I'm exhausted, you want the TV leaving on?"

"No, I'm zonked. Sleep sounds good. Thank you, for coming here, I'd still be sobbing in the bathroom otherwise."

"Anything for you. Night, Penny. Love you."

"Love you too. Always."

He kissed me, soft and slow, then turned onto his side, fidgeting for a moment before he settled down.

I felt like I'd never sleep, not with this space between us, but the events of the day must have overtaken any anxiety, as I found myself inside a horrible dream, where Lucy and Rocket were trapped in Ryan's car, as it was raced away by a mysterious woman, although I suspected I knew who she was. It said a lot about the state of my mind that the memory of *her* was mixed in with this, it said things that I didn't want to acknowledge, alongside the paralysing dread that lurked oppressively within my chest.

Instinctively I reached out for Ryan as I awoke, my body rested but my head still aching. The other side of the bed was barren, no warmth left in his space.

I reached out for my phone, before cursing at my reliance on the item I no longer had. Through squinted eyes, I saw the remote control on Ryan's side and flicked the tv on, turning the volume right down.

The morning news told me it was a little after six, I left it playing, as I lay back down. If it was so early and his side of the bed was cold, meaning he'd been up at a ridiculous time again. That had never happened to him with me, until now, until I'd landed all that worry on him.

His car keys were still on the bureau under the television, so I knew he hadn't left entirely. I opened my laptop to access my contacts again and found his number, dialling it from the hotel landline and crossing my fingers that he was OK.

"Hello…" he answered, and I realised of course that an unknown number at six in the morning was usually a bad omen.

"Hey, sorry, it's me," I said, before adding. "Penny."

"I knew the voice, Penny," he replied, and I could almost sense a smile. "Is everything OK?"

"Yeah, I just woke up, was worried about you."

"I'm fine. Was awake early. Came for a walk, it's beautiful around here."

"Shall we get breakfast?" I asked, my stomach now unimpressed at the meagre offerings of yesterday.

"To be honest, I'd like to head home. Get your phone and car sorted out. I didn't want to disturb you but if you're awake anyway, shall we head off soon, miss the traffic?"

"That's a good idea," I said, although I wasn't entirely sure it was.

"I'll be back in ten minutes."

"See you then," I replied, wondering if he wanted to hear that I loved him, but he'd already ended the call.

The drive home was tense, we made polite chit chat but there were more silences than anything else. I listened intently to every news report and traffic announcement to save having to make my own form of conversation. I didn't know what he wanted me to say or do.

He was hurt, that much was obvious, but I felt powerless to help. Jess had described it, but it was now all too real. A wave of nausea built up inside me as we neared our town, and from the turns he took it was obvious that Ryan was heading to my place.

He pulled up outside my house, his car making that ominous electric motor noise that freaked me out at times. "I'm meant to be in meetings today, can you give me an hour to nip home and re-jig things? Then I'll come and help you with everything."

I nodded my head but, even as I did so, burst into

uncontrollable sobs. "I'm sorry I ruined everything, please tell me what I can do to make this better."

He stroked tears from my cheekbones, as he rested his head back on the seat and let out a long sigh. "You didn't ruin anything, you haven't done a thing wrong. I..." He twisted his hands together. "I need to process. Yesterday was traumatic. Knowing you were in the car and not being able to get hold of you. I thought the worst. I just need to figure how to handle this. But please, Penny, please believe me when I say you have nothing to be sorry for."

"I love you, I want to help you."

"I know. But I'm used to carrying the weight of this, I don't want to burden you with it too." He reached forward and stroked my cheek with a smile, but it didn't reach his eyes. "You lift it, you remind me how to escape it. But any escape is temporary, yesterday showed me that. If I lost you, that weight would double, and it would kill me. I don't know what to do anymore."

"But you won't lose me, Ryan, please..." I reached for him, but he tensed up and I let my hands drop.

"I'll be back soon, we'll sort all everything out. We could get you a hire car or something?"

"I just want to help you, cars and phones are nothing, you're everything."

"Just time, Penny. Give me a little time."

I opened the car door, unsure of what to say or do. Half of me wanted to respect his pain and his space, the other half of me wanted to throw myself at his feet and scream and beg for him to stay with me.

My footsteps were like lead as I trudged to my front

door, glancing back at him every second, his knuckles white as he gripped the steering wheel. His eyes met mine for a second and he graced me with the saddest of smiles, before the car droned into life again and he slowly pulled away down the road.

I waited there, like an ever-loyal stray dog at the side of the road, hoping beyond hope that he'd screech to a halt and run back for me. But he didn't. Reluctantly, I let myself into the empty, cold, silent house, where I proceeded to slide to the floor, my head against the letterbox, fists curled up into balls, as I flooded myself with self-pity.

An insufferable amount of time later, the doorbell rang. A little spark of hope combusted in me that maybe it was Ryan, but then I heard the tell-tale yipping of Rocket and a high-pitched voice commanding he "shut up!".

I opened the door with a plastered-on smile, but Zoe's mouth dropped in shock at my appearance. Rocket jumped up at my legs and I absentmindedly stroked his head, but my eyes remained on Zoe's as her gaze questioned me. I shook my head sadly, tears flowing hotly down my cheeks.

We still hadn't spoken a word as she stepped into the hallway, closing the door behind her, arms wrapped around me, the familiar tang of her spicy perfume rolling over me. Rocket had run straight into the kitchen in search of his food bowl, and she took my hand, leading me after him.

"Are we at the strong cup of tea or the shot of brandy stage?" she asked.

"Tea please," I replied as I sank down at the dining table, my head in my hands.

She didn't need to ask how I took it; one of the joys of close friends was they could soothe you without speaking, make perfect cups of tea and had similar taste in books meaning we could always do a swap. She sat beside me, two steaming mugs on pretty coasters between us, and looked at me.

"This isn't all about a stolen car, surely?"

I shook my head and blew out a shaky breath.

"Ryan messaged me," she continued. "To say you were back. What happened?"

"I think it was too much for him, what happened yesterday. He was worried about me driving all that way, to begin with. Then, he began to think the worst when he couldn't get hold of me." I stopped for a long sip of the hot drink, letting the steam flow over my face and keep me focused. "Even once he knew I was OK, he drove up to me and he hates motorways. He wasn't like the Ryan I know by the time he got to me. It was like he'd gone back to when it all happened, all tense and hidden behind these barriers that I couldn't cross."

She reached out her hand and placed it on my arm. Not rushing me, just letting me know she was there.

"He said he needs some space. I kept apologising, but I don't know what to do. I didn't plan any of this. I love him, Zo. So fucking much it's ridiculous."

She pulled me to her as I dissolved into heaving sobs once more, my eyes and nose streaming over her beautiful blouse. "Penny, listen to me."

Her arms held me back a little as she smiled, forcing my eyes to focus on her. "I'll try, you know it's not my strong point," I joked with a feeble grin.

"He hasn't said it's over, has he?" I shook my head. "I think you're in shock, what happened yesterday was horrible. And I think he is too, for different reasons. The two of you need to process it all and talk it through when he's ready."

"What if this is it though?"

She blew on her tea, before considering. "Then that's out of your control. We pick you up and move forwards. But honestly, I don't think it will be. I know you aren't sure about Jess, but she tells me how he's changed, how happy he is, besotted I think was the word. He isn't going to give that up because of a bad day."

"I'm sure she doesn't like me," I whinged, before blowing my nose on a tissue, another ridiculous panda one which took me right back to the day she had sat in this kitchen, and I'd said there was nothing going on between Ryan and me.

"She doesn't let people in easily, that's all. It's a family trait. She's had a tough time recently. When's Lucy back?"

"Tomorrow morning." I wavered as I said it, knowing I'd have to keep a brave face on for her.

"Saturday, perfect. How about we go somewhere for the day then? You, me, Lucy, and Emma?"

"Maybe…" I said. "But shouldn't I be here in case he comes round?"

"Penny, give him his space. You know what guys are like. Let him retreat to his man cave, you can't force him out. I'll check in with Jess and see what she knows. But you moping around here won't help. Let's do a yes day for Lucy, hey? Just relax, have fun."

I didn't have the strength to argue so I simply nodded

and rested my head on the table, cradled in my arms as I emitted the deepest yawn.

"Right, you." She stood and pulled me with her. "Bed. You've had tea and a hug. You look like death, no offence. Go, get some sleep. Also, that hair isn't a good look on you." She grinned impishly as she headed to the front door, my heavy feet padding after her.

I'd called Ryan straight after Zoe left. She was right, I did need to rest, and Ryan needed some time. Insurance companies and ridiculous paperwork could wait. He accepted that, and begrudgingly admitted it was a huge client meeting he'd been trying to rearrange for me, so maybe this was best for today. As it was, I barely slept, but those few hours of rest were better than nothing; between that and a long hot shower, I looked vaguely human for when Lucy got back home the next day. She hugged me and then ran to Rocket, tearing around the kitchen with him as she laughed.

Simon's eyes narrowed, as we stood on the doorstep together. I didn't often invite him in now. "Everything alright?" he asked.

"Yeah, it's been a nightmare with the insurance company. My phone is being delivered in the next hour, so at least I'll feel connected to the world again then. Cost me a fortune for weekend delivery, but I should be able to claim it back."

"Are they replacing your car?" he asked.

"Eventually yes, until then I get a hire car. Managed to

arrange that for tomorrow. I still don't understand how they stole it when I had the key; apparently, these contact-less keys are easy to clone or format, I don't know."

"Ok, well as long as you're coping. You can always call me, you know, if you need anything." His face softened and, for a moment, I saw the guy I fell in love with, but it was a fleeting glimpse, too much had moved on.

"Thanks, Simon, I'm OK, though. I'll drop Lucy back to you on Tuesday evening. Don't forget it's her nativity next week."

"It's on the calendar. I'll be there." He smiled, as he backed up the driveway and I felt an unerring sense of relief. In spite of all the absolute chaos and hurt that being an adult seemed to entail, at least I knew we were good parents to Lucy. We got on better than some of the parents who weren't divorced to be honest. I'd seen some of the kick offs and angry whispers at the PTA cheese and wine night.

I'd been infatuated with Simon when we first met, utterly convinced I wanted to marry him, and proud as punch to carry his baby. I didn't think I'd find love like that again, but Ryan... Ryan was a whole other level. And was it really all at risk now because of some idiot car thieves?

I loitered in the doorway even after Simon had driven off, breathing in the cold air, somehow Christmas had infiltrated even that. As if the combined effects of all the pine and cranberry in these houses gave the entire neigh-bourhood a festive scent. My face was cold, but it didn't matter, what did any of it matter?

A delivery truck pulled up and the driver, tight on his festive schedule no doubt, positively sprinted up the driveway and threw the small box at me. I carried it in, pulling the phone from the package and inserting the sim before plugging it in. Everything on it would restore to a backup, revert to normal, as if there'd been no issues... why couldn't the rest of life be that easy?

TWENTY-FOUR

*L*ucy had been beyond excited at the prospect of a day out with Zoe and Emma, even more so with the knowledge it was a yes day. I loved how her creative mind whirred, as she sat in the back of Zoe's car with me and gave us her wish list.

"I want Cinnabon for breakfast," she began, even though it was almost eleven already. "Then I want to go to the toy shop by the supermarket, you know the big one, Mummy?" I cringed; it would be hellish in a toy store this close to Christmas, but I kept the smile plastered on my face. "Then can we go to the place where they let you make your own pizza?" That place also had amazing wine: I was happy with that.

"That all sounds brilliant, sweetheart," I said.

"Erm, I'm not finished!" She put her hands on her hips and I struggled not to laugh, even though I could see Zoe's shoulders shaking in the front seat. "The new movie about the squirrels is out. Can I see that too?" I nodded. "There's one more thing, mummy, but I don't want to upset you."

I leaned closer to her, wondering what this was. Had she picked up on something about Ryan? She hadn't mentioned him, but kids were intuitive. "You won't upset me, Luce. What's the last wish?"

She reached forwards as far as her car seat (luckily, I'd had a spare in the garage) would allow her, hot, sweet breath tickling me as she whispered into my ear. "I really, really, really, really want to have a sleepover with Emma and Zoe."

"Oh, my love, we can do that another time, but I happen to know that Emma and Zoe are going to a party tonight." I met Zoe's eyes in the rear-view mirror. She'd mentioned last week that they were at an 80's themed party tonight for a friend.

"To be honest," said Emma in that beautiful accent that would soothe the worst insomniac to sleep. "I don't want to go. I'd love a sleepover if that's what Lucy wants. We did promise a yes day after all?" She looked at Zoe, her large green eyes pleading.

"Well, I'm not going to the party on my own," Zoe batted back. "And I can't not turn up. So, there's only one way this works." She twisted round to face me after easing her car into a space. "Penny comes to the party with me. Lucy stays over with Emma. Easy-peasy."

"Woah, woah, woah!" I said. "I'm not up for a party. I'm up for moping in a darkened pub, listening to Portishead while I chain-smoke, nothing more."

"Penny, it's not 1995. Jesus… nobody has smoked in a pub for years. What's up with you?"

Guilt washed over me as my façade slipped, in front of Lucy who looked at me questioningly, not that she knew who Portishead were. I also wasn't sure if she understood about smoking, but I immediately felt guilty. Her brave, wide eyes pulled a decision up in me. "Emma, do you honestly not want to go?"

"I don't," she shuddered.

"Can I borrow your neon wristbands and rah-rah skirt?" I asked.

"How did you know I had them?"

"It's an 80's party, of course you have them! So, can I?"

"All yours, can I borrow your daughter?" she winked at Lucy, eliciting sharp giggles.

"It's a deal," I said, thinking that even if my heart was crushed, I could escape into another decade and screw adulting, for one night at least.

"There's my gorgeous boy!" My mum beamed with happiness as Rocket galloped up the drive towards her, the entire back half of his body wriggling and wagging with doggy happiness.

"Thanks for having him again," I said as I pressed a kiss to my mum's soft cheek, Rocket had already let himself in, in search of grandad and the inevitable bag of treats that had been bought for him.

"I love having him here, and your dad does too, but you know he can't let that grumpy old man act drop too often."

I laughed, as I followed her into their cosy bungalow. My dad was the biggest softie I knew, but on first meeting him you'd be forgiven for thinking he was entirely unimpressed by everything.

"Afternoon, Petal," he said as he placed a cup of tea down for me and ruffled my hair. Rocket was at the foot of his chair, munching on some ridiculous-sized chew that I probably wouldn't have bought or approved of. "Is that young man of yours whisking you out tonight then?"

"Oh, erm, no." I screwed my toes up in my shoes, trying to attract some blood flow that way instead of it reddening my face. "Zoe invited me to a party, it's an 80's theme."

"Oh, we had some amazing parties in the 80's." My mum clasped her hands together as she reminisced.

"I remember some of them! Used to love those New Year's Eve do's, when I could stay up and we'd all conga in the street."

"It's not the same anymore," she said. "Maybe we should throw a party for Lucy this new year?"

"Oh, Mum…" I began, as a further explosion of guilt burst to life within me. "She'll be with Simon, remember? I'm meant to be in Edinburgh too, but I haven't finalised it all yet." Would I still be going? I had no idea at this point.

"I forgot, of course, never mind." She took a drink from her 'best nana' mug and my heart twinged with hurt, I never felt like the daughter they deserved. "We've got all of Christmas Day together. I know what, why don't you both come and stay over on Christmas Eve? Then you get the full experience, early wake up, floor covered in wrapping paper. Smoked salmon and champagne for breakfast?"

My Dad grumbled at the TV, as he flicked between channels looking for the football; the derby had been on that afternoon I remembered hearing on the radio. He'd basically go along with whatever me and Mum decided though, anything for a quiet life and as long as he got fed.

They had that traditional, old-fashioned marriage where they drove each other mad half the time but stuck together through thick and thin. And I knew they'd had a lot of both, I didn't always appreciate it when I was younger, but they'd had money troubles, health worries, and insecurities like anyone else. Maybe everyone struggled with adulting, and it wasn't only me. Perhaps some people just hid it better.

"That sounds perfect! Will Ryan be staying too?" She was charmed by him, obviously it ran in the females of my family.

"I don't think so. I imagine he'll be with his Mum."

"Have you asked him?" She said, her nose crinkling up a little in a way I often saw in Lucy.

"No, I'll talk to him." I gulped, would I? Would I ever get to have that conversation? This was why I'd never introduced men to Lucy or my folks before, because when it all ended it was just more strings to untangle, more disappointment to shoulder. Another failed relationship.

I'd sent him some photos throughout the day, not too many, just enough to ensure that he knew I was thinking of him. Plus, who wouldn't want a selfie from their girlfriend with Cinnabon icing on the end of her nose?

I downed the tea even though it was still too hot, purely to stop the tears that burned behind my eyelids. They would fall so easily, I feared they'd never stop. I crouched down and cuddled Rocket, rubbing his soft ears while his eyes began to close in contentment.

"I'd better go get some neon on, I suppose." I smiled, as I looked between them both. "Thanks again. Are you OK with him until lunchtime? I'll get Lucy first and bring her round when we pick him up?"

"No rush at all. Have a good night, you deserve it. You know Lucy could have stayed here."

"We'll get her over to you for a sleepover soon, she just wanted to spend some time with Emma. Her and Zoe are the closest things to aunties she has."

My dad walked me out to the door, while mum fussed over Rocket. He leaned forwards and hugged me; somehow, he felt frailer than he had mere weeks ago.

"You sure you're ok, Petal?" he asked.

"I'm fine, thank you so much for helping."

"What are the insurance company doing about your car? You can't keep walking everywhere. Do you need me to speak to them?" It made my heart ache with love that he still tried to look after his little girl.

"The walking is good for me, I spend too much time on my bum at that computer. I'll have the hire car soon, waiting on an email."

"Do you need any money?" he asked.

"Dad," I smiled and wrapped my arms back around him. "It should be me asking you that. I'm fine, promise." Despite them living off a pension and me having a good job, he always took me back to seventeen when he'd slip me the odd five-pound note without my mum knowing, so I could enjoy a night out with friends. Five pounds went much further in those days obviously. "I'll see you tomorrow, love you. Get back inside where it's warm."

He waved goodbye and closed the door to keep in the heat, one of his favourite sayings. As I wandered up the path, my hands tucked in my coat pockets to protect against the chilly wind, I could already hear him call to my mum that he'd put the kettle on. I dreaded to think how many tea bags they got through in a week.

My feet brushed along the pavement at a sluggish pace as I headed home, and my fingers trailed across the screen of my new phone continually, I longed for one of our light-hearted, flirty little chats.

I knew in my heart of hearts though that Zoe was right. Ryan had retreated, and only he could deal with the anguish that my unfortunate incident had stirred up in him. Crowding or pushing him would achieve nothing. I had to wait this out, but every second of not knowing if he still wanted me was like a chain tightening around my body, squeezing the air from me, restricting my blood flow.

I'd bought some hot pink hair crimpers earlier in the year when Lucy wanted mermaid hair for a party – hers had been so pretty, I went for full-on 80's frizz and volume with mine. I dragged out every eyeshadow palette I had, using all the random and weird colours to create some peacock-style shading alongside an electric blue eyeliner Emma had passed me earlier. Hot pink lips perfected; my head was done at least.

I sipped from an extremely large glass of Sauvignon Blanc, as I flicked through my wardrobe. Along with the blue eyeliner, Emma had loaned me a neon pink rah-rah skirt and some neon orange wristbands. What to put on underneath was another matter entirely. I had some random leather look leggings that I think were left over from a Halloween costume a couple of years back; they'd have to do with a fluorescent yellow workout top that had never even been worn, never mind worked out in! Lucy's jewellery box also came in very handy; she had some old, beaded necklaces and bracelets that my mum had bought her at a charity shop one day, all good for this outfit along-side a trusty pair of black heels.

I was vaguely pulling off retro sexy, I thought, as I looked myself up and down, the wine glass still in my hand as I worked my way through its chilled contents. What I'd normally do at that point was either Facetime Ryan or send him some selfies, but there was little point taking any pictures to show to nobody. Lucy would appreciate the giggle though, I told myself, as I pinged a couple of cheesy smile shots through to Emma, knowing they could giggle together, along with another thank you for keeping her overnight.

I messaged Zoe, as I stepped into the cold air outside. I was going to rely on alcohol to keep me warm tonight.

PENNY

Getting the taxi now, be with you soon. Promise me, that no matter how much I beg, or how sneaky I get, you will not let me drunk text Ryan? Or drunk facetime? Or drunk anything?!?! x

ZOE

I'd already planned to take the phone off you! See you in a few mins, you're in safe hands x

The taxi driver beeped his horn as he pulled up outside, his face already in a smirk as he looked me up and down. "Thought it was Cyndi Lauper," he joked as I slid into the backseat, smiling politely as I gave Zoe's address and the destination of the party, The Fox and Ginsmith, a new bar in the town centre. I'd wanted to try the place for a little while, I just didn't expect to do it with hair that could be seen from space.

TWENTY-FIVE

*W*hy is it that the moment you don't want to meet any men, they're around you like flies? It was as though the 80's outfits had sent the testosterone levels in the bar through the roof. By the time we had three cocktails in us, the dance floor was the best place to be. We'd perfected a technique where we both turned our backs on any advancing males and made the 'stay the hell away' message quite clear.

The party was for the 50th birthday of one of Zoe's colleagues and the place was full of friends and family of assorted ages. Apart from the creeps, who, let's face it, got everywhere, it had a fun, jovial atmosphere. If I'd been in a better mindset, I would have been in my element.

"Zoe," I puffed. "I need to sit down, I need a drink. Do you mind if I go to the terrace for a few minutes?"

"With the smokers?" She pulled a disgusted face. "They won't be playing Portishead you know," she teased with a wink.

"I'm not going to smoke. I want some space for a few minutes, and it looks pretty up there."

"Well…" She looked around. "I do need to catch up with some folks. You sure you'll be OK?"

"Yeah, I'm good, I promise," I said with a smile, as I began to turn away.

"Penny…" she scolded, holding her hand out. "Phone please."

I sighed as I handed it over, but knew it was the best. I couldn't be trusted. Those cocktails had been high in both alcohol *and* sugar content, and I wasn't entirely sure which was vying for control of me at the moment.

The party had the exclusive use of one floor of the bar, but the area downstairs was still open to the public so, of the people gathered on the terrace puffing away, only a couple were in 80's get-ups like me.

I'd grabbed a wine on the way out; water would have been more sensible, but I wanted to drown my misery. I leaned against the half wall of the terrace, taking in the noise of the town centre, the lights, traffic, litter, and drunkenness … but also the couple holding hands as they walked, the teenagers kissing outside the cinema. Ugh, how the hell was I in my forties and still such a bloody mess?!

This bar wasn't a party atmosphere aimed at revellers, an older clientele I guess, and the people who were on the terrace were huddled in conversation, laughing. It wasn't full of lads and louts and of that I was glad. Saturday nights in some places felt unbearable to me these days.

I pushed a little further forward, smiling as the girls walking below gossiped about someone's new boyfriend. I loved friendship groups, always there for each other. Well, apart from the odd bad egg but I'd moved on in that case, she'd been my final mistake as far as friends went. Between her and the subsequent divorce, the number of people on my Christmas card list had plummeted, but the ones that remained were true and that was all that mattered.

I froze, as I felt a hand sweep across my upper thigh, rubbing below my bum cheek. "Damn, I really *have* missed that arse."

My stomach dropped at the sound of *his* voice; revulsion twisted in my belly where once he'd only conjured lust. I stepped backwards away from the edge, attempting to turn to the left and march back inside, but he sidestepped, and stopped me.

"Penny, I've missed you. Why did you block my number like that?" He slurred his words, his eyes flitting greedily across my body and back up to my mouth.

"How have you even got the nerve to speak to me, never mind touch me?" I hissed the demand, not wanting a scene but in absolute disbelief at him.

"I'm not with my wife anymore, it's fine."

"What the actual fuck!" My hiss turned into more of a screech now. "You told me that the *first-time* round, remember?"

"Penny, Penny, Penny..." He shook his head, his hair still shiny, his suit expensive, his teeth obviously absolutely perfect as he looked at me with a smouldering smile, but it did nothing for me anymore. "You don't know what it's like to be trapped in a loveless marriage, to be so unhappy every day. And then BAM!" he clicked his fingers. "You turned up and, I know it was wrong, but I've never wanted anyone as badly as I did you. We were so good together. I wish I'd met you first, I still love you."

He watched for my reaction, as if expecting me to throw myself at him, or thank him. "But you didn't meet me first. You got married, you had children and then you hid them, you hurt them, you hurt me, you lied to us all. I detest what you put me through. How can you say you love me? When she found out, you did nothing to try and help me, nothing!" I spat the words out.

"What would you have done if I had?" he asked, leaning towards me, a tiny spark of something that looked like hope, if I'd be pliable to his lies, still gleaming in his eyes.

I took a steadying breath. "I'd have told you to go fuck yourself. *You* are my biggest regret."

"That's not very ladylike, Penny. Although..." He winked conspiratorially. "That was always one of my favourite things about you. Definitely not a lady in the bedroom."

I stepped back, in total disbelief, needing to be out of the path of his whisky breath; but this left me with no way out, as my heels pressed against the wall, and I realised I'd literally backed myself into a corner. The music from the party blasted out and I focused on the lyrics of Blue Monday as I watched him, wondering what the hell would come from his lips next. I didn't feel in any danger, not physically, he wasn't *that* type of guy, but this was definitely not a situation I wanted to be in, and the last thing I needed was to be in his wife's crosshairs again.

"What do you want?" I asked, hoping to end the encounter.

He shrugged. "I saw you looking all sexy and thought...

maybe now I'm single and you're single that we could..."
His mouth clamped onto mine and I shoved him with a
shriek. I wasn't very strong, but he was drunk, and it
pushed him off balance as he tumbled into a table behind.

"You bitch," he growled. "As if I was going to come back
for sloppy seconds anyway." He shot towards me, and I
flinched, throwing my hands up over my face, but before
he reached me, another voice joined the fracas.

"I'd suggest you leave now, before the bouncers get up
here and I tell them how you were treating the lady." The
voice was firm, but with an undertone of threat. I'd
squeezed my eyes shut and was too afraid to open them
right now; the voice was familiar, but I couldn't place it.

"Stay out of it, you don't know what you're talking
about. She's another prick tease."

"You had to go too far, didn't you? Lads, give us a
hand?"

I heard the hurried scrape of chairs and a scuffle
ensued. By the time I felt ready to open an eye, wanker
dentist was being hauled away by two heavy-set, bearded
men. My hand flew to my chest in an attempt to steady my
breathing which fluttered, rapid and chaotic as a baby bird.
He looked back, as he bellowed. "You'll regret it tomorrow,
trust me!"

"It is Penny, isn't it?" A kind voice spoke, and I twisted
my head toward my saviour, my eyes still darting around
in panic, as if this was some setup and his wife lurked
nearby, ready to attack me.

"Rob?" The voice suddenly placed, as I saw his face.
"Thank you, I..."

At that point, I burst into ugly sobs for approximately

the thousandth time that week. He pulled me to him, removing his jacket and wrapping it around my shoulders. "He'd been hassling someone else earlier, do you know him?"

"He's my ex," I begrudgingly admitted. "Let's say my judgement was very off in that period of my life."

Rob led me over to his table which was thankfully situated under one of the powerful heaters. He passed me an unopened bottle of water which his friends seemed to have brought back after depositing the bollocks of a man outside. I sipped at it, murmuring grateful thanks to all of them.

"This is Ryan's girlfriend, Penny," he explained to them. There were greetings and questions about how he was, how they wished he got out more. I don't think he realised how missed he was, and I promised myself to let him when I got the chance. "I'll be heading home in ten minutes, this was a quick catch-up. Want me to drop you at Ryan's?"

"I'm staying with a friend tonight, I need to find her actually. We were at the 80's party together. I only came out here for some air, I didn't know he was here. I haven't seen him in months."

"I was going to ask if you always dress like that or if it was a special occasion, didn't want to seem rude." He grinned and I laughed along.

"Thank you, I mean it. That was pretty nasty."

"I wouldn't have let him speak to any woman like that, never mind the woman who made my best friend smile again."

His words almost summoned tears again, so rather than dwell on the mess I stood up, thanking them all hurriedly before insisting that I really must find Zoe, at which point I scarpered like Cinderella, barely remembering to return Rob's jacket. Finally, I spotted Zoe back in the party. I jogged over and filled her in on the whole sorry tale.

It seemed as if another night was ruined, and I was exhausted at it always being because of me, I hated that. The party atmosphere was gone, though, and I was frankly drained and emotional, so we headed to the taxi rank together. I considered asking for my phone back, but I knew she'd say no, and I also knew it was for the best. I couldn't be trusted right now. I was a disaster.

TWENTY-SIX

I'd woken up in a hungover, dry-mouthed state of confusion. While I waited for my mind to kick into consciousness, I frowned, confused. I could hear Lucy laughing somewhere in the house... but someone was in bed with me. Who was Lucy playing with and where was I?

I rolled over, the pain in my head asserting itself, and realised I was in Zoe's spare room. With Zoe. We were still in our 80's clothes, Zoe's face was covered in make-up streaks, and I suspected mine was the same. She rolled over with a loud snore, and I crept out to the bathroom, closing the door softly behind me.

Zoe's handbag was discarded on the bathroom floor, my phone sticking out of it. I grabbed it as I sat down on the loo, slightly nauseous. Yet, my heart sank once again when I saw no messages, no missed calls. I wanted to go home and wallow.

I washed up, said my thank you's (to Emma at least, Zoe was still out for the count) and began the walk home with

Lucy. She pointed out every interesting thing she saw, I smiled and nodded, but I was in pain. My head hurt from alcohol, my body hurt from dancing and my heart and soul ached with worry and stress. This also proved I wasn't the type of woman who could live without a car.

I ushered Lucy inside and settled her with YouTube and a bowl of sugary cereal; this wasn't the Sunday morning to try and play perfect mother, it was a morning to try and survive.

I slumped down with a large, black coffee and a gaping yawn. I needed to pick up Rocket, but I was beyond exhausted. I decided to take the coward's way out and dialled my parents' house phone.

"Hello!" My mum's cheery tone greeted me and raised a smile on my face by some miracle.

"Hi Mum, it's me," I said.

"Did you have a good night?" she asked.

"Yeah, it was great," I lied. "I'm... not feeling so good today, though. Think I ate something that didn't agree with me."

"Do you mean drank?" she asked, and I could picture the pursed lips.

"No, I didn't drink much, honestly. I feel awful, like I'll throw up."

"Spit it out. Do you want me to keep Rocket?" She sounded stern, but I knew she wasn't really.

"Would you mind? I might feel better later, and I'll come for him, but I can't at the moment."

"I don't mind, just ring me later and let me know, OK?"

"I will, thanks, Mum. Love you."

"Love you too, sweetheart," she replied, before ending the call.

Lucy had fallen fast asleep on the sofa. I guessed it had been a late night for her and Emma. I grabbed a throw and covered her, before I moved over and snuggled up alongside; we'd nap Sunday afternoon away if we needed to. My eyes could barely stay open, but there was something I needed to say to Ryan before I let them close. I had to let him know that I was thinking about him, that I missed him.

PENNY

I'm adrift without you xx

Eventually, the click and thrum of the boiler turning on woke me, meaning it was mid-afternoon. I always set the timer to warm the place up for Lucy returning home from school. We'd been out for the count, and my gorgeous girl remained that way. I knew I should wake her or else she'd never sleep tonight.

I squinted at my phone; there was a message from Zoe, saying sorry she'd missed me and she hoped I was OK. There was a whole string of messenger chats about this month's book club and whether we were having Christmas drinks instead of, or as well as, the normal meeting. Then there was a message from Ryan, short and straight to the point, but still... a message from Ryan...

RYAN

I was thinking something similar but couldn't have said it as poetically. Could I come round this evening? x

This could be bad news or good news, but whatever it was I needed to know. Plus, I was desperate to see him, and the thought of being near him again almost consumed me. I could picture his perfect little cupid's bow and how badly it begged to be kissed.

PENNY

Yes, of course. 8 pm ok? x

RYAN

See you then x

I felt like the most selfish woman in the world, but this now changed how I felt about Lucy napping the afternoon away. I needed to wake that girl up and tire her out so she'd sleep tonight, and I could talk to Ryan properly. I also decided that work could do one tomorrow. I'd been thoroughly traumatised by everything that had happened and, for once, I needed to put myself first. Tomorrow would be a sick day and, with that in mind, I messaged my mum.

PENNY

> So sorry Mum, I can't get Rocket today.
> I'm taking tomorrow off work though so
> how about I pick him up in the morning
> and then I'll take you shopping? We can
> have lunch out, my treat to say thank you x

MUM

OK x

I smiled to myself; it might have sounded short or annoyed, but my mum was terrible at texting and most things got that reply of – OK.

So, 'Operation Exhaust Lucy' began, and it wasn't a hard job in all honesty, I dreaded to think what time Emma had let her stay up until. We ordered pizza for tea and then, while Lucy played in the bath, I hopped in the shower. A nice Horlicks, some toast, a bedtime story and she was sweetly snoring in her bed for a quarter to eight.

I didn't look great, I knew this, but I hoped I pulled off cosy and welcoming, someone Ryan could trust and turn to. I lit the fire, mine was electric and not as fancy as his, but it was still cosy, even more so with the Christmas tree lights lit in the corner of the room. I plumped all the cushions up on the sofas as I waited for him, expecting to hear that drone of his electric car. But the drone didn't materialise, so I jumped out of my skin when a quiet tapping came at the door.

I knew the knock was his, I'd heard it so many nights before, but it had always been easier than this.

I ran my tongue over my teeth before I slowly opened

the door and, in a second, my every resolve to be strong melted away as I looked at him. How had this man claimed my heart so entirely?

"Hi," he said.

"Hi…" I replied, full of anxiety.

"You going to invite me in or…"

I laughed with nerves. "Of course, sorry. Come in, it's frozen out there tonight, did you walk?"

"I did. Helps with my ridiculous mind." He smiled, but there was sadness. I wanted to pull him to me and kiss him, but I was out of my depth. I had no idea what was going on between us right now.

"Want some wine?" I asked as he kicked his boots off, hanging his jacket on a hook in the hallway, a random hook that had become his over these last few months.

"Definitely." He looked around, confused. "Empty house?"

"Lucy is fast asleep upstairs, Rocket's with my parents, I wasn't feeling great earlier. Take a seat," I pressed on, not wanting to converse about why I hadn't been great. "I'll be back with the wine in one minute. You hungry?"

He shook his head. "No, I'm good, thank you."

God, why did things feel formal? I took some deep breaths and rolled my shoulders as I poured two large glasses, hoping they would relax us both, before I headed back to him.

"It's that Portuguese one you like," I said as I handed him a glass and settled onto the sofa, my legs tucked under me as I faced him, my own wine cradled in my hand in between sips.

"I met Rob this afternoon, he told me what happened.

That guy sounds like an absolute dick. You should've called me; I would've picked you up."

"Rob and his friends were brilliant, sorted it all out. It was too late to call you and I didn't know if I should, if I could... It's good you saw him today, the others said that they missed you too."

"I know, I keep meaning to make arrangements." A further silence ensued, and I could see words whirr through his mind but not make it onto his tongue. "I had to see you to make sure you were OK. That's twice in one week I've felt this fear about you, and I hate that I'm hurting you by being distant. I need to assure myself that I can cope with this."

"'You mean our relationship?" I asked, already knowing the answer. "I'm sorry if I pushed you into it, I didn't mean to, I just—"

"You didn't push me into anything," he interrupted. "I couldn't stop thinking about you from the day we met. I need to know I'm ready before we go any further, that's all."

"I understand, I do. But none of us ever know what's around the corner, what we will or won't have to face. I've never been as happy as when I was with you, when you drove off on Friday afternoon, I didn't know what to think. I can't quite believe it's only Sunday evening now, this has been the weirdest weekend..."

"Penny, I'm sorry that I did that, it wasn't fair." He gulped at his drink, his free hand resting on his knee. I reached forwards for it, desperate to touch him.

"You don't have to say sorry, I feel awful that you got dragged into that whole mess."

"I wanted to come and save you, be the knight in shining armour, and the fact it set off this utter dread in me. It..." His breath shuddered. "It made me feel helpless, and then that made me feel out of control. And the only way I've dealt with everything is by staying in control. I was helpless with what happened to Tara, and I was helpless as I fell through all those 'stages' after." He quote marked the stages before he carried on, his hand slipping on top of mine now. "And so, all I could keep thinking was, if I couldn't even help you without feeling that way, then I didn't deserve you. And also, if my worst fears had come true and I'd lost you too, I couldn't handle it. I couldn't handle twice what I already did, I don't think anyone in the world could. It's why I evaded relationships but you Penny, you... I don't want to evade you."

"Do you have any idea what you mean to me?" I asked.

"I do because you mean the same to me. I'd got so used to not caring what happened to me. I'd never have hurt myself, no matter how much Jess and my Mum worried that I would, but if I'd known I was going to die the next day, I wouldn't have cared either way. And now that's all flipped again. I *do* care about the future, about making sure tomorrow happens, it's painful in a way. But I know it's good and healthy and I know from the bottom of my heart that you're the right person to be doing this with Penny..."

His hand covered his forehead as he leaned down, his breath shuddered. I took the glass from him and placed it on the coffee table alongside my own, before shifting towards him, my arms wrapped around him as I kissed his cheek, tasting his tears, wishing I could remove his pain, but at the same time knowing I wouldn't change a thing about him because *this* was the man I'd fallen in love with, with his scars and flaws and fears... I wouldn't swap him for the world.

He held me tight against him, then eased me down so my head rested on his chest as he continued to talk. "I couldn't see my counsellor today, too short notice, but I talked to Rob, more openly than we ever have."

"That's good," I said. "He wants to help you. Everyone does."

"He made me realise that there will be days I can't handle, and events like the past few days, whereby there'll be nothing in the world I can do to stop myself from feeling like rock bottom. And that's fine, I *can* spend some time at rock bottom, it's inevitable. But what matters is when I pull myself back up, when I keep moving forwards. And I want to move forwards, I really do, Pen."

I remained against his chest, listening to his heart, but I let my hand wander up and stroke his neck. "You know I'll always be there to help you. I love you ... That means thick and thin, good, and bad."

He leaned forward and kissed me, we were both crying, and it turned into a wet, salty, emotional tangle, but I wanted to kiss him over and over and over.

"I know it'll be different, after Tara, and I'd never want to try and replace her—" I began.

"I love you for *you*, Penny. I'll always love Tara, of course I will, but this is different. I need a future. I *want* a future, and you're the one I want. I want forever with you, but I've planned for forever before and had it snatched away, I'm scared. So scared."

I kissed his forehead and held him close to me. "I guess

nobody can ever promise forever. But what I can always do is promise you I will love you tomorrow. Every night, before we fall asleep, after all the sexy sex…" He laughed, and I continued with a smile. "I can promise you that I'll love you the next day."

"You're amazing, truly. I've booked some extra sessions with Caroline, switched some things around." He stroked my cheek as he spoke. "It's two weeks until Christmas, and I'd love for us to spend it together. But between then and now, I need to do a little stocktake of me, I think." His forehead wrinkled up with worry again.

"Hey," I said as I rubbed at his arm. "Don't stress. I don't know if you're aware that the two weeks before Christmas for a single mum with a job and a dog and eight million tasks to finish are insane. I'm going to be meeting myself coming backwards and I was worried you'd be offended I had no time for you. So how about we have a more relaxed couple of weeks? Some dog walks, some late-night calls, just take a little step back and breathe?"

"You wouldn't be offended by that?" he asked, his eyes darting between mine.

"No, we don't need to take the straight path, let's go on the detour, I'd go any route if you were at the end of it."

"Thank you." He mouthed the words almost silently, as I stroked my fingers through his hair.

"I've invited my parents to stay for Christmas, so if you want to join us, that would be amazing."

"I'd love that, so much. Can I be really cheeky though?"

"Go on…" I was intrigued.

"Would one more make any difference? My mum insists she's fine on her own, but I can't have that. I was going to bring her to mine, but your house is so homely, she'd love it. Don't worry if not, just an idea."

"It's a great idea. I offered to invite her round a few weeks back and there just hasn't been time. I'd love for her and Lucy to meet. Honestly, I always cook enough for about twenty people anyway. Just promise me if it's too much you'll tell me?"

"I promise, can you send me that Christmas list of Lucy's though, please? I am fully prepared, of course." He winked. "But mum will want to get her something. And you, but I have ideas there." He kissed me once more and stood, his wine glass empty. "I'm going to head home, I'm exhausted."

"Me too, to be honest," I confessed. "You can be exhausted here with me. No funny business, I'll behave. We can just sleep."

"I do sleep better with you…" he said, interlacing his fingers with mine.

"Decision made. Come on, Big Spoon," I teased, as I grabbed the keys to lock up.

Bea blushed as we all raised a glass to her, in thanks for another year of book club fun and shenanigans. I loved that fiction had brought us all together, both bad and good, but friendships outside of that had bloomed nevertheless.

"Thank you everyone for bringing the presents tonight," She said, almost salivating at the stacks of wrapped books that covered the table between us. We'd eaten our gorgeous pub Christmas dinners, complete with

Christmas pudding, prosecco and gin; the chat about last month's book had been brief, we were all frankly too giddy in our Christmas jumpers and hairbands.

Bea brought my stack of bookish presents round to me, giving me a hug as she squidged in on the bench next to me. "I bet you can't wait for Christmas," she said. "You and that lovely man. I feel like it's a bookclub love story."

"Bea, you big softie," I grinned. "I seem to remember us saying this last Christmas and look what a shit *he* turned out to be."

"It only takes one to not be though. And I think you've found your one."

"I hope so. I want him to be the one."

"You deserve it. Even if you haven't read all the books since he's been on the scene."

She scooted away to the next person with a wink, always organised and on top of things. I envied the ease with which she seemed to meander through life, but then you never knew the struggles people hid, the pain they didn't publicly show.

I mentally whirred through my to-do list. In the next few days alone I had Lucy's play, a GP appointment for my mum, the hairdressers for me, the groomers for Rocket, a monster food delivery, and of course work had to fit in somewhere too. Council planning didn't stop because it was December. The boiler needed a service and I kept forgetting to book it, and then stressed about carbon monoxide. At least I'd been able to keep hold of the hire car. I'd have been lost without four wheels, and my replacement should be available soon. I'd bought all the presents, but they needed wrapping, and I daren't open my wardrobe while Lucy was in the house, as they were at dire risk of toppling out at any moment. I was probably forgetting a million things, but at least my nails had been done that lunchtime; pretty little snowflakes for the white Christmas we wouldn't get.

I sent a photo of my book stack to Ryan with a happy emoji. He replied with the big eyes emoji and a couple of kisses, telling me he'd be there in thirty minutes to walk me home. We'd get there, I was sure of it. Things had got very intense very quickly, and this lovely flirting and anticipation was delicious. I had to admit. Christmas together would be the ultimate gift.

After hugs and wishes for a wonderful Christmas, I bundled up warm, my scarf around my face and my mittened hands clutching heavy gift bags. I headed out of the pub, immediately spotting Ryan who sat on one of the picnic benches, once again looking up at the moon.

"You didn't have to meet me, you know?" I said, as I reached up to give him a kiss.

He grabbed my gift bags in one hand and rubbed at my mittened hand with the other.

"I'm just making sure you're safe, and, attempting to be chivalrous whilst simultaneously being totally selfish because I love walking with you."

"Can't promise I'll walk in completely straight lines." I giggled.

"Nothing like a drunken book club woman to get my attention," he teased.

"You'd be sickeningly jealous, I've had roast turkey *and* Christmas pudding. Plus, I got that bag full of presents."

"Judging by how heavy this thing is," he raised the sparkly bag slightly. "I'm guessing more books?"

"Yey!" I grinned and squeezed his hand.

"I love how you're all animated after book club."

"You wanna know a secret? It's the mix of prosecco and gin, gets me drunk as hell every time."

"And that's even more reason to not walk home alone." he said, his serious face back on.

"I'm Goldilocks drunk," I replied.

"You're what now?" asked Ryan with a chuckle.

"Goldilocks drunk, happy and merry and tipsy, but I won't be throwing up in the morning and dying of a hangover."

He pursed his lips for a moment. "I was going to make some comment about the three bears, but it sounded pervy as hell."

"I mean… That's one of my favourite moods of yours,"

He grinned at me. "Anyway, you're my Cinderella story, right? Can't mix up our fairy tales."

"This week is ridiculous," he said as we meandered towards my front door. "But I want to see you. Quick coffee tomorrow maybe?"

"Or…" I turned to face him, wrapping my arms around his middle. "You could come in now for coffee."

"I suppose I *should* come in and make sure the place is safe for you…" He rubbed his ice-cold nose against my own equally chilly tip. "I'd have to get going really early though, got a tight deadline on some ridiculous changes a client needs signing off by the end of the week."

"That's fine, I'm meeting Simon and Jane at lunch to head to Lucy's play. I only got three tickets, it was ages ago

I filled the form in. But maybe next time, you could come too?"

"Definitely. Wish her good luck from me, she'll be the most amazing camel in the history of nativities."

I grinned at him, lost in how happy he made me feel, not realising I was dopey faced and tipsy.

"Penny…"

"Yes, Ryan," I replied, ready for some huge romantic moment.

"Could you let us in now? I can't feel my toes anymore."

I shrieked, as he pressed his cold fingers on to my back. Then, with the door unlocked, I revelled in the moment as he chased me upstairs with those icy digits that I knew exactly how to warm up.

TWENTY-SEVEN

"He's been!" screeched Lucy as she barrelled into my bedroom on Christmas morning.

"Lucy," I groaned, fumbling around for my phone. "What time is it?"

"I don't know, Mummy. But it doesn't matter, he's been!"

"Luce... it's four-thirty. Go back to bed."

"I can't, why aren't you excited? Look!" She bounced up and down next to me.

"Show me what he left, Darling," I said, knowing full well her stocking was just a few little bits of tat (that she'd love!) and the real presents were clustered under the Christmas tree. Albeit, beyond an old baby gate as Rocket couldn't be trusted not to eat them.

Lucy screeched with delight as she opened miniature dolls, fidget toys, hair bows, and chocolate coins. I heard my dad cough and shuffle into the bathroom from my spare bedroom, and I couldn't help but giggle as I imagined his grumpy face. It didn't feel like forty years had passed since I'd been waking him and mum up at ridiculous hours on Christmas Day like this. The presents hadn't been as extravagant, and the food hadn't been from Marks and Spencer's, but we'd always had the most amazing family Christmases and I still remembered them with fondness now. My parents had made Christmas magical year after year, and I cherished the fact they could now see those traditions passed onto Lucy.

It had been a late night as we'd drunk Baileys and played silly quiz games, my dad assembling some god-forsaken pink, plastic, Barbie contraption that Lucy was desperate for. I'd wanted to buy something a little more classic for her main present, but then she'd told Father Christmas (and she was convinced he was the real one) that this was all she wanted, so how could I not give in? There'd also been approximately my own body weight in cheese and crackers before I'd fallen into bed and spent an hour talking to Ryan when I should've been sleeping. He'd be over mid-morning with his mum and my body buzzed with anticipation. Although we hadn't seen as much of each other, I felt even closer to him. We'd talked on the phone a lot; he'd had extra counselling sessions and some-times he'd tell me about them, sometimes not. We flirted incorrigibly and he'd asked if he could stay over on Christmas Day, (just him, not his mum!) which felt like the best present he could ever have chosen.

I acquiesced to Lucy's request to eat the chocolate coins immediately; after all, back in the day I'd been known to eat a full selection box for Christmas breakfast. She promptly fell back asleep, foil wrappers all over the duvet, as she wedged against me cuddling a tiny, strange-looking doll – I had some ridiculous Roblox game to thank for that one.

Cooking Christmas dinner was seldom simple, but I'd never laughed through it like this. Ryan and I danced around each other in the kitchen, helped by the homemade Bucks Fizz we'd consumed (it was a lot more Fizz than it was Bucks). Lucy played with my parents and Elsbeth in the living room; her shrieks of laughter and joy needed to be bottled and passed around on sad days, to remind everyone of happiness. Rocket point blank refused to leave the kitchen, beside himself with the smells of roast turkey, stuffing and of course... pigs in blankets. We all liked them, but my dad and Lucy were obsessed, so I always cooked double what I expected we would need. This was Rocket's first Christmas, so I'd chucked a few extra in for him too, although he'd already had some fancy doggy Christmas dinner that I'd been conned into buying for his breakfast. Such a pampered pooch.

"They seem to be getting on well," said Ryan, his arm wrapping around me as I peeped out of the kitchen door to check how the 'in-laws' were mingling.

"They do, if we aren't careful they'll still be sat around drinking Merlot at midnight and I'll never get my presents."

"Be patient," he said as he kissed the top of my head. "I thought opening them on our own might be nicer, that's all."

"If mine is edible underwear I won't be impressed," I

teased.

"My lips are sealed, you'll have to wait." He twirled me around so I faced him. "Now, we have thirty minutes until we need to plate up, no more excuses. You're going to have to join in."

"Come on, Mummy!" shouted Lucy, right on queue. "Grandad got it ready."

My parents had bought her, amongst other things, a game that involved wearing a mouth guard, the other players having to guess what you were trying to say. I don't think they expected she'd make them join in.

I burst into laughter, as I saw my dad with the mouth guard already in place, a bib over his festive shirt. Much hilarity ensued, as he tried to communicate 'spaghetti bolognaise' with absolutely no success. I grabbed another glass of wine before my turn, mortified to have Ryan and Elsbeth see me looking so daft, but also overjoyed with how well the day was going.

"This is my best present ever!" Lucy jumped between her grandparents on the sofa and hugged them tightly. "Oh, and this!" she exclaimed, touching the pretty beaded bracelet on her wrist and smiling widely at Elsbeth.

Dinner was an absolute triumph, and it wasn't just the roast potatoes that made me feel warm inside as I looked around the table. My nearest and dearest wearing paper party hats and managing to fit in 'just one more slice of turkey'. Lucy insisted on calling Elsbeth 'Ryan's nana," and I was mortified, but in her innocent eyes, anyone that age was a nana, not a mum. Luckily, Elsbeth seemed to find it endearing and as my dad snoozed his dinner off, she began a serious tournament of Hungry Hippos. The Snowman played in the background, Ryan was restacking the dishwasher for the umpteenth time. All was calm, as the song goes, it seemed a good opportunity for me to pop out with Rocket. He'd worn himself out chasing all the wrapping paper and had stuffed himself silly at lunchtime as, despite my protestations, many titbits of turkey were dropped under the table for him.

"Can I join you?" My mum asked.

"I'd love that," I replied, and we bundled up warm in readiness. The house was boiling with all the bodies and cooking, but it was a frosty day outside.

The streets were silent as we walked, nobody else was about but, as I glanced into windows of the houses we passed, I could see laughter and happiness. It made me wonder what Ryan's last couple of Christmases must have been like. I knew not everyone had a happy time, some people dreaded the season, but I'd never truly contemplated how hard it must be when love and perfection is thrown in your face for weeks beforehand.

"Lucy is having the best day, I bet she's flat out by half seven though, she hasn't stopped," Mum commented.

"She might not be the only one, I'm exhausted."

"I'm sure you'll get a second wind once we're all gone. You and Ryan deserve a lovely evening together."

"Can't wait to see what he's got me."

"If he proposes you have to phone me, immediately."

"Could I say yes first?" I laughed at her silly idea. "Not that he will, it's way too soon."

"I notice your first thought was yes though." She smiled to herself as she called Rocket over for a treat.

"Shush," I said. "Stop embarrassing me. Come on, it's

freezing, the cold always makes me need a wee."

Safely back home, I settled Rocket before sliding onto the squidgy end of the sofa with Ryan. I smiled over at my mum and dad, absorbed in nostalgia and love. I adored Christmas and it was for moments such as those, not the gifts… although I *was* intrigued to know what Ryan had got me. Elsbeth's 'friend,' whom she insisted was nothing more than a kind-hearted old gent from her bridge club, had offered to drive her and my parents home in the evening and, despite all her protestations, she blushed at his mere mention.

I'd been worried about how the 'in-laws' would get on together, but they seemed to be having a jolly old time, no animosity or reluctance; not that there was a need for there to be, but it had bothered me the last week or so – what if they didn't like each other? Fortunately, it had just been my usual level of over-thinking kicking into action.

Elsbeth had bought a restaurant voucher for me and Ryan as a joint present, a very generous one for a celebrity chef place in a nearby city. She also made it clear she was happy to babysit both Lucy and Rocket if needed. She seemed made up with her beautiful, gift-wrapped Jo Malone set. My gorgeous, adorable parents had bought a traditional wicker picnic basket filled with accessories down to tiny plastic wine goblets and a thick, checked rug, and alongside it was a mini doggy version with a teensy water bowl and a drying towel. The note accompanying it wished us happy days out for many years to come, and they were enamoured with the photo book I'd created, full of happy memories, plus the bumper box alongside it full of luxury tea and biscuits.

I grinned with excitement, as I opened the gifts from my book club. We'd all chosen a book for each person, so the eight differently wrapped, but similar-sized, rectangles of endless promise blew my mind, as I opened them up and looked forward to reading every single one. It was almost as much fun as I'd had selecting the books to give, that had been a fantastic afternoon and the lady working in the shop had been as excited as me as she had scanned them all.

Ernie, Elsbeth's 'friend,' was of course invited in for drinks; we were all merry as hell by that point and thoroughly engrossed in a game of Cluedo which was abandoned as we found an excuse to pull out yet more food and make Ernie welcome. I had no idea how we fitted in turkey sandwiches and profiteroles, but we did.

At some point Lucy fell fast asleep on the sofa, still in her party dress, a little smile on her lips and her cheeks rosy with warmth and happiness. I held my finger to my lips with a shush and, as everyone noticed her, they began to gather coats and bags, stopping to blow kisses to the beautiful little girl. Rocket was asleep in the kitchen, still loathe to leave the smell of the food even though his tummy was full to bursting.

I held everyone tight to me at the front door, the chill of the frosty air seeping into the hallway as we kissed and hugged goodbye, all full of thanks for a beautiful day, when really it was *I* who needed to thank *them* for their presence, their love. That was what had made it a day to be cherished.

Elsbeth held onto my hand as the others wandered to the car, her eyes glinting wet and full of emotion as she

looked between me and Ryan. It was a look that I understood, as a mother, and I hoped one day I'd look at Lucy
and see her so settled, so content. I held my hand to my
heart, and she smiled, before heading along the path to
Ernie.

Ryan carried Lucy upstairs for me, she was getting too
big for me to lift now, but I'd never miss tucking her in. I
kissed her warm forehead as she murmured and just about
managed to waggle a toothbrush inside her mouth, all too
conscious of the amount of sugar she'd had today, but also
not wanting to disturb her sleepy, sweet dreams.

"I'll take Rocket for one last walk before bed," Ryan
whispered with a soft smile as he left her bedroom.

"Thank you," I mouthed back, feeling like the luckiest
woman in the whole damn world.

I was downstairs within five minutes; Lucy was out for
the count. She'd had an amazing day and been spoiled by
everyone. I grimaced, as I glanced around the kitchen;
despite the dishwasher having been on repeated cycles
since breakfast, the place was still covered in piles of
washing up. My mum had wrapped all the leftovers up and
put them in the fridge. I'd make sure to send them a lovely
Boxing Day treat tomorrow.

I emptied the dishwasher and loaded it up one final
time, thinking that any items that wouldn't fit or needed
washing by hand would have to wait until tomorrow.
There were bags of discarded wrapping paper by the back
door, and I thought back on the months of hiding presents,
the late-night wrapping sessions, and all the money spent,
but it somehow all seemed worth it.

I poured two generous portions of Baileys over ice,

savouring the crackle as the thick, creamy liquid glugged to the bottom of the tumbler. Then I retreated to the living room, where the tv still quietly played, some old Christmas re-run. It didn't matter what it was as I basked in the glow of the tree lights and the warm ambience. The room was messy and perfect and under the twinkling lights of the tree sat a small pile of presents.

I heard the patter of four excited little paws in the hallway as Ryan and Rocket returned, the familiar clangs of his harness and lead being hung up, followed by slurping from his water bowl.

By the time Ryan entered the living room I was sprawled on the sofa, my head on the arm, Baileys in hand, and my legs dangling off the edge as I grinned up at him. I had my cosy elf pyjamas on and some fluffy socks, but I knew he'd love me regardless, there was a lot to be said for that level of comfort.

"Present time?" I asked hopefully.

"Definitely." He leant down and kissed me. "Bailey's lips... perfect."

"There's one for you on the table," I said, pulling him over towards the tree, as I knelt cross-legged on the floor.

"It was wonderful everyone being here today," he said as he joined me, sipping from his glass, a smile erupting on his lips. "But I'm glad we're alone now."

"Me too," I said. "Things feel good between us..."

"They do, better than good."

"We need to move onto presents before I implode with anticipation!" I pressed a kiss to his mouth. "And I think *you* should open this one first."

I handed him the slim parcel, wrapped as best as I

could. I wasn't known for neatness or perfect ribbons, but I'd tried.

"It's heavier than it looks," he said as he began to slowly unfasten it, teasing me with delicate fingers, when I wanted him to rip it open.

Inside was a handmade forest green dog collar and lead; it could have been mistaken as a present for Rocket, but the inside of the lead handle was lined with a rich, deep green velvet, so as to be soft on Ryan's hands; stitched at the point where the collar and lead met were the words – 'Dog Dad'.

"Me and Rocket both hoped you'd agree to be his dad. He said he loves you more than I do, we fell out about it," I said with a serious face, nodding towards Rocket who was flat out at the base of the radiator on his new fleece blanket, a present from my parents that, in all honesty, I was worried he'd have chewed holes in before new year.

He turned the lead and collar over in his hands with a contemplative smile. "Thank you, that means a lot. I know it's not easy to let people into your family, thank you. I may need some form of legal ownership document though." He leaned forwards to kiss me, but I pulled back with a grin.

"Maybe when you get some kind of legal document about me…" I challenged, biting on my lip suggestively.

"I'm working on it," he laughed, before attempting another smooch.

"Erm… presents before kisses if you don't mind!"

"You never said you were high maintenance," he grumbled as he reached under the tree for a rectangular gift that was wrapped neat and tidy, the architect in him obviously having given it perfect corners and straight edges.

"Only at Christmas," I replied as I took the present from him, the weight of it surprising me.

"Don't drop it," he said as I dove in and tore the paper, noticing him flinch which made me grin even wider.

I found myself looking at the back of a photo frame and, as I turned it over, I recognised the same beautiful frames that lined Ryan's staircase. And there we were, in one of those beautiful monochrome shots. I recognised the moment, we'd danced to Norah Jones at the end of the wedding reception, moments before he'd asked me to stay with him. My arms were wrapped around his neck, my fingers laced together, his the same around my waist. Our gazes were locked, as I looked up and he looked down and, even though we hadn't been 'together' at this moment, the photo showed me that we were absolutely meant to be.

"This is so much better than a Beyonce CD," I said, turning to humour as a wave of emotion overtook me.

He took the frame from me and placed it safely against the wall. "Nobody even sells CDs anymore, you know this right?"

I laughed and he wiped a stray little tear from my cheek, where it had dripped. "I know. Who took the picture?"

"Jess. I struggled with what to buy you and she told me she'd taken this at the wedding. I thought it was very 'us.' So, I had it framed at the same place I always use, and I've re-arranged the photographs that are around the house. Because you should have a place there, I want you to have a place there, always."

I wrapped my arms around him, pressing kisses to his cheek and neck. "No getting rid of me now. I'm surprised

Jess took it though, she wasn't pleased about us being close that night."

"No, but she knows a special moment when she sees one. I always said she should have pursued photography." He kissed my lips and I settled back down, selecting a second gift for him.

"Speaking of that night..." I said, as he carefully began to open the next present, my knees jiggling up and down with impatience.

Inside was a canvas print. Ryan studied it, tracing his finger over the moon. "Waning gibbous?" he asked.

I nodded with a smile, "It's the sky on the night we met. Drinking stolen Champagne and eating sexy pizza as we looked up at those stars, that moon."

"Best night of my life..." he said, blinking as if the realisation had taken even him by surprise. I didn't want to get introspective, nobody should have to compare, as was the night he met me better than the night he had met Tara? It didn't matter as, in the grand scheme of life, things didn't have to be listed in such a way. For people who had multiple babies, was one being born more special than another? Surely not. Multiple nights could be incredible, without needing to compete.

He shook whatever it was off and reached for a smaller box, handing it to me. Smaller, but not *that* small.

Once again, I tore into it with an excited giggle as I noticed the name of the famous jewellers on the lid. I opened the box to be greeted by my favourite rose gold in a stunning bracelet, with a singular charm attached.

Ryan fastened it onto my wrist as he spoke, and I lifted it to admire the charm, two entwined love hearts. "I thought this would be perfect because our adventure is just beginning, and we can chronicle it on this bracelet, so you carry all our stories with you."

"How are you so bloody perfect?" I asked, as I kissed him again.

"Ahh well, my last one isn't that good." He handed me a small white envelope, which I opened to find a very generous book voucher for my favourite shop. "Given all your books from your friends today, I don't think this will be needed for a while."

"Are you kidding me?" I exclaimed, as I beamed. "You know they do that hardback sale every January? This will be amazing, thank you, thank you, thank you!"

I sprang into his lap, kissing him as we both grinned and his hands slid inside my top, stroking over the warm skin of my back.

"I did get you a third present," I whispered into his ear. "But it's a surprise. I need you with a weekend bag to meet me here early on the twenty-ninth."

"I'm intrigued..." he whispered, as he nuzzled at my neck. "Do I need a passport?"

"Nope, just you... Now shh, no more clues."

"That's not good enough," he teased. "I'm upset, I demand compensation."

"I'm afraid I'm not sure what I could ever do to make it up to you..." I replied, as I rubbed myself against him, my teeth nibbling on his bottom lip.

"Let me show you..." He lay me down under the Christmas tree, paper rustling beneath us, Baileys long forgotten. I had naught but dreams of Ryan and our future together on my mind.

TWENTY-EIGHT

*T*ypically for me, I'd been unable to hold my own water and had told Ryan all the plans. I was excited to meet his business partner, thrilled to explore Scotland but mostly... desperate to get this man to myself for a few days. There was no other way I'd want to bring in the new year than with my arms around Ryan Grayson. I'd been sad to say goodbye to Lucy for a longer period of time than normal, but equally delighted to have this time alone with my man.

"What does Joshua's wife do?" I asked, as Ryan parked outside a magnificent Victorian villa in Morningside, Edinburgh.

"She's an obstetrician. Don't ask her how many babies she's delivered, got me a fierce eye roll when I first met her."

I nodded thoughtfully as I glanced behind me. Rocket was curled up asleep on the back seat, all clipped into his doggy seatbelt. It was as much for our safety as his, otherwise, he'd be bouncing around Ryan's face halfway up the motorway.

"I promise we won't talk business for long, there are a few things we need to sort out while we're together. Doesn't matter how many zoom meetings we have each week, it's not quite the same."

"I don't mind, don't worry," I replied as I opened the car door and stepped out, glad to stretch my legs, which had been getting fidgety to the extreme. "I want to Facetime Lucy soon anyway. Simon messaged and said they'd be back from the beach early afternoon. They're taking siesta's very literally."

The grand, royal blue front door opened, and a woman walked towards us, her smile wide and beautiful. She was one of those effortless types, tall and willowy with flared trousers, tall heels, and a silky cream blouse that I never would have dared to wear.

"Ryan," she said as she pulled him into air kisses, her face creased just the right amount to show sympathy. I knew it would drive him mad, that she still looked at him that way, as though he were nothing but grief everlasting. "It's so good to see you. Is this Penny?"

She stepped away from him and drenched me in the same air kisses, a beautiful rose-tinted scent flowing over me. "Hi," I said self-consciously. "Lovely to meet you, Louisa."

"Call me Lou," she replied with a wave of her hand. "Joshua will be back soon, he got called on-site, some disaster or other. He said you were bringing a dog. Buffy will be so pleased to meet him."

"Buffy? Like the vampire slayer?" I asked, wondering if

once again you shouldn't judge a book by its cover; she looked more Bridgerton than Buffy to my eyes.

"Yes! Are you a fan? It's my all-time favourite. So, where's your little guy?"

I opened the back door of the car. Rocket eyed me sleepily before stretching his front legs out and having a little shake.

"This is Rocket," I said as I unclipped the seatbelt, grabbing his lead in time as he bolted for freedom from the car. His first job was, of course, to cock his leg against the back wheel. I was relieved it wasn't against her very expensive-looking trousers.

"What breed is he?" she asked as she crouched down to fuss him, rubbing his ears and dissolving into baby talk.

"A barbet," I replied, smiling at Ryan as he pulled our bags from the boot.

"I need one, I'll tell Josh tonight. I'll send all the Christmas gifts back and get another puppy instead." She rose to her feet again, that wide smile more natural now. She was classically beautiful but also had a sternness about her. I wasn't sure I would have wanted her near me with my legs in stirrups mid-contraction.

"They're not a well-known breed, but I got him from a family friend. I can pass their details on if you're interested, they're down in Cornwall, they'll breed again at some point."

"Yes! But first of all, priorities, let's get you inside and open some wine."

The interior reminded me a little of Ryan's house, albeit a lot tidier, not a thing was out of place. The kitchen was light and airy, with the widest bi-fold doors I'd ever seen.

They were of course closed given it was late December in Scotland and we were lucky if the days got above freezing.

Rocket yipped with excitement, or possibly hormones, as he smelled Buffy. She was absolutely adorable, about half his size though, and I prayed to god he wouldn't squash her, hump her, or any combination of the two. A whole corner of the den area of the room seemed to be dedicated to doggies, and housed water, treats, blankets, toys, and every canine luxury. Rocket wasted no time at all making himself at home, his puppy shyness seeming to disappear by the day. It made me sad to think how quickly he'd grown, he was almost adult sized now, could I still legitimately call him my puppy?

Lou spoke, as if reading my mind. "I didn't want children, the horrors I see occur to women's genitalia every day, not for me! So Buffy is our baby."

"She's gorgeous, I hope he behaves himself."

"Oh, they'll be fine," she breezed. "Red or white?"

"Red please," I replied. I was generally more of a white wine girl, but it was gorgeous and warm in here, and a glass of red sounded wintery and perfect.

Lou grew on me more and more as time passed and we chatted; she wanted every detail of how Ryan and I had met and my heart bloomed to recall it all, and to hear the tale from his side as he interjected with his slightly different memories.

Buffy flew out of the room with a yip. Rocket looked confused for a millisecond before he followed, definitely in the throes of a little Buffy crush. Seconds later, the two of them barrelled back in, springing up and down at the legs of a man whom I assumed to be Joshua – in fact, there was no mistaking it having seen his photo on the Grayson and Williams website. Perhaps in the early days of meeting Ryan I'd spent far too long perusing images on there, familiarising myself with Ryan's features.

Joshua was shorter than Ryan, his sandy hair close-cropped. The two of them had met as junior architects during the intake at a large firm post-graduation and had hit it off from there, both climbing career ladders at different firms, before coming together to form their own company in their mid-thirties. The fondness between them was evident as they shoulder clapped and greeted each other, the volume growing as they worked out how long it was since they'd been together in person, which turned out to be a week or so before I'd 'Beyoncé'd' into Ryan's life, as he liked to label it.

Joshua turned his attention to me, smiling as he shook my hand, his head tilted to one side. "Lovely to meet you, Penny." He pursed his lips, as if he was chewing on his gum. "Have we met before? You look familiar?"

I shook my head, searching through my mind but coming up with nothing. "I don't think so, sorry. I must have one of those faces."

His head tilted the other way, before he spotted Lou pour him a large glass of red, at which point I became far less interesting. "Ryan!" he declared loudly. "Why don't we go get all the business out of the way? I've booked this incredible restaurant for later. So hard to get a table, but the owner wants to use us for his Manchester branch. I met him at that conference in Bristol, do you remember?"

They sauntered out of the room together with their full

glasses, raucously laughing as they moved outside to Josh's office.

"I'm so sorry, this is frightfully rude, but I need to do some work too. All this post-covid video consultation is wonderful, but it means I can't even escape when I'm at home."

"It's not rude at all, you're so kind to let us stay in your home, don't worry."

"Let me show you to your room, you can have a nice relax. There's a gorgeous bath in the ensuite. Ryan told us all about Lucy, you must be exhausted after Christmas. Take some time for yourself."

And that was precisely what I did. The bedroom was beautiful, lots of dark blue with mustard-checked sheets and assorted cushions. It was dark and warm, like a little boutique hotel. The large Victorian sash window looked out over the garden, which was akin to a fairy trove with beautiful borders, a pond, a rockery, and centre stage a large, wooden office building, very scandic and deeply stylish.

The bathtub was indeed stunning, deliciously deep and, on the recessed shelf, sat co-ordinated bottles of bath oils and salts. I created my own little concoction and sank happily into the water, my glass of red wine at my side, a favourite playlist drifting out from my mobile phone. I'd had a really lovely chat with Lucy, who was obviously loving the time with Simon and Jane. I missed her, of course I did, but equally I knew she was perfectly safe and cared for and would be back in my arms before I knew it.

I thought back to last New Year's Eve and how far I'd come, how things had changed. This time last year I'd been in love, but little did I know that by Easter I'd have a broken heart and be sworn off men for life, only for those barriers to crash down as Ryan entered my existence.

Wanker-dentist had seemed so disappointed that I couldn't see him that New Year's Eve, but I was spending the night with Lucy and no way did I want the two of them to meet. Looking back, it was likely a relief to him that he hadn't had to make excuses to his wife, plus my firmness that Lucy not meet him or know about him *had* been obstructive, and I wondered if that had been my subconscious protecting me.

The day it had all fallen apart had been crushing, far beyond the pain of a normal breakup because of that stigma of being the 'other woman.' I hated it to this day, that people thought that of me. Sometimes I'd still get ugly glares in the supermarket, or wandering around town, and I could only assume they were friends of his wife as she'd bad-mouthed me to every possible person she could. I didn't know if the two of them were together now or not. I didn't believe a word that passed his lips, and more importantly, I didn't care. That was the past, and I was living in this amazing present with Ryan; my heart told me our future was only going to get better.

"Hey, daydreamer," Ryan said as I startled, water sploshing over the side of the bath. I bit my lip self-consciously as I sat up, mortified that *anyone* could have walked in and seen me. "Thinking about anything nice?"

"That would be telling," I replied, as he knelt down at the side of the tub and pressed a kiss to my forehead.

"Should I be jealous?"

"Extremely. I like to think about this guy I met over the

summer, he's sort of supremely sexy. I might proposition him later."

"Mmmm," he mumbled as he kissed my damp lips. "What are you going to offer him?"

"Whatever he wants…" I whispered before returning his kiss, my hands reaching over the bath edge to link with his, wrinkled fingers and all.

"What if he wants to throw you on the bed right now?" he said, as his lips moved across my neck. He stood, pulling me up with him as more hot water rippled over the sides.

"I wouldn't want to drip all over the sheets of our very kind guests." I stepped out of the bath, his hands supporting me as he kissed my wet shoulder. My dripping body, still oily from the bath, pressed against him and soaked through his clothes as I unfastened his belt.

"I don't think they'll care," he said as he pulled his t-shirt off, letting it fall to the wet floor.

"OK, but don't throw me, you'll put your back out." I grinned, rubbing my nose against his before he led me to the bed, haphazardly throwing a towel down before he pressed me into the mattress.

"I love you," he sighed as he buried his nose into my neck.

"I love you, too," I replied, delirious, as the wet bed sheets were relegated to the last thing on my mind.

No matter how many times we did this he took my breath away, more than that, he took my mind away. To a place where nothing but our bodies existed, nothing could worry me or touch me except him, always him, I knew I'd never want another.

We lay face to face afterwards, breaths still fast and

heavy with lust, dozing on and off, utterly satiated before we eventually dressed, ready for dinner with Josh and Lou.

The restaurant was minimalist chic, with minuscule portions of very fancy food. Personally, I was worried my stomach would still rumble when I got into bed and was secretly glad I'd packed chocolate in my suitcase, as I might need a midnight snack at this rate.

The only things that weren't miniature were the wine top-ups and the conversation, which got drunker and rowdier as the evening ran on. Lou looked a little glazed over as Ryan and Josh told stories of their early careers, the shenanigans, the girls, and the all-nighters. She had heard them all before but, for me, it was all brand new and I loved learning more about my beloved, from a time I'd never known him. It had shaped him, made him the amazing human he was today, and I felt eternally grateful that I was in his life.

"I'm still sure I know your face from somewhere," slurred Josh.

"Maybe you saw me around town when you've been at Ryan's. We sat and worked out all the times our paths almost crossed, amazing it took this long for us to meet in such a small town."

"Remind me," Lou joined in. "Ryan's sister was the bridesmaid for her best friend. And her best friend goes to your book club?"

"Basically." I smiled at Ryan. "Ryan was only there because his brother-in-law had food poisoning. I almost didn't go to the wedding because I'd had this awful breakup from an utter wanker of a dentist, so it's a miracle we met at all."

Josh spluttered on his drink, gasping for breath as the wine went down the wrong way. Lou slapped him on the back, very matter of fact until the coughing stopped, and he looked across at us, all bleary-eyed. I was horrified he'd been about to choke but Lou took it all in her stride as she called over for the bill, rubbing his hand affectionately.

The giddiness gave way to sleepy drunkenness, and we were all quiet in the cab on the way back. Lou had given me some wonderful tips for how to spend the week, some amazing countryside walks, a spa that specialised in couple's massages, the best places for brunch and a dog walk. I was fired up with excitement and the thought of seeing in the new year with Ryan Grayson. I loved his name, I loved everything about him. I can't deny I'd reverted back to full-on teenager mode on Boxing Day and practised my signature as Penelope Grayson – then I'd ripped the paper to shreds and hidden it at the bottom of the bin in case he ever saw it.

Josh hung back as we made our way inside, the dogs greeting us as if we'd been gone for weeks and they'd been left alone to fend for themselves. I heard him mumble to Ryan, who took hold of my arm as I grabbed some water to take upstairs.

"Hey," he said with a sleepy smile. "Josh wants a drink before bed, he's got some rare whisky and he's been saving it. Is that OK with you?"

I chuckled, it was so sweet he'd even check I didn't mind, not something I'd been used to with other partners.

"Of course, it's OK, I know you guys speak most days, but you hardly ever get to see him properly. Enjoy, stay up all night if you want to, I'll be starfished in the bed."

He kissed my forehead. "Duvet-hog. See you later." He sauntered off after Josh with a slight stumble. I grinned to myself, noticing Lou watch me.

"You're so good for him," she said. "I'd say he's like the old Ryan, but he's not. That's not it, I don't think he could be that Ryan again. But he's not carrying that same sadness he was, I can see light and life in him again, plus he's besotted with you, that's obvious even to me."

"Thank you. And for letting us stay here, I'm so looking forward to it."

"You're doing us a favour too; I hate having to put Buffy in the dog hotel. Anyway, must sleep, we're flying early afternoon and I'm a horror if I'm too tired. Night, Penny!" she exclaimed with air kisses before heading upstairs.

I made a fuss of the dogs for a minute or two, giving her a chance to get into her room before I followed up. I could see lights outside from the office/man-cave and guessed that's where the whisky was. I chuckled at the phrase 'dog hotel;' there was one near me, a far cry from the kennels, with every luxury for pampered pooches. I'd best hope Buffy wasn't telling Rocket all about it, because he was highly unlikely to ever see the inside of one.

I watched myself in the bathroom mirror as I brushed my teeth, my cheeks rosy with drink, my eye makeup smudged and the lipstick all gone, but all I saw now was happiness. I didn't care anymore about the dark circles that grew under my eyes each day, or the wobbly bits that I'd never gotten under control after Lucy was born. I didn't have to parade around in ridiculous lingerie to be loved, adored, or wanted. I'd found my place, my person.

By the time Ryan headed into the bedroom much later, I was probably still grinning deliriously while I slept. Therefore, I didn't notice as he lay with his back to me, his mouth tight with worry.

TWENTY-NINE

I woke up late, far later than I ever normally would. The curtains were still drawn but I could see the daylight as it crept in between the gaps. It wasn't often I had the luxury of this, so I pushed away the guilt that began to form, instead reaching for my tall glass of water, aware that last night's plethora of wine was making itself known to all of my internal organs. It would be best to have a day off the booze and let myself recover before the big night tomorrow. New Year's Eve again... where had the time gone?

I reached around for Ryan, but the other half of the bed was empty. I momentarily worried he'd had one of his early wakeups, before realising he'd probably just gotten up at a normal time and it was me being slovenly.

The hot water from the shower streamed all over me, before I dried and dressed in black jeans and a red jumper – the one Lucy had told me not to wear for that dog walk so long ago, I realised with a smile. Well, it was fine to be

Christmassy now, it was still December after all, for a little while at least.

The house was quiet as I tiptoed downstairs, no sound but the distant hum of a television. I went through to the kitchen, which seemed to be the hub of the house with its large den area, but it was deserted, not even the dogs were in their usual spot.

I was aware of a more formal living room at the front of the house and followed the sound in that direction. My mouth broke into a smile as I rounded the door and saw Ryan snoozing on the sofa, the two dogs curled up around his feet. Some ancient James Bond movie played on the television, typical for the bizarre scheduling of Twixmas.

I had no idea what time he'd made it to bed, but he was obviously as exhausted and hungover as I was. I left all three of them asleep, Ryan, Rocket, and Buffy, and headed into the kitchen where I set about fathoming out the fancy coffee machine. A quick rummage in the bread bin also uncovered a stash of pain au chocolat. I carried it all through on a tray, careful not to drip or spill a crumb as I placed it down on the coffee table. I then knelt and stroked the side of Ryan's face.

"Hey, sleeping beauty. I have coffee." Ryan's eyes seemed to stutter as he awoke and my heart sped up a beat as I anticipated that slow, sexy smile, but this morning it didn't come. Instead, his eyebrows squashed together over his nose in a tense line, and his eyes darted away from mine quickly.

He sat up, displacing both the dogs as he did so, raking his hands through his hair with an awkward cough. "What time is it?" he asked as he looked around, patting his pockets before retrieving his phone and checking it through bleary eyes.

"Almost twelve," I replied. "Are you OK? Was it a rough night? How much whisky did you two drink? Where are they both anyway? I didn't miss them, did I?"

"Penny," he groaned as he held his head in his hands. "Too many questions, please, let me think."

I handed him his coffee, taken aback at the alien reaction I was getting from him. I sipped from a porcelain coffee cup as I waited; at least the coffee was amazing, it had been worth persevering with that machine.

He took a large swig, oblivious to the quality, before he turned to me with one of those expressions that filled me with dread. "We need to talk."

The four words set terror coursing through my body; what had happened? Had Lou and Josh thought I was awful and told him to dump me? Had he had enough? Was he about to end things on our first trip together?

"What's wrong?" I asked as I stood, taking an involuntary, but protective, pace backwards.

"Come and sit down." He patted the seat next to him. "Josh and Lou have gone to the airport early, she booked some fancy lounge." He sucked in a deep breath. "Something happened last night, we need to talk."

I sat, more like hovered, at the edge of the seat, as I picked at the skin around my nails. "What happened?" I said, aiming to sound confident but the words crawled out of me in a hoarse whisper.

"Please know that I'm not telling you this to be horrible, or because I judge you. I…" he ran his hands through his hair three or four times, his knee bouncing up and down. "You need to know."

"I need to know what? Ryan, you're scaring me." My voice trembled at the same speed as my hands.

"Josh went to Uni in Newcastle for his BA. In his last year, he shared this huge old house with a load of students from various courses. It was a total party place, by all accounts."

"You didn't know him then though, did you?" I asked. "I thought you only met him after. When you had jobs?"

"I did, I've only heard stories of it. A couple of weeks back, they had a reunion, all the students from this house. Met up in Newcastle to relive youthful memories, revisit their old haunts, those sorts of things. Using Christmas as an excuse for it all, basically."

"OK…" I said, "What's this got to do with us?"

"Penny, on blokes' trips like that, things can get pretty lairy, rightly or wrongly. Stuff gets shared that shouldn't be. It sounds like a miracle they all made it back without anyone ending up in the hospital." Ryan looked at me as if he anticipated another question, but I had none, I didn't understand where this was going. "One of Josh's old house-mates studied dentistry when they lived together. He's a dentist now, obviously…"

Ryan's knee tapped so rapidly now I couldn't bear it. I pushed my hand down to stop its motion as the information sank into me, like a sickening wave that landed in my belly and pooled in a revolting whirl.

"My ex?" I asked in a whisper. My eyes met Ryan's as he nodded, and I sank my head into my hands. "What did he say about me?"

"It's not so much what he said, sounds like it was random bollocks about blaming you for his divorce. It was more what he shared..."

The room seemed to fall away from me and I slumped to the floor in absolute anguish as vivid memories crashed into my mind, assaulting me as I remembered his late-night messages asking to see me as he told me how he missed me, his fondness for using his camera when we were together.

"Penny," called Ryan as he slid off the sofa next to me, wrapping his arms around me as he tried to soothe me, but he sounded as if he were too far away, the room tipping as my mind tried to process what this meant. "Penny, look at me." He tugged at me, his fingers on my chin but I screwed my eyes closed, unable to look at him as the realisation dawned on me.

"What did he share? Tell me. I need to know." My voice was deadpan, muffled. I heard the gulp before Ryan spoke.

"I didn't look, OK? Please believe me. When Josh asked me to go with him last night, it was because he'd realised where he recognised you from. He showed me one picture, one of the less..." He didn't finish the sentence. "He wanted to check it was you, and it was. Penny, I'm so sorry. I didn't know if you knew or... Fuck!" He bawled as he stood up, kicking the coffee table and spilling crumbs which the dogs soon hoovered up, although warily. "I want to kill him."

"I didn't know he was still with his wife. When he couldn't see me, I thought it was because of his kids, I thought he was just an amazing, attentive dad." I breathed the words, more for myself than anyone, but they wouldn't make anything better. "He'd ask me to send him pictures and videos, said he missed me, and it made him feel close to me. I was stupid, I know I was stupid, but..." I gasped for breath, panic overtaking me as my eyes bulged and my lungs burned. I couldn't deal with this, it was too much, it couldn't be happening. Who'd seen them? How many people? Had he posted them online? Were my parents going to see them? My baby girl... not my baby girl.

I stood, fight or flight kicking in as I lunged towards the front door, grabbing at the car keys on the little hooks in the hallway, not even knowing whose keys they were or which car they opened, just certain I had to get out of here as I was suffocating. I felt as if I might die as my heart hammered, hurting my head and bruising my chest, maybe *that's* why I couldn't breathe properly. I raised a hand to the hot skin of my torso, hearing the wheeze but not associating it with myself; it was as if I weren't in my body anymore, just living on some plane of pure panic and idiocy.

"Penny!" called Ryan as he raced after me, grasping at my hands as I fumbled with the strange locks on the front door, not standing a chance of opening it when I couldn't even focus on my surroundings. I struggled and fought, trying to push Ryan away only for him to grip my upper arms. He was talking the whole time, trying to soothe me, trying to still me, but I couldn't stop, I couldn't listen, I couldn't be here.

He was so much stronger than me, it didn't matter how I twisted and turned and battled, I couldn't get away. Eventually drained, so tired, I let myself sink to the floor, his grip on my arms loosening as he sensed my submission, defeated.

He gathered me in his arms, cradling me like an injured child as he rocked me, kissing my forehead and trying to appease me, bargain with me, calm me down. But in my head, all I did was replay everything I had sent to that man in utter trust. Sexy selfies, which had led to tasteful nudes, I'd sent them on quite a few occasions; he adored them, they'd drive him wild, and he made me feel so desired, so wanted. Then there'd been that night he'd whisked me away to a luxury hotel and we'd lain in the oversized bed, the air thick with sex and sweat and I'd let him take some of his own.... We'd been drinking but we were just high on each other at that point. The thing was, I trusted him completely, we were in love and had a future and he'd keep me safe, that's what I'd thought. But instead, he'd betrayed me and caused my heart to break once more.

At this point I vomited all over the hallway, myself, and Ryan. He ushered the dogs away as they tried to crowd us, excited by the tension and acrid smell of my shame, mixed with last night's wine. Ryan got them out and brought towels, continually talking to me, but I couldn't make sense of the words. I lay down, my hair in the mess, as I wished the ground would swallow me up, take me away, anything to not have to deal with this.

I couldn't judge how much time had passed as he cleaned up, speaking to me in words that didn't register. He led me upstairs by my hand and I sat on the edge of the bed, mute, as he ran me a hot bubble bath.

All I could do was run those nights through and through my mind, trying to recall the detail of everything, to think how bad the situation was. Was I going to get fired? Or was I thinking the worst and they were simple, sexy selfies? My mind couldn't focus, the consternation was simply too much.

"Penny." Ryan's voice floated through from the beautiful en-suite. "Bath's ready, sweetheart."

I wandered through in a daze, greeted by his kind smile but buried under anxiety. All I could wonder was whether it was pity or disgust. So, as I undressed and slipped into the hot water, covered in bubbles, I didn't meet his eyeline.

Just being this little bit more north than normal meant the darkness arrived earlier, the day seeming to have drifted away as I noticed the darkening of the afternoon outside. Ryan lit two large candles. I hoped Louisa wouldn't mind as I spotted the designer brand.

"You feeling any better?" he asked, pulling the dressing table stool next to the bath, his eyes still wide with... something.

"Shall I call him? I don't know what to do..." I leaned forward, resting my elbows on my bent knees as I sighed heavily; even my tears were confused about if they were needed or not.

"I think you should go to the police, they take this revenge stuff really seriously nowadays. So no, I wouldn't call him, let him find out from them."

"Revenge stuff?" I asked, feeling unfairly angry at him. "You mean revenge porn? Are photographs porn? I don't know, maybe I'm overreacting, maybe I... Ugh he is *such* a wanker, I hate him!"

I slid down under the water, wanting to hide, escape, let the water take everything away. But how could it? Seconds later I surfaced, spluttering and wiping water from my eyes.

"I'm sorry I let you down."

"What? Penny, how the hell have you let me down? *You're* the victim here. I just want to help you. I mean, I also want to drive home and beat the living shit out of him, but I'm fully aware that'll only make it worse."

"How many people were there?" I asked, trying to stay pragmatic and sensible.

"I think ten or eleven. If we go to the police, and we *should*, but that's your decision, Josh said he'd provide all the evidence they need." Ryan poured a jug of steaming, scented water down my back, rinsing the bubble bath from my hair as he reached for shampoo and began to lather it for me, massaging my scalp in a way that, on any normal day, would have had me purring in pleasure.

"I'm so stupid…"

"You're not stupid, Penny. Not at all. You're loving and trusting and open, it's him that's the absolute fuckwit here."

"Can I be alone for a while?" I asked timidly.

"Of course. Guess my hairdressing skills aren't up to scratch, hey?" His little joke was sweet, it made my heart ache, but I couldn't laugh along, it didn't feel possible. "Shall I bring you a glass of wine?"

I nodded, turning to him and attempting a smile, but instead silent tears curled down my cheeks.

"I want to go home" were my first words to Ryan the next morning. He perched anxiously on a Chatsworth style armchair opposite the bed, his face creased with worry as I sat up and my eyes met his for a millisecond before he looked away. The glass of wine in the bath had turned into almost two bottles and my stomach felt vile. We'd sat and watched something I couldn't even remember, before retreating to bed where cuddling felt wrong, comfort felt impossible, and I thought I'd never sleep soundly again.

"I'll speak to the dog hotel, see if we can drop Buffy off."

"Will you call Josh?" I asked. "Let him know."

Ryan mumbled words I couldn't make out as he left the room. The previous day had felt like a blur, as if I hadn't quite been in my own head as it all happened. Once I was sure Ryan was asleep, I'd spent over an hour googling myself, in some vague attempt to see if anything was online, but I didn't even understand how this stuff would work, would my name be linked to them? Where would they be? I ended up in a warren of sites I wished I hadn't known existed, and my sickness had grown with each swipe of my phone.

It seemed Ryan had been busy while I'd dozed this morning, he'd printed off the details for a helpline which were on the bedside table next to me. I knew he longed to comfort me, but I felt wrong, in so many ways. As much as I'd hated being the 'other woman,' feeling as though I'd betrayed Ryan was a million times worse. How could he ever want me as a girlfriend, wondering who had and hadn't seen me naked as we walked into a bar?

Thankfully, the dog hotel had a cancellation and would take Buffy. Ryan had spoken to Lou and Josh, I didn't ask for details. We ended up setting off home around lunchtime.

"Will I have to show them to the police?" I asked, as I chewed on my bitten down nail and Ryan headed towards the southbound entrance to the motorway.

"Does that mean you're going to report it?" he asked.

"Yes, I think so. Did you and Josh fall out? You looked annoyed when I mentioned him earlier.

"A little..."

"It's not his fault. Don't blame him."

"He could have said it was out of order when they were sent, that it was going too far." His hands were clamped on the steering wheel as we merged onto the motorway.

"He could, yes, but he's not the one who caused the problem. Be mad at me before you're mad at Josh."

"For the last time, I'm not mad at you," Ryan snapped. I turned my head and looked out of the window, not even caring about the travel sickness that brewed within me, it was nothing compared to the stomach pains that troubled me every waking moment. "Sorry," he said a moment later, his hand resting on mine for a moment.

When we'd driven to Scotland less than a week ago, we'd laughed and touched each other's knees, sung along to the radio, stopped for coffee and kisses, his hands in my jeans pockets as he held me to him for a lingering embrace that got us filthy looks from the staff at the service station.

The drive home was a million miles away from that. The radio played but we didn't sing. I angled myself so I faced away from Ryan. I remained uncomfortable meeting his gaze. So ashamed, guilty, dirty, used. Was he wondering why I hadn't sent *him* pictures like that?

"The relationship I had with him back then..." The words flew out of me as we turned off the motorway, only thirty minutes from home now, so I needed to say these things. "It was different, it wasn't like me and you, it wasn't good, it wasn't healthy, I couldn't see it at the time. I don't want you to think that because I sent that stuff to him it means he meant more, he didn't, he never could. I'm so sorry, I hate that I was ever that stupid. I'm so sorry, Ryan."

He kept his eyes on the road but his hand reached for mine and rubbed over my knuckles. "Penny, stop. Just stop. You can't keep saying sorry when you did nothing wrong."

"I don't know what else to say, Ryan," I exclaimed as tears welled yet again. "I trusted him. I was falling in love, and I was blind."

I wanted to ask if he forgave me. If we had a future. If things could ever be the same. But his hand withdrew and moved back to the steering wheel, plus in reality, I was too scared to hear his truths, his thoughts. I hurt so bad right now that the idea of adding more onto that wasn't viable, I couldn't handle it.

And so, the conversation ended. He stopped his car outside my house, not pulling onto the driveway, an audible swallow breaking the silence as he exited the car, grabbing my bag from the boot and placing it on the pathway to my front door.

I followed and, as I closed the passenger door behind me, he was already unclipping Rocket and lifting him from the seat. The pup was sleepy and disorientated, licking Ryan's face as he whispered, before passing him to me.

I blew out a long breath and walked up the path, letting Rocket down as we neared the door so he could christen his favourite shrubbery once again before we went inside.

I wanted to invite Ryan in, I wanted him to make everything better for me, but it wasn't fair of me and besides, he couldn't, nobody could. He placed my bag on the doorstep and rubbed at his temples.

In the end, we both spoke at the same time.

"Ryan, I—"

"Penny, I—"

This normally would have resulted in a 'jinx' or a laugh, but instead he pulled me into his arms, holding me tight against his body, as he peppered kisses into my hair. All too soon he stopped, his hands rubbing up and down my upper arms as he looked at me.

"I love you, you know this. Penny, please... don't give him the satisfaction of ruining anything else for you. It's New Year's Eve, I want us to be together."

I shook my head, barely holding back tears, my throat stinging with the pressure of stopping them, as if they pooled there, burning, punishing me like tiny shards of glass. "I need to be on my own. I can't... I... I don't know if things can ever be the same."

"I think you're in shock. I'm worried about you being alone, I can't leave you like this."

I inched backwards, desperate to throw myself under my duvet and remain there, hidden.

"I'll call you later, I just want to get in my bed and stay there for a while. We'll go to the police, let me rest, and we'll go to the police."

His forehead was wrinkled, his lips pursed as he watched me. "If you change your mind, if you need anything at all, call me, text me. Doesn't matter the time, I'll be here within a few minutes. Promise you will?"

"I will," I replied meekly, but I knew I wouldn't.

"I hope I'll see you later but if not I'll pick you up at ten tomorrow morning, is that OK? To go to the police?"

"Ten is good, thank you." I tried to smile but my mouth trembled with the pressure of the tears, so I turned and shakily slid my key into the lock, balancing my bag and Rocket as my chest heaved. "Bye, see you later…"

I slammed the door, too late to stop Ryan from witnessing the tears that streamed down my cheeks as if they wouldn't ever stop. But I didn't want to hear his words, couldn't bear to know his truth.

I sank to the hallway floor, sobbing so hard I couldn't breathe as ugly, painful gasps overtook me, my stomach convulsed as I shuddered and shook. Rocket nuzzled at my face, licking the tears from me, as I cried until I thought my body would give up. I cried rivers, tears for being so foolish, so trusting. Tears for the shame my family would feel when they knew. Tears for the loss of that final chance I'd had at everything being perfect. Because losing Ryan was the final pain I couldn't take, the final heartbreak I'd sworn I wouldn't put myself through. And I honestly wasn't sure how I'd survive it, I only knew that I had to for the sake of my baby girl, and I had to raise her and educate her to never give a man the power to destroy her life, to never give herself away like I so foolishly had.

I'd climbed into bed fully clothed, my phone on silent and discarded on the floor. I'd set the heating to stay on continuously, it had been on its timer anyway to keep the place warm while I was gone, but for some reason I couldn't stop shivering, I couldn't warm up. I slept like the dead, no dreams, no thoughts, just silence and darkness, which was exactly what my mind craved. The whole sorry situation burst back to life within moments of my eyes opening though, escape wasn't quite that easy.

There was only one person who I wanted to talk to, so I dangled over the edge of the bed to reach my phone and connect to them.

"Penny, are you OK? We tried to call earlier but there was no answer." Simon sounded annoyed and I realised they were probably out, as he'd mentioned a big family, New Year's meal at a local restaurant. I'd been there many times when we were together and knew it would be a warm and wonderful evening for Lucy.

"Yeah, sorry, dodgy signal. I haven't missed my chance to talk to Lucy, have I?" I could hear laughter ring out in the background amid the clattering of cutlery.

"She's here, hang on, I'll step outside so she can hear you better."

I heard mumbling and the banging of a door, then there she was, my baby.

"Mummy!"

"Hey, beautiful," I replied, sucking in a deep breath to steady my tone, the emotion of simply hearing her voice affecting me. "Are you having a wonderful time?"

"I went down the big water slide six times today. Six times!"

"Oh wow, you're braver than me." I giggled along with her, her enthusiasm contagious as ever.

"Nanny said I can stay up until midnight. I'm having

pasta and Alvaro and Lucia are here. I wish you were here too."

"You just have a great holiday, my darling. And when you're home, I want to hear about everything."

"Are you and Ryan having a lovely time too?" she asked, as the jagged edges of my heartbreak melted a little.

"We are, thank you, baby."

"Tell him I miss him too."

"I will…" I could no longer stop my voice from cracking. "I have to let you get back to the party. I'll call you again tomorrow."

"Happy New Year, Mummy," she trilled in her little sing-song voice.

"Happy New Year. I love you forever."

"Forever and ever!" she called.

And then she was gone. I could picture her ending the call as she ran back into the restaurant, the evening air in southern Spain would still be warm and fragrant. I held the phone to my chest, wishing I had her soft hair tickling my nose, her baby soft smell flowing into me.

I missed her so much it was a physical ache, but I had to be strong for her. There was no choice here, I couldn't fall apart because that little girl depended on me, and I would never let her down.

It was just gone eight and I knew if I didn't send Happy New Year's messages to friends and family it would look suspicious, so I barrelled a few off with a gorgeous shot of Edinburgh at night time that I'd taken on the way to the restaurant just a couple of nights ago: it felt like a lifetime ago. I sent an obscene amount of love and soppiness to my mum and dad. Then, I found Ryan's number and let my fingers hover over the message icon… Maybe after a cup of tea. Maybe.

Tea was soothing, as ever, but also gave me a raging appetite. I hadn't eaten properly since that meal with its teensy portions. I had a craving for a stack of hot toast, smothered in real butter, but of course as I hadn't planned on being home, there was nothing that comforting in. Instead, I had to put an uninspiring frozen pizza in the oven and drag out a bottle of wine from the back of the pantry.

Ryan had sent a couple of messages, worrying, wanting to come over, but I just didn't know what to do for the best. I couldn't stop the train of thought that I'd let him down, that I'd sullied what we had and that things had irrevocably changed.

I knew I couldn't ignore him, it wasn't fair to punish him when he'd done nothing wrong, this was another Penny-style mess. So, in the end, I did pick up the phone again, just before eleven.

PENNY

Sorry, didn't mean to ignore you. Had a big sleep, a chat with Lucy, and an awful pizza. What are you up to? x

RYAN

Just wishing I could make this better for you x

PENNY

I was thinking I might wrap up warm and see the new year in. Have a great view of the fireworks from my garden. I've got some really cheap wine too, am I tempting you? Come join me? x

RYAN

I'll be there soon x

Twenty minutes later, I heard a soft knocking on the back gate. Rocket was fast asleep inside, bonfire night hadn't bothered him, so I wasn't worried about the bangs. I'd lit the firepit and dragged out two recliners from the shed, plus a couple of warm blankets.

"Hey." I smiled in spite of myself as I unbolted the gate and let Ryan in. He reached forwards and kissed me on the cheek.

"I couldn't leave you with the cheap wine," he grinned sheepishly as he handed me a bottle of champagne, the condensation wet against my fingers.

"You saving me again? Thank you."

"I'd always save you…"

He opened the bottle with a satisfying 'pop,' as the cork flew away over the fence and fizz bubbled up over the rim. Then he filled our glasses and pulled the two chairs close together. I sat and reclined my seat, he mirrored me, and we lay looking up at the stars, our breath clouding above us in the cold as he reached for my hand and gripped it tight.

"Reminds me of the night we met," he murmured, his fingers stroking mine.

"The moon is wrong, but I know what you mean."

"I wouldn't want to be anywhere on New Year's Eve but with you, do you know that?"

"Even with what I've done?" I bit my lip, forcing away any tears that may threaten.

"Penny please, I know it's still a shock, but you haven't done anything wrong."

"You must think less of me."

"Never."

"Can we talk about something else?" I asked before any energy I had left was drained away.

"Anything you like." He turned on his side to face me, and I mimicked him, drinking from the bubbly champagne.

"What were you doing last New Year's Eve?"

"I stayed with Jess and Matt. They had a party. I hated it. Every minute of it. How about you?"

"Was just me and Lucy, we watched movies and ate cake, sat out here for the fireworks. There was no Rocket then, of course."

"Did you make any resolutions?" he asked.

"The usual. Lose weight, save more money. I had high hopes for the year, had no idea it was going to be such a rollercoaster." I blew out a breath, watching the hot mist dissipate into the cold air. "You?"

"Not really, I always promised myself I wouldn't forget her, I guess that was the only thing. It's weird going into a new year without someone, experiencing something they'll never know."

"You never have to forget her."

"I know. And I won't. But if anyone had told me that night that I'd be head over heels in love next year, I would have laughed in their face."

"I was in love, I really was, this time last year. But sometimes we love the wrong people."

"We do, but equally, sometimes we love the right people."

We drained our glasses in silence, our fingers still entangled. As always, one party a couple of streets away set off their fireworks a couple of minutes early, but we knew it was close. So, with a refill of glasses, Ryan pulled me close, murmuring in my ear how much he loved me, how he wanted every year with me, until I couldn't hear him over the booms and bangs, the cheers from the street, and the sound of my own sobs as my heart broke at what I'd brought to him. A man burdened as he was did not need *this* landing on his doorstep. Yet I loved him so much it tore me up.

Was it fair on him to start a whole new year with a potential court case and world of humiliation? Maybe I shouldn't report it after all, maybe it would disappear like a bad memory? It didn't feel as if I had the luxury of time, because if this was it, I definitely needed to rip the plaster off in one, smooth motion.

THIRTY

Of all the things I'd expected to worry about on New Year's Day, what to wear to the police station wasn't one of them. I didn't want to look attractive, or provocative, or as if I was the type of woman who liked strangers seeing her naked.

In the end I opted for boyfriend jeans, a long black cardigan over a t-shirt, and some tatty old converse that always felt comfortable. Without any make up I looked pale and tired, but I didn't care as I scraped my hair back into a loose ponytail.

The familiar knock on the door came just before ten. I still had my nose in my coffee mug. I don't think I'd slept a wink the night before once Ryan had left, he'd wanted to stay but I had needed my space.

I let him in with a quiet hello, happy that Rocket took the attention from me, as he jumped all over his best friend. I poured a small coffee for Ryan, who looked as exhausted as me.

"Happy New Year again," he murmured as he kissed the top of my head and grabbed the mug, sipping from it.

"Have you got all the information you need from Josh?" I asked, drumming my nails against the dining table.

"I've got everything, you don't need to worry about that. Just focus on yourself. I'll be right at your side, always." His comment was meant to calm me, I was sure, but it bristled in case it wouldn't be long until I was alone again, and I had to toughen myself up for that if I was going to get through it.

"Let's go," I said decisively, as I tipped the rest of my coffee down the sink and grabbed my handbag. I needed this next step over.

———

It took some time before an officer was free to see us. It hadn't occurred to me that New Year's Eve would have been insanely busy and now I felt idiotic as we sat at the back of the waiting area, surrounded by people from all walks of life. Yes, there were drunks still sobering up, but also an older couple, a frantic mother whose teen son was missing, and various other individuals all waiting on the plastic seats which were attached to the walls.

Eventually we were called into a small interview room by a female police officer, ready for my written statement. Her male colleague was already seated, a giant bear of a man but with kind eyes. I can't remember their names, I went into autopilot, showing no emotion, to the point I worried they'd think I was making it up.

"When were the images taken and by whom?"

"Between January and March. Mostly selfies taken on my phone but some by him, on his." I didn't know if Ryan knew that, and my stomach knotted up tighter as his hand squeezed around mine.

"And how many people were in the group he shared the images on?"

"Twelve people," Ryan replied. New information for me this time... Twelve people... it didn't take much maths to figure the numbers if they'd all shared too. "One of them knows we're here, my business partner. But we haven't told the others in case it affected the investigation."

"Are you able to provide their details?"

"Yes," replied Ryan, pushing a stack of paper towards the officer. Everything is in there, details of all the people in the group, which includes the..." He paused. "Offender. Plus, screenshots of the messages and images as they were shared."

I reached for the plastic cup of water that had been left in front of me, my hand trembling as I thought of my pictures being in that stack of paper, of Ryan having to sit and print them out.

The interview continued, but I struggled. I was so thankful that Ryan was there to help me, but it only added to my guilt at him being pulled into the situation. How mortified must he be to have to sit and discuss his girl-friend in this way with the police?

Nausea buffeted my body as I explained everything to them, and I found myself wishing that Ryan weren't there. We'd talked about ex's, of course we had, but hearing about it in this bare way, in these circumstances, surely that was too much for anybody to handle? I touched on how things had been after the breakup, and felt Ryan tense beside me. I'd never fully opened up about just how much the newly discovered wife had frightened me, her threats, and insults.

The police officers glanced at each other as they handed me some documents to sign. Were they thinking what a foolish, sad, pathetic middle-aged woman I was? Or was it more along the lines of how ridiculously slutty I was to have sent the photographs? Maybe it was more weariness, that I was wasting their time with this when there was much more important work for them to be doing.

They told us they'd be in touch soon, gave me a stack more leaflets about support and the Criminal Prosecution Service, plus the next steps, which I shoved in my handbag before we left the building, not wanting anyone to see them. They'd explained a lot about the revenge porn laws and how they'd changed in recent years, the progress that had been made. But I couldn't stop this feeling that it was my own fault for starting it all off by sending him images. I was an adult for god's sake, not a silly teenager. I should have known better.

"They were very understanding..." said Ryan as he reversed out of the parking space and headed onto the main road. "You want to go get coffee?"

"I want to go home, go back to bed," I said as I gazed out of the window at the people out shopping in the January sales, not a care in the world except buying more stuff they didn't need. "Actually," I said, unfastening my seat belt as Ryan stopped at a red light. "I'll walk, I need the air."

"Stop, Penny!" Ryan reached for me, but I'd opened the door and clambered out. I needed air and space, I couldn't breathe in the car, I couldn't be that close to him knowing what I'd done, what he'd had to do for me.

The blaring of car horns rung out as I strode around the corner, my vision blurred, and my body felt distant and cold. The hard slap of footsteps pounded on the pavement after me before I was twisted around, hands gripping my arms, hands I knew and trusted and loved but hands I didn't deserve anymore.

"You saw all the pictures, didn't you? To have printed them out, you must have seen them all?" I sobbed; my eyes planted on the floor.

"I had to print them for the police, Penny. Think about it, I *had* to. I'm trying to help you, but you keep pushing me away." He sounded exasperated.

"I've caught you looking at me, as if you don't know me anymore."

"That's not true. I'm just riddled with concern for you, I feel helpless. I'm not saying this is the easiest situation in the world." He let go of me, running his hands into his hair and keeping them clutched at the back of his head. "But I'm not giving up on us. It feels like you're the only one doing that right now."

The blaring of horns and yelled expletives continued.

"I need to be on my own. Can you give me a few days. I can't think, I just don't know what to do..."

"Pen..." He didn't have words, and I understood entirely, because neither did I.

"You'd better go before someone steals your car."

He looked torn, so I took the choice away from him as I wriggled from his arms and sprinted away, unsure of my direction but certain I needed to be alone.

THIRTY-ONE

I fell into what I can only describe as an absolute funk. As soon as I arrived home that day, I retreated back to my bed with Rocket, forgetting all the house rules. I just wanted some comfort from someone who would never judge me. Not that Ryan had... I knew that deep down. I could see I was behaving like a brat by pushing him away, but self-preservation had kicked in, and when combined with the fear that dwelled inside me, I just couldn't bring myself to let anyone in.

Ryan called me multiple times, but I didn't answer. I replied by message but that brought a new issue to me. Every time my phone beeped, the most intrusive and painful thoughts hounded me. I imagined my boss had seen the photographs, or my mum, and they were messaging me in shock, bitterly disappointed by my behaviour. Or I imagined it was his wife, laughing that I'd gotten my comeuppance for wrecking her marriage, as she saw it.

I wanted to throw the phone away, but my baby girl was still away, so I needed it nearby for our calls, to see the photographs that Simon sent me of her smiling face, her cheeks freckled and rosy from the sunshine. Hearing her voice kept me going, because otherwise I never wanted to leave the safety of these walls again.

I explained this to Ryan, in the form of awkward, stilted messages. He sent me voice notes, adorable voice notes about how much he cared, how worried he was. He offered to bring anything I needed around, to walk Rocket, to get in touch with the helplines... but none of it eased my mind. His helpfulness only made me feel worse, it would be easier to take this if he were not such a good man. He reluctantly agreed to give me space for a few days, as long as I promised to call him immediately should I change my mind or need him. To be out of touch with him felt like torture, but also necessary. Still though, he sent me a message every morning and at bedtime to tell me he loved me.

There were a couple of days before Lucy was due home, and I knew I had to be visibly OK for then, even if all the pain was hidden away until she slept. I scrubbed every inch of the house from top to bottom, it gleamed as it never had. I threw all my sexy lingerie into bin bags, never wanting to see it again as I drove it to the tip, then on the way home I dropped bags and bags of glamorous clothes and high heels at a charity shop. My bottom drawer had already been emptied and disposed of. I didn't think I'd ever want to be desirable again, to have sex again, to be 'that' person again.

I told Zoe and Emma over many bottles of wine at their

place. The night ended with me vomiting in the back garden and Zoe desperate to rush out and 'lamp him one,' as she put it. They were brilliant, amazing, and supportive, but the shame still filled my body and mind until I felt there was no space for any other emotion. I felt so full I could burst with it. I longed to run, escape, sprint until my lungs burned and then keep going. But I couldn't; I had to keep myself here and grounded for Lucy.

Talking to my mum and dad was more troubling, I hated that I'd let them down and I didn't want to worry them, they had enough with their hospital appointments and general day-to-day struggles. They needed to know though. I had considered not telling them, pretty confident that neither of them browsed porn after Wednesday bingo sessions, but there was always the chance someone else would know and tell them, and I couldn't risk that. I underestimated them though, they were miraculous. They rallied around me, taking me out to treat me to lunch in Marks and Spencer's, sitting over endless cups of tea and bashing the male species in general (my mum), recalling old Boxing Days and threatening to knock all of his teeth out (my dad). I stayed over with them the night before Lucy got home, it was as though they shielded me from the horrors outside of their protective bubble, like being back at primary school and they were going to sort out the school bully and then take me to Wimpy for burgers and fries to ease the pain.

I sobbed again as I left, telling them over and over how wonderful they were, the best parents I could ever have imagined. For as much as we might have been short of money or holidays or new cars as I grew up, I never for a single second of my life felt unloved.

The house remained spotless, I'd even re-wrapped all the toys Lucy hadn't had the chance to play with at Christmas, wanting to make things sparkly and new for her. I'd bought all her favourite food; the cupboards and fridge were bursting and tellingly... the second fridge in the garage was now full of wine. I knew I was drinking too much but I wasn't sure what else to do to get any sleep.

Thankfully Jane, all tanned and smiling, dropped Lucy back and she didn't know me well enough to spot that anything was off. My amazing little girl was full of excitement, as was Rocket who once again peed everywhere when he saw his friend was home. She was jet lagged and exhausted though and, when she fell asleep by seven, I joined her, cuddled up tight in bed as I sobbed into her soft hair and prayed she'd never go through something like this. I'd closed all of my social media in case anyone tagged anything or linked me back, I was scared to even be on the internet full stop, the idea of casually scrolling like I used to filled me with apprehension. I wasn't used to being controlled by fear, but its icy grip held me in place in this new normal that I had not asked for, did not want.

The police rang me a couple of days later, asking if I could go and see them for an update. Lucy was back at school and I told my boss I needed an emergency day off. I didn't mention it was so I could head to the station. My dad offered to accompany me, as did Zoe, but I knew the only fair thing I could do was to ask Ryan, as there wouldn't even be evidence without him, I likely wouldn't have reported anything, just slunk away and hidden even more deeply than I currently was.

"Hey," he said, his voice hushed as I opened the front door that next morning. "Thank you for letting me know. I wouldn't want you going alone."

I blew out a long breath as I looked at him, it hurt me to look at him. I missed him so much it was like an open wound that wouldn't heal, instead constantly bursting open and reminding me with each sting of what I was losing.

"You look so pale." He reached out to touch my cheek, but I flinched backwards, grabbing my handbag and keys and stepping outside before the situation was further complicated by Rocket.

"I had to drop Lucy at school early, that's all. Early start."

"I've walked to the end of the road so many times, I've been desperate to see you. I wanted to respect your wishes though."

"I appreciate it, I just don't feel very me. I can't think about this now, I need to just focus on the police. Is that OK?"

"Of course, whatever you need." The glabellar lines between his eyebrows deepened.

The drive to the station was quiet. I filled Ryan in on Lucy's adventures in Spain, and he told me he'd been working on designs for some old warehouses on the docks that were to become office spaces. Mundane, safe, easy to navigate topics of conversation, as if we were nipping to a garden centre rather than a police station.

Upon arrival, we were taken to a small interview room

without too lengthy a wait, but unlike last time there were no tape recorders or notepads. Just a weak coffee in a Styrofoam cup that I clung to as if it were my last connection to the world outside of this situation.

"Dr Deane has been interviewed under caution, he admitted sharing the images via the messaging app with a group of his friends. He was remorseful; his explanation was that following an altercation between the two of you at 'The Fox and Ginsmith,' he had a partial breakdown and had wanted to lash out and hurt you. His marriage had broken down, he was living in a small bedsit above his dental practice, having been forced to move out of the marital home. His children had ostracised him, and he had begun to drink heavily. When he saw his friends a few days later, again under the influence of drink, he shared the images in their group chat."

"That's why he did it? Because of what happened at the bar?" I asked in disbelief, at how five minutes of that night had led to these devastating events.

"Apparently so."

"So, what now?" I asked, my voice barely a whisper as I sipped at the tepid coffee.

"He willingly deleted all of the material from his phone, as witnessed by two of my colleagues. Our cybercrime team have found no trace of the material online, and he willingly agreed to his laptop and phone being examined. Given the evidence from yourself and Mr Grayson, plus Dr Deane's confession, the case has been forwarded to the Crown Prosecution Service."

"And that's it?" I asked.

"The CPS will pursue charges, so they'll be in touch

with you soon. There's a leaflet here with all their details and what the next steps will be."

I tore the edges of the lip of the cup, unsure what to say or do.

"Here," the officer said. "There are helplines and support networks you can utilise. I don't think Dr Deane will trouble you again, but please do come straight to us should you have any concerns."

I left the police station in a numb sort of shock, imagining *him* in there, using all his rich, white male privilege to charm them, tell them how I'd wrecked his marriage and humiliated him. All complete lies. I detested him with a hatred I'd never felt before.

"How do you feel about that?" Ryan asked, as we headed back to his car.

I shrugged, deadened and still exhausted; it was as though I couldn't sleep enough at the moment.

"Want to come back to mine? To talk?"

"Yes…" I replied, knowing I needed to have one of the hardest conversations of my life.

"It's good news. They absolutely should press charges," Ryan said, pouring coffee into a mug for me as we sat at his breakfast bar.

"I'm still so mad at myself for getting into this situation."

"Penny, I don't know how else I can say that this isn't your fault."

"You haven't known me that long, not really. This is the

latest in a long line of fuck ups. You deserve someone who can be a normal adult, not a huge, laughable mess."

"You're driving me insane right now, Penny. Stop, just for a minute will you stop blaming yourself and look at your life. Look what an absolute inspiration you are. Your job, Lucy, Rocket, your friends, your parents. You're amazing, people love you. You do so much for people, you bring light everywhere you go. But now you're burying yourself away over that arsehole."

'I need to stop pretending I live in a romance book. Life isn't happy ever after. It was bad enough being the one talked about as a marriage wrecker, but when this is in court..." I sighed and drank slowly from the steaming mug of coffee.

"Do you think I haven't been there? Hiding away, wanting to get off the world? Knowing people whispered and pitied me everywhere I went? You laugh and joke about how I saved you at the wedding but really, it was you who saved me. I'd given up on ever being happy again and then you sat at that table opposite me and it was like I came back to life. Slowly, bit by bit, you saved me."

"I hate myself, I hate this situation. I'm not going to be the one to bring you back down." A tear splashed into my drink as I stared downwards into the coffee and the mug trembled in my hand.

"Please, don't do this. I love you. I will be here for you every step of the way. Always, Penny. Don't push me away."

"I have to go, Ryan. I have to. Maybe we can talk soon, but I can't right now. I can't..." My voice cracked and trembled, as I jumped down from the tall stool and bolted towards his front door, memories flooding my mind of the first time I'd seen his house, how enthralled with him I had been. He was a decent guy, the best guy, and he would stick with me through thick and thin, I knew it, but he deserved more, and I had to put him first.

He strode after me, quickly catching me and twisting me around to face him.

"You can't just walk out on what we have. I know you're in absolute turmoil at the moment, I understand. But let's get through it together."

"I need more time, Ryan. I'm sorry, I truly am. For everything." I sobbed and he pulled me to his chest, squeezing me tightly as my heavy tears soaked into his shirt.

"I know more than anyone that time runs out..."

"We'll talk soon," I whimpered as I felt his body chest shake with tears to match my own. "I'll walk home, I need the air. I'm sorry... so sorry."

I left before it could get worse, heaving for breaths as I walked home, not aware of which streets I passed. A vivid memory rocked my mind, of the day we met, and how pleased he was that I didn't say 'I'm sorry,' upon learning about Tara. How come now that was all I seemed to say?

That was the point I pretty much withdrew from my life. How could *he* carry on so free, running his business, probably meeting more women, while I was still coated in shame and living in fear, every single day, that these images would pop up elsewhere and somebody in my life would recognise me, see them, and think the very worst of me?

Over the next few weeks, I let the colour fade out of my hair, keeping it swept back in a greasy ponytail when I did the school run, make-up free, and with oversized sunglasses hiding my face no matter the weather. My work continued at home, but it didn't seem to matter so very much anymore. I left book club, blaming my job, but the reality was, I couldn't sit in the pub and wonder who knew. The school run and dog walks were the only times I went out, my shopping was delivered, and Simon took over most of the activities and parties for Lucy. I'd asked Zoe to explain to him, being too ashamed to let my shitty ex know that I had managed to find an even worse one after him. Because, for all Simon had done, at least I knew he wouldn't have ever humiliated me in that way.

Sometimes, Rocket would mope by the front door, and I knew it was for Ryan, but if I could learn to live without him, so could a little dog. Lucy was trickier; I hated lying to her but I said he was working away on a big project. It was a temporary solution, but I didn't seem able to plan for any further than a few days at a time. Maybe I'd fooled myself all along that our little meet-cute could ever amount to anything.

The only thing that did make me feel more comfortable was the news, passed on via Zoe, that the dental practice had closed down. *He'd* moved away to god knows where, hopefully to never be seen again.

And so, my very full life changed, for better or worse was down to individual opinion. But it was easier, there was less I could screw up. Work, school run, dog walk, shopping with my parents, the odd hospital or GP appointment, and a lunch out once a week with them - somewhere quiet, and I'd always phone ahead and ask for a secluded corner table at the back. My beloved books were even replaced with the trashiest reality tv, I didn't want to think, to dwell, I wanted to camouflage myself away and hide. From everything. But my self-loathing remained with me at all times, some things are impossible to avoid.

THIRTY-TWO

*J*anuary rolled frostily into February. Ryan and I exchanged some messages, the odd phone call when I had updates on anything to do with the case, but I still couldn't bring myself back into the relationship, couldn't shake the feeling that I didn't deserve him. He hadn't been around to see what people thought of me when the 'marriage-wrecker' label was being banded around, and the 'slutty-selfies' reputation was going to be even worse. I couldn't let myself rely on his support and love, only to see it withdrawn when he realised how unworthy I truly was.

As on any other day, I threw myself into work. I was engrossed in complex schematics that the finance department wanted, pages and pages of plans and calculations that would be enough to drive me insane usually but, nowadays, focusing on those facts and figures, the cells of the spreadsheet, kept my mind from travelling anywhere else.

The doorbell rang, but to be fair it did that a lot these

days as my online shopping accounted for most of my spending now that I avoided the busy stores and weekend crowds.

Rocket had grown up so much since Christmas. I no longer had to shut him away when I opened the front door, he wouldn't run away or bite anyone's ankles, but would happily sit behind my legs and sniff the air to suss out who had arrived.

And so, as I opened the door that morning, still in my pyjamas, hair ruffled and wavy, an adorable dog peeping out from behind my legs, it was surreal to be taken back in time. Because there, once again, was Jess.

"Hi," she said, bouncing on her toes. "I'm sorry to disturb you, but could we talk?"

"I'm working..." I countered automatically, before I could even think about if I wanted to see her or not. Her eyes were so like Ryan's it was disconcerting.

"They give you coffee breaks, don't they?" she asked. "Please, it's important."

They did indeed give us coffee breaks and, to be honest, I didn't even need to finish this bloody schematic in any timely fashion. I'd volunteered to tidy it all up, anything to keep my mind busy.

"Come in," I said as I stepped backwards, leaving space to invite her into. She knelt and fussed over Rocket.

"Hey, boy. I've heard so much about you." She stood, still smiling at him. Everyone smiled at him, it was inevitable. Good job I hadn't chosen him to be a guard dog.

She followed me through to the kitchen. I kept Rocket with us this time, he was always a good 'awkward silence' breaker, and I didn't harbour any high expectations for this visit.

"Can I use your loo?" she asked, her eyebrows furrowed up.

"Sure, upstairs and first door on the left."

I set about making the coffees, my memory serving me well as I remembered our previous encounter. Milk, no sugar. By the time I placed them on the dining table, she'd returned.

I gestured towards a chair for her as I sat opposite, clutching the hot mug between my hands. My fingers looked bony as I contemplated them, maybe I hadn't eaten very well these past few weeks.

"Penny?" Jess asked, shaking me from thoughts of my chubby thighs.

"Hmm?"

"I asked how you were."

"Oh…" I sipped at my drink, which was scalding, but I needed to buy time before I answered. "Busy, really busy. You know, work, Lucy, cleaning, my parents… all that stuff. How about you?"

"Well… I'm pregnant," she declared proudly as a blush rose up her cheeks.

"Congratulations!" I said, an authentic smile spreading across my mouth as I was genuinely made up for her.

"That's why we didn't see you at Christmas, it was early days, I couldn't stop throwing up. Feel better now, just can't stop needing a wee!"

"I was the same with Lucy," I replied. "Couldn't be more than five minutes away from the bathroom. Oh! Do you want me to make you decaf?" I asked, remembering all the caffeine and food restrictions that had worried me every single day.

"It's fine." She shook her head. "I have one proper cup a day, and this is delicious."

"You must be made up. I bet your mum can't wait!" I said, imagining Elsbeth's contained excitement, and all the crochet blankets she'd no doubt produce.

"She's overjoyed. Matt and me, we went through a rough patch, and you don't expect that so soon after the wedding. It's partly why I wasn't very welcoming to you, and I'm sorry for that."

"Hey, everyone has rough patches, you can't dictate when they happen."

"No, but..." She blew a puff of air out, her cheeks still flushed. "I cheated on him. I'm not proud. A work conference, too much to drink... I thought I was going to lose him, but I *had* to tell him the truth. It's not been easy, but we've worked through it. Many painful conversations, times that felt excruciating, but we're stronger now."

"It takes a big person to admit to their mistakes, most cheaters I've known don't want to even confess when they're caught." Her face paled, and I berated myself for the harsh language. "I didn't mean to lump you into the same category, sorry, that was wrong."

"No, don't worry. It's true, what I did was vile. I'm lucky Matt is such an understanding man. It doesn't excuse it, but I hope this goes some way to explaining why I was so prickly."

"I'm glad you two are working things out and its wonderful news about the baby. Truly. Don't be too hard on yourself, self-forgiveness is important."

"It is, isn't it. That's what I wanted to talk to you about," she began, her teeth grazing her bottom lip.

"What do you mean?" I asked, as my heart plummeted into my stomach; was this a conversation I'd rather avoid?

"Ryan told me what happened. I haven't let on to Matt, and my mum doesn't know, but he's needed someone to talk to. He's beside himself."

I cradled the coffee mug in my hands, gripping it tightly to stave away the tremble. "He must hate me."

"He doesn't hate you, he could never. He's worried sick about you. Why would he hate you?"

"Because things were going so, so well. And then I screwed it up, again. Does he know you're here?"

"No," she shook her head. "I wanted to... I don't know, make amends I guess, for taking my own shitty situation out on you. I acted like a brat when you two got together. He's like a little lost soul without you, Penny."

"I don't want him to see those pictures every time he looks at me, it's not fair on him. And he must question the type of woman I am, to do what I did."

"Come on, who hasn't sent stuff like that these days? I've seen some pretty bad shit on dating apps. The only thing that was 'wrong' was that knobhead showing them around when he had no right to."

I looked up at her in surprise, to be greeted with that same mischievous grin that Ryan flashed from time to time. We both laughed, and I headed to the biscuit tin for my emergency stash of chocolate digestives. Maybe, in the grand scheme of things, they weren't that bad? Could she be right?

Jess grabbed a couple, biting into the biscuit with a little sigh. "I am starving all the time, it's ridiculous. I'll be the size of a house by six months."

"What does he think, really?"

"Obviously," she began, wiping crumbs from her mouth. "He wishes it hadn't happened, but only because it hurt you, *not* because he thinks less of you or anything like that. He did drink copious amounts of whisky one night and was determined to find the guy, but luckily whisky also makes him sleepy. I told him getting arrested wouldn't help anyone."

"Definitely not. I've no doubts that the knobhead would've pressed charges. Ryan's not drinking too much, is he?"

"No…" Her eyes flitted across to my recycling tub next to the kitchen window which was stuffed full of empty wine bottles. "Like I said, he's lost. He's hurt and he's upset, but basically, he wants to be with you. Would you see him, listen to him? There's no need for the two of you to split up over this, it feels so sad." She wiped a tear from her eye. "Bloody hormones!"

I smiled sympathetically. "When I was pregnant, I cried at everything, it was ridiculous."

"He's miserable without you, and no offense, but you don't exactly look like you're living your best life."

I looked down at my tatty pyjamas, my chipped nails, and considered the horrid empty feeling that lurked in my stomach.

"I'll think about it," I said. "But I do have to get back to work, I'm sorry."

"Don't worry," She stood at the same time as me, stepping around the table for a hug, her perfume sweet and floral as she squeezed me. "You two seem like something special and this little bean..." She pressed my hand to her stomach. "Is going to need an auntie. Ryan will buy Lego architect sets for its first birthday without your guidance. He's desperate to see you Penny, he's giving you the space you asked for, but that has taken a toll on him, please don't forget that."

A shiver ran through me at the thought of us, me and Ryan, our lives and our families blending together into one happy mishmash. Playing auntie and uncle, maybe living together How did it all sound so good but, at the same time, as though it were a galaxy out of reach?

"I don't know if he's ever said, somehow it never seems right to discuss the flaws of someone who has passed away, but him and Tara," She looked a little unsure, as she continued. "They weren't perfect, not by any means. She had a ridiculous jealous streak. She'd get in these furious rages, accuse him of all sorts when he'd done nothing wrong, he spent many a night on Rob's sofa. It wasn't all hearts and flowers, no relationship is. He doesn't expect you to be perfect, Penny. Nobody's perfect."

I couldn't focus on my work for the rest of the day, the numbers on the screen swimming as my eyes glazed and I contemplated what to do, how to feel. That was part of the problem, I couldn't control my feelings about Ryan or around what had happened. I wanted to, I wanted to reach out from this tar that it felt like I was struggling through, always on the verge of being pulled down. But I was scared, and nothing saps strength away like fear.

I sat all evening with my mobile in my hand, Ryan's

number displayed on the screen, my thumb hovering between the call icon and the message icon.

PENNY

I'm sorry if I'm hurting you x

RYAN

I just want you to be OK x

PENNY

I'm trying. Do you think I'm overreacting? x

RYAN

No, I think you're very hurt, and you're just trying to process that. I only wish you'd let me help. Will you do something for me? x

PENNY

I'll try. What is it? x

RYAN

If I book you in with Caroline, will you go and have some counselling sessions with her? x

PENNY

Do you think it will help? x

RYAN

Yes, definitely. I can book you in and send you the details, if you're happy with that? x

PENNY

Thank you. I miss you x

RYAN

I miss you too. More than you know. I wonder if I'm doing the right thing, keeping away, or if I should be pounding on your door every day x

PENNY

I'm scared x

RYAN

I know. But you're punishing yourself for no reason x

PENNY

The GP gave me a prescription. I'll see Caroline. Take it from there? x

RYAN

Good, now, shall we talk about the dreadful auditions on this show tonight? x

I laughed, despite myself. I wished I could see a way through this, but at the moment it all felt too dark.

THIRTY-THREE

"*H*appy birthday, darling," I said with a smile as Lucy rolled over next to me and stretched like a perfect little warm and cosy angel.

"Is it today?" she sprang up, instantly awake. "Am I seven!?"

"You are indeed. Happy Birthday!" She wrapped her arms around me; even though they were longer, slender, and more grown up these days, they'd always be those chubby baby arms that reached for me with such love, in my mind at least.

"I've been waiting so long, Mummy. I thought it would never be my birthday."

"Well, it finally is. My special little Valentine's girl." I held her tight to me, the love within her like a positive force that kept me on track because she was everything, no doubt about it. And that was why I was going to make the effort to be the mum she deserved today, not one who hid inside with her curtains closed, shutting out the world.

Somehow, over the last few weeks, Rocket had started

to sleep at the end of my bed, so between him and Lucy I rarely had it to myself. He was so big now, not much growing left to do, but still an absolute ball of fluff and tomfoolery.

"Shall we go see what we can find downstairs?" I asked, as excited as she was. I'd spoiled her rotten, the focus of purchasing such adorable little gifts and wrapping them all had been the most fun I'd had recently.

I made her favourite French toast for breakfast. I'd even found a little heart template to sprinkle the icing sugar on in a pretty votive for her and, with it being her birthday, there was no limit on syrup.

She adored each and every one of her presents, from the mermaid hair accessories to the novelty lip balm, the new box set of books and the denim dungarees she'd been hankering after since Christmas. But the icing on the cake, her pride and joy, was the scooter with light-up neon wheels and as soon as breakfast was shovelled down, she raced up and down the garden pathway on it, Rocket chasing her and woofing happily.

A familiar knock sounded on the front door, and I flicked the kettle on before jogging through to let Zoe and Emma in.

"Morning," I said as I embraced them both. "Thank you so much for getting up early on a Saturday, she'll be made up."

"Ahh, the rampant Valentine's sex can wait for tonight, don't worry," said Zoe with a wink as she moved past me towards the kitchen.

"As if…," said Emma. "She forgets we're married now."

I poured large mugs of creamy coffee, smiling to myself

as Lucy spotted my friends and screeched their names, the scooter abandoned against the garden wall as she ran over, content to be scooped up into hugs. She might not have had actual aunts and uncles or godparents, but these guys were even better. Lucy was loved, protected, wanted, and beyond that, they didn't see her out of obligation, they actually loved to spend time with her.

"Do I still get another yes day?" Lucy asked, as we sat around with our drinks. Lucy had a yoghurt smoothie, the latest trend that *had* to be in school lunchboxes and, once again, probably contained too much sugar.

"You get half a yes day..." I began, her face drooping into a pout. "Don't sulk, half a yes day is still awesome. But we have to meet Nana and Grandad for lunch, they're desperate to see you. And then I'll drop you at Daddy's house, he's got a big birthday tea planned with Jane. I heard a rumour there might even be more presents."

"Fine," she sighed, in full-on teenager vibe which soon reverted back to her cheeky grin. "Can we take Rocket to the beach this morning then? And get giant ice creams?"

"You know it's February, right Luce? It'll be freezing," I advised, but the rules of a yes day meant I couldn't really say no.

"Yeah, I'll wear many layers, we'll be fine." How was this girl so wise?

"One compromise then," I countered. "It's too cold to eat ice cream on the beach, so how about after lunch I buy you one of those huge desserts that they do at the pub?"

"Knickerbocker Glory?" She gasped in excitement, before dashing back out to the scooter, Rocket bouncing after her like a little lamb. I could almost taste my childhood come back to me, it had been a family treat for good school reports when I was little and had always felt so special, the tall glass stuffed full of ice cream, fruit, and sauce, as we all dug in with long spoons.

"That OK with you both?" I asked, addressing Emma and Zoe. "I've got warm clothes if you need them."

"It's fine by us," answered Emma. "And I booked the pub table last week, so we're all set."

"Did you book the table I like?" I asked, my stomach flipping around.

"I did, it's all fine." She smiled, they both knew I was struggling but they didn't preach to me about it, they just let me be and it meant a lot. The last thing I wanted to do was push them away as well.

My baby girl's birthday continued in style. She was in her element, and it warmed me to witness it. The beach gave us all cold toes and rosy cheeks, but that only made the pub even more inviting as we barrelled in, picking up my mum and dad en route and roughly drying Rocket before he covered everyone in muddy sand.

They'd also spoiled Lucy, with clothes and games and books, plus vouchers to spend on her favourite online games which I wasn't sure was a habit I wanted her to get into, but who was I to deny the whims of doting grandparents? I was fortunate that Rocket was good in public spaces like this, he always had been, and today he was exhausted from the beach run so, after a few long licks from the communal water bowl, he settled under the table, happy and warm after some sneaky treats from Nana.

Pub grub was just so soothing, the familiarity, the stodge, the carbs, I adored it all. I had homemade steak pie with chips, peas, and my own little jug of gravy. Lucy tucked into a kid's size gammon, but still pinched the onion rings from Grandad's plate after he whispered to her with a wink. It all made me a little emotional, it scared me to see my wonderful mum and dad growing older and frailer, to not knowing how long I had left with them. I couldn't bear to think about it.

The meals and drinks were soon finished. I'd had just one small red wine from the two bottles ordered, as I was the driver. But Lucy had been more excited about dessert than anything else. Zoe had obviously given the staff the heads up, as they brought over her ice cream monstrosity, complete with sparkler and a chorus of happy birthday. They also sent spare spoons, but I was happy with my cappuccino, just sitting back and taking it all in, fading into the background and hoping nobody noticed when I hid my face every time waiting staff came to the table or people passed nearby. My dad smiled at me kindly, placing his hand over mine and squeezing. The small action brought a tear to my eye which I hastily wiped away.

"So, Lucy," I said. "What's next on yes day? Depending on what you choose we might have time for two before I take you to Daddy's place, we definitely have time for one."

"Well... you know Ryan sent me some money?" She twirled her hair around her little finger. She'd been overjoyed when the envelope arrived from the postman this morning. We'd continued our messaging, but I was still wary to see him. I couldn't explain it, but it scared me. I was booked in with Caroline next week and hoped she'd be able to make some sense of my jumbled thoughts.

"Yes…" I leant my chin on my hands as I watched her, faux serious.

"Could we go to the bookshop?" Her eyes widened as she looked at me.

"Of course, we can!"

"Fab," said Zoe. "I need the new book club read. Maybe you could get a copy?"

It was a dig that I should have returned, but I wasn't ready. I let it slide and raised my coffee back to my lips.

I hadn't physically stepped foot inside the bookshop for ages as most of my shopping had been done online, books and clothes included. I doubted the staff would even recognise me, so different from the vibrant girl with the plum hair and the winged eyeliner – I was now the pale, mousy brown-haired girl who hid inside a big coat. I never had got to have that loyalty card shopping spree but, in spite of all that, this felt a little like coming home. Just not quite enough to stop the tremble in my hands or the accelerated heartbeat that pounded in my ears.

My parents headed to the little café next door for a cup of tea, after all it had been almost forty minutes without one, bless them… There was much activity in the kid's area of the shop, where they had Valentine's activities, plus a signing and book reading by a local kid's author. I hadn't heard of the author myself, but Lucy was desperate to take part.

"We'll take her, you browse," Zoe said, as she saw my

worried grimace at the crowd. That whole section of the shop was packed full of people.

"Thank you," I mouthed as she walked away, Lucy's fingers gripping onto her arm as she skipped merrily alongside her.

I made my way upstairs where the whole ambience was quieter and calmer, this was the more serious section. Non-fiction, study guides, cookery, and travel. That's what I was looking for. I still hadn't booked that trip with Lucy, and I was determined this would be the year, I wouldn't let another winter pass. Plus, I was pretty sure I'd be anonymous in Lapland amongst the snow and the huskies.

I let my fingers pluck along the books on the shelves until I found my desired destination, my fingers delving between its neighbours and pulling it free. A quick flick through the pages showed it was the type of thing I was after, so I turned towards the counter, ready to go flash my loyalty card again and pay.

But there was someone between me and the counter. Someone who stared at me, as if he'd seen a ghost as he clutched his own book. I wasn't sure how to deal with this, especially on Valentine's Day, with everything that had occurred between us.

He stepped towards me, could the salt and pepper in his hair have spread in these few weeks? He looked tired too, and that only caused another wave of guilt to crash through me.

"How are you?" I asked, as Ryan took a step towards me; a long sigh escaped his lips. He didn't answer the question.

"What are you buying?" he asked with a nod towards my hand, which was turning white as it clung to the book.

"Travel guide," I replied. "What about you?"

"It's about eco-builds. I know that's very dull."

"Not at all."

"How are you, Penny? Really?"

"I'm fine, work's good, I've been so busy I've not had time to catch up with anyone. You?" I garbled, full of guilt and mortified that he'd bumped into me when I looked like crap, although that was my standard appearance nowadays.

"Every day I wake up at five, and then I battle ceaselessly to stop myself from turning up at your place, begging you to speak to me. Then there's the odd days I'm so incensed and angry I feel like I need to destroy things."

His sincerity was disconcerting, painful, and I tried to back out of his gaze, but he trapped me in it with his honesty and conviction.

"Angry at me?" I asked.

"No. Angry at him and desperate to intervene, to hurt him. Angry at me that I couldn't protect you."

"I'm sorry…" I whispered.

"You need to stop with the sorry. You did nothing wrong, and I get how hurt you are… I get it, Pen, I really do, but… I love you. I can't switch that off. I miss you. I want you. Every single day I want to come and get you, to make it better, and I can't, and I abhor being that helpless."

I sensed the young girl behind the till watching us, her senses on alert that there was something going down in the usually quiet upper floor of the shop.

"You know what the worst thing is?" he asked. I shook my head, chewing on my gum as a pained distraction.

"I can't even listen to Beyonce anymore. You've ruined Beyonce for me."

My eyes shot upwards in disbelief. "You don't even like Beyonce," I spluttered out, before I noticed the sly smile on his face, the little sparkle of mischief in his eyes.

"Nope, but it made you smile, wanted to check that still worked at least. How about we pay for these and go get a coffee? I'll even let you have my loyalty points again."

"I can't…" His face fell and that only drove home to me how badly I wanted to spend some time with him. "Lucy is downstairs with Emma and Zoe. My mum and dad are waiting too. She's spending the money you sent her, takes after me, rubbish at saving."

"I hope it was a nice surprise for her?"

"She loved it, the llama card was perfect. The sweets lasted about forty seconds."

"I'd better not interrupt then, it seems…" he paused. "Serendipitous that fate bumped us into each other today of all days. And here, of all the possible places. The place that sells the pages that you fall in love with time and time again."

"Do you think it's possible to fall in love over and over?" I asked.

"I do, and I don't mean with multiple book boyfriends." His gaze burned into me as I rubbed at my face awkwardly, suddenly exposed and uncomfortable. "There's nothing I wouldn't do for you."

I let my hand brush against his, my fingers instinctively reached out as if seeking long-lost friends. The very touch of his skin against mine sucked the air from my lungs and I spluttered as I stepped back, my gaze firmly on the floor.

"Maybe you need more time, I get that. But I've got this dad dog lead that I have no use for." He smiled. "Could we maybe meet in the park one day soon? Walk Rocket, be in the same space for a while?"

"Tomorrow?" I asked. This was a rip the band aid off situation, if I said I'd text him next week I'd likely chicken out and not follow through.

"Tomorrow," he confirmed. "Eleven? The usual park bench?"

"Yes."

"I'm going to leave a gift on your doorstep later today. All I ask is that you read it before you meet me. Can you do that?"

"What is it?"

"Can you read it before you meet me?" he repeated. "I've had it for a week or so now but wasn't sure when to give it to you."

"I will, I promise."

"Give Lucy some extra birthday hugs from me," he said as he backed away, placing his book back on the shelf.

"Of course..." I mouthed as I watched him walk away. Had there ever been a man on this earth who deserved love as much as him? I was petrified in case I wasn't the one to give it.

The whole day had been amazing and seeing my little girl smile so wide and true meant everything. I dropped my mum and dad home first, who held me and Lucy tight, once more springing tears from me. Then it was Zoe and

Emma's turn, they were all high fives and tickles, eliciting squeals of laughter from Lucy. I couldn't deny the feeling of relief though that we were almost done, and nobody had recognised me or pointed or laughed, as unlikely as it was. That's what was maddening, I knew it was hugely unlikely anyone had seen anything, but my mind wouldn't stop with its ridiculous anxiety.

Last stop was Simon's place. I pulled up outside and glanced towards the house; the daylight had begun to fade, and the living room looked warm and cosy, illuminated against the cold and the dark. It looked as though the two of them were dancing, as if Simon had caught Jane as she walked past. She was laughing and play-fighting him away, but her hands wrapped around him eagerly as he pulled her to him for a kiss.

I sighed at the sight, not through envy, but in acceptance, that our split had been the right thing because he was happy, Lucy was happy, and everything that had gone wrong with me since had been of my own doing, not his.

Simon caught my eye and I looked away, not wanting him to think I'd been spying. The front door was already open by the time Lucy and I reached it, and she was scooped into more hugs and happy birthdays. A glance inside showed me the kitchen at the end of the hallway was bedecked in birthday banners and balloons.

"I'll see you in a couple of days, my gorgeous seven-year-old," I said to Lucy as I crouched down and hugged her tight to me. "I love you, forever."

"I love you forever, Mummy," she said, pressing her hot mouth to my cheek in a sloppy kiss that from anyone else I would have wiped away. Then she grabbed Jane's hand and the two of them wandered away, chatting animatedly, the joy in Lucy's gait pronounced.

"Are you OK?" Simon asked, as I dabbed my tears away; drop offs hadn't felt this emotional for a long time, not once we'd got used to the process.

"Yeah…" I mumbled, biting my lip.

"Has something happened?"

"No… I'm wondering how our baby got so big. Feels like yesterday she was born."

"It really does…" he said as he tentatively pulled me to him. I tensed up, but the familiarity of it was soothing, we hadn't touched each other like this in years; this was a hug borne from the bond of bringing a tiny, sparkling life into the world together. It didn't matter that we fell out of love, we'd always be bound by our little girl.

"Do you want to come in for a drink?" he asked.

I shook my head as I pulled back, rolling my shoulders and drying my cheeks. "No, it's your turn. She's had an amazing day, but I know she's been equally as excited to get here. She adores being with you two."

"We're always here if you need us. I've said it before, but I mean it."

"I know, thank you, Simon. I'm sorry, by the way…"

"For what?" he asked with a look of surprise.

"I've said a lot of horrible things to you over the years, I spent so long not forgiving you, it was childish, and I'm sorry."

"Honestly, I don't blame you. I still don't really understand why I did what I did. There's still a part of me that wonders where we'd be today if I hadn't…"

"Life's too short for what ifs," I interjected. "You have an amazing woman in there and we are raising the best daughter in the world. Maybe that's how everything was meant to be."

"Don't miss your chance to be happy, Pen."

"See you at drop off," I said with the nearest thing to a smile I could summon, as I headed back towards my car and drove home with all the windows open, as if the frigid February air could still my emotions.

As I pulled onto the driveway I saw a package on the doorstep, all wrapped up in brown paper and string like an old-fashioned bookseller might wrap a purchase. I grabbed it and headed straight inside, popping it onto the kitchen counter before I made a huge fuss of Rocket and let him into the back garden. I wouldn't normally have left him alone for as long as I had today, but it had been a special occasion.

I filled his bowl with food and poured myself a large glass of wine, as he careered around flattening yet more plants and bushes, before finally sliding back inside and wolfing his dinner down. I grabbed the parcel and headed through to the living room, flicking the tv to a mellow music channel before I began to unfasten the string.

As I pulled the paper back, I saw a large book in a beautiful indigo blue, golden stars illuminating the edges of the paper, as I focused in on the title, "The Book of Us." It wasn't a long book, but each page had photographs of me and Ryan alongside small boxes of text. I traced my finger over our faces as I absorbed each image. Us at the wedding, in the woods laughing as we tried to keep Rocket still for a photo, cuddly selfies on the couch in our PJs, holding hands as we drank coffee in our favourite little spot...

nothing major, we weren't travelling the world or running marathons, we were just us, together, living life and loving each other and I missed it so much at that moment my heart almost cracked.

I took a large gulp of my wine, steadying myself before I began to read.

If I can't say the words to you right now, maybe you will read them instead?
Because if we were the characters in a book, I hope you'd be reading one more chapter before bed until we found our happy ever after. I know you, my beautiful little bookworm, you wouldn't go to sleep leaving us on a cliff-hanger, or with tears and sadness.

I wonder how many more nights I need to be patient until you're ready to move on to the next paragraph, to come down from that story arc. To get to the ending and tell me you have a book hangover and can't possibly start another, only for me to find you sneaking a new book up to bed.

You once told me it's the middle parts of a relationship that count, not how it begins or how it ends. I want our end to remain unwritten for many, many years. I want to hurl myself into the middle as if it were some ginormous bed, and we could bury ourselves under the covers and enjoy every moment yet to come.

I want holidays and adventures and romance. But I also want drizzly weekdays and gas bills and squabbles about who used the last of the milk. I want you. I want you and me to live our forever, with Lucy and Rocket and our family and friends.

You've taken my life from empty and cold, to bursting with love and warmth. I want to give that back to you. I want to be the book boyfriend you deserve.

But I've spoken too much about what I want. This should be about what you want, and I'm here when you're ready to tell me.

If this is the end, then I want you to know that I will never regret the middle we got to experience, the love we grew, the kisses we shared, the spark you gave back to my life. But also know that I want to spend forever with you, and there is nothing we can't get through together.

Ryan x

I gasped as my diaphragm forced a breath into me, my face was soaked with tears. I dropped the book onto the soft cushion next to me, as if it singed my fingers. What the hell was I supposed to do with that? Those words were everything I'd ever dreamed about, but as much as we wished it might be, this wasn't a book, and things weren't that simple.

Or could they be?

I grabbed a box of tissues from the bookcase and wiped

the tears away, blowing my nose in a way very unfitting for the heroine of this 'book.' With great caution, I placed the book on the coffee table, exchanging it for my wine. As I did so, a folded piece of paper fluttered from the back page and landed on the carpet.

Rocket spotted it at the exact same moment I did and dived for it. He had a thing about eating paper and had upset Lucy on more than one occasion by ruining her precious artwork from school.

"Rocket, no!" I yelled. "Bad dog!"

I grabbed the paper, the corner of it tearing between his teeth as I yanked it away, I overbalanced, landing back on the couch with a shrill screech, as cold wine sloshed all over my face and dripped down my top.

Rocket had scarpered to the kitchen, and, for a moment, I just sat there, dripping, cold, and thinking how ridiculous I was. But at least the book was dry. I checked it nervously, but it was fine. I'd borne the brunt of the wine.

I wiped my eyes, at least not due to tears for once and slumped backwards, no longer caring if the sofa was wet or it left a stain; thankfully it wasn't red wine. I carefully unpeeled the soggy paper. Fortunately, Rocket had grabbed a blank corner, so I could still make out the blurred, hand-written words.

Penny,
I didn't want this to be in the book, but I needed you to know.
The twelve people in that group - minus

Josh and the one whom the police are dealing with, that leaves ten.

I have spoken to all ten of them. I've explained what he did, and how wrong he was.

And mostly, they agreed. A lot of them had been uncomfortable on the night, it simply seems that nobody took the step to speak up and stop him.

None of them appears to have uploaded or shared anything and they all told me they'd delete the images from their message history. A few of them left the group completely, I'm not sure there'll be any more reunions.

Even if you never want to see me again, I'll never stop trying to keep you safe.

Love, Ryan xx

How was it possible to cry as much as I did without turning into a shrivelled-up husk, desiccated and dry? I dripped wine onto the carpet as I leaned forwards with my head in my hands and sobbed, gulping ugly, heaving sobs with snot and dribble and the weirdest feeling of relief, but also dread.

What had I done to him? Why had I shut him out when all he wanted to do was help me? I'd judged him by other's standards, something I'd never wanted to do because any other man I'd dated would have run a mile at the situation I had found myself in. But not Ryan, never Ryan.

I read through the book and the note once more, cuddling Rocket as he sheepishly trotted back into the room, the paper in his tummy by now no doubt. He took one lick of the wine from me but, with obvious displeasure, lay down with a sigh.

I knew what I had to do.

THIRTY-FOUR

I had the quickest shower of my life and bundled my hair into a damp, messy bun, applying some concealer, mascara, and tinted lip balm. I didn't look great, but at least I smelled nice.

My mind darted from idea to idea, thinking of things to say, pondering back on his words, to the point that I couldn't even focus as I dressed, ending up in mismatched underwear, fluffy socks, black jeggings, and a long tunic-style jumper.

I grabbed some trusty old cowboy boots that I'd dug out from the back of the wardrobe, whistling for Rocket as I did so, who bounced around excitedly as I grabbed his harness and lead, the prospect of an extra walk filling him with delight.

The temperatures had been low since the New Year, and every morning saw people scraping their cars and stocking up on de-icer, so my winter coat, hat, and gloves were already waiting by the door. With keys and phone pocketed, plus the inevitable poop bags and dog treats, there was nothing left to do but be brave.

It was a chilly walk to Ryan's, but I'd drunk too much to drive and, regardless, this gave me time to compose myself and plan what I would say and do when I saw him. It was late to turn up unannounced, but I knew he'd be awake, probably working, knowing him.

I marched at a brisk pace to Rocket's delight, but every phrase I came up with in my head sounded cliched and ridiculous. I slowed as I rounded into Ryan's street, not wanting to turn up huffing and puffing like some wheezy slob.

The downstairs lights were on, but the pristine, white shutters were all closed. His car sat in its usual spot; it all looked as I'd seen it countless times before, but this time was the one that could change everything.

My bravery diminished with every footstep I took along the driveway. I wanted to tiptoe, slow and quiet, but Rocket recognised where he was and pulled me with every ounce of his now considerable strength.

I took a deep breath as my finger pressed on the video doorbell, stuck in that weird moment of trying to look nonchalant whilst knowing it was recording me and my every movement.

The door opened almost immediately. "Did you forget something?" Ryan asked, as he greeted me with a smile which soon sank into a confused frown. "Penny?"

I looked him up and down. He was in one of his best suits, tie removed, and his top button undone, exactly the kind of look on him that made me weak at the knees. I felt horribly underdressed but then I realised... it was still Valentine's Day, and here he was looking like sex on legs.

"Shit, sorry. I shouldn't have turned up unannounced," I mumbled as Ryan knelt down and made a fuss of Rocket who was crying and whimpering with excitement, reunited with his one true love. "I forgot, you probably had plans tonight. I'll go."

"Penny." He grabbed my hand, the one holding Rocket's lead so we held him together. "I was playing chauffeur for my mum and Ernie, they're an official item now. They'd been to a dinner dance. What did you think?"

"That you'd maybe had a Valentine's date…" I mumbled.

He shook his head in disbelief, that slow smile appearing and thawing out my frozen features as it did so. "You are insane, officially. Come inside, you look frozen."

He unclipped Rocket's harness, as I hung up my coat and accessories; it was only as I stepped inside the warm hallway that I realised how frozen it had been outside. The night sky was clear of clouds and the moon shone bright, stars twinkling in every direction; it was beautiful, but the distinct lack of clouds also meant the frost and ice would grow treacherous overnight.

Rocket was running laps of the house, bounding back to Ryan every few seconds as he led me through to the kitchen, where I was grateful to see the fire blazing. Ryan ushered me over to the sofa, before heading to the fridge.

"Wine? Or do you want a hot drink?" he called over.

"Wine please," I replied as I rubbed the end of my nose which still felt like an icicle in danger of snapping off.

He came and sat next to me, leaving two glasses on the coffee table. Rocket wasted no time in curling up at his feet and gazing at him with loved-up puppy dog eyes. I sort of felt the same way to be honest.

"He's grown so much."

"I know. The vet reckons he won't get much bigger now. He's daft as ever though, as you can tell."

"So," he said, his foot tapping against the carpet. "Is this a good visit or a bad visit? I wasn't expecting to hear from you so soon."

"That book... Ryan... I..." I exhaled, trying to quiet the jumble in my head.

"Was it too much?"

"No," I said with a quiver in my voice. "It was perfect. And you are so right, if this were a book, I'd be screaming at the stupid female lead right now for letting love slip through her fingers." He took my hands in his, squeezing but not interrupting me. "Hiding away was the easy option but I can't do that forever. I've been scared."

"Why would you ever be scared of me?"

"Nobody wants to see their girlfriend act..."

"Stop!" he said forcefully; even Rocket looked up in surprise, a chew dangling from his mouth that Ryan had obviously slipped to him in the kitchen. "Stop. We aren't doing that again. Tell me why you were scared."

"I was scared that if I saw you, you'd say it was all over, that you couldn't look at me in the same way now. So, it was easier to hide than face up to that, even though we were stuck in this weird limbo," I confessed, looking down at my nails which hadn't been manicured since Christmas and still had vague bits of snowflakes on what remained of them.

"I love you, those things never even occurred to me. You recall when we first met?"

I nodded in reply as I looked at him, my eyes watery but his smile soothing as he inched closer. "Yes. I have vague recollections of it." The tease got me one of his lovely smiles.

"That whole time we were not really dating but having lovely walks and coffees and messaging each other a million times a day. That entire time I felt like I didn't deserve you. Because I saw how much love and attention you put into everyone; Lucy, Rocket, your parents, your friends, your work, even your bloody never-ending 'to be read' pile…" I laughed, and he squeezed my fingers again. "I thought that I didn't deserve to be part of that, because of the sadness I carried, and you didn't need that to dull your light. As much as you two wind each other up, it was Jess who gave my head a wobble in the end. Told me all the changes she could see in me, and that Zoe saw the same in you. And I realised it isn't about what people deserve, it was about what my head and heart said. And for the first time in so long, they agreed, they wanted you, Penny. You and your busy, chaotic life which is full of people and love and laughter, and yeah maybe too much wine and chocolate but it's perfect."

I realised I had tears on my cheeks only when he reached forwards and wiped them away, so enthralled had I been in his words, his intent, that I hadn't noticed my reaction.

"Let's not talk about who deserves who because all I know is that I love you, you light up my entire life, and I think we were meant to meet that night at the wedding.

Because there were a hundred other opportunities before that when the world could have put us together, but it didn't. Because one, or both of us, wouldn't have been free. So instead, it waited until a time we were both full of hurt and it showed us how we could love again. I fell in love with you so fast, Penny."

I was in full-on blubbering mode, as I wrapped my arms around him. He slid me up onto his knee and held me tight against him.

"I'm talking a lot and you're not saying much."

"I... can't... speak... when I...cry..." I sobbed, half giggling, half breathy, as I wished I could be composed and beautiful but, after all, I don't think it really mattered.

"I know. You don't do anything half-heartedly, not even crying. You go all in, and I love that about you," he said as he pulled back with a smile, kissing the cold tip of my nose. "Tell me what you want, Penny. Forget the rest of the world, tell me what your heart wants."

"You, Ryan. I want you, I'm so..." He pressed his finger to my lips, cutting off the next word.

"No more sorries, no more doubt. Are we OK?"

"We're so much better than OK," I said, relieved yet still hiccupping.

"Good, I've run out of Cinderella lines for the next girl who leaves a button in my room."

"You're my future, Ryan Grayson," I grinned as I shuffled forward, pressing my body to his as I kissed him, slowly...

The last man I'd ever kiss, my last love, my last everything – Ryan Grayson – with all his scars and pain and passion, he was indescribable to me and, somehow, we'd found our way back to each other.

One kiss to remind me I adored him.
Two kisses to warm up hearts.
Three kisses to fill us with desire.
Four kisses to promise our souls.
Five kisses to fall in love, forevermore.
Just as we'd begun.

ACKNOWLEDGMENTS

A million thanks to Sam & Sophie - for sharing your special day, which led to Penny & Ryan.

Thank you to Stephen Black (@stephenRB4) for some wondrous editing - and for pointing out there were just too many Rocket moments.

My gorgeous cover is by the very talented Rebecca (@CatGraphic) - thank you for putting up with my indecision over Penny's legs.

A big shout out to my own book club - and just to re-iterate - I promise none of these characters are based on you.

I'm lucky to have the two best alpha readers - Renee & Kit - thanks for all the advice and encouragement.
Also, thanks to my fab beta readers, who helped give me the confidence to share Penny & Ryan with the world.

A special shout out to Jasmine Luck - how one lady can be so talented, so kind, and so lovely all at once I don't know!

Last but never least, my family, who astound me each and every day with their unwavering support and affection.

ABOUT THE AUTHOR

Olivia Lockhart (Livvie to her friends) is an English author who can't quite decide if she wants to write contemporary romance or paranormal romance. Either way, it HAS to be romance.

She loves to write about the underdog, the one who got away, the bits of love stories we can all relate to.

When not writing she can be found drinking wine, cuddling her beloved pooch or with her head buried in a book.

twitter.com/livvieharts
instagram.com/bubblybookstagram
tiktok.com/@livviehartsauthor

ALSO BY OLIVIA LOCKHART

LIAR